Italian for Beginners

Kristin Harmel

little
black
dress

First published in the USA in 2009
by 5 SPOT
An imprint of Grand Central Publishing

First published in Great Britain in 2009
by LITTLE BLACK DRESS
An imprint of HEADLINE PUBLISHING GROUP

A LITTLE BLACK DRESS paperback

5

ISBN 978 0 7553 4743 8

Typeset in Transit511BT by Avon DataSet Ltd,
Bidford-on-Avon, Warwickshire

Printed and bound by CPI Group (UK) Ltd,
Croydon, CR0 4YY

Headline's policy is to use papers that are natural, renewable and
recyclable products and made from wood grown in sustainable forests.
The logging and manufacturing processes are expected to conform to the
environmental regulations of the country of origin.

HEADLINE PUBLISHING GROUP
An Hachette Livre UK Company
Carmelite House
50 Victoria Embankment
London EC4Y 0DZ

www.littleblackdressbooks.com
www.headline.co.uk
www.hachettelivre.co.uk

To all my wonderful friends, who have taught me volumes about love, trust and faith, just by being yourselves. Words can't express how much you all mean to me or how lucky I feel to have you in my life.

Acknowledgments

I feel like my life gets better and better each year because of all of the wonderful people in it. I'm so lucky to have so many great friends and loved ones.

A special thank you to Amy Tangerine, whose creativity and kindness inspire me; Gillian Zucker, who keeps me grounded; Lauren Elkin, who broadens my world; Kara Brown for all the smiles (and for being my Rome traveling partner); and Kristen Milan Bost, who can complete my sentences and whose wedding I was so honored to be a part of (congratulations!). Thanks also to my amazing mother, who gave me a solid foundation and continues to surround me with love; to my sister Karen and brother David, who are two of my favorite people in the world; and to my dad, who I understand more the older I get. I'm also fortunate to have a great extended family too – especially my wonderful grandparents, Donna, Steve, Anne, Pat, Fred, Merri, Derek, Jessica, Gregory and Janet.

Thanks to all those who I have the pleasure of working with, especially my talented, insightful editor, Karen Kosztolnyik, my wonderful agent Jenny Bent, the publicity team of Elly Weisenberg and Melissa Bullock, and the 360 Media team of Tara Murphy and Ashley Hesseltine. Thanks also to Michelle Rowell of Piper-Heidsieck, Katarina Maloney of Pierce Mattie, and Jessica Eule and Mara Piazza of Mediabistro.com. Thanks to my film manager, Andy Cohen, who becomes a better and better friend each year (I owe you a burger at Barney's!), my *People* magazine editors Nancy Jeffrey and Moira Bailey, my UK editor Cat Cobain and her assistant Sara Porter, and of course Caryn Karmatz Rudy at Grand Central. And a huge thanks to the writers who have become my dear friends, especially Megan Crane, Liza Palmer, Jane Porter, Alison Pace, Sarah Mlynowski, Lynda Curnyn, Melissa Senate, Brenda Janowitz, Laura Caldwell, Lauren Myracle, E. Lockhart, Robin Palmer, William McKeen, and Lisa Daily.

Thanks to my many wonderful, amazing, talented, kind friends, including: Scott Moore, Lisa Wilkes, Courtney Spanjers, Ryan Newell, Kendra Williams, Wendy Jo Moyer, Elizabeth Rivera, Chris Loomis, Leonard Holman, Megan Combs, Amber Draus, Willow Shambeck, Melixa Carbonell, Julie Walbroel, Sanjeev 'Jeeves' Sirpal, Trish Stefonek, Krista Mettler, Don Clemence, Michelle Tauber, Christina Sivrich, Zena Polin, Wendy Chioji, Courtney Jaye, Ryan Dean, Ben Bledsoe, Lana Cabrera, Pat Cash, Courtney Harmel, Janine Harmel, Megan McDermott Lewis, Ryan Moore, the real Marco Cassan, Evan Lowenstein, Kate Atwood, Samantha Phillips, Steve Tran, the Rock Boat Girls (Maite, Amanda, Gail and Michelle), Barry Cleveland, Michael Ghegan, Denny Hamlin, Steve Helling, Vanessa Parise, Amy Green, and the Pearson family: Susan, Carleigh, Cole and Luke.

To Amy, Courtney and Gillian: May our TIC-TAC

adventures continue as we raise a Harmtini, a Tangerine-tini, a Courtini, and a Gilli-tini to our friendship at Katsuya! And of course to the Kristin Convention.

A 'woof' and 'meow' to some of my favorite four-legged friends: Duke Harmel, Bailey Harmel, Ty Cleveland, Buster and Bamboo Tan, Josie Atwood, Carly Pace, and Parker and Miles Newell.

And to all of you whose belief in love has been tested: If there's one thing I've learned so far, it's that things work out the way they're supposed to in the long run, even when life gets in the way. So just be you; treat others the way you'd want to be treated; and enjoy the ride.

It all began with a wedding.

My little sister Becky and I, along with a few cousins and friends, had been brushed, buffed and polished to perfection that morning at our favorite salon on the Upper East Side. Vows had been written and rehearsed, something blue had been borrowed, and, as I stood on the altar, watching my baby sister prepare to promise forever to a man she'd known for a year, I couldn't help feeling a bit like I was the something old to her something new.

'Rebecca, do you take Jay to be your lawful husband, to have and to hold from this day forward, for better, for worse, for richer, for poorer, in sickness and in health, until death do you part?' asked the priest, gazing down at my sister.

'I do,' she said softly.

Her fiancé, Jay, echoed her vows as he looked at my red-headed sister, whose pale, freckled skin looked perfect swathed in the silk of her ivory Carolina Herrera dress.

Just as the priest was moving on to his next line, something serious about the vows of forever, I heard a low mumbling from the front row of the church. I tried to block it out, knowing full well what it was. *Not now*, I thought. *Please, not now.*

But the mumbling got louder.

And then it took on the distinctively raspy Irish brogue of my grandmother.

'What's this?' she asked loudly as my dad tried in vain to shush her. 'Is that little Rebecca getting married?'

A mumble ran through the church as my grandmother's voice rose and floated through the congregation. Becky turned around, glanced at Grandma and then looked at me in horror. I shrugged, helpless. What could I do? I was standing at the altar, several long yards away from the front row of pews. And clearly, Dad wasn't having much luck shushing her.

'Mum!' I heard my father whisper desperately. 'Shh! It's Rebecca's wedding!'

'Rebecca, you say?' demanded my grandmother loudly, her Irish brogue sharpened around the edges by a lifetime of smoking addiction. She coughed to punctuate her question. 'Rebecca? But Rebecca's the younger one! What about Cat?'

I closed my eyes briefly, hoping that perhaps my father would have the good sense to drag his mother from the church. But of course this was an Irish Catholic wedding – a wedding in our large Connelly clan, no less – and how complete would it be without a little disruption from my grandmother?

'Yes, Mum, Rebecca's the younger one,' Dad whispered soothingly. 'You know that. Let's talk about it after the ceremony, okay?'

There was silence for a second, and I thought with a

slice of hope that Grandma had agreed to delay their little chat. Slowly, I let out my breath, and I could hear the small swoosh of others throughout the church doing the same. Becky shot me a look of tentative relief and turned back to Jay.

The priest had just opened his mouth to continue when Grandma piped up again, her loud, raspy voice punctuating the still air of the church.

'But where's Cat?' she asked. I glanced around nervously, wondering if I should respond. 'Where's *Cat*?' she repeated, more loudly this time.

'She's just there, Mum,' my father said. I could hear the weariness in his voice.

'Where?' Grandma demanded. 'Not the one in the white dress, then?'

'No, Mum, that's Rebecca,' Dad said as Grandma continued to scan the church wildly.

I looked from side to side nervously. Perhaps if I ignored her, she'd just disappear. I held my breath and tried counting backwards from ten, a trick that had often worked to calm me down when I was a little girl. *Please, God*, I said, *Please make Grandma stop talking.* After all, this was a church. He had to listen to me here, didn't He?

But instead of quieting down, Grandma began insistently repeating my name. 'Cat?' she asked raspily, her voice rising. 'Cat? Where's Cat? Cat, dear?'

Gradually, her voice drowned out Dad's protests. I squeezed my eyes shut, wishing for the deluge of words to stop. When I cracked them open a few seconds later, Becky was staring down at me, her cheeks flushed with color.

'Do something!' she whispered urgently. 'Please?'

I braced myself, took a deep breath and turned around.

'I'm here, Grandma,' I croaked. My voice seemed to echo off the cold stone of the altar.

'Cat, dear!' Grandma exclaimed, her face lighting up. 'I hardly recognized you, love! You're wearing a dress! And you've done your hair!'

A small ripple of laughter ran through the church.

'Er, yes,' I said. 'Listen, do you think we could discuss this later, possibly? Rebecca's in the middle of getting married, and we're causing a bit of a disruption.'

'But that's what I wanted to talk to you about, dear!' Grandma exclaimed, coughing once again to punctuate her words. One slim, bony hand flew to cover her mouth, and the other smoothed down her kelly green dress, the one she wore to every family wedding, despite the fact that it had gone out of style approximately fifty years ago.

I glanced at my father. Dad, towering over his mother at six foot one, was staring at me helplessly with eyes full of apology.

'Everything's fine, Grandma,' I soothed. 'Let's talk later.'

'But Cat!' Grandma exclaimed. She paused to cough violently while Dad rapped on her back. 'Cat, dear!' she resumed, after the coughing fit. 'Your sister is much younger than you! And now she's getting married? What about that nice young man you were dating, dear? Dennis, was it? Did you screw it up?'

A fresh wave of snickers ran through the church as I felt my mouth dry out, as if someone had filled it with a handful of cotton balls. The room began to swirl around me – just a little, not as if I was about to pass out, but the way it does sometimes when you're dreaming.

That's it! Perhaps this was all a dream. Of course it was! I mean, in what kind of twisted world did a thirty-four-year-old woman attend her twenty-nine-year-old sister's wedding and have her grandmother ridicule her in front of a hundred and twenty friends and family members? Obviously, this was some sort of devious trick on the part of my overactive imagination.

Just to be sure, I pinched myself. Hard.

Ouch.

Right. Well. Evidently this was a *deep* sort of dream, the kind in which a pinch didn't always work. So I pinched harder. Still nothing. I turned to glance at Rebecca.

'This isn't really happening, is it?' I whispered. 'I mean, this is obviously some kind of nightmare brought on by my subconscious reaction to you getting married before me, which, by the way, I'm *very* happy about. Right?'

Becky looked at me strangely. 'Noooo,' she said slowly. 'We're all very much awake. Now please, Cat! Do something!'

'Right,' I muttered, horror finally beginning to set in. 'Um, Grandma,' I said gently. 'Let's talk after the ceremony, okay? I promise we can have a full discussion about just how grandly I've screwed up my life. Okay?'

My father was bent toward Grandma, trying to shush her, but it was clearly too late. She had something to say, and she was going to say it.

'I just don't understand, dear!' she said loudly, pushing my father away with surprising strength. 'You're not ugly.'

'Thanks,' I said, glancing around at the faces of the congregation, some amused, some horrified.

'You're not a dimwit,' Grandma continued.

'Thanks,' I repeated through clenched teeth.

'I'm sure you've held on to your virtue, if you know what I mean,' she said quite seriously. She winked and added in a theatrical whisper. 'I'm talking about *the sex.*'

'Er,' I said, my face turning bright red. The snickers in the church seemed to get even louder, and Father Murphy cleared his throat. I closed my eyes for a moment, wondering about the odds of spontaneous combustion, which sounded like a lovely idea at the moment.

'So what's the problem?' Grandma demanded after I had not, in fact, burst into flames on the spot. I glanced from side to side, seeking some escape, but of course there was none.

'Um,' I began again.

'You're nearly an old maid, dear!' Grandma chirped as I contemplated how nice it would be to simply die on the spot at that very moment. She paused. 'You're running out of time!' she shrieked suddenly, flapping her arms above her head like a demented bird. And then, just as quickly, she sat down in the pew, smiled sweetly at me and waved, as if we hadn't just had a lengthy, revealing exchange in front of all my sister's wedding guests. 'Hello, dear!' she said brightly after a moment. 'When did you get here?'

The congregation sat in stunned silence for a moment until Father Murphy cleared his throat again.

'Um, right then,' he said awkwardly. 'That was, um, enlightening. Now if we could just return to the wedding?'

Becky glanced down at me with concern in her eyes and mouthed, 'Are you okay?'

I nodded, forced a smile and mouthed back, 'Of course!'

But the truth was that I was mortified, disgraced and humiliated, all to the umpteenth degree. But I'd felt that way before Grandma even opened her mouth. After all, when you're six weeks away from turning thirty-five and your little sister has found the man of her dreams while you're remaining steadfastly single after yet another emotionless breakup, it's difficult not to feel like a failure. Even when you're so happy for her that you could burst, there's always a little voice in the back of your head that sounds suspiciously like your grandmother, asking, 'What's wrong with you? Why doesn't anyone love you?'

That was a silly question to ask, of course. When you got right down to it, I had plenty of people who loved me. My dad did, of course, and Grandma. And since Dad was a first-generation Irish-American, I had the requisite seven uncles, five aunts and several billion (okay, twenty-five) cousins on his side alone. And then of course there was my only sister, Becky, my best friend in the world.

I suppose our close relationship was unusual, especially given our six-year age gap. But our mother – a fiery, temperamental Italian woman – had left us without so much as a note just a week and a half before my twelfth birthday, and major events like that have the effect of bringing people together. Dad had fallen apart for that first year or so, and it had been up to me to keep things together.

I had quit the soccer team, my ballet classes and my dream of playing the trumpet in the high school band, and I'd become, in effect, an adult before I was even a teenager. I'd taken Becky to all her lessons and classes, cooked meals for the three of us every night and even kept the apartment clean when Dad worked overtime. I hadn't minded; I had always figured it was my job.

Then our mother came back, a few months after I turned seventeen. And she'd expected to pick up just where she left off.

She'd been there for my senior year of high school and for Becky's sixth grade year. She had lived in an apartment just down the street at first, and she and Dad went out on dates with each other, and seemed to be falling in love with each other again. Becky, who had been too young to truly feel abandoned the first time around, had been thrilled when she came home. I'd felt the opposite; in the five years she'd been gone, I'd grown to hate her for leaving us.

So when she returned, I kept waiting for her to break our hearts again. I wanted to strangle my father every time he'd shrug helplessly and say in that deep brogue of his, 'But Cat, girl, she's my one true love. And she's your mum. Can't you give her another chance?'

She moved back in with us three months after coming back. And every day, I waited for her to leave again. I knew she would. I knew it in the core of my soul.

And then, one day, she did. But not the way I thought.

She died. A massive heart attack at the age of forty-nine.

And for the second time in my life, I'd been left by my mother. But this time, it was for good. And it wasn't her fault, which was the hardest part of it to wrap my mind around. I couldn't hate her for leaving this time. But I could hate myself a little for failing to let her back in when I still had the chance.

Dad sank into depression. Becky locked herself in her room and refused to talk to anyone. And I quietly changed my plans to go off to UCLA for college and instead stayed at home to go to NYU. When I'd graduated with my degree in accounting, I'd taken a job at a tax firm in the city. I'd been there ever since, old reliable Cat Connelly.

It was better that way. I could take care of Dad and Rebecca. And that's what I did. It was in those next several years that the three of us grew inseparable. We had all been changed by Mom's leaving. Dad had learned that sometimes you have to let go of the people you love the most. Becky had learned that there would always be people there to take care of you.

And me? I learned to trust my instincts and to know that even the people who are supposed to love you can leave you one day for no reason at all.

'I miss Mom,' Becky whispered to me a few minutes after we'd sat down for dinner at her reception at Adriano's Ristorante on the Upper West Side.

'Yeah?' I asked noncommittally.

She made a face at me. 'Don't do this, Cat,' she said. 'Not today.'

'Do what?' I asked innocently.

'The Mom thing,' she said.

Becky remembered all the good things and revered our mother. It was the one thing in our lives we'd never been able to see eye to eye on.

'I'm sorry,' I mumbled. 'I won't.'

Becky looked at me for a moment and nodded. 'Thank you,' she said. She took a deep breath. 'It would have been nice for her to be here. I think she would have been proud.' She paused again and added, 'She would have liked this.'

'Yes,' I agreed after a moment. 'I think she would have.'

I meant it. The reception was beautiful. Not that I'd expected it to be any other way.

The Roma ballroom at Adriano's, Becky's favorite Italian restaurant, was packed to capacity with Becky and Jay's family and friends. Exposed brick walls gave a warm, intimate feel to a room dotted with high-backed chairs covered in clover green, and the fireplace in the corner crackled brightly, lending a glow to one end of the room while crystal chandeliers bathed everything else in soft light.

While most of the wedding guests continued to eat and chat, I got up and walked to the back of the room, where I'd left my tote bag tucked under the gift table. I pulled out my camera, one of my most prized possessions. It was a Panasonic Lumix DMC-FZ50S, the only major purchase I'd made in the last five years, a thirty-fourth birthday present to myself last year, and I'd meant to use it more. In fact, I'd spent many mornings wandering my neighborhood, photographing people in their normal environment, sitting on their brownstone stoops, walking their dogs, taking out the trash. I'd caught couples arguing down the block, mothers fixing the collars of their young children's jackets, grandchildren helping elderly grandparents out for a stroll. I somehow felt most in my element when I could capture the world inside my lens, anonymous, unobserved, blending into the scenery while life happened around me.

I had taken Becky's engagement photos, and she'd loved them, but she told me not to worry about shooting the wedding. 'That's why we hired someone to take pictures,' she'd said. 'Just relax for once, okay?' I had agreed at the time, but with Becky fully absorbed in Jay, I couldn't resist sneaking in a few shots. I knew she'd appreciate them later. Becky loved having her picture taken, and she looked more beautiful tonight than I'd ever seen her.

'Hey, kiddo,' Dad said, coming up behind me and squeezing my shoulder after I'd shot a few dozen frames. 'How you doing?'

I turned around and lowered the camera. He looked so handsome in his dark suit, his crisp white shirt and his clover green tie that perfectly matched my maid of honor dress. I smiled. 'Good,' I said. 'This is beautiful, isn't it?'

'I thought you were on camera suspension for the wedding.' He winked. 'Bride's orders.'

'I couldn't resist,' I said. 'She looks beautiful, doesn't she?'

He nodded and we both looked at Becky for a moment. 'Listen, kiddo,' my dad finally said. 'I'm sorry about your grandmother.'

I shook my head. 'It's not your fault,' I said. I swallowed hard. 'I just hope Becky's not too upset.'

My father fixed me with a stern look. 'Your grandmother humiliated you in front of over a hundred people, and you're just worried about your sister?'

I glanced away. 'Whatever.'

A few minutes later, after I'd put my camera reluctantly away, I headed toward the bathroom to touch up my makeup. I was stopped by well-intentioned aunts who told me 'Your time is coming, dear,' and, 'You look beautiful today. Don't worry about what your grandmother said,' and cousins who said things like 'That color is great on you!' and, 'When are *you* getting married?'

I smiled and gave the appropriate responses, issued the proper excuses. I'd almost made it safely to the back of the restaurant when my cousin Melody, a tall, plump woman with bad hair, stopped me with a firm, icy hand on my arm.

'So where's Dennis?' she asked, her eyes boring into mine. Melody was just a year older than me, but we'd never been close. She lived just outside Boston, like most of my relatives. She had been married for a decade and was heavily pregnant with her sixth child.

'He's not here,' I said, not wanting to get into it. I smiled pleasantly, hoping that could be the end of it, and began to walk away. But she maintained her death grip on my arm.

'Why not?' she asked with a syrupy smile. Sweat glistened at her brow and threatened to smear her heavy-handed makeup job.

I'd thought that the story had already made the rounds of the Boston Connelly clan. But perhaps Melody had somehow missed it. Or maybe she was just trying to rub it in. 'We broke up, Mel,' I said through gritted teeth.

She looked at me for a minute. I could have sworn that there was a little bit of satisfaction in her expression. She always had been competitive with me. 'I'm sorry to hear that, Cat,' she cooed. 'It must be tough to be dumped at your age.'

I took a deep breath. I knew she was trying to get under my skin. I also knew it would be better to walk away. But I felt like I needed to defend myself. 'I wasn't *dumped*,' I said. 'I broke up with him.'

Real shock crossed her face this time. Then she laughed. 'Oh, come on, Cat,' she said. 'You don't have to say that. It's all right to be broken up with. It happens to all of us.' She paused and smiled. She patted her pregnant belly. 'Well, not me, obviously.'

'He *didn't* break up with me, Melody,' I said. 'He just wasn't the right person for me.'

'You can't be serious.' Her eyes looked like they were going to pop out of her head. 'You had a man who loved you,' she recapped slowly. 'Who made a good living. And you dumped him because you didn't think he was right for you?'

'Yes,' I said.

'You're thirty-five,' she said flatly.

I cleared my throat. 'Well, I will be in a few weeks.'

She ignored me. 'Don't you think you're running out of time? I mean, really!'

I took another deep breath and tried not to react. This had, after all, been the general reaction of everyone I'd told. Apparently, when you were thirty-five, you were supposed to hang on for dear life to anyone who happened to show the slightest bit of interest in you. It seemed that in everyone else's opinion, I'd been damned lucky nine months ago to land Dennis Zcenick, a mild-mannered senior-level accountant who worked at the same firm as I did.

'He just wasn't right for me,' I repeated calmly. I swallowed hard again. 'Now if you'll excuse me, I need to go to the bathroom.'

I yanked my arm out of her meaty grip and strode quickly away, hating that I could feel tears prickling at the corners of my eyes.

*

In the bathroom, all three stalls were full, so I stood in front of the mirror for a moment and splashed cold water on my face. If I could make it past my grandmother's humiliation at the ceremony, surely I could brave Melody's superiority without crying, right? I dried my face, took a deep breath and studied my reflection, trying to steady myself.

The face looking back at me in the mirror looked as out of place as it always had at family gatherings. Whereas my sister was the spitting image of my father and his Irish clan, I looked like a carbon copy of my Italian-born mom. Becky was a petite five foot four, while I towered over her uncomfortably at a long-legged five foot nine. Where Becky's hair was curly and carrot-colored, mine was pin-straight and dark brown. Where her alabaster face was sprinkled with pale freckles that my father always called 'pixie dust,' my pale face was devoid of any such magical sprinklings, save for a tiny beauty spot just below my right cheekbone. My dad always said it was eerie, because my mother had had the same single mark in the same place on her face. Where Becky's eyes were brilliant and blue, mine were a stormy green, just like my mom's had been. Without Mom around I looked like I had just dropped out of some alternative Italian universe into my dad's perfect little Irish world.

And on days like today, when my self-confidence was flagging anyhow, I wished I could look at my own reflection and see something comforting. But instead, all I saw was a face that was, with each passing year, becoming more and more like that of my mother, a woman who couldn't be trusted, a woman who didn't know how to love.

'Get a hold of yourself, Cat,' I whispered to my reflection as I gave myself the evil eye. I took a few deep breaths. I was just about to turn and leave when I heard a high-pitched voice come from the middle stall.

'You sort of have to feel sorry for her.' I thought I recognized the shrill tone as belonging to my cousin Cecilia. I cocked my head to the side and listened, wondering who they were gossiping about now. I started to smile at myself in the mirror. Honestly, they never stopped. My cousins were, in effect, a bunch of little old ladies in thirty-something bodies.

'I don't,' said another voice, which I was fairly sure belonged to another cousin, Elinor. 'She's had every opportunity in the world. Who's she waiting for, Prince Charming?'

'Apparently, Cat thinks she's better than the rest of us,' said a third voice, which I was sure belonged to my cousin Sandy.

I started, the smile falling from my face. They were talking about me?

'Too good to settle down with any of the perfectly good guys she's thrown away,' Elinor chimed in.

'I don't know,' said the voice from the middle stall. 'I mean, maybe she's just all screwed up because of her mom, you know?'

'Oh, c'mon,' scoffed Sandy. 'You can only blame your problems on a dead mom for so long. It's pathetic. The way she dumped the most recent one? That Dennis guy? It's terrible.'

'Seriously,' said the one I thought was Elinor. 'She's running out of chances.'

One of the toilets flushed, snapping me out of my

horrified trance. I glanced quickly from side to side. The last thing I needed was to be caught eavesdropping on a humiliating conversation about myself.

Before I could think about it, I yanked the bathroom door open and ducked back into the hallway, hoping none of my cousins noticed. I glanced around quickly. On one end of the hallway was the door to the men's room. At the other end, there was the entrance back into the restaurant. I sure wasn't going back there yet; all I needed was to face a room full of a hundred and twenty judgmental faces while tears still prickled threateningly at the back of my eyes. The only other option was the restaurant kitchen. Heart pounding, I looked from side to side and quickly made my decision. Just as the bathroom door behind me started to open, with the voices of my gossiping cousins seeping out from behind it, I took a swan dive toward the swinging doors across the hall.

I landed in the entrance to the kitchen with a crash, flat on my face. I narrowly missed knocking over a stack of mixing bowls and a table full of utensils, but I wound up in a pile of flour that had escaped from a big sack on the floor. As I stood up, blushing, and began to dust myself off, a few cooks looked up at me with mild curiosity but went quickly back to stirring, chopping, kneading and whatever else they were doing, as if diving maids of honor were a regular occurrence there. I took a quick step to my right, so that I wouldn't be knocked over by the next waiter to bustle through the swinging doors, and looked around to get my bearings.

The kitchen was huge, much bigger than I would have expected. The walls were a sterile white, and stainless steel pots, pans and mixing bowls seemed to hang from every surface. A small team of washers-up ran hot water over plates and piled them into massive dishwashers, while several white-frocked young men and women in chef's hats seemed to be an assembly line chopping vegetables, tossing pizza dough, spreading sauce and cheese and sliding raw pizzas into a massive wood-burning oven in the far corner of the room.

I was half hidden behind a giant rack of hanging fresh pasta, and the cooks who had seen me enter seemed to be fully absorbed in their work once again. I was forgotten, invisible.

I backed up a few more paces and sat shakily down on a barrel in the corner. I put my head in my hands and closed my eyes, trying to collect myself.

I'd been so sure about my decision to leave Dennis. At least, I'd told myself it was the right thing. But had I made the biggest mistake of my life? I held my head steady, trying to stop the wave of an approaching migraine. Maybe the relatives were right. Maybe I was being foolish and much too picky. After all, all my friends were married, and now my little sister was too. Was I condemning myself to a lifetime of being alone?

A moment later, I was snapped out of my self-pitying trance by a deep voice above me. 'You must be Cat.'

I jerked my head up, surprised, and saw a man in a suit and tie staring down at me. He had unruly dark brown hair that seemed at odds with his buttoned-up appearance, and boyish dimples that didn't seem to entirely fit on a face with crow's feet around his pale green eyes and smile lines like parentheses at the corners of his mouth.

I just stared at him for a moment, not quite sure how to respond.

'Maybe,' I said finally. 'Who are you?'

'Michael,' he said, extending his hand formally. I stared at it for a moment but didn't shake it.

'Michael?' I repeated. He'd said it like the name was supposed to mean something to me.

'Yes,' he said. He grinned and glanced around. 'You're in my kitchen, actually.'

'*Your* kitchen?'

'Yes,' he said simply. He raked a hand through his thick hair, making it stick up at even stranger angles.

I looked him up and down and narrowed my eyes. 'But you're not a chef.'

He laughed and held up his hands defensively. 'Well, not professionally, anyhow,' he said.

'And you're not the restaurant manager,' I said. 'I've met him.'

'Right again,' he said mysteriously. He arched an eyebrow at me and offered his hand. I took it reluctantly and stood up. As I did, I was surprised to realize that, even in heels, I was still shorter than him by a few inches, which meant that he had to be at least six foot two.

'So what are you talking about?' I asked. I was running out of patience.

'This is my restaurant,' he clarified once we were face to face. 'I mean, I own it.' He was studying me with an amused expression. 'You're tall,' he added.

I sighed. 'Yes, you're the first person to have ever pointed that out.' I paused and added, 'Your restaurant? Your name is Michael, but you own a restaurant named Adriano's?'

He laughed again. 'It's named after my father, who ran a restaurant in Italy with his brother before he died. Is that acceptable to you?'

'Oh,' I said.

'So,' he said after a moment, looking amused, 'do you want to tell me what you're doing back here?'

I felt a little color rise to my cheeks. I did look pretty foolish. 'Well,' I said slowly. I didn't know where to begin. 'I'm the maid of honor in the wedding.'

Michael smiled again. There was something about the way his green eyes danced that made me melt a little. 'I know,' he said. 'I was sent to look for you.'

'You were? By whom?'

'The groom. He said you vanished, and he was worried. Actually, come to think of it, so am I. Or is hiding among the olive oil barrels some strange new wedding tradition I'm not aware of?'

I laughed, despite myself. 'Yes, the hiding always precedes the cutting of the cake.'

'Ah, I see.' He looked at me closely. 'So do I have to guess what's really wrong? Or do you want to tell me?'

I looked down and felt the smile fall from my face. 'No,' I mumbled.

'No?' Michael repeated.

'I'm totally okay,' I said.

'Of course,' Michael said. 'Women who are totally okay are always sneaking away to hide in my kitchen.'

I rolled my eyes, but I didn't say anything. After a moment, Michael sat down on one of the barrels and motioned for me to do the same. I paused, glanced from side to side, and reluctantly followed suit.

'So it's your little sister's wedding?' he asked after a moment. 'How much younger?'

'Five and a half years.'

'Is that why you're upset? Because she's getting married before you?'

I looked up sharply. 'What? No!' I took a breath. 'I mean, she's my sister. I'm nothing but happy for her.'

'Of course,' Michael said slowly. He was looking at me like he didn't quite believe me.

'I'm really not upset about that,' I insisted. 'I mean, I'm *so* not ready for that, you know?' I paused and took a deep breath. I didn't know why I was telling him all this, but I didn't seem to be able to stop once I'd gotten started. 'It's just that my grandmother made a scene in church, and everyone keeps asking where my boyfriend is and what's wrong with me that I'm about to turn thirty-five and I'm not married yet,' I blurted out.

I looked at him miserably. He raised an eyebrow.

'And?' he asked.

I stared. 'What, now *you're* asking me why I'm not married yet?'

He laughed. 'No, I'm asking you where your boyfriend is.'

I narrowed my eyes at him again. I hesitated, then mumbled, 'I broke up with him a month ago.'

'Hmm,' Michael said instantly. 'Why?'

'Is that any of your business?' I asked, bristling.

Michael shrugged. 'Probably not.' But he seemed to be waiting for an answer.

I glanced down at the barrel I was sitting on and took a deep breath. 'Fine,' I said. I thought about my answer for a minute. 'He just wasn't the right guy,' I said. 'I liked him, but I didn't love him. And I'm pretty sure I never could.'

'Okay,' Michael said. He looked interested.

I took a deep breath, looked down at my lap and continued. 'He was good on paper. We should have fit. I guess I thought that if I stayed with him long enough, maybe I'd fall in love, you know? But it doesn't work that way.'

'No,' Michael agreed. 'It doesn't.'

I looked at him again, then back down. 'It just seems like everyone wants me to settle, you know? Like I'm about to turn thirty-five, and I apparently just turned down the best chance I had at getting married.'

Michael was silent for a long moment. Finally, he said, 'No matter how pleasant he was, would you really want to spend the rest of your life with someone you're not in love with?'

'No,' I said softly.

'Then you did the right thing,' Michael said. 'And who cares if you're thirty-five?'

I rolled my eyes. 'Everyone, apparently.'

'Yeah, well, that's stupid,' Michael said. 'No offense to any of your family and friends. But thirty-five is just a number.'

I shrugged.

'You want to hear another number?' he asked.

I looked up, wondering what he meant.

He smiled and continued. 'Sixty. Or, if you're lucky, sixty-five or seventy.'

'What?'

'The number of years in the rest of your life,' he said. 'By that count, you're only a third of the way through, right? Do you really want to spend the second two thirds of your life with someone you *know* isn't right for you?'

I smiled. 'No.'

'Okay, then. Now we're getting somewhere.'

Our eyes met, and for a moment, I couldn't look away. I had this sudden, crazy, overwhelming feeling that there was something more between us than there should have been. I held my breath without meaning to, and I had the distinct feeling he was holding his too.

And then, just as quickly as it had started, the moment was over. I blinked and took a deep breath. He coughed and looked away. And Becky chose that moment to come bursting through the kitchen doors in a cloud of ivory silk.

'Cat!' she exclaimed, her eyes alighting on me. She glanced at Michael and looked confused. 'Hi,' she said warily.

'Hi,' he responded cheerfully, as if this was the most normal situation in the world. 'It's the new Mrs Cash! How's the reception going?'

'Um, it's good,' Rebecca said. She cleared her throat and looked at me. 'Are you okay?' she asked. Her eyes darted to Michael and then back at me.

I smiled. 'I'm fine. Michael here was just helping me out with something.' Becky still looked confused, so I added, 'This is his restaurant.'

Becky just looked at me. 'I know,' she said. 'I met with him last month about the food. A meeting *you* skipped, by the way, because you were supposedly too busy with some accounting emergency.' She looked back and forth between us. 'What on earth was he helping you with in the kitchen?'

I opened my mouth to reply, but Michael answered for me. 'Your sister was just asking me about various olive oil varieties,' he said quickly. 'I was just explaining the difference between virgin and extra-virgin.'

I stifled a laugh. Becky still looked suspicious.

'Okay. But maybe you could rejoin the wedding now,' she said, 'considering you're the maid of honor. Maybe you could find out about olive oil later?' Now she just looked annoyed.

'Yes, of course,' I said quickly. 'Sorry.'

I turned to Michael and smiled. 'Thanks,' I said. He smiled and I added, 'For the lesson about olive oil.'

'I hope it made you feel a little better,' he said. Then he glanced at Becky and back at me. 'About olive oil,' he added.

I grinned. 'Thanks,' I said again. I turned to follow Becky, who had already flounced out of the kitchen, muttering to herself. But Michael's deep voice stopped me before I made it to the door.

'Listen,' he said. 'If you want to talk olive oil again, maybe we could have dinner sometime.'

My heart was thudding suddenly. I looked at him in surprise. I didn't think it was my imagination that he looked a little nervous.

Before I could stop it, a voice that didn't sound like my own said, 'That sounds great.'

'Like Monday?' he asked.

I took a deep breath. 'Monday sounds fine.'

'Good,' Michael said. He smiled at me as I scribbled my name and number on a piece of paper. He glanced at it before slipping it into his pocket. 'I'll call you, Cat Connelly. It was nice to meet you.'

'Yeah,' I said. I shook my head and smiled. 'You too.'

O n Monday morning, I arrived at work at seven thirty a.m. on the dot, earlier than almost everyone else, as usual.

'Why, Miss Connelly!' exclaimed the building's security guard, Miles, who greeted me each morning. 'Didn't your sister get married this weekend? I thought for sure you'd be late getting in today, for once.'

'Why, Mr Parker,' I said back, refusing, as usual, to address him by his first name until he addressed me by mine. It was a longstanding joke between us. 'I would have thought you'd know me better than that by now.'

He smiled. 'That's true, Miss Connelly,' he said. 'I can set my watch by your comings and goings, you're so consistent!'

I laughed, but it sounded hollow to me as I stepped onto the elevator and wished Miles a good day. I knew he was joking, but he was right, wasn't he?

As I settled down behind my desk in my cubicle on the deserted forty-second floor, his words rattled around in my head.

Consistent Cat Connelly.

Consistent.

Consistent meant boring. No surprises. No taking chances. Not a second spent living on the edge.

But consistent was good, wasn't it? It was safe, reliable, predictable. I had always been proud of being the person everyone could count on, the one who would always be there, whom security guards could set their watches by, who arrived to work early and stayed late, who held everything together while everything around them fell apart.

I hadn't always been that way. But after my mother left the first time, it had been survival. The mortgage and the bills still had to be paid, food still had to be on the dinner table, the house still needed to be cleaned.

Becky was too young. Dad was too broken.

There was only me.

And there had been solace in the routine and consistency I'd found after my mother left. It was harder to feel sad when I had a list of twenty chores and a timetable everyone had to stick to.

Not that there was anything wrong with that. Indeed, I think it was that attention to detail, that consistent reliability, that propelled me to straight A's in high school, a scholarship to NYU, and a stable job as an accountant at Puffer & Hamlin, one of the foremost firms in Manhattan. I'd been here for a dozen years now, and every six months, like clockwork, I earned reliable performance reviews and a regular raise. In fact, this progression up the ladder was so steady that I even started factoring in the raises before I received them, because after a decade I knew exactly when they were coming and how much they'd be. That was one of the nice things about working for an accounting firm: the people in charge were just as consistent and predictable as I was.

I supposed that the only flaw in my carefully laid out life was that I hadn't seemed to be able to quite figure out dating.

'That's because you can't control people's reactions and feelings the way you control numbers,' Becky told me once. Easy for her to say. She was a giggly, scatterbrained part-time nanny, part-time dog walker who lived paycheck to paycheck but never seemed to worry about it. She didn't exert an ounce of control over her life, and yet things *always* fell into place for her. Her apartment, a dirt-cheap Village walk-up, had practically fallen into her lap, thanks to an elderly client whose unit became available the exact week Becky was being evicted from her old place. Every time she lost one nannying job because the family moved or the kids outgrew her, another one magically materialized within a few weeks. She'd never gone more than two months without a serious boyfriend since she first started dating Jamie Allen in the eighth grade.

Becky broke all the rules and seemed to be living in a fairy tale.

I lived by the rules and seemed to be barreling toward a dead end.

By eleven thirty that morning I'd hardly gotten any work done, which was unusual for me. Even Kris, who sat in the cubicle beside me and had, in the last six years, become my best friend at work, had noticed.

'Head in the clouds over there?' she asked me with an arched eyebrow as I once again sighed at the computer screen. As usual, she was decked out in a brightly colored outfit that looked as if it had dropped straight out of 1969.

Before settling down, getting married, having two kids and going into accounting, she had spent the latter part of the nineties waving peace signs and doing silent sit-ins in San Francisco.

I felt a little color rise to my cheeks, and I hastily closed the window I'd been looking at on the computer.

'No,' I lied. 'I was just looking something up.'

'Mmm,' Kris said. I knew she didn't believe me. 'You know,' she added with half a smile, 'you *are* allowed to goof off sometimes.'

'Not on company time,' I responded quietly.

Kris rolled her eyes and shook her mass of black curls. 'Oh, please!' she said. 'When else would you goof off? You're always here!'

I smiled at her and shook my head. She always teased me for my perfect attendance record and my tendency to arrive early at the office and be one of the last to leave at the end of the day. When she had first started working here, I think she was wary of me, wondering if perhaps all my diligence meant I was gunning for some sort of big promotion. I think she wondered vaguely if she'd have to compete with me. But she realized soon enough that it was just my way. Not that she encouraged it. In fact, she had actually stood up and booed me, only half joking, at last year's Christmas party, when I was given the award for best attendance for the third year in a row. 'That's just weird,' she had murmured.

But it wasn't weird. Not to me. I hardly ever got sick, so why waste a sick day when I didn't have to? I didn't really have anyone to go on vacation with, so what was I going to do, take time off and sail around the world by myself? My friends from college were all married; my sister had only ever taken trips with her boyfriends, and my dad lived in Brooklyn, close enough to mean I didn't have to take time off if I wanted to go see him. Plus, if I took a vacation, my work would just pile up and stress me out when I got back. Who needed that hassle?

The only impulsive thing I'd ever done was a summer abroad in Rome between my junior and senior years of college. And that was only because Dad had convinced me that I had to get out and see the world, and that he and Becky would be fine without me for two and a half months.

It had been a big mistake. I'd worried obsessively about the two of them for the first twelve days. And then I'd met Francesco, a Vespa-riding, dark-haired, green-eyed Italian guy seven years older than me. It was the only time in my life I'd ever really been irresponsible. It was the only time I'd really been in love, though now I wondered whether I really had been. Could you fall in love that quickly? Maybe it was just the excitement of being somewhere new, somewhere where I didn't have to take care of anyone but me for a few blissful months. But it was also the only time my heart had been broken, although I was the one to end it. I still couldn't believe I'd lost control so totally. After that, I had vowed not to be so careless again.

But as the years ticked by, I was beginning to wonder, just a little bit, if maybe that was a mistake.

I snuck a look at Kris's desk. She had turned her back to me and was once again typing furiously.

I turned back to my own computer and, looking once more at Kris, I reopened the page I'd been browsing a moment ago. I had, in fact, been goofing off. But the thing was, I couldn't shake the cute restaurant owner from my mind. And worse, he still hadn't called. Granted, I'd only met him a day and a half ago. But hadn't he specifically asked me out for tonight?

So there I was, on a Monday morning when I should have been hard at work crunching numbers, instead browsing the website of Adriano's and, when I discovered there was no bio of its owner (only a listing of his full name, which was Michael Evangelisti), Googling him, hoping for some tidbit of information.

The only thing I could find was a brief article in the *New York Post* about the opening of Adriano's two years ago. I clicked on the link and leaned in hungrily, waiting to digest whatever scraps of knowledge the Internet might throw my way. I snuck another glance at Kris, who was absorbed in her work, and reasoned that if she glanced over I'd look equally absorbed in mine.

The *Post* article, which was brief, materialized on my screen, and I read it quickly, taking note of all the scant facts and gazing a little too long at the thumbnail-sized headshot of Michael, who looked just as attractive as I remembered him.

Michael was forty-two when the article was written, making him forty-four now. Older than I'd thought. Older than me by a decade, in fact, despite his boyish dimples and youthful laugh. He had been in publishing before opening the restaurant. He'd gone into business with a silent partner, who financed the start-up of the business while Michael agreed to be the managing partner. As for why Michael had quit his old job and suddenly started the restaurant, the article quoted him as saying it was because his mother had just died, and opening a restaurant was always something they'd talked about together. Her unexpected passing had made him realize that you couldn't just sit and wait for dreams to come true. You had to make them happen before it was too late.

'My dad died when I was twenty,' he said. My heart thudded with the familiarity of the statement as I read on. 'He was hugely into cooking, and he used to take me back to Rome with him all the time to visit his family. I spent every summer there with my cousins. They all live there; it's where my dad grew up. That's where I learned to cook and where I learned to be passionate about food. My mom and I always talked about opening a restaurant incorporating that passion, and what better way to do that in my dad's honor than to name it after him?'

The article ended with a brief note from the reviewer that called the cuisine 'haute Italian' and lauded the restaurant's low lighting and lofty ceilings, its rustic wood-fired pizzas and its appetizing aroma of breads and olive oil. Reading the last quote, I laughed aloud, recalling the conversation I'd had with Michael on the olive oil barrels. Unfortunately, this made Kris look up with a smile on her face.

'You *are* goofing off!' she said triumphantly. 'I *knew* it!'

I felt the color rise to my cheeks. 'No, I'm not,' I protested weakly.

She rolled her eyes. 'Oh, please,' she said. 'When's the last time someone's expenses made you giggle?'

I tried unsuccessfully to stifle a small smile. Arching an eyebrow, Kris stood up and crossed the few feet between our cubicles to come stand behind my chair. 'So?' she asked. 'What are you looking at?'

I shrugged, but she was already reading over my shoulder.

'You're giggling at a restaurant review?' she asked after a moment. I glanced back at her. She looked confused.

'It's where Rebecca's reception was,' I responded weakly.

'Oh,' Kris said slowly. 'Okay. But I still don't get what's so funny.'

She leaned over me and grabbed the mouse. She clicked a few times and scrolled up on the page. As Michael's headshot came back into view, she stopped scrolling. 'Ah,' she said simply.

I waited for her to elaborate, but she was silent. So I tentatively asked, 'What?'

'Could it have anything to do with the cute restaurant guy?'

I looked up guiltily.

She grinned. 'Ah, so your weekend was even more interesting than you let on!' she said.

'Nothing happened,' I said quickly. Too quickly, perhaps.

Kris laughed. 'I'm not implying you had your way with the guy over a barrel of olive oil or something,' she exclaimed.

The color drained from my face. Why had she mentioned olive oil?

'But I'm assuming you met him?' she persisted.

'Yes.'

'And?' she prompted.

'And . . . nothing.' I shrugged. 'He just seemed nice.'

'Nice?'

'Yes,' I said. 'Nice is good. Nice is . . . nice.'

Kris made a face at me. 'Yes, thanks for the definition. Now are you going to tell me about what happened or not?'

I paused and then gave in. Kris listened intently as I filled her in on the conversation I'd overheard in the bathroom, my snap decision to hide in the kitchen, and Michael's discovery of me among the olive oil barrels.

'So there was definite chemistry,' she filled in when I finished.

I blushed. 'He, um, asked me out,' I mumbled.

'Wait, what?' Kris was suddenly grinning. 'Like on a date?'

'I don't know. I thought so. But he hasn't called.'

Kris had her mouth open to respond when my cell phone, which was lying on my desk, began to vibrate. We exchanged glances and looked down at the screen. The call was coming from an unfamiliar 212 number.

'Did you give him your cell number?' Kris asked.

'Yes.'

'That has to be him, calling from the restaurant!' she said. 'Answer it!'

I paused. It vibrated again.

'Answer it!' Kris repeated more urgently. When I still didn't move, she reached down, pushed the 'send' key and handed me the phone. Now I had no choice.

'Hello?' I said.

'Cat?' I recognized Michael's voice immediately. 'It's Michael. From Saturday night? I'm so sorry I didn't call yesterday. It just turned into a crazy day, and by the time I was done it was eleven o'clock, and I thought that might be too late to try you.'

'No problem,' I said as breezily as possible. I mouthed to Kris that it was him, and she did a happy little dance. I put my hand over my mouth to stifle a laugh.

'So, um, are you still interested in grabbing a bite to eat

tonight?' he asked. 'I know it's kind of last minute, but there's a great little fondue place a few blocks from my restaurant that I've been meaning to check out, if you're up for it.'

I grinned. 'That sounds great,' I said as casually as possible.

'Good.' He sounded relieved. 'I'm so out of practice with this.'

I wanted to ask what he meant. Had he just gotten out of a relationship? Did he not have time to date? But I didn't want to have that conversation on the phone. So instead, I told him I could meet him at eight at his restaurant, if that worked for him.

We hung up, and I looked sheepishly at Kris, who was still standing at the entrance to my cubicle, grinning down at me.

'Fondue, eh?' she asked. 'Sounds romantic.'

I smiled. 'Yeah, it does.' I took a deep breath. 'I know this sounds dumb, but I have a really good feeling about this guy.'

Kris winked at me. 'I know. I can tell. I haven't seen your face this shade of red since you collided with that waiter at the company party and spilled a whole tray full of red wine on Mr Hamlin.'

I laughed. 'You know, I think I actually have butterflies in my stomach. Is that crazy?'

'No,' Kris said. 'That's a good thing. That's how it's supposed to feel.'

'Yeah,' I said. I smiled and looked at Michael's face, smiling back at me from my computer monitor. 'It is, isn't it?'

*

I took a cab across the park from my one-bedroom walk-up on East 76th and arrived at Adriano's five minutes before eight. I couldn't believe how nervous I was; I was normally cool, calm and collected before a date, but then again my dates were usually set-ups from well-intentioned friends, or guys I'd met through work and had to talk myself into being excited about.

I walked into the restaurant and asked the hostess for Michael. She looked me up and down, snapped the gum she was chewing, then pursed her lips and sauntered off to find him. He appeared a moment later, smiling widely.

'So this is what you look like when you're not crouching in my kitchen,' he said, looking at me in amusement.

I could feel myself blushing. 'And?' I asked, looking self-consciously down at my khaki skirt and pale pink tissue-weight tee.

'I think you're the most beautiful woman to have ever graced an olive oil barrel,' he said.

I laughed. 'Okay. I'll take that.'

'And I want you to know, I don't go around saying that to all the women I meet in my kitchen,' he added seriously.

'Well, that's good,' I deadpanned. 'I was worried for a minute.'

He stood there for a moment, rubbing his hands together and shifting his weight from one foot to the other. I had the sudden feeling he was a little nervous too.

'Shall we?' he asked, stepping forward and offering me the crook of his elbow formally, the way ushers do when they walk you down the aisle before a wedding.

I smiled and threaded my arm through his. As we

strolled toward the front door of the restaurant, I couldn't help but notice the hostess staring after us.

It would be no exaggeration to say that the date with Michael was the best one I'd had in years – even better than those first few magical times I'd had with Francesco in Rome.

I'd never been with anyone so easy to talk to or anyone who made me laugh quite as much. He was a great storyteller, and as we walked the few blocks uptown to the fondue place, our arms still comfortably linked, he told me about deciding to open the restaurant and how he had to fight the bank to prove why he was worthy of a loan.

'It's just not that easy here,' he said, shaking his head. 'When my grandfather opened his restaurant in Rome fifty years ago, all he had to do was promise the bankers free meals for life.'

I laughed. 'Your grandfather owns a restaurant in Rome?'

'Well, he did,' Michael said. 'He passed away a number of years ago. My uncle has been running it since I was a kid.'

He paused as we reached the door to the fondue place, which was called the Big Dipper. I smiled at the logo on the door: a cartoon image of a cat sitting on the edge of the moon, holding out a fondue utensil into a cheese-filled constellation.

'Cute place,' I said.

Michael smiled. 'You have to hand it to them for creativity.'

As we sat down at our table a moment later, Michael continued his story. 'My father used to take me to Rome for a few months every summer when I was a kid,' he said.

'I don't have any brothers and sisters, but I have about a million cousins over there. I taught them and their friends to speak English; they taught me how to run a restaurant. My cousins still work in my uncle's place. I'm sure they'll take it over some day soon. That's one of the nice things about Italy: everything is family-run.'

I smiled and nodded. 'Where's the restaurant?'

'It's near the Pantheon,' he said. 'Do you know Rome?'

I nodded. 'I lived there for a summer.'

'You're kidding!' he said. 'Don't tell me you have family over there too.'

I hesitated. My mother's parents and sister still lived in Rome, as far as I knew, but the summer I'd lived there I had deliberately avoided seeking them out. I knew exactly where I could find them if I wanted to – they owned a scarf shop near the Piazza Colonna – but I couldn't bring myself to go. What if they rejected me too? But I spent a great deal of time anxiously studying strangers' faces on the street, wondering if I'd see my mother's deep green eyes on an unfamiliar face or hear a tinkle of laughter similar to hers. It was like looking for ghosts.

'No,' I said finally. 'I don't.'

The word felt heavy between us, the way lies sometimes do.

'So, did you like it?' Michael asked after a moment.

I blinked at him, confused. 'What?'

Michael smiled. 'Rome. Did you like it there?'

I hesitated. I thought of the feeling of being surrounded by my mother, a sensation that, oddly, made me feel both anxious and protected. I thought of Francesco, the first man I'd ever fallen in love with, though our relationship lasted only the length of the summer. I'd only heard from him a few times after I returned to the States; he'd said he couldn't do long-distance. I thought of the feeling of being free, if for only three months – free to come and go when I pleased, free to wander the streets and do what I wanted, free to worry about myself for once.

'I loved it,' I said softly.

Michael beamed. 'Me too,' he said. 'What was your favorite place in the city?'

I didn't even need to think about it. 'The bridge near the Castel Sant'Angelo.'

Michael looked surprised. 'Really? Wow. That's always been one of my favorite places too.'

I smiled, took a breath and continued. 'It was sort of my place. It sounds silly, but whenever I felt sad or needed to think about something or make a big decision, I went there. I mean, you've got a million people walking by, but no one looks at you. It feels like you're sitting in this bubble, just looking out over the world.'

'I agree,' Michael said softly. He was looking at me differently now. I liked what I saw in his eyes.

We ordered a cheese fondue and a bottle of Sauvignon Blanc, and we talked and laughed over the meal, telling stories about our childhoods, our favorite things about Rome and the things we loved and hated about our jobs.

We discovered that we'd both been voracious readers as kids, and that we'd even shared an interest in the same kinds of books. He sheepishly admitted to reading his mom's old Nancy Drew hardcovers once he had finished reading all the Hardy Boys books, and I laughed and said that I'd read the Hardy Boys along with Nancy Drew. In high school, we'd both developed an interest in F. Scott Fitzgerald after reading *The Great Gatsby*, and we'd both gone through a Tom Robbins phase in our twenties. We had both been raised as Catholics, but we admitted that although we still believed in all those things we'd been taught in church as kids, we didn't go to Mass nearly as much as we should, and we felt a little guilty about it. We both loved *Flight of the Conchords* and *Entourage*. And we discovered we liked similar eclectic mixes of music. We'd both been to see Elton John and Billy Joel when they toured together; we'd both attended Radiohead's most recent concert in New York, we'd been to see Guillaume Riche twice, and we'd both been in the audience at a Sister Hazel show at Irving Plaza a few years earlier where Pat McGee Band from Virginia had opened up. We both had Mandy Moore's new CD and Courtney Jaye's old one on heavy rotation in our iPods, and we both thought that Paul McCartney and John Lennon were the most talented songwriting duo in history.

By the time our chocolate fondue dessert arrived, my stomach was full of butterflies, and I found myself feeling even more nervous than I had when the date began. It all felt so perfect. I suddenly felt like I was waiting for something to go wrong.

'So, how many times have you been back to Rome?' Michael asked, interrupting my self-destructive line of thought as he dipped a banana chunk into the vat of chocolate on our table.

'I haven't.'

He paused mid-dip and stared at me. 'You haven't been back?'

I shook my head slowly.

'Why?' he asked.

I shrugged. 'No real reason to go,' I said. 'My life's here, you know? I have a good job. My sister needed me for a while, when she was younger. I like to be close to my dad in case he needs anything. You know.'

Michael studied my face. 'No,' he said. 'I don't know.' He looked a little troubled. 'So it's a place you love. But you haven't tried to return there? Because you feel like you shouldn't?'

I shrugged, feeling a little silly. 'I don't know,' I mumbled.

Michael was silent for a long moment. I looked up at his face, expecting to see judgment. But instead, there was only concern. 'You should go back,' he said softly. 'You and I both know that life can sometimes be too short, right?'

I shrugged again. I pretended that his words didn't mean much to me. But the truth was, they cut deep. He was right. Life was short. Even if you got to live all the years a normal person was allotted, it didn't feel like enough time sometimes. And I hadn't really *lived*, had I? My stomach lurched a little.

'Anyhow,' Michael continued, seeming to sense that I was getting lost in my own head again, that his words were doing something to me. 'Enough about that. We'll have plenty of time to talk about Rome in the future, right?'

I smiled at him. 'Yeah.' I liked that he had mentioned the future, like it was a given. It made me feel a little safer. I liked safe.

He cleared his throat. 'I've had a really good time with you tonight.'

I smiled. 'Me too.'

'I'd love to do this again sometime soon,' he said. 'If you'd be up for getting together.'

'I'd like that,' I said. We smiled at each other for a long moment.

Fifteen minutes later, we were strolling back toward Michael's restaurant. He had suggested a walk around the neighborhood, and then maybe a glass of wine somewhere, but he had to stop quickly and drop an overdue check off for his head chef, he said. He'd meant to do it earlier, but he'd forgotten.

Once we reached the doorway to Adriano's, Michael paused and took a step closer to me. The world around us seemed to slow as he put one hand on my waist, drawing me closer, and the other hand on the side of my face. He gently stroked my cheek with his thumb as he gazed at me. I held my breath as he closed his eyes and dipped his head slowly closer to mine until our lips touched, ever so slightly.

It felt perfect.

We stood like that for a moment, suspended in time, our lips just barely touching, and then the kiss grew more passionate. I should have felt silly, kissing a man I barely knew right in front of the restaurant he owned on a busy Manhattan street. But instead, I only felt butterflies. My head swirled. It was the most perfect kiss I'd ever had. He continued to hold me gently, stroking my cheek with soft fingers while he threaded his other hand through my hair. The kiss seemed to last forever, and when we finally pulled slightly back from each other, I was breathless. He seemed to be too.

'Wow,' he said, gazing into my eyes. He took a step back and raked a hand through his hair. 'Wow,' he repeated.

'Wow,' I echoed. I could tell that I was blushing, but I no longer cared.

Michael cleared his throat and blinked a few times. 'I, um, have to run that check inside quickly,' he said, nodding at the door to the restaurant. 'Do you want to come in for a moment and wait? And then maybe we can take that walk?'

'Sure,' I said.

'Good,' Michael said. He smiled at me. 'Because I was thinking maybe I'd like to kiss you again.'

My heart thudded. 'I think that sounds like a very good idea.'

He stared at me for another moment, looking a little dazed. 'That might have been the best kiss I've ever had,' he added softly.

I swallowed hard. My heart was pounding and my cheeks were flaming. 'I couldn't agree more,' I said honestly.

A slow grin spread across his face. 'I'll be right back,' he said. He gave me a quick peck on the lips. Then he opened the door for me, and we ducked into the dark interior of the front room of Adriano's. He showed me into his office, a small room just off to the right of the waiting area, and told me to make myself comfortable. I sat down in one of the padded chairs facing his desk and waited while he went off to find his executive chef.

A few minutes later, he returned. 'You know, I was thinking,' he said as he strode into the office. 'I should give you the number of a woman I know in Rome who rents rooms by the month. She's an old friend of the family.'

I smiled. 'You're really convinced I need to go back there, aren't you?'

He laughed. 'I'm just looking for an excuse to come visit. Would you let me crash on your couch?'

'That's a long way to go for a second date.'

'I was hoping we'd have our second date before then,' he said, holding my gaze for just a moment longer than necessary. I could feel my cheeks heating up as I smiled at him. He scribbled something on a piece of scrap paper and handed it to me. I glanced at it quickly. It had a woman's name – Karina – a phone number and the word Squisito.

'That's the restaurant where she works,' he clarified. 'It's right near the Pantheon. I haven't talked to her in a few years, but if you tell her you know me, I'm sure she'll give you a great rate.'

'I feel like I'm meeting with a travel agent,' I said with a smile. But I folded the piece of paper and tucked it into my wallet, knowing that if I did indeed make it to Rome, I'd probably stay at a hotel. But I didn't want to insult Michael, who was obviously going out of his way to help me.

'Ready to go?' he asked.

I nodded and stood up. He took a step closer, and we looked at each other for a long moment. He pulled me close, leaned in again and kissed me slowly, tenderly. I felt like I was in a dream. I could have stayed there forever.

But the spell was broken by the restaurant's gum-snapping hostess, who appeared suddenly in the doorway of his office. 'Um, Mr Evangelisti?' she asked hesitantly. We stepped away from each other quickly, as if we'd been caught doing something wrong. She looked tentatively between the two of us and then cleared her throat. 'There's, um, a phone call for you.'

He glanced at her. 'Can you take a message?'

She looked nervous now. She glanced at me and cleared her throat again. Then she looked back at Michael. 'Well, uh, it's your mother-in-law,' she said.

My stomach dropped.

Michael's eyes darted immediately to my face, which, I was sure, had turned ashen in a moment.

No. There must be some mistake.

'His mother-in-law?' I repeated in a voice so high I didn't recognize it.

The girl glanced at me and nodded slowly.

'Oh my God,' I murmured. I felt like someone had just slapped me across the face, and I was still reeling from the impact. Had I just imagined the connection between us, the electricity in the air, the chemistry? What game was he playing? Was I supposed to have become his unwitting mistress? Or did he think I'd be on board with this plan, just because I was almost thirty-five, pathetic, boyfriend-less and boring? Like I couldn't do any better than a smooth-talking restaurant owner who was *married*?

I couldn't believe I'd almost fallen for it.

I felt physically ill. The butterflies had been replaced by an almost overwhelming wave of nausea.

'Great,' Michael muttered under his breath, as if discouraged that the inconvenient little detail of his marriage had come up so soon. 'Um, listen, Cat, it's not what it sounds like.'

I wanted to cry. But I had never cried in front of a man. And I wasn't about to start now, in front of someone I barely knew at all and had very clearly misjudged entirely. 'No need to explain,' I said crisply. I was already gathering my things to go.

Michael looked wounded by my sudden coldness. I don't know what he had expected. Was I supposed to be jumping up and down with glee that I had begun falling for a married man, that I had just shared the best kiss of my life with someone else's husband?

'But Cat!' he exclaimed. He raked both hands through his hair in obvious agitation. 'It's ... I mean, I ...' He didn't seem to be able to spit out words. I waited, glaring at him. 'It's just ... I mean, she lives with us, and, um ...' His voice trailed off.

'Your mother-in-law *lives* with you?' I repeated in horror. I snorted. 'Oh, perfect! This just keeps getting better.'

'No, it's not what you think!' Michael said. 'I mean, it is, but it's not. I mean, you don't understand.' He looked desperate. He paused and turned to the hostess. 'Anneliese, can you ask if I can call her back in a few minutes?'

She hesitated and glanced at me. 'Mr Evangelisti, she says it's about your daughter.'

My jaw dropped.

'*Daughter?*' I repeated. 'You have a daughter too?' Is this what my life had come to? He had a wife *and* kids? I felt short of breath, like something heavy was suddenly pressing down on my diaphragm.

'Listen, please, wait right there, and I'll explain everything,' Michael said. He looked panicked. 'I, um, I really have to take this. She never calls. It must be an emergency. I'm ... I'm sorry.'

And with that he strode quickly out of the office, while I stared after him, slack-jawed and momentarily frozen to the spot. After he'd disappeared toward the kitchen, I took a deep breath and shook myself. I had to go. I suddenly wanted to be as far away from this place as possible. I glanced at the hostess, who was still standing there staring at me.

'Unbelievable,' I muttered to her. 'He has a wife?'

She looked at me for a long moment and nodded. 'Duh,' she said noncommittally. Then she rolled her eyes, looked bored again and went back to snapping her gum. And why shouldn't she? She was all of eighteen or nineteen. Her whole life stretched before her.

Mine, on the other hand, seemed to be rapidly closing in on me, leaving me fewer and fewer chances for happiness every day.

'That bastard!' my sister declared later that evening, her voice sounding closer and clearer than it should have given that she was thousands of miles away in Cozumel, in the midst of her honeymoon. She had called to say hello, but she had noticed right away that something about my voice sounded off.

I told her what had happened with Michael. 'The worst part of it,' I said, 'is that I can't believe my judgment was so off, you know?'

Becky sighed. 'It's not your fault, Cat,' she said. 'You're just in a bad place right now. And he took advantage of it. Or he tried to, anyhow.'

I blinked a few times and tried to steady myself, even though I was sitting down at my desk at home. 'It was just that he made me feel . . .' I searched my mind and then filled in, 'hopeful. He made me feel hopeful, for the first time in a while. Like maybe I'd finally met someone who was different, you know?'

'He was playing games with your head,' Becky said softly.

'I know,' I said. 'But it got me thinking. I just keep sitting around waiting for life to happen to me, don't I?

I mean, maybe I'm not meeting the right guys because I'm not out there living.'

Becky was silent for a moment. 'I don't know if that's it,' she said.

'But what if it *is*?' I asked, suddenly feeling like time was sifting too quickly through the hourglass, even as we spoke, and I needed to do something right away to stop it. 'What if I'm just sitting in my little cubicle every day and going to and from work and living in this routine that I don't know how to get out of?'

Becky sighed. 'But Cat, that's *you*,' she said.

Her words stung. She was right. That *was* me.

Becky tried to give me a few words of support, but I could hear Jay's voice in the background, and I could tell she was distracted. I didn't blame her. It was her honeymoon. She didn't need to be counseling me.

'Go have fun,' I said firmly. 'And take lots of pictures.'

'You got it, sis.' I could hear her smiling through the phone. 'And honestly, don't worry about Michael. He was just a jerk. The world's full of them. You simply haven't met the right guy yet.'

For no reason at all, except maybe that speaking of Rome had reminded me of him, Francesco's olive-skinned, chiseled face suddenly popped into my mind, as clear a vision as if I had seen him just yesterday.

'Yeah,' I said vaguely, shaking my head. 'Maybe I haven't.'

But as I wished my sister safe travels and told her to say hi to Jay for me and to make sure to have fun, I couldn't shake Francesco's face from my mind.

Maybe I hadn't met the right guy yet. Or maybe he'd

been right in front of me all along, and I'd been too scared to take that leap into the unknown and find out.

At midnight that night, I was still wide awake in my bed, tossing and turning. The later it got, the more distressed I felt. I hated nights like this. I had to wake up again at six in order to get in my daily half-hour of yoga before showering, blow-drying my hair quickly and leaving for work by seven fifteen. I knew I'd be miserable tomorrow if I didn't get enough sleep.

But that wasn't the primary thing that was on my mind. What was really bothering me was that I couldn't shake the thought of Francesco. The more I tried not to think about the married restaurateur, the more I focused on the guy I'd fallen for in Italy more than a dozen years ago.

So at twelve fifteen I finally snapped on my bedside light, got up and walked into my living room. I switched on the lamp on my desk and opened the bottom drawer. Slowly, I pulled out the small, wooden keepsake box I'd placed there years ago.

I sat down on the living-room sofa with the box in my lap and cracked it open slowly, as if doing so with less caution would invite my old life to come lumbering into my present one more quickly than I was prepared for.

The first thing I saw was the photo of Francesco, the last one I'd taken the morning I left Rome. I'd snapped the shot just hours before I last saw him. It was my favorite picture of him. I had gotten up early that morning to pack the rest of my things, most of which had migrated from my tiny dorm to Francesco's much larger apartment over the course of our two-month relationship. I had set my neatly packed suitcases by the front door and crept back into the bedroom to wake him. But when I stepped through the doorway, he looked so cute tangled up in the sheets, his mouth just a little bit open, the muscles in his bare, darkly tanned shoulders rippling perfectly, that I couldn't resist grabbing my camera and snapping a shot. He never knew I'd taken it, but I'd looked at it so many times, especially in that first year after leaving Rome, that the edges were tattered and worn, and the photo looked many years older than it was.

Of course, the photo *was* old. In the thirteen years that had passed since my time in Rome, so much had changed. *I* had changed. As I started flipping through the rest of the photos, which I had never actually put in an album, because it made me sad to look at them, I marveled at how young and how happy I had looked. I was like a different person. Not that I wasn't happy here. I was, of course. It was just that in Rome there was a lightness to my smiles, a carefree look in my eyes. I looked so excited to be there, so excited to be exploring the city, so excited to be on my own.

I flipped through various poses of me and Francesco at the Trevi Fountain, me and my roommate Kara at the Colosseum, me and Francesco doing shots at his favorite bar near the Pantheon, me by myself outside the museum in Vatican City. I smiled as I passed photos of me kissing Francesco on his smooth, darkly tanned cheek, or posing near his Vespa. I felt like I'd made a lifetime of memories in that summer. And yet there were only a few dozen photos to prove it. I'd been through them so many times over the years that I almost didn't know whether my memories of Rome were real anymore, or whether I was just remembering the things that the pictures showed me.

I quickly flipped through the rest of the box. There was the diary I'd kept, the one I hadn't looked at once since I returned. There were ticket stubs from my train rides around Italy, brochures from the museums I'd visited, pressed sunflowers that I'd picked by the side of the road in Tuscany. There was also the butterfly necklace that Francesco had given me two weeks after we met. It was costume jewelry; he'd probably bought it for a few dollars from some guy on the street. But to me, it might as well have been Tiffany silver and diamonds. I had stopped wearing it a year after I came home from Rome, eleven and a half months after I'd stopped hearing from Francesco. It had almost completely fallen apart by then anyhow.

I picked up the keepsakes one by one, letting the memories wash over me, and I studied the pictures for a long time. I had almost forgotten how much I'd loved his bright green eyes, the way he'd furrow his brow when he was concentrating on something, the way he'd wink at me when I said something funny or referenced a private joke between us. I'd nearly forgotten how good we looked together. He had driven me crazy all the time with his haphazard, devil-may-care approach to life, his constant disorganization. I liked to think that we had balanced each other out perfectly, me with my obsession with order; him with his total lack of a schedule. I think he made me loosen up a little, if only for the summer. And I think I helped make him a little more responsible.

But I had no idea where he was now, or what he was doing. He had never specifically asked me to stay – but I wouldn't have in any case; I had to come home to help take care of Becky and finish up college. He had told me he couldn't do long-distance, and I had left anyway. I could have stayed. I knew I could have stayed and built a life for myself in Rome. But Becky and Dad needed me. And so I'd turned my back and left.

So in the end, I suppose it was my fault. I didn't even blame him when he stopped calling or responding to my emails two weeks after I'd left Rome. I knew I had hurt him. But I'd thought then that the world was wide open for me, that I'd fall in love again with someone new, that Francesco would one day be a fond memory.

Instead, I was nearly thirty-five, and despite the fact that I'd been in and out of several relationships in my adulthood Francesco remained the only man I'd ever really loved.

How had I walked away from that so easily?

I put the keepsakes, diary and photos away, back in their box, and closed the lid decisively, as if banishing the memories into the past, where they belonged. But of course they lingered, and even after I climbed back into bed, turned out the light and tried to fall asleep, Francesco was still there, lurking at the edges of my mind.

That Saturday morning, after avoiding nine calls from Michael and deleting the six messages he'd left without listening to them, I arrived at my dad's narrow rowhouse in Brooklyn, juggling a big brown bag of pumpernickel bagels (our favorite), a container of cream cheese and two cups of coffee, one of which I had managed to spill on my white T-shirt en route.

'Hello, beautiful,' my dad greeted me as he usually did, taking the bagels and cream cheese from my hands as he bent down to kiss my cheek.

'Hey, Dad,' I said, stepping inside and pulling the door

closed behind me while balancing both coffee cups in the crook of my arm.

We settled in the kitchen nook with our usual Saturday spread of bagels, cream cheese and the lox Dad always bought from the deli two blocks away. He poured us two glasses of orange juice from the jug in his fridge and sat down across from me, a serious expression on his face.

'Becky told me about your date with that young man from the restaurant,' he said without any preface.

I could feel myself turning red. 'It's no big deal.'

'Cat, it is a big deal,' he said firmly. He paused and didn't speak again until I looked at him. 'You've had a lot of bad luck, kiddo. But it's not your fault.'

I took a deep breath and exhaled slowly. 'Yeah, well,' I said, 'at some point, I think we have to start tracing it back to me. After all, I'm the one making all these bad decisions, aren't I?'

'I don't think the restaurant guy was a bad decision,' my father said. 'How were you to know?'

'Don't you think I should have sensed that something was off?' I picked up a knife and began to violently slather a bagel with cream cheese. 'But all I thought was, *Wow, this guy is so nice.* I actually thought I'd finally met a good one, you know?'

My father looked at me sadly. 'You will.'

I set the knife down and stared at my bagel. 'I don't know why we're even talking about this,' I said. 'It's fine. Let's talk about something more exciting. Like the wedding. Or Becky's honeymoon. Or your new golf clubs.'

My dad arched an eyebrow at me. 'You always do that,'

he said. 'But not this time. We're going to talk about you for a minute.'

I took a bite of my bagel and ignored him. 'The bagels are great this morning,' I said cheerfully.

'Cat . . .' My father looked at me sternly.

'What?' I played innocent.

My dad rested his chin in his hand and shook his head slowly at me. 'You need to make some changes.'

I set my bagel down. 'What is this, an intervention?'

'I think you need more than one person for an intervention.'

'Okay, so it's a really bad intervention.'

'Cat,' he said, 'it's not an intervention. But Becky and I have talked about it, and we have a suggestion for you.'

'You and Becky talked about me?'

He frowned. 'You can let other people help you sometimes too, you know,' he said. 'You don't always have to take care of everyone.'

'Okay. So what's your big suggestion for how to change my life?' I took a giant, defiant bite of my pumpernickel bagel, steeling myself for what was to come. Had they signed me up for speed dating? Posted my profile to several online sites? Sent up a blimp with my number, photo and a message that subtly screamed, *Desperate and Dysfunctional? Call Cat Connelly!*?

My dad took a bite of his bagel and avoided meeting my gaze. 'Go to Italy,' he said with his mouth full.

I swallowed too soon and choked on my bagel. After a moment spent dislodging a giant chunk of creamy pumpernickel from my throat and downing half the glass of water my father had jumped up to pour me, I wiped my eyes and repeated, 'Um . . . go to Italy? What are you talking about?' I had the disturbing thought that my father had turned into a mind reader and knew I'd been obsessing over Francesco last night.

My father looked surprisingly calm. 'It's the place where you were the happiest,' he said. 'Becky and I think it would be good for you to go back there for a little while.'

'What are you talking about? I'm happy right here.'

He just gave me a look. 'Cat.'

'What? I am.'

'Oh yes, I can tell,' he said. 'This is what you've always dreamed of. Working fifty-hour weeks at a dull job and delivering me pumpernickel bagels every Saturday morning while your love life goes down the drain.'

'I take exception to that.' I paused. 'All of that.'

My father sighed. 'Look. You certainly have the vacation time saved up. And knowing you, you have plenty of room on your credit cards.'

'I do not,' I responded. 'Are you forgetting I just bought an apartment?' It had been one of my proudest accomplishments yet; I had scrimped and saved for a decade to put enough away for a down payment late last year on my one-bedroom on the Upper East Side.

'You didn't pay for your apartment on your credit cards,' Dad reminded me.

'No,' I grumbled. 'But I save my credit for emergencies. And I've been using my cards to make ends meet while I earn back some of the money I spent on the down payment, okay?'

'So spend a thousand on a plane ticket and another fifteen hundred on a month in a hotel.'

'Wait, you want me to go to Rome for a *month*?'

'You can't change your life in a week,' he said. 'Go over for a few weeks, at least. Make it worth your while.'

'You've got to be kidding me,' I said flatly.

My dad looked away. 'Maybe it'll give you some time to deal with your issues with your mother, too.'

'My *issues* with my *mother*?' I asked, standing up.

'Stop being so dramatic,' my father said. 'Sit down.'

I glared at him for a moment and then slowly sank back into my chair. 'I don't have any issues with my mother,' I said softly.

'Aside from hating her,' my father said nonchalantly. He wrapped his hands around mine before I could move to protest again. 'Relax, Cat. I don't blame you for feeling that way. But maybe you could pay a visit to her family while you're there. Maybe they can help you to understand that she never meant to hurt you. Perhaps once you understand that, you'll be able to move on.'

'Whatever,' I mumbled. I looked away. 'Look, this has all been very enlightening. But I have a really busy day ahead of me. So I'm afraid I have to get running.'

My dad sighed and let go of my hands. 'Fine. But will you think about it, at least? You don't even have to see your mother's family, kiddo. Just go over there and remember what it feels like to be happy again.'

'I was a lot happier before I came over here this morning,' I muttered.

I stood up, and we awkwardly kissed goodbye. I expected to feel angry with my father and Becky as I marched out of his house and headed up the street to the subway. But all I felt was a strange emptiness surrounded by a question. And at the center of it all, I kept coming back to Francesco.

That night, after running errands, cleaning my apartment from top to bottom, watching TV for a few hours and trying to fall asleep, I finally gave up, got out of bed again and turned on my computer. It booted up slowly, and I found myself tapping my foot impatiently, way too eager to get onto the Internet.

I logged into AOL and pulled up my address book. I'd been on AOL since college, and I still had Francesco's old email address saved. I hoped he still used it. I clicked on his name in my AOL address book and watched <u>FrancescoValeti11@hotmail.com</u> come up in the 'Send To' field of a blank email. Just seeing his email address again made my heart leap. I remembered how many mornings in Rome I'd started with emailing him a brief *Thinking about you . . . xoxox, Cat* note. I also remembered with a pang how many times I'd written to him in vain after I returned home. I must have sent him fifty unanswered emails before I finally let it go and decided to salvage the remainder of my pride.

Thirteen years had passed since I'd last tried to reach out to him, yet he was burned into my mind as clearly as if I had seen him just yesterday. What if he didn't feel the same way?

I took a deep breath and began writing.

Forty-five minutes and six drafts later, I finally had an email I felt okay about. I read it over one more time.

Dear Francesco,
Hi. It's been a long time. I hope you remember me;
I know I could never forget you. You meant more to
me than you could have known. I wonder where

you are and what you're doing these days. I still
think of you often. I'd love to hear from you.
xo,
Cat

I closed my eyes and hit send before I could reconsider. I
hoped I wouldn't regret this in the morning.

I logged off, shut down the computer and crawled back
into bed. And for the first time that night, my mind was
silent. Finally, I slept.

By the time I got to work on Monday, I felt like I had
kicked up a huge sandstorm of dormant emotions. What
had I done?

My work inbox was filled, as it usually was, with
dozens of messages from over the weekend. I read
through them quickly and gritted my teeth when I saw
michaelevangelisti@adrianos.com on one of the return
addresses. I hadn't given him my email address, so he'd
obviously Googled me to find it. It annoyed me to no end
as I pictured him holing up in his den and furtively
searching for me while his unsuspecting wife played with
their children in the other room. I hit delete before I
could think anymore about it.

There was nothing in my AOL inbox from Francesco.
And a strange gnawing had begun in the pit of my
stomach.

By noon, I had gotten a little work done, but I had also
wasted a ton of time refreshing my AOL mailbox every
few minutes and hoping that Francesco had responded.
With every hour that ticked by without an email from him,
I was growing more and more nervous – and feeling sillier

and sillier for even trying. I kept doing the mental math in my head. By noon our time, it would be six p.m. in Italy, and he'd be heading home if he was still working as a computer programmer, like he had the summer I'd known him. Did he check his email at home too? Maybe he had read the email at work and was at war with his own emotions about how to respond.

'You look deep in thought.' Kris popped her head up over my cubicle wall with a grin.

I cleared my throat. 'No. Just busy with some emails,' I said innocently.

'On your AOL page?' she asked with a smile, nodding at my screen.

I reddened, which was evidently all the answer she needed.

'So who are you waiting for an email from?'

I glanced nervously at the screen. 'No one,' I said quickly.

She raised an eyebrow. 'No one?' she repeated. 'Interesting, considering you've checked your email like a hundred times today, and you seem to be breaking out in a cold sweat.'

I could feel the blood rise to my cheeks.

'And now you're blushing,' she continued smoothly, 'which pretty much confirms my suspicion that it's a guy. I'm hoping it's not the married restaurant dude.'

I shook my head. 'Definitely not.'

She was silent, staring me down. 'Then who?' she finally asked. 'You have *another* new guy?'

'Well,' I said. 'He's not exactly new . . .'

Just then, my computer made a little pinging noise, alerting me to a new message. My breath caught in my throat as I turned to look and saw the familiar email address I'd been waiting to hear from all day. FrancescoValeti11@hotmail.com

Francesco had written back.

Ignoring Kris, I turned quickly back to my computer and clicked on the message. My heart was pounding. In a second, the email popped up on the screen. I read it hungrily.

Bella!
Greetings from Italia! I think to you still. You are written in my memory. Please, you must come back to Italia to see me. My heart longs for you.
Love and kisses,
Francesco

I read and re-read the email breathlessly. I could hardly believe that he had replied at all, but to tell me I was written in his memory? That his heart longed for me? That I should come to Italy to see him? I felt a little woozy.

'Who's this Francesco?' Kris cut into my thoughts, sounding amused. She had come up behind me and was reading over my shoulder.

'No one,' I mumbled, hastily closing the email and blinking a few times to steady myself.

'No one?' she repeated. 'Come on, Cat.'

And so, after a brief pause, I told her the whole story, beginning with the day I first saw him at a nightclub in Rome and ending with my email to him last night. When I finished, she was staring at me with her jaw hanging open.

'How come you've never mentioned him before?' she asked.

I shrugged. 'I don't know. He was in the past, you know?'

'Well, he's not in the past anymore,' Kris said.

I looked up at her hopefully. 'You think?'

'Um, yeah!' Kris said, looking at me with wide eyes. 'He said his heart *longs* for you!'

I could feel myself blushing again. 'Yeah, he did, didn't he?'

'So?' Kris asked. She paused and looked at me closely. 'What are you going to do?'

'Do?' I asked.

She rolled her eyes. 'The man of your dreams, apparently, has just invited you to Italy. Don't tell me you're not going to go.'

My face turned even hotter. I recalled my father's words. Then I recalled my last bank statement. 'I can't go to Italy!'

'Why not?'

I didn't have a good answer for that. 'I don't know,' I stammered finally. 'I mean, it's just impractical. I can't afford it. I have work to do.'

'You haven't taken a vacation day in years!' she said. 'You could probably vanish for a month with all the time you have saved up.'

I cleared my throat. 'Nine weeks, actually,' I said.

Kris widened her eyes. 'Seriously, girl? What are you waiting for?'

I shrugged uncomfortably. 'What if my dad needs something? Or maybe Becky will need some help getting settled in the new apartment. Or what if one of my clients needs me?'

'Cat,' Kris said slowly, as if talking to someone whose comprehension skills were delayed. 'You have a hot man in Italy who wants you to come visit him. Isn't it time you put yourself first for once in your life?'

'But I—' I began to say, but Kris cut me off.

'Seriously, Cat,' she said. She sounded stern now. 'It's truly ridiculous if you don't go. You deserve this. You *need* this.' She paused and added, 'If you don't go, you'll always wonder about what could have been. And that's no way to live.'

'I don't know . . .' I said, my voice trailing off.

Kris stared at me for another long moment. Then, without a word, she stepped into my cubicle, nudged me aside and hit the reply button on Francesco's email.

'What are you doing?' I asked.

She didn't respond. Instead, she typed something into the computer. I watched nervously over her shoulder as the words appeared on the screen.

Are you sure you want me to come? It's been a long time . . .

She hit send before I had a chance to protest.

'Kris!' I exclaimed. 'I can't believe you just did that! What if he was just kidding? What if he didn't mean it! What if—'

Just then, my email pinged again, to let me know I had an incoming message. I stared in disbelief as Francesco's address came up on the screen again. Wordlessly, Kris maneuvered the mouse and clicked. Holding my breath, I read over her shoulder.

Of course I want you to come. True love, it lives forever, no? Please come to Roma. Soon, my bella.

'Oh,' I breathed.

Kris smiled at me. 'Okay, Juliet,' she said. 'Let's send you off to your Roman Romeo.' I tried not to think about how that particular story ended. 'Do you have your passport?'

I nodded, numbly.

'Fantastic,' she said briskly. 'Give me your credit card, and I'll get started on booking you a flight. You start on filling out the vacation request paperwork.'

'But—'

'Just do it,' Kris said firmly. 'I'm not letting you back out of this one. Now when would you like to go? Thursday? Friday?'

I snorted. 'Are you kidding me?'

Kris shrugged. 'Do I sound like I'm kidding?'

I felt like I was in a fog – or perhaps living someone else's life – as I walked down the hall to HR to pick up a vacation request form. Amber, the HR coordinator, looked at me like I was nuts.

'*You* want to take a vacation?' she asked.

I nodded.

'My God!' she exclaimed. 'Hell has frozen over!'

I stared at her, not sure how to respond. 'I don't have to go,' I backpedaled. 'I mean, I can take the vacation whenever it's convenient so that I don't put anyone else out.'

Amber rolled her eyes. 'Are you kidding? I've been waiting for you to request a vacation for the last five years. Please! Go!'

'But—'

'Don't say another word,' she said firmly.

While Amber was still laughing behind me, I walked

out of her office with the vacation request form clutched in my hand, still not really believing that I was going to do this.

Until I got back to my desk.

'So I've booked your outgoing flight for Thursday night,' Kris said cheerfully. 'When would you like to return?'

'Wait, *this Thursday*?'

Kris turned and shrugged at me. 'I found a great deal on Travelocity. A last-minute fare. Don't blame me.'

I took a deep breath. 'Kris. This is crazy.'

She smiled at me. 'Yeah,' she said. 'It is. And that's exactly why you have to do it. When have you *ever* done anything crazy or irresponsible in your life?'

'Nothing good has ever come out of being irresponsible,' I said stiffly.

She studied my face for a moment and sighed. 'Cat, life is messy. Sometimes you have to take chances. You have to step outside your comfort zone. You have to do things that are irresponsible or downright stupid. Does it leave you open to getting hurt? Yeah, of course it does. But how can you say you've lived if you've never really gone out on a limb for anything?'

I considered this as a knot formed in the pit of my stomach. 'It just seems like such a dumb thing to do,' I said.

'Cat, sometimes you *have* to do dumb things,' she said. 'Life works out the way it's supposed to anyhow. For goodness' sakes, do you think I was supposed to be with Dani's dad? Was he really the smartest choice for me? Of course not. But I followed my heart, and now I have my little girl, and I have absolutely no regrets.'

'You don't?'

'Not one,' she said firmly. 'It's all part of the adventure, you know? Sometimes you have to break out of your comfort zone to get to where you need to be in life.'

I considered this. I glanced at the computer, where Travelocity's return flight options loomed in full, vibrant color. I thought about Francesco's email. *Please come to Roma. Soon, my bella.* I thought about how I'd never taken any real chances with my life since that summer in Rome. I thought about how it felt to fall asleep in Francesco's arms and hold his hand and look into his eyes, and how I hadn't felt that with anyone since I'd last seen him.

I swallowed hard. I had nine weeks of vacation time accumulated. My sister was all grown up. My dad could certainly take care of himself.

'I'll go for four weeks,' I heard myself say. 'I can afford four weeks in a hotel.'

Kris stared at me in disbelief then broke into a wide smile as I gaped, stunned by the words that had just come out of my mouth. As I fumbled to take them back, I watched in horror as she quickly clicked select, filled in my credit card information and hit 'Buy Ticket.'

'You're going to Rome,' she said, sitting back in the chair, her face glowing with satisfaction.

'But . . .' I said weakly.

She grinned. 'Too late to back out now,' she said. 'The ticket is nonrefundable.'

'Oh my God,' I muttered. It was all sinking in now. I was going to Rome. By myself. In three days. To reunite with a man I hadn't seen in over a decade. What if he didn't find me attractive anymore? What if he had changed and I no longer liked him?

While I agonized, Kris was cheerfully emailing Francesco back. I gazed weakly at her response, feeling suddenly disconnected from the whole situation.

Francesco,
I've gotten some time off work and can be there Friday afternoon. I'll try to find a hotel.
Cat

He wrote back immediately.

Cat,
Friday? You make my heart sing. I will wait for your arrival. Send me your flight information, and I will arrive to pick you up. I can not wait to see you again, bella.
Molti baci,
Francesco

'There you go,' Kris said, turning to me triumphantly after I read Francesco's reply. I felt like I wanted to pass out. 'You're all set.'

'I can't believe I'm doing this,' I murmured, still staring blankly at the computer screen.

'I can,' Kris said happily. 'It's about time you stopped living life on the safe side.'

5

Becky and Jay came back from their honeymoon the next morning, and I met them for dinner at my father's house. They'd already gotten prints of a hundred of their honeymoon pictures, and my sister chattered nonstop while she talked us through all the minute details of their trip. Jay looked bored, and I could see my father's eyelids beginning to droop by about the sixtieth photo, but I tried to focus on what she was saying. After all, it was important to her, and I always tried very hard to pay attention to the things that mattered to my sister.

She didn't finish her honeymoon stories until long after Dad and I had cleared away the remnants of the butter walnut pasta and chopped salad I'd made for dinner. It wasn't until the four us had settled down for coffee in the living room that I finally dropped my bomb.

'I'm going to Italy on Thursday night,' I said casually, hiding my smile behind the rim of the cracked *Daughters Are Life's Greatest Gift* mug my father always insisted I drink out of.

Becky spat her coffee out. 'What?'

Jay wiped her coffee splatters off his shirt and echoed, 'Italy?'

My father simply stared at me with a smile on his face. 'Good girl,' he said finally.

I looked at Becky and Jay and then locked eyes with my dad for a long time. Then I shrugged. 'I think you were right,' I said. 'I think maybe it's something I need to do.'

'Thursday?' Becky said, still staring at me. 'But that's, like, two days from now.'

I nodded. 'Blame Kris for that,' I said. 'She found me a cheap last-minute ticket. But it's probably better. It won't be enough time to talk myself out of it, will it?'

'That's great,' Jay said, nodding. 'Italy. Wow.'

'But that's really sudden, Cat,' Becky said, laying a hand on his arm to quiet him. 'I mean, are you sure about this?'

I glanced at my father and then back at her. 'I thought this was your idea,' I said to her.

'Well, yeah,' she said. 'But I didn't think you'd actually *do* it. You never do anything.'

Uncomfortable silence settled over us for a moment. My father cleared his throat. 'Well, she's doing this, and I think it's wonderful.'

'Thanks,' I said softly, feeling suddenly uncertain. Becky was right, wasn't she? This was completely out of character for me, completely foolish. My heart started to sink. But then she clapped her hands together and smiled at me.

'You're right,' she said. 'Totally right. It sounds super-fun. I'm just jealous I can't go.'

'Where are you staying?' Jay asked.

'I didn't want to spend a fortune, but I wanted to be somewhere decent and safe,' I said. 'There's actually a great little place near the train station where rooms are about seventy-five dollars a night, which is really reasonable for Rome. With all the taxes and everything, it comes out to about two thousand five hundred for the month.'

Becky whistled, long and low. 'Whoa,' she said. 'That's a ton of money. That's, like, twice what our honeymoon cost.'

'Yeah, well, I'll be gone for four weeks,' I said. 'It's actually not that bad for that amount of time, I think.'

'You have that kind of money?' she asked.

I shrugged, suddenly uncomfortable with the conversation. I talked about other people's money all day long, but hated talking about my own. 'I'll manage,' I said. I shot my dad a weak smile. 'Plus, I've been told that's what credit cards are for.'

'Wow,' Becky said. Then she smiled. 'Well. Good for you.' She paused and added, 'So, are you going to call that guy? What's his name? Francisco?'

I swallowed. 'Francesco,' I corrected. 'And yes. I mean, I've emailed him already.'

For the second time that night, Becky's jaw literally dropped. 'You did? That's so unlike you.'

'Yeah, well, I'm trying to step out of my comfort zone a little more, you know?'

'Well, wow,' Becky said. She shook her head. 'I don't know what to say.'

'I do,' my father said firmly. 'I'm proud of you, honey. You're going to have a great time.' He raised his coffee mug. 'To Cat!' he said.

'To Cat,' Becky and Jay echoed as all four of us clinked mugs.

*

By four the next day, I was so excited I could hardly concentrate on my work. Kris kept assuring me that she'd be fine in my absence and that Puffer & Hamlin wouldn't fall apart without me. I knew she was teasing me, but I still felt uneasy. I'd never been away for more than a few days since I'd started working here. What if one of my clients needed me? What if some disaster happened when I was gone, and I wasn't here to fix it?

'We can always reach you by email,' Kris soothed me with a slightly amused expression on her face. 'And since you also have three hundred capable coworkers, I have the feeling that someone here will be able to solve any problem that comes up.'

'But—'

'No buts,' Kris said firmly. 'Seriously. Just go. Stop worrying. Have a good time for once in your life.'

I avoided two more cell calls from Michael that day and deleted the messages he'd left without listening to them. There was a sliver of me that wanted to tell him that I was going to Italy, but I knew I shouldn't even be thinking about him still. I called the cell phone company and asked them to up me to an international plan for the next thirty days. And I called my cable company and suspended service while I was gone.

'Geez, is there anything you don't think of?' Kris asked, shaking her head in amusement.

'I like to be prepared,' I said.

Just then, my cell phone rang. It was Becky's number. She never called during the day unless something was wrong; I answered immediately.

'Cat?' Her voice sounded small and far away. I could hear her whimpering a little.

'Becky?' I asked. 'Are you okay?' Kris shot me a worried look.

Becky paused. 'Not really,' she said. 'I kind of messed up.'

I closed my eyes for a moment. I'd heard those words from her more times than I could count. 'What happened?'

More sniffling. 'I, um, borrowed Mrs Cohen's car.'

I sighed. Mrs Cohen was a sweet old lady whose miniature poodle Becky had been walking for years. 'Becky, you don't have a driver's license.'

'I know.'

'And?'

She paused. 'Well, I just wanted to use it to take Mitzi up the Central Park for a walk. And you know, I couldn't exactly take her on the subway, because they don't allow dogs, and I didn't have the money for a cab ride all the way uptown.'

'A cab would have been cheaper than paying to park up there.' I couldn't help interjecting a little logic into the story.

'Cat, as *if* I couldn't talk some young parking lot guy into letting me leave my car there for an hour while I walked the dog,' Becky scoffed.

I considered this. It was true. Becky batted her eyes, and men lined up to do what they could to assist her. When I batted mine, people just thought I needed eye drops.

'True,' I said. 'So what went wrong?'

She heaved a big sigh. 'Well, everything was fine, and I was just driving uptown when this total jerk cut me off, so I took a left to avoid him, and I wound up on Broadway, heading north.'

'But Broadway is southbound,' I said.

Becky paused. 'Er, yeah,' she said. 'That was the problem.'

'You drove into oncoming traffic on Broadway?' I demanded. I glanced up to see Kris shaking her head. *Typical*, she mouthed.

'Uh-huh,' Becky whimpered.

'And?' I asked.

'I kind of got hit.'

'Are you okay?'

'Just a little banged up,' she said. 'I'll be fine. Mitzi's okay too, thank goodness. But the car . . .'

'Totaled?' I guessed.

'Not exactly,' she said. 'But it's pretty bad. I talked to the guy at the repair shop, and he said he could knock the price down, since I was so sweet to him and everything, but it will still be a lot to fix it.'

'Doesn't Mrs Cohen have insurance?' I asked.

'I haven't exactly told her,' she said. 'She doesn't even drive the car anymore. I mean, it's a waste, if you ask me. How can you just let a Porsche sit in a garage and rot?'

'You wrecked a *Porsche*?' I asked in disbelief.

'The guy can fix it,' Becky said in a small voice. 'He says that when he's done with it, Mrs Cohen won't even notice.'

I took a deep breath and pinched the bridge of my nose, trying to channel calm. 'What do you need?'

'I don't exactly have the money to pay for it,' she said. 'We kind of spent everything on our honeymoon. My credit cards are maxed out.'

'Can't you just come clean with Mrs Cohen?'

'Well, the thing is, she's friends with all the other ladies whose dogs I walk,' Becky said. 'So if she gets mad at me, I know she'll tell her friends, and I'll lose, like, all the business I've built up over the last five years. It would be devastating.'

'So you want to borrow money from me?' I guessed.

'Only a little bit,' she said quickly. 'And I'll pay you back. I swear.'

I paused for a moment. I knew I'd say yes. I always said yes. I'd bailed Becky out of messes at least a dozen times. But I'd always had a cushion in the past too. Now, between buying my apartment last year, using my credit cards for a few months to scrape by while I made the initial mortgage payments, and putting the airline reservation and Rome hotel on my card, I was pretty much out of spending power. Because of my good credit, I'd been allowed to take out a higher loan amount than I should have, but that also meant that I couldn't request a credit line increase any time soon; I was already overextended.

'How much do you need?' I asked. I held my breath, hardly wanting to know the answer.

'Two thousand, nine hundred fifty-one dollars and sixty-five cents,' she said quickly.

'Three thousand dollars?' I repeated. Across the narrow hallway, Kris's jaw dropped.

'Now you're exaggerating,' Becky said. 'It's not quite that much! And I'll pay you back, Cat! You know I will!'

'Becky,' I said slowly. 'I can't. I'm out of room on my cards.'

She was silent for a moment. 'You're out of room?'

'Hang on,' I said. I logged on to the websites for the

three credit cards I owned and did the math. 'Becky, I only have about fifteen hundred dollars between my three cards.'

'But I need twice that,' she whimpered. 'I'll lose my jobs. And if I lose my jobs, we won't be able to pay rent. It'll, like, ruin our lives.'

I closed my eyes. 'Becky, isn't there anything else you can do?'

'I can't ask Dad.'

We both knew our father didn't have the money. He was barely scraping by as it was. In fact, Becky didn't know it, but I'd had to loan him his rent money a few times this year when he didn't have it. 'I know,' I sighed.

I thought for a moment. I glanced up at Kris, who was just shaking her head. I knew exactly what she was thinking. She would be furious with me if I bailed Becky out of yet another mess at my own expense. But Kris didn't have sisters. She'd never been in this position. You had to help your family if you were capable of doing so.

I closed the credit card websites and opened the site for the hotel in Rome, which I had bookmarked. I gazed longingly at it for a moment. 'Give me five minutes, and I'll have the funds available, okay?' I said.

'Thank you,' Becky said in a small voice. 'You're the best. I promise I'll pay you back.'

'I know,' I said.

'You can just read me the numbers, and I can give them to the guy,' she said helpfully. 'You don't even need to come down here.'

I told her I'd call her right back, then I slowly pushed end. I typed a few things in the computer and hit enter. Then I looked up to find Kris exactly where I'd expected her to be, standing over me, glaring down.

'What did you just do?' she asked accusingly.

'Becky got into a car accident and needed some money,' I mumbled.

'You told her you were out of money,' she said.

'I was,' I said. I paused. 'But she needed me.'

'And?' Kris asked impatiently.

'And I cancelled the hotel in Rome,' I said in a small voice.

'*What?*' Kris demanded. 'Cat, are you insane? Where are you going to stay?'

'I don't really need to go,' I said. 'I mean, maybe this is a sign. I'm just not meant to go over there. And what's more important? Some frivolous trip? Or my sister?'

'That's a ridiculous question,' Kris snapped. 'In this case, the trip was more important. Your sister has asked you for money and favors more times than I can even count!'

'But that's what you do for family,' I said.

'That is *not* what you do for irresponsible, selfish family members who always take advantage of you,' Kris said. 'And besides, your airline ticket is nonrefundable.'

'So I lose seven hundred dollars,' I said. 'The world won't end.'

Kris took a deep breath. 'How much do you have left between your cards?'

I did a quick calculation and told her. 'Not enough for a hotel,' I said. 'I guess it just wasn't meant to be.'

She stared at me for a moment. 'The hell it's not,' she muttered. She bent down next to me and pushed me aside. She opened up my AOL inbox, which I was already logged into, and scrolled down my incoming messages until she got the last note from Francesco. She opened it, hit reply, and typed something quickly. She hit send before I could see what she'd written.

'What did you just write?' I demanded.

She crossed her arms defiantly. 'None of your concern,' she said.

I pushed her back aside and opened the sent mailbox. My jaw dropped as I scanned her message.

Hi Francesco,
I made a really, really stupid mistake and decided to loan my sister some money. Now I won't be able to pay for a hotel in Rome anymore. Do you think it would be possible for me to stay with you?

'Kris!' I exclaimed. 'I can't believe you just did that!'

She shrugged and narrowed her eyes. 'Someone had to. You are way too ready to keep living on the safe side.'

We both stared at the computer for a moment. I knew Francesco had just been scared away, that he wouldn't reply, and that I'd feel even more foolish than I had when this whole fiasco began. After all, he hadn't seen me in years. Surely he wouldn't want me to be his random house guest.

And then a new email popped up in my inbox.

'Told you he'd write back,' Kris said as she clicked to open the message. We both stared at the words on the screen.

You with me would be perfect. I am counting the moments until I see you on Friday.
Love,
Francesco

'Oh my goodness,' I said.

'Cat Connelly,' Kris said, grinning triumphantly, 'you're out of excuses. You're going to Rome.'

Thirty hours later, I was sitting in a middle seat of an Alitalia flight from New York to Rome, still in disbelief.

Even after Francesco had said I could stay with him, I had fully expected something to go wrong. Perhaps, I told myself, my boss will tell me I can't possibly go off with so little notice. But in fact, my boss was so pleased I was taking vacation time that he even ordered me a going-away bouquet from the florist in our lobby.

As I sat on the plane, unable to sleep thanks to my racing mind and the full fleet of butterflies flapping around in my stomach, I tried to conjure what it would be like when Francesco and I saw each other for the first time again.

I knew I'd recognize him, of course. But how would he look after thirteen years? Would he have gained weight? Would he have lost some of his muscular physique? Would the laugh lines around his eyes have grown much deeper?

Of course he was older than me, I had to remind myself. A good seven years older. So he was already into his forties. It was a strange thought; the last time I'd seen him, he'd been twenty-nine. It seemed like nearly a lifetime had passed.

Could he have married and divorced since I'd last seen him? Could he have had a child? I wondered if he frequented the same bars, rode the same moped, still liked to twirl his spaghetti twice and then suck the strands messily in through his front teeth. I wondered if he still smoked when he drank or whether he'd out-grown that. Had he started shaving every day rather than letting his sexy stubble accumulate? Did he get haircuts more regularly instead of allowing his curls to grow a little wild? Did he wear business suits now, or was he still wearing collared shirts and jeans to work? Would he still laugh at my jokes and smile at me like we shared a special secret?

It was just past two p.m. Italian time when I finally cleared customs and began walking toward the inter-national arrivals exit of Rome's Fiumicino Airport, a sprawling, old-fashioned place that seemed as if it hadn't changed since I'd seen it last. My heart was pounding as I dragged my suitcase behind me, moving as fast as I could. I knew that Francesco was just yards away. The dark-tinted automatic doors loomed up ahead like the entrance to another world. Taking a deep breath, I quickened my pace and strode through, my eyes scanning the waiting crowd.

And then, there he was. It was like something out of a dream.

I recognized him right away. Thirteen years had done little to dull his sharp-edged good looks. In fact, as he moved toward middle age, he looked even better. His hair was still thick and jet black; his smile lines were few but looked deliciously sexy; his darkly tanned skin was still taut across his strong-featured face. He was wearing dark jeans and a gray designer T-shirt that clung to him in all the right places, showing me that he'd lost none of the muscular structure to his arms and shoulders that I'd found so attractive long ago.

He was scanning the crowd too, and I lifted a hand to wave as he glanced in my direction, but he seemed to look right at me and look away, as if he hadn't seen me. My heart sank a little, but that was silly. He continued scanning, slowly, leisurely, while I hurried toward him, my heart hammering.

'Francesco!' I said loudly, once I was in shouting distance. 'Over here!' I raised my right arm above my head and waved it madly, trying to get his attention.

Finally, his eyes focused on me, and I saw the spark of recognition in his face. He blinked a few times, seeming to take me in, then he smiled as I rushed forward.

'*Bella!*' he exclaimed. '*Che sorpresa!* I cannot believe you are here!'

I let go of my suitcase just a few feet from him and rushed into his arms. It felt a bit like being enveloped in the past as he kissed me on both cheeks and pulled me into a tight hug. It felt amazing. It was the way Francesco had always held me, every time we embraced, and it felt so familiar now that I almost wanted to cry.

But there would be no crying today. It was too good to see him. I couldn't stop smiling.

'What are you doing here?' Francesco exclaimed, pulling away from me finally and studying my face.

'I know!' I said. I couldn't wipe the grin from my face. 'It's the most spontaneous thing I've ever done, just emailing you like that and hopping on a plane.'

His brow creased and he stared at me. 'But why?' he

asked after a moment. 'Why did you come all this way?'

'I never . . . I never forgave myself for leaving the way I did. For not following up on what could have happened between us. I'm sorry.'

'Ah,' Francesco said, his lovely green eyes boring into mine and making me tingle. '*È bel niente*. It's nothing. *Non si preoccuparti.*'

Francesco spoke proficient English, but he had an endearing habit of peppering his words with Italian phrases. It had always seemed to me to be very charming, very cosmopolitan. The fact that he was releasing me from blame as he stood there gazing down at me made my insides do back flips.

'I've missed you,' I said softly.

He paused and then smiled. '*E tu.*' He glanced down at my suitcase. 'So. Shall we go?'

I nodded, and as Francesco grasped my hand tightly with his right hand and began effortlessly dragging my suitcase with his left, my heart swelled. I felt like part of a couple, part of a pair again. But as we exited into the bright afternoon sunshine outside the terminal and made our way toward Francesco's little Fiat, it occurred to me that I had no idea where we were going or what his life was like now.

We made small talk as we sped toward the city. Francesco drove the way I remembered, quickly and aggressively, cutting off other drivers, cursing under his breath when someone got in his way. I supposed I'd expected that he would have grown out of this Italian-specific form of road rage. But, strangely, it wasn't a turnoff to me that he was still like this. It made me feel closer to him, like less time had passed and fewer changes had occurred. Maybe I *did* still know this man. Maybe he still knew me too.

'So, you were able to just leave your job, like that?' Francesco asked as he cut off an old woman in a coupé and wove deftly between two helmetless moped riders.

'I hadn't taken much vacation time,' I said, trying not to feel paralyzed with the fear of dying in a fiery car crash on the A91.

Francesco glanced at me and smiled slyly. 'You must have a good job, no? Very good?'

I laughed. 'It's all right,' I said. 'Same thing I've always done. I work in accounting.'

It felt strange, having a getting-to-know-you talk with someone whose birthmarks I could locate with my eyes closed (one directly over his left hip bone, one on his right elbow), whose whole life story I already knew, whose hopes and dreams I'd once found impossible to separate from my own.

'But you make a lot of money, no?' he pressed on playfully. He turned his attention back to the road and darted in front of an old pickup truck, whose driver leaned out the window and unleashed a string of expletives and hand gestures, which only made Francesco laugh. He glanced back at me. 'You are rich?'

I rolled my eyes. 'Hardly. I've just been good with saving my money. How about you?'

'Am I rich?' Francesco asked in obvious amusement. 'Is that what you ask me?'

'No! I meant, what's your job? What are you doing these days?'

'Ah, my job,' Francesco said. He stroked his chin with

his right hand thoughtfully, as if this was a question that needed to be mulled over. 'This is an interesting thing, *bella*. I do a lot of things. I paint a little. I do, how you say, handiwork? Yes, handiwork around town.'

'Handiwork?' I stared at him in confusion.

'Yes, yes,' he said. 'Like that character on your TV show. *Desperate Housewives*. Er . . . Mike Delfino?'

He pronounced the character's name slowly and respectfully, as if talking about a real, revered individual. I had to laugh; like many Romans, Francesco had always been enamored with American pop culture.

'Yes,' I said. 'You're a handyman?'

'Yes, yes,' he said. He was distracted again as he shot through a spot between two cars and zigzagged into the right lane. 'I fix things. You know. Wires. Pipes.'

'But what happened to your job as a computer programmer?'

He glanced at me, and I thought for a moment that I saw something like annoyance flash over his face. 'That job, it was not for me.'

'I'm sorry,' I said.

He blinked a few times and changed the subject. 'And you? Where do you live?'

'New York,' I said.

'Oh, New York! I visited New York six years ago. I love it. The Big Apple!'

I stared at him. My mouth felt dry. 'You were in New York?' I said slowly. 'Why didn't you call?'

He glanced at me sharply. 'I did not know that is where you live.'

Now I felt confused. 'You didn't? But I always lived there. Remember? I told you it was the only place I ever wanted to be, because my family was there.' Surely he'd remember that from all the times we'd lain in bed, talking about our futures and our pasts.

'Ah, yes,' Francesco said vaguely. 'I remember now.' He paused and cut the wheel sharply, sending us shooting off the road on a side street to the right. I grasped the door handle for dear life. Seeing this, Francesco laughed. 'Relax, *bella*. It is the way we drive here.'

I was being reminded of that quickly enough as Francesco wove in and out of side streets, cutting other people off, being cut off, slamming on his brakes and cursing in rapid Italian approximately every forty-five seconds. How had this not bothered me more when I lived here?

But then, as we shot off a side street, lurching onto a main drag, I recalled immediately why the erratic driving of Romans hadn't bothered me as much as it should have. It was because the town they drove like maniacs through was so ridiculously, achingly beautiful that one could hardly blame them for wanting to race from one gorgeous spot to the next.

I sucked in a deep breath as the Tiber and its beautiful, arching bridges stretched out ahead of us. The afternoon light gave a soft, milky glow to the ancient buildings across the Ponte Garibaldi, and the sun seeped through their arches and crevices, caressing them with its rays.

I felt suddenly like I was home.

'I'd forgotten how beautiful it is here,' I murmured.

Francesco glanced at me. 'Ah yes? Yes, it is beautiful. A little bit of *colpo di fulmine* for you, no?'

'*Colpo di fulmine?*' I repeated.

'Love at first sight,' Francesco said, pulling up to a stop

sign and turning to stare at me meaningfully before hurling the car forward again.

He cut another hard right and we whizzed past a rectangular piazza, presided over by a hulking statue of a stern-looking, hooded man who looked like a monk.

'Campo de' Fiori,' Francesco announced like a tour guide as he saw me straining to look. 'Remember?'

I nodded, wishing we hadn't just shot by it at the speed of light. But, I reminded myself, I'd be here for a whole month. I'd have plenty of time to visit my old haunts.

Francesco turned down a side street then down a narrow alley and screeched to a halt in front of a building painted a faded rusty orange color. 'Here we are,' he said after parallel parking. 'Home.'

Home. The word lodged itself in my mind.

Francesco hopped out of the car and, ever the gentleman, came around to open my door too. He grinned and held my arm gently as I stepped onto the sidewalk.

'*Grazie*,' I said with a smile.

'*Prego*,' he replied with a wink. 'So you speak Italian now?'

I laughed. It had been a joke between us that summer, that even though I had taken two semesters of Italian and was studying in Rome I was horrible at speaking the language. Two semesters of college Italian was barely enough to get down the basics, never mind verb conjugations and sentence construction. So I could say all kinds of useless words – *mucca* for cow, *mela* for apple, *finestra* for window – but much as I loved the way the words rolled off my tongue in that smooth Italian legato that made you want to gesture with your hands, they didn't do me much good.

Understanding Italian was a different story. My mother had, of course, been born in Italy, so, like Francesco, she peppered her English with Italian words and phrases. I remember sitting at the kitchen table many times as a child, coloring pictures or eating apple slices with peanut butter while I listened to her having rapid-fire telephone conversations with her parents and sister. I worshipped her then and used to ask her to teach me words in Italian. So she did, patiently some days, with impatient agitation on others. By the time she left, I could understand a good fifty per cent of what she said, although I wasn't capable of repeating most of it.

It was during one of those phone conversations that I'd heard her say she was leaving. I was so sure I'd misunderstood that I never said anything to my dad, or to her. And then, a week later, she was gone. I'd always felt guilty for having advance notice and failing to stop her – even if I hadn't been sure. To this day, I'd never told anyone.

Francesco grabbed my suitcase out of the trunk and pointed toward the door of the burnt-orange building. 'This way,' he said. 'Up those stairs.'

I nodded and set off up the stairs with Francesco following close behind me. I wondered if he was checking me out from the back. Granted, I didn't have the same body I'd had at twenty-two. But I wasn't bad for a thirty-four-year-old woman, all things considered. I hoped Francesco agreed.

Four flights up, we stopped at a door just off the landing, and Francesco set my bag down while he fiddled with his keys and inserted one in the lock. He pushed the door open and gestured for me to step inside.

Even though it was a different apartment from the one he'd lived in thirteen years ago, a wave of familiarity washed over me as I walked through the door. It was a studio loft, much like Francesco's old place had been, and I was moderately surprised to see the same worn leather sofa, the same cream-colored throw rug, the same wrought-iron coffee table and the same dented wooden kitchen table that I remembered from there. It even smelled like him; the faint smell of cigarette smoke mixed with a touch of Trussardi cologne. I breathed in deeply, loving the way the scent transported me back in time.

The floor of his new apartment was mostly a glossy, brick-colored tile with a small rug separating the living room from the rest of the space. A small TV sat on a wooden stand opposite the old leather couch, and a sturdy wooden ladder was propped against the loft, where I could just glimpse the end of a bed covered in a navy comforter. The kitchen was tiny and clean, but I guessed Francesco didn't use it much; I remembered him eating out most nights and complaining that he wasn't even capable of cooking spaghetti correctly. The counter was lined with a dozen bottles of Chianti, two tall bottles of Campari, and several bottles of Piper-Heidsieck champagne. Francesco had been cheap in many areas, but never with his alcohol; he drank only the best. Sunlight poured in through a narrow pair of French doors just off the living room.

Francesco followed my eyes to the patch of sunlight and smiled. 'That's why I rented this *appartamento*,' he said. 'The *terrazzo*. Wait until you see it.'

He gestured toward the French doors and I walked over to peek out. He came up behind me, and touching my waist lightly in a way that sent tingles shooting through me he opened the doors to the terrace.

I stepped outside and breathed the ash-scented Roman air in deeply, falling in love immediately with the view, as he must have the first time he saw it.

The terrace was longer and wider than I would have expected. It had two dark green reclining chairs and a small table between them, on which sat a pair of over-flowing ashtrays. A few steps away, a wrought-iron railing separated us from a steep, four-story drop down the side of the building. But it was the sun-soaked view over the edge of the rail that made my breath catch in my throat.

The scene was nothing extraordinary, and perhaps that's what made it so beautiful. It was exactly the Rome I remembered and missed every day. A cobbled street below gave way to several cream-colored buildings roughly the same height as Francesco's. Windows were open across the small piazza, and flowers in all colors spilled out of rust-colored window boxes and haphazardly balanced pots on windowsills. A block down, a partially obscured dome rose up from behind another apartment building, its rounded, slate-colored top glowing in the afternoon sun and ending in a narrow cross. Below, I had no doubt, Catholics had probably worshipped for centuries. Perhaps my mother's grandparents' grand-parents' grandparents had even knelt beneath it. The sense of being steeped in history – not just textbook history, but the history of the people themselves – was one of the things that I'd always loved most about the Eternal City.

'Beautiful, isn't it?' Francesco said. He had come up behind me as I stared out on the cityscape. He was holding two drinks in his hand, both of them clear, bright red concoctions on ice, with thin, floating slices of orange.

'It is,' I said. I glanced at the drinks. 'A spritz?' I guessed.

He nodded, handing me one. '*Si, naturalmente. Cincin.*'

It was the Italian toast I remembered so well. I clinked his glass, looking into his eyes, then I took a long sip of the drink. It was a Venetian classic that had become popular in Rome in recent years: two parts prosecco, two parts soda water, one part Campari or Aperol bitters, with a sliver of orange just to sweeten it a bit, all served over ice. It had always been the drink Francesco served, along with a small bowl of potato chips, on the afternoons when we'd sat by his window, trying to catch a breeze, in the deepest days of that stiflingly hot summer.

'The river and the Ponte Sisto are just a hundred meters that way.' Francesco pointed after he'd taken a long sip. He took another sip and smiled at me. 'Sometimes, I go run by the river now.'

'You run?' I asked, incredulous. Francesco had always prided himself on being a couch potato who only stayed in shape because he worked hard on the weekends, helping friends lift furniture, mowing his mother's lawn outside town, hiking with his buddies in the hills nearby.

He smiled. 'A lot has changed.'

I nodded. 'But a lot has stayed the same too.'

Francesco furrowed his brow then nodded. He turned away and looked out over the city. Then he turned back to me. 'So. Shall we go to dinner after you freshen up?'

Francesco took me back inside, brought me an extra towel and led me into the bathroom, where he turned on the shower for me, explaining that sometimes it was tricky to get the temperature just right. I loved the feeling of being taken care of by someone else for once – even if it was something as simple as someone turning on the hot water for me.

I rinsed off quickly, washing away the remainder of New York from my skin while I quickly sudsed my hair with the bottle of Joico shampoo I found lying on the edge of the tub. I wondered for a moment, with a pang of jealousy, if it belonged to a girlfriend of Francesco's, someone who had shared his bed much more recently than me. I had to remind myself that I had no right to be jealous; I was the one who had walked away so many years ago, and I had certainly dated since then. Besides, he was with me now, wasn't he?

It took me about thirty minutes to blow-dry my hair with the travel dryer I'd brought (complete with a voltage converter plug) and slap on some tinted moisturizer, cheek stain and a swipe of mascara – my quickest get-pretty routine. I'd have more time to dress up later, but tonight, I wanted to look effortlessly pretty and casual, like I wasn't trying too hard.

When I stepped out of the bathroom in a pale pink sundress with a white cardigan thrown jauntily over my shoulders, Francesco was sitting on the couch, one leg crossed over the other, reading a book. He had changed too, into inky-blue jeans so dark they were nearly black and a gauzy white shirt that he left unbuttoned almost to the middle of his chest, exposing his sleek, tanned muscles and a little chest hair. I swallowed hard. He was gorgeous.

He looked up and smiled.

'You look beautiful,' he said. 'Shall we go?'

I nodded and let him take my hand as we crossed the room toward the door. I didn't know where the evening would lead, but I had the feeling that it would be a decisive step away from my life of safety and security in the States. New York and all my responsibilities there felt far, far away as we stepped out the door into the twilight and headed off down the street, where all roads led to Rome.

After a stroll around the neighborhood, down to the river, up the Via Arencia toward the Pantheon and back over toward the Piazza Navona through a series of side streets and alleys, Francesco led me to a quaint, brick-walled restaurant just off the busy tourist square on a street tucked away behind an apartment building whose façade was crumbling, exposing worn, chipped brick underneath.

We'd run out of things to talk about by the time we reached the restaurant, which was more than a little worrisome. How had we both been able to sum up the events of the last thirteen years so quickly? Surely more had happened to us than that, but I found that once I'd skimmed over what was happening with Becky and Dad, what had developed with my job, where exactly I was living and a brief, un-detailed list of the major relationships I'd had since I left Italy, I was out of things to say.

Similarly, Francesco seemed at a loss after telling me that his mother was still living outside the city, that his sister Alessandra had moved to Venice and had fallen in love with a gondolier (a big scandal, apparently), that he had decided to leave his computer programming job to go out on his own and start a handyman business, and that he hadn't dated anyone for more than a few months since me. So we sat through our salad courses in awkward silence, commenting only about the food and the wine, which I noticed both of us were drinking quickly.

Sure enough, two glasses of Chianti and fifteen minutes later, I was feeling bolder and less self-conscious about how uninteresting I might have seemed, how lined my face was, how jiggly my thighs had become and whether Francesco had noticed any of this.

'I see you like *il vino, bella,*' Francesco said in amusement as I started in on a third glass.

I raised an eyebrow. 'You're drinking just as much.'

He smiled, nodded and beckoned for the waiter to bring us a second bottle.

Once we were halfway through our entrées – seafood pasta with a light cream sauce for me, and rosemary T-bone steak with a side of alfredo pasta for Francesco – we were talking comfortably again. All the edges of my self-doubt were softened now. I even told him about Becky's wedding and how Grandma had embarrassed me in front of the congregation.

'But why is this the situation?' he asked, his face growing more serious after he had finished laughing about my admittedly amusing humiliation.

'Why is what the situation?' I asked.

He seemed to struggle for words. 'You. You are still single. Why? You are a pretty woman. I am sure a man would want you.'

I tried not to take his words the wrong way.

'I just haven't found the right one yet,' I said. Then, seeing an almost wounded expression cross Francesco's face, I backtracked. 'But maybe the right one isn't in New York.'

We let the words dangle meaningfully between us. I noticed that Francesco didn't argue, and I knew from the look on his face that he understood exactly what I meant.

'Perhaps,' he said finally. He studied my face for a moment more and then winked at me. 'Perhaps he is here in Roma.'

My heart leapt. He was definitely flirting with me. All of the awkwardness I'd felt earlier had been in my own mind, a product of my own subconscious trying to defeat me with a barrage of doubts. I cleared my throat, smiled, and said in my sexiest voice, 'Maybe he is.'

We rushed through the rest of our meal, and the remainder of the bottle of wine, taking long sips as we stared at each other over the rims of our wine glasses. Francesco kept making *cin-cin* toasts – to us, to the past, to the future, to Rome itself, to the good fortune that had brought me back to him after all these years.

Still, something felt off, and I couldn't put my finger on it. As I downed more wine, I resolved to chalk it up to the inevitable discomfort of two lovers who had become strangers and were slowly finding their way back.

Francesco paid the bill quickly, and after downing a shot each of ink-black Lavazza espresso, we stumbled out into the street, Francesco's strong right arm around me, pulling me close. I could feel his weight on me, and I liked it.

The walk back to his apartment was short; we had taken a roundabout, scenic way to get to the restaurant. Francesco fumbled urgently with the lock to his fourth-floor door, then we fell inside together. Before he had even

closed the door, he was all over me, kissing me passionately, pulling me close to his taut body.

The next few minutes were a blur of murmured words
of passion, shoes being kicked off and landing with loud
thuds on the tile, items of clothing flying almost cartoon-
ishly into every corner of the room as we undressed each
other frantically. I think we both felt an urgency to the
moment, a feeling of being given a second chance, a fear
that if we didn't take hold of it quickly, it would slip away.

We didn't even bother climbing up the ladder into the
loft. I'm not sure we could have made it. Instead,
Francesco pushed me backwards onto the couch, landing
gently on top of me without separating his lips from mine.

'I want you,' he murmured in my ear, as if I couldn't
tell already.

'I want you too,' I murmured back between kisses,
feeling the power behind the words, still hardly believing
that I was here. Naked. In Rome. With him.

And then, just like that, he was inside me. I gasped,
taking him in, adjusting my body. My head was spinning,
and I wasn't sure whether it was from the Chianti or from
being with Francesco again. But it didn't matter. It was
amazing. For the first time in years, I felt loved by a man
again. I closed my eyes, pulled him closer and let myself
slide into the moment as he whispered Italian endear-
ments in my ear.

Afterwards, as we lay sweaty and panting on the couch,
Francesco traced a finger slowly down my face and tilted
my chin toward him. 'That was good,' he said. 'Very good.'

I laughed. Talk about the understatement of the year.
'Yeah,' I agreed. 'It was.'

We lay there for a while, catching our breath. His left

arm was still around me, and I felt safe and protected as he pulled me closer. I closed my eyes and tried to imprint the moment on my mind. I never wanted to forget the way his body felt against mine, the way our breath rose and fell together, the way he was gently stroking my hair, almost absent-mindedly, the fact that we didn't have to speak to be together; we were beyond words.

A few minutes later, he leaned over and kissed me again, tentatively at first and then more passionately. He pulled me on top of him, and after a moment he asked in a husky voice, 'Shall we go upstairs?'

'Yeah,' I whispered. He scooped me off the couch, like a prince carrying his princess, and deposited me at the foot of the ladder to the loft. I climbed up quickly, momentarily feeling self-conscious that he was behind me, getting a full view of my cellulite-ridden thighs. But he didn't seem to care. Seconds later, he was on top of me again, in his bed, kissing me everywhere.

I woke the next morning feeling strangely disconcerted. In fact, it took me a second to register exactly where I was. It all came back in a flood of moments, though.

Francesco touching me.

Francesco's lips on mine.

Francesco ripping my clothes off like he couldn't wait to be with me.

Francesco holding me as we fell asleep.

I turned my head and smiled. His familiar form was beside me. He was deeply asleep, curled away from me on his side. I watched his smooth, tanned back rise and fall for a moment, his muscles stretched taut. I shook my head in astonishment. How could everything feel so perfect? It was like the last thirteen years had never happened. I was twenty-two again, waking up in bed next to the man I was madly in love with.

As I lay there, watching Francesco sleep, I thought it just might be possible to get back to that place, to love him with the same intensity I once had, to let go of common sense and fall recklessly in love. If we were still so connected after so much time, it seemed almost as if we were meant to be together.

For no reason at all, an uninvited image of Michael Evangelisti popped into my head. I scrunched my eyes tightly closed and banished it. What was wrong with me? I was with a man who loved me for me – and, more important, was single. Why was the married restaurant owner even a sliver of a thought in my mind?

I swung my legs over the side of the bed and climbed down from the loft. After pouring myself a glass of water in the tiny kitchen, I found an extra towel on a shelf in the bathroom and turned on the shower.

As I lathered up with the olive oil soap Francesco kept there – the same kind of soap he'd been using the last time I saw him, which meant that the scent propelled me back in time – I looked down at myself and frowned.

With the morning light pouring in from the window above the shower stall, my body's imperfections were all illuminated, as if a spotlight were shining down, pointing out all the things that were wrong.

My own shower at home in New York was dimly lit, which was exactly how I liked it, because here in the bright light of day I could see every flaw. Too much fat around the waist. Breasts that weren't quite big enough. Arms that were starting to get jiggly. Dimpling in my thighs.

God, when did I get so old? I wondered what Francesco had thought of me last night. The body I lived in now was a different one from that I'd inhabited when he'd seen me last. Could he possibly still love this older, aged version of the girl I used to be?

Of course he can love you, I chided myself. *Don't be silly*.

After all, hadn't last night – and the ease with which we fell so comfortably together once again – proved that? Hadn't he looked at me with that intoxicating mix of love and lust in his eyes?

I looked down at my imperfect body once more and didn't hate it quite as much as I had a moment ago. It was *me*, and if Francesco was capable of seeing past the imperfections, then I was too.

I finished my shower, toweled off and washed my face at the sink. Feeling suddenly self-conscious and wanting to look my best for Francesco when he woke up, I dipped into my makeup bag and quickly applied my usual concealer, tinted moisturizer, gel blush and mascara, until I looked halfway human. I smiled at myself in the mirror and, with the towel still wrapped around me, opened the bathroom door.

Francesco was already up, sitting in the center of the couch, holding an espresso cup in his hand. He looked devilishly sexy with his dark hair mussed from sleep, his white T-shirt stretched tight against his contours, his dark gray boxer briefs gaping slightly, ever so enticingly. I smiled at him. I almost wanted to throw myself at him again, but first I needed some caffeine. I still felt like I was moving in slow motion.

I could smell the brewed coffee and wondered if he'd

made me a cup too. There were few things I liked more than strong Italian espresso, and Francesco always brewed it perfectly.

'Good morning,' I said, trying to remember how to be seductive and flirtatious. Geez, I was out of practice. 'Last night was wonderful.'

I said it in my best sexy purr, but to be honest, I thought I sounded kind of silly. Oh well, I supposed there was no need for further seduction, right? Francesco was obviously interested.

He gave me a half-smile. 'Good morning.' He gestured to the empty space next to him on the couch. 'Can you sit down? I need to talk to you.'

For the first time, I noticed that he didn't look quite right. A strange feeling washed over me, and the smile fell from my face. 'Okay,' I said tentatively.

I crossed the room and sat down on the couch next to him. With only the small white cotton towel around me, I felt suddenly overexposed. My pasty skin looked even whiter against the pale towel, and the couch didn't do me any favors by splaying my thighs wide against the worn leather.

Francesco opened his mouth and then closed it again. He looked nervous. My stomach swam uneasily.

'We have a problem,' Francesco began slowly. He wasn't looking at me; he was looking away from me, as if meeting my eyes was too hard.

'A problem?'

'Si.' He still wasn't meeting my eye. 'I seem to have made a mistake.'

'A mistake?' I stared at him, my heart pounding.

Francesco nodded, met my eyes briefly and looked

away again. 'I, well, it seems I mixed up your email address with someone else's.'

I stared at him. A lump formed in the pit of my stomach as he went on.

'This is awkward,' he said. 'But the truth is, I thought when I got your email that it was from an American girl named Caty whom I met two months ago in Roma. Your email addresses are very similar, you see, and since I hadn't seen you in years I thought it was her writing to me. She's a junior at UCLA. Very smart girl, you know.'

I gaped at him. 'A college *junior*?' was all I could muster. I wanted to ask him if maybe at the age of forty-two he wasn't a little too old for a college kid. For goodness' sakes, he could be her dad! But that didn't seem to be the most pressing issue at the moment.

'Well, yes,' Francesco said a bit defensively. His face lit up. 'But she seems very mature. Very passionate. And love shouldn't be restrained by age, no?'

I threw up a little bit in my mouth. 'Love?' I managed to choke out.

'Anyhow,' Francesco continued, glancing at me nervously, 'I am sorry. I know this is, ah, a very awkward thing to say. But it was not you whom I intended to share my bed with. And, well, you are not quite the woman you were when I met you, I think you'd agree.'

He raised an eyebrow meaningfully and glanced down at my body, my dimpled thighs, my wobbly arms, my general lumpiness.

Suddenly, I was humiliated and furious all at once. I felt like he had slapped me across the face, hard, snapping me instantly out of the dreamlike state I'd been in since arriving in Rome.

'Wait a minute,' I said, feeling my temper flare. 'You're telling me that I'm the wrong girl and you screwed up and oh, wait, I'm not pretty enough or young enough for you, but you still figured you'd sleep with me last night before telling me?'

Francesco didn't look nearly as embarrassed as he should have. 'Well, ah, yes,' he said. 'But do not worry. It was my mistake. Entirely. So you may stay here, if you wish, until you are able to book a flight home. I will sleep on the couch. I am a gentleman, Cat. You know that.'

I stared at him. I wasn't sure whether to die of shame right on the spot or to punch him.

Instead, I stood up, clutching my towel protectively around me, and walked quickly to the bathroom. I grabbed my suitcase, dragged it awkwardly inside and slammed the door behind me. I would have locked the door too if it wasn't one of those stupid, antiquated Italian doors with no lock.

I couldn't have felt lower. I was an idiot.

'I will not cry,' I said firmly to my reflection in the mirror. I blinked quickly, hating myself a little more for being stupid enough to have not seen this situation for what it was, for being foolish enough to have believed that there was anything redeeming about this arrogant, shallow man outside the bathroom door.

Breathing hard, I rooted through my suitcase and grabbed the first two clothing items I could find – a pale pink A-line skirt I had planned to wear on a dinner date with Francesco and a green and blue striped collared shirt. I tugged them on angrily, not even caring that they didn't match at all. All I wanted, suddenly, was to get out of there as quickly as possible.

I zipped my suitcase back up, left the wet towel in a heap in the corner and looked balefully at myself in the mirror. I was a mess. Non-matching clothes. Sopping wet hair. Red-rimmed eyes. Great.

Steeling myself, I yanked open the bathroom door and dragged my suitcase out behind me. Just as I'd predicted, Francesco was sitting calmly in the middle of the couch, one leg crossed over the other, holding his tiny cup of espresso in one hand and his folded magazine in the other. I rolled my eyes, and he looked up, almost pleasantly. A hint of amusement crossed his face as he looked me up and down.

'Nice clothing,' he said with a smirk.

'Shut up,' I snapped.

He looked surprised. He furrowed his brow and shrugged. 'So. Do you need to call the airline?'

'I'm fine.' I began dragging my suitcase toward the door, hating how unwieldy it was. Would I have to carry it down all four flights by myself just to maintain my pride? Great, I'd have a strained back and pulled shoulder muscles to keep my wounded ego company.

Francesco didn't move from the couch, didn't offer to get up and help.

'But where will you go?' he asked casually.

'None of your business.'

I dragged the suitcase across the rest of the room.

'Well!' I huffed as I reached the door. I yanked it open dramatically and shoved my suitcase into the hall, where it promptly tipped over on its side with a dramatic crash. A dog began barking frantically in the apartment next door. 'I hope you and your little college student are very happy together,' I added haughtily.

'Thank you, Cat,' he said calmly. Francesco had never really grasped sarcasm, which was one of the things I didn't like about him. Funny how I'd managed to forget all the negative things. But suddenly, they were all flooding back. He paused and raised his espresso cup in a sort of wave. 'What is it they say in your American TV shows?' He tapped the folded magazine against his knee, a far-off look in his eyes as he tried to conjure up the words. 'Ah yes. *It's not you. It's me.* Is that right? *Si*, I think so. It's not you. It's me.'

He smiled pleasantly, as if we had just run into each other on the street instead of rolling around naked in bed all night. Then, to make the slap in the face complete, he winked at me – he actually *winked* – and went back to reading the magazine in his hand.

I knew I should walk out then, with my pride intact, but his aura of calm was infuriating. I stood there for a moment, feeling the heat rise to my cheeks and the veins in my neck and forehead bulge. 'Go to hell, Francesco,' I finally said in a low, calm voice that sounded a lot more confident than I felt.

Then, with every shred of my remaining pride, which wasn't much, I held my head high, sniffed at him and strode confidently into the hallway, slamming the door decisively behind me.

While the dog next door barked madly, I hefted my duffel bag and purse over my shoulder and began dragging my giant suitcase down the stairs, step by step, thud by thud, my back aching with the effort. I was on the verge of tears again, but I vowed I wouldn't cry. No way. Not here. Not because of Francesco. He wasn't worth my tears.

It wasn't until I was out on the street in front of Francesco's building, my stair-dented suitcase by my side and sweat dripping down my face, that I realized I had absolutely no idea where to go.

The smart thing to do would have been to hail a cab, head to the airport and book the first flight back to New York. After all, I'd just walked away from the only person I knew in Rome.

But as I stood there on the cobbled street, looking up at the flower boxes on windowsills, the flimsy curtains flapping in the breeze, the domes of ancient buildings rising around me in the distance, I knew I couldn't go back. Not yet.

Much as I knew my friends and family back home loved me, I also knew they looked at me as a boring failure. And who could blame them?

Coming to Rome was finally something different, brave and out of character for me. I always lived my life on the safe side, and for once I had stepped out of the box.

To admit that I'd failed miserably, that once again my life hadn't worked out, was more than I could take. I couldn't stand the thought of crawling back to New York with my proverbial tail between my legs, admitting to everyone that my imaginary love affair with Francesco had probably never existed in the first place.

'So I'll stay,' I said aloud. A squat, middle-aged woman

strolling by with a little dog looked at me in alarm and quickened her pace, no doubt assuming I was a crazy person. Not that I blamed her. 'I'll stay,' I repeated to myself, almost in disbelief.

I took a deep breath, soaking in the smells around me; baking bread from a nearby bakery; a hint of lavender perfume hanging in the air from the giggling pair of twenty-something girls who had just passed by; the slightly salty, slightly muddy smell of the Tiber river, drifting in from a block away. This was the Rome I remembered. And, I reminded myself, I had loved it here even in the time before I met Francesco. He hadn't been single-handedly responsible for making Rome feel like home to me. It was the city itself, its faint, dusty smells, its rich, flavorful food and wine, its being steeped in ancient history, that wrapped its arms around me and made me feel like I belonged.

'I'll stay,' I said once more. I swallowed hard, hoisted my duffel back onto my shoulder, grabbed the handle of my suitcase and began dragging.

The problem was, I had no idea where I was going. It was one thing to decide to stay in Rome, but it was quite another to figure out exactly how to do that. I did the calculations in my head; I didn't have enough to stay in a hotel for the next thirty days, but a new airline ticket home would cost me a fortune too. What was I doing?

I headed away from the river. I doubted my decision more with every step. As the sun rose higher in the hazy Roman sky and the dust began to rise in the air like it always did when the streets began to bake in the heat, it was becoming harder to breathe. I was sweating everywhere now, and my pathetic date skirt and too-heavy polo shirt were sticking to me like glue. I knew without looking at my reflection in one of the shop windows that my hair was a mess. I usually blow-dried it straight, but left to its own devices it looked like a pile of burned straw.

I glanced up and recognized the top of the Pantheon ahead. Its perfectly rounded concrete dome seemed to glow like a beacon, and for some reason Michael Evangelisti flashed into my mind again. He had mentioned the Pantheon, hadn't he? Wasn't that the neighborhood he'd said his friend Karina lived in? I stopped and dug in my wallet until I found the folded piece of paper he'd given me with the name of the restaurant where Karina worked. I stared at it for a long moment, just thinking.

I couldn't stay with some Italian woman I only knew through a cheating, lying man with whom I was barely acquainted, could I? I thought about it. It wasn't like I'd be forgiving Michael. Staying in a room rented by someone he'd known years ago wouldn't bring me back into contact with him. And if I wanted to stay in Rome, I had few other options.

So with nowhere else to go, I crossed the street and began walking toward the Pantheon. I made my way down a side street and, as often happened in the twisting, turning alleys of the city, I lost sight of the dome for a moment. I felt strangely lost, even though I knew it must be up ahead still, simply obscured by the buildings along the way. I felt oddly deflated. The road was more uneven here, and it was getting harder to drag my suitcase.

And then, as if I hadn't had enough to deal with in one morning, one of the wheels of my case snapped off suddenly and rolled cheerfully away, down the cobbled street, heading straight for a gutter.

'No!' I cried. I dropped the handle of the suitcase, and it flopped decisively on its side as I dashed after the escaping wheel. People around me stopped and stared. I dived for the little black wheel, landing flat on my belly, but I was a second too late; it was already disappearing into the entrance to the sewer.

'No!' This time it was more of a whimper. I was lying face down in the middle of the street, covered in dirt, grime and sweat, gazing into the mouth of a sewer. I closed my eyes for a second, collected myself and stood up, gathering as much of my dignity as I could. Around me, people were still staring. I saw an old man dressed in faded, suspendered corduroys make a face at another man and wind his index finger in a circle near his ear, making the universal sign for crazy.

I raised a hand and waved faintly, forcing a smile, like an actress acknowledging her audience. The onlookers turned quickly away, some clearing their throats loudly as they went back to their business, pretending that they hadn't just been staring at me.

I brushed what grime I could off my outfit, resigning myself to the fact that I now had a streak of dirt down my front to tie my mismatched outfit together. I crossed the street back to my tipped-over suitcase, righted it, and with as much pride as I could muster while pulling a one-wheeled suitcase down the street on its side I held my head high and began walking again, knowing that the suitcase was mere minutes from being ripped wide open, thanks to the harsh cobblestone surface digging into its fabric.

Scanning the street, I searched desperately for some place to stop before my suitcase tore, spilling my underwear all over the street as a final indignity. To my relief, up ahead on the right, I saw a little outdoor café that looked open. I squinted at the sign. Squisito, it said. It was the place where Michael had said his friend Karina worked.

'Thank God,' I said to myself. I glanced at my watch. It was only ten in the morning; most restaurants in the city didn't open until at least eleven. But despite the fact that it appeared devoid of customers, the pavement tables and chairs were already out, the forest-green umbrellas extended as shields against the sun, and the doors to the interior all flung open. I decided to try my luck.

A moment later, after using all the muscle power I could muster to drag the suitcase the remaining half-block, I collapsed into one of the outside café seats, pulling my luggage up next to me so that I didn't block the pathway in and out of the restaurant. I glanced around for a waiter or waitress, and seeing none I took a moment to flop forward onto the table. The shade of the umbrella felt good, as did the cool stone of the tabletop under my arms and face. I tried to catch my breath and wished desperately that someone would see me soon and bring me a glass of water.

Okay, Cat, I said to myself. *Let's get a cappuccino and some breakfast and we can go from there.* I was trying desperately not to cry.

What was I doing? Had I really decided to stay in Rome? I tried to comfort myself with the thought that it could be as temporary as I wanted it to be. I could stay a week, for instance, and concoct a story that Francesco unfortunately had to depart on an important business trip to somewhere far away and I'd chosen not to go with him. Or perhaps I could say that he'd been called away suddenly to a family emergency and I hadn't wanted to intrude, but he'd promised to come visit me soon because he knew he'd miss me terribly.

Just then, I heard footsteps from the direction of the restaurant. I looked up hopefully, expecting to see a polite waiter making his way toward me with a notepad in hand, maybe even with a glass of water balanced on a tray already.

But instead, the sight that greeted my weary eyes was that of a tall, slender woman, about my age, flying toward me, her gypsy skirt swirling around her like a cloud and her eyes blazing. Her pale cheeks were flushed, and her mass of long, black curls, streaked with red highlights, shot haphazardly every which way from her head. As soon as my eyes met hers, she started speaking to me in sharp, rapid Italian, shaking her index finger at me for emphasis, in case I couldn't tell by her tone that I was being scolded.

But for what, I didn't know. I tried in vain to follow her words, but they were so rapidly spoken, and they ran together in such fluid succession that I couldn't make out more than a bit of what she was saying.

'*Mi dispiace, ma non parlo bene l'italiano,*' I said haltingly, using one of the first phrases I'd learned when I spent the summer here. *I'm sorry, but I don't speak Italian very well.*

But this only seemed to anger the crazy-looking woman more. 'Oh, I should have known!' she snapped, switching to sharply accented but near-perfect English. She was practically dripping sarcasm as she arrived at my table. 'An American woman! Of course! Ah, *mi scusi*! If you are American, apparently you can go to any café you want and sit down, even if it clearly does not open for another hour! Who am I to tell you no?'

I stood halfway up and tried to apologize, to explain, but she wouldn't let me get in a word in.

'Apparently, if you are American, you own the world!' she continued angrily, waving her arms around. I shrank back into my seat, staring at her. She was clearly nuts. 'Do rules mean nothing to you in America?' She was gesticulating wildly and rolling her eyes. 'Do you get to just come over to my country and do what you please?'

I gaped at her. She raked a hand through her curls and made a disgusted face. 'Oh, so you have nothing to say for yourself now, Miss America?' she asked dramatically.

I found myself without words. I opened and closed my mouth.

The crazy woman rolled her eyes. 'Oh, now you can't talk?' she demanded.

'Well, I—' I began.

She cut me off. 'You are looking so good.' She looked disdainfully at my clothes. 'You do not have the words to back up your fashion sense?' She laughed at her own joke.

'No, I . . .' I began again. I fumbled for words, but I was entirely at a loss. And to my horror, I felt tears welling up in my eyes. *No, no, no*, I thought to myself desperately.

But apparently my tear ducts weren't listening to the voice in my head, because before I knew it, big, fat teardrops were rolling down my cheeks.

The woman stared at me for a moment in disbelief. She opened her mouth, and for a moment I fully expected her to unleash another tirade. Perhaps she was going to tell me that I was pathetic, that only wimpy Americans cried.

But instead, her face softened a little, and she said, 'Okay, so maybe I was being a little hard on you, but there's no reason to cry.' She looked uncomfortable now. She glanced from side to side. 'Really,' she added. 'I didn't mean it.'

I wiped my tears away angrily and stood up, hating that my dignity was being stripped by the pathetic rivers racing down my cheeks. 'It's not *you* I'm crying about,' I said, glaring at her. 'I was just looking for a friend of a friend who supposedly works here. But I've had the worst morning of my life, pretty much, so it's no big surprise that I wander in here and encounter the most unpleasant person in this city.'

The woman stared at me.

'I was just looking for someone named Karina, okay?' I continued. 'But excuuuuuuuuuuse me.' I drew the word out dramatically and made a big show of collecting my things. 'I clearly walked into the wrong place. So I'll just be going now.'

I grasped the handle of my beat-up suitcase and tried to storm huffily away. But thanks to the missing wheel and my growing exhaustion, I could barely budge it. I tried again. No dice. I looked down and noticed that the one remaining wheel had somehow gotten wedged in a crack in the ground.

'You've got to be kidding me,' I muttered. I tugged again, but to no avail.

And then, to my surprise, the Italian woman began to laugh. I looked up and noticed that the anger had melted from her face.

'Sit down, sit down,' she said, rolling her eyes as she gestured to the chair I'd just been sitting in. I looked at her uncertainly. 'Sit, sit!' she commanded. I glanced at her once more and sank slowly back down into the seat.

'I am sorry,' she said. 'I am just so tired of these American tourists who come in here like they own the world. But I have misjudged you, I think.'

I rolled my eyes. 'Yeah, no kidding.'

'Okay then,' she said. 'Let me start over. I am Karina. Welcome to Roma.'

I just stared at her. She was smiling now and looked almost pleasant.

'Usually, when someone introduces herself, the thing to do is introduce yourself too,' she said after a moment. 'At least in Roma.'

'You're Karina?' I continued to regard her warily.

'That is what I said.'

I took a deep breath. 'You're kidding, right?'

'That would not make a funny joke,' she said.

'No,' I muttered. 'No, it wouldn't.'

'Do you have a name?' she asked. 'Or do I have to guess?'

I stared at her. I couldn't imagine what I was still doing here after receiving such a bizarre welcome. But the more she smiled at me, the more my icy exterior melted. There was something oddly warm – albeit crazy – about her. 'I'm Cat,' I finally said.

She looked puzzled. 'Cat . . . like *gatto*?'

I sighed. 'No. Cat, like short for Catherine.'

'Ah. Well, Cat-short-for-Catherine. You are welcome to sit here, okay?'

I just stared at her.

She cleared her throat and went on. 'Really. I am sorry. I will go get you a cup of cappuccino, okay? On me. On the house, as they say in America.'

I started to protest, but she cut me off with an amused look at my suitcase. 'I don't think you're going anywhere, anyhow,' she said. 'So why don't you relax for a moment? Okay?'

I slowly nodded my assent.

She strode away, her long, black curls swishing behind her from side to side. She swung her hips in that well-practiced way many Italian women had and Americans didn't seem able to master. Maybe if I'd possessed that sexy swing I wouldn't be sitting at a café table by myself in the middle of the morning with filthy clothes and a tear-streaked face.

Karina returned a few minutes later carrying two steaming cups.

'Cappuccino is okay?' she asked, setting one before me. I nodded. She smiled, reached a hand into the pocket of her apron and withdrew it a second later with two spoons, two packets of sugar and two pieces of gold-wrapped dark chocolate. 'The best way to drink cappuccino, no?' she said with a wink.

I felt myself starting to warm to her, but only a little. It was obvious that she was trying to make up for her initial reaction to me. 'Thank you,' I said. I put the piece of chocolate into the coffee and stirred until it melted.

Karina watched me until I took a first sip. 'You drink your coffee like me,' she said. 'No sugar, just *cioccolata*.'

I nodded. I didn't feel particularly compelled to make conversation with her.

But Karina didn't seem to understand that. Instead, she sat down across from me at the table and took a sip of her own coffee. Any passer-by would have assumed we were a pair of close friends, out for a morning chat.

'So,' Karina said after a moment. 'You have been sent to me by a friend?'

I paused, unsure whether I should correct her terminology. I wanted to tell her that Michael was no friend, that he was a cad and a scumbag. But that didn't seem to be the correct way to ingratiate myself to my prospective landlord. So I nodded. 'Michael Evangelisti,' I said.

Her whole face lit up. 'Ah, Michael! I adore him!' She leaned forward and patted my arm. 'Any friend of Michael's is a friend of mine!'

'Good thing we're friends then,' I muttered.

She nodded pleasantly, my sarcasm having flown over her head. 'So you are upset, no? Allow me to guess. You have had an encounter with one of our famous Italian cads? And you are disappointed?'

I sighed. 'It's not exactly like that,' I said.

Karina nodded. 'Okay. So tell me.'

I stared at her for a moment. I didn't know if I wanted to tell this stranger anything. But what did I have to lose? 'I should have known better,' I began. 'It's a guy I dated thirteen years ago. I came back to see him, and it turned out he'd made a mistake. He thought he was emailing with a college kid, not me.'

She looked at me in disbelief. 'But you, you are beautiful!' she said. She truly looked astonished. 'And surely you know more about the ways of womanhood than a college girl, no?'

I couldn't help but laugh. 'Probably not,' I said. 'I'm not exactly the most feminine person in the world.' I looked pointedly down at my mess of an outfit.

Karina smiled, but she shook her head. 'Nonsense,' she

said. 'You are more feminine than you realize. And this
Italian man, he is an idiot if he doesn't see it.'

I looked down at my coffee. 'Thank you,' I said softly.

Karina nodded. 'So tell me.'

'What?'

'Tell me about him. About this man. About why you are
here.'

I hesitated. I looked at her and was mildly surprised to
see her leaning forward and looking at me with intense
interest. 'Are you sure you want to hear this?'

'*Si, assolutamente.*'

I nodded. 'Okay.' And so I told her briefly about my
history with Francesco, my desire to break out of the
dullness of my life in the States, my snap decision to
follow my heart to Rome again, and what had happened in
the last twenty-four hours. I wasn't sure why I was being
so honest with her, but her mouth fell open in horror when
I told her that I'd slept with him last night and that this
morning he'd told me it had all been a 'mistake.'

She cursed under her breath in Italian, which made
me feel a little better. She seemed to find his behavior as
appalling as I did.

When I was finished, Karina stared at me long and
hard. 'So you are to stay in Rome, then?'

I shrugged and shook my head. 'I don't know. I'll look
like such a failure if I go home. But honestly, I had to loan
my sister some money before I left. And now I can't afford
a hotel. It's why I came here.'

'How much money do you have to spend?'

I hesitated. 'I guess about four hundred euros,' I said.
'And that would get me, what, maybe a week in some one-
star hotel?' I sighed in discouragement. 'Then, if I want to

go home sooner than my ticket is booked for, I know I'll have to pay a big change fee.'

Karina studied me for a moment. Then a slow smile spread across her face. 'Okay. You will stay with me,' she said, as if it was the most obvious thing in the world. 'My apartment has a small maid's chamber above it; it is a studio apartment with a separate entrance. I need some-one to rent the room. It might as well be you. You look clean – even if you seem to have a little problem matching your clothes.' She paused and smiled. 'And you say you can pay. Four hundred euros is fine for one month. So why not?'

I couldn't believe I was even considering it. But the offer *did* sound enticing. And the price was right. 'I don't know,' I said finally. Could I spend the next four weeks living under the roof of this raven-haired lunatic? Although I had to admit that she didn't seem nearly as crazy now as she had half an hour ago.

'Okay,' I heard myself say. Karina's face lit up, and I swallowed hard. 'I'll do it,' I added, as confidently as possible. After all, what did I have to lose?

An hour later, the restaurant had officially opened for lunch, and I had filled out a four-page, handwritten rental application that Karina had whipped up quickly in the back. Along with asking me for my home address and three references, it also asked for my favorite food, my worst childhood memory and my zodiac sign.

What had I gotten myself into?

After bringing me a huge cornetto, a little glass bottle of apricot juice and another cappuccino, Karina came back out on the restaurant's patio at eleven thirty to see if I'd completed the application.

'*Meraviglioso!*' she exclaimed enthusiastically when I handed it to her. She stood there for a moment, reading carefully. Then a shadow passed over her face.

'Your mother left your family?' she asked, looking at me in surprise.

I swallowed hard. Why had I answered the childhood memory question so honestly?

'I shouldn't have written that,' I backtracked. 'It's in the past.'

'No, no,' Karina said. 'That is horrible. What kind of mother leaves her children? I can't imagine!'

I swallowed hard.

Karina continued. 'You do not feel this makes you unreliable?'

'What? No.'

Karina's face softened. 'I just do not want you to run out on the rent.'

'I'm not my mother,' I shot back.

She looked hard at me. 'No,' she said after a moment. She nodded. 'You are most likely not.' She went back to studying the rental application. 'I see you are a Cancer. Good, good. I'm a Pisces. We're a good match.'

I raised an eyebrow, expecting her to laugh and say she was just kidding. But she seemed completely serious.

'Okay,' she said after a moment. 'It is decided. You give me half the rent now, the other half in two weeks. Okay?'

I nodded warily. 'Okay.'

'Good,' Karina said. She seemed to be waiting for something.

'Wait, *now* now?'

She looked bewildered. 'Of course. You have the money?'

I hesitated. This was foolish, wasn't it? For all I knew, I'd never see this woman again. But there was something about her that struck me as intrinsically honest. Sure, I was being impulsive and making a decision I never would have made at home. But in my gut, I felt like it was the right thing to do.

'Yes,' I said. I pulled out my wallet and counted ten twenty-euro bills into Karina's outstretched hand.

She smiled once the counting was done. 'Good. Shall we go? I will help you with your bags. I told my boss I needed just a half-hour, and he said fine. We are not busy.'

I nodded and stood up, prepared to take the handle of my suitcase. But Karina grabbed it instead and began dragging.

'Wait, I can do it,' I said.

She shook her head. 'You are a wimp,' she said over her shoulder. She was already pulling it down the street. She was freakishly strong.

I hurried along after her with my tote and my purse slung over my shoulder. Karina chattered along the way about things we were passing: the meat market where she liked to buy sausages; the greengrocer who stared at her chest whenever she picked out fruit; the wine shop that gave her a discount if she tried a new kind of wine. After we'd walked a couple of blocks, zigzagging in and out of alleyways, she stopped in front of a tall, old-looking building that was painted in a faded copper color.

'We have arrived,' she said. She dug in her pocket for her keys and turned one in the front lock. The massive wooden door cracked open, and Karina threw her weight up against it and tumbled, along with my suitcase, into the foyer. 'Sometimes the door sticks,' she said. 'You have to push.'

I shook my head and followed her inside. She glanced back. 'Can you help me with the suitcase?' she asked, pointing to the stairs.

'Of course.' Together, we lugged my bag up three flights of stairs. I was sweating again by the time we reached the landing, but Karina looked as cool and unfazed as ever.

'Wait here,' she said crisply. She turned another key in the lock of a door just to the right of the landing, and I craned my neck a little to catch a glimpse inside her apartment. All that I managed to see before she slammed the door were her burnt orange walls, her cream-tiled floors and several pieces of dark wooden furniture that seemed to match wooden beams on the ceilings. It looked nicer and more richly furnished than I would have expected for such a wacky waitress. Maybe she was more normal than I'd given her credit for.

She emerged a moment later and held up two keys. 'Yours,' she said simply. She nodded back to the stairway and added. 'Up one floor.'

Lugging the suitcase once more, we walked up one more flight of stairs. Karina turned one of the keys in the lock of a door just at the top of the stairway and pushed it open. 'Welcome home,' she said cheerfully.

I stopped in the doorway and stared. The room was tiny; it looked more like a converted walk-in closet than an actual apartment. There was a single bed pushed up against the far wall, and there appeared to be a complicated set of drawers underneath the mattress. My bureau, I concluded glumly. Gauzy white curtains fluttered at the edges of a big picture window above the bed. Against the right wall was a small door that I guessed led to the bathroom. Against the left wall was a small archway.

'There's a little kitchen in there,' Karina said, following my eyes. 'You'll find a closet in the kitchen where you can hang your clothes.'

'In the kitchen?' I asked tentatively.

'I didn't say I was renting you a palace.'

'This is definitely not a palace,' I said under my breath. I swallowed hard and gazed around. It was even smaller than my college dorm.

'I know it is small,' Karina cut in, her voice softer around the edges now. 'But please. Before you judge, look out the window.'

I took a deep breath, crossed the room and knelt on the bed to push the curtain aside. The sight made me gasp.

The noon sun was beating down on the streets of Rome, and from my window I could see the ancient roads stretching out before me, with angular, brick-red rooftops, short chimneys and arched windows the only signs of modernity. Straight ahead, down a dusty brick road, behind a series of stout apartment buildings, the Pantheon loomed, immense, hulking, its sturdy walls scuffed from nineteen hundred years of wear. From where I sat, I could see three of its great columns holding up the entrance, the base of the dome, and its curved side disappearing behind a neighboring building.

'It's beautiful,' I said softly.

Karina was smiling when I turned around. She shrugged and held her hands wide. 'Naturalmente,' she said simply. 'It is Rome.'

Karina had to return to work, and she invited me to go back with her, but I shook my head and told her I wanted to unpack and settle in. The truth was, I just wanted to be alone. The questionable wisdom of my decision to stay in the tiny maid's quarters belonging to the crazy friend of a cheating jerk from New York was weighing on my mind.

Karina told me she'd come back when her shift ended. After she left, I spent thirty minutes unpacking my suitcase, hanging dresses, skirts and shirts in the little kitchen closet, folding pants and underwear into the drawers beneath the tiny bed.

When I was done, I gazed out the window for a while, watching the people below pass by. I felt like some sort of secret voyeur, high above the action and undetectable, as raven-haired young mothers in long skirts and floaty blouses strode quickly down the street, clutching the hands of toddlers who were trying to dawdle and gaze into shop windows. A pair of old women, dressed in black, their heads bent together conspiratorially, hobbled along the road, one of them using a cane, the other one drawing her head back every few moments to emit a guttural cackle. Two elderly men, one in a tweed golf cap, his friend wearing a huge pair of dark-framed glasses, set up a chessboard outside a small coffee shop just down the way and began moving their pieces slowly around without saying a word to each other.

The apartment was situated on a side street, so although we were near a touristy area, the view from my window seemed purely residential, purely Italian. For a moment, as I gazed out, I felt almost Italian too, as if by virtue of overlooking these private, everyday scenes, I belonged here.

I thought for a moment of my camera, which hadn't seen the light of day since Becky's wedding. The street scenes below almost begged to be captured. But there would be time for that. For now, I needed to sleep.

I pulled the blinds and tugged the gauzy curtains closed over them. I changed quickly into a T-shirt and sweatpants, pulled my hair into a ponytail and crawled under the covers of my new single bed.

But despite the fact that I was exhausted, I couldn't seem to drift off, no matter how much I willed myself to. I tossed and turned for hours. As the daylight disappeared from behind the blinds, I snapped my light on and tried to read for a while, hoping that it would make me sleepy. No luck.

Finally, in desperation, eight hours later, I resorted to taking one of the prescription sleeping pills Kris had pressed into my hand before I left. 'In case you need them on the plane,' she'd said. I had protested that I'd never taken anything that strong before, but she had insisted they would change my life.

I was reluctant to try. But I couldn't quiet my racing mind. I swallowed the pill, and moments later I felt it beginning to take effect.

And finally, finally, as my bedside clock neared ten p.m., I fell asleep.

'Wake up!'

I awoke with a start to a shrill voice, inches from my face. My heart nearly banged out of my chest, I sat straight up and screamed.

'Relax!' Karina said, backing away with an amused look in her eye. 'Relax!'

I stared at the crazy Italian woman in disbelief. She was perched on the edge of my bed, not looking the least bit embarrassed to have broken into her new tenant's apartment.

'What are you doing here?' I demanded. I blinked groggily at her. She looked blurry. The room swam in front of me. It took me a moment to realize that I was still very much under the influence of the sleeping pill.

She looked at me blankly. 'Waking you up,' she said slowly, as if talking to someone with comprehension problems.

'Yes, I got that. But *why* are you waking me up?'

She stared at me for a moment. 'Because, Miss America, you have been in your room all day and evening. You are feeling sorry for yourself. And that is not permitted here.'

'It is not *permitted*?'

She shook her head triumphantly and whipped a sheaf of papers out from somewhere in the folds of her skirt. I recognized my rental application from this morning. She pointed to a paragraph on the third page, a quarter of the way from the bottom. I had skimmed it, my tired eyes registering only that it required me to give seven days' notice if I wanted to renew my month-long lease, that it asked me to keep hot showers to a minimum since we shared a water heater, and that it required me to take out the garbage at least once every three days to prevent bad smells from drifting through the pipework into Karina's apartment.

But now, Karina was jabbing at something near the bottom of the page. I blinked a few times, clearing the sleep from my eyes, and bent forward to look.

Tenant will not sulk, the contract said in Karina's scratchy handwriting.

'You have to be kidding me,' I said. 'You put a no-sulking clause in the contract?'

Karina shrugged. 'No one forced you to sign it.'

'Karina, I could barely read your terrible handwriting,' I protested. 'This is ridiculous.'

'Well, you should know better than to sign something you can't read,' she said. She shook her finger at me. 'What if I had required you to give me your firstborn child? You would have just signed away your rights to your baby.'

I stared at her. I didn't even know where to begin. 'You're insane,' I said.

She shrugged, widening her eyes in faux-innocence.

'Plus,' I continued in a mutter, 'it's not even like I'm ever going to *have* a baby, at this rate.'

Karina leapt to her feet dramatically, startling me. She jabbed at the contract again. 'You are doing it again!' she exclaimed. 'Sulking! Feeling sorry for yourself! How do you know what your life will hold?'

I blinked at her.

'Anyhow,' she said a moment later when I didn't answer, 'it is time.' She brushed her long dark hair over her shoulders and stared at me, as if I should know what she meant.

'Huh?'

'It is *time*,' she repeated.

'Time for what?'

She clapped her hands together. The sound made me jump. 'Time to get up and go! Time to get out of self-pity mode. Time to stop sulking!'

I shook my head and sighed. 'I'm really not in the mood for this right now. What time is it anyway?'

She checked her watch. 'Eleven.'

'At night?' I asked, incredulous. I'd only taken the sleeping pill an hour ago. No wonder I felt so woozy. I was supposed to be fast asleep.

'*Si*. You are being lazy. It is time to get out of bed.'

'But—'

'No buts!' she interrupted. 'Now get up. If you're not dressed in five minutes, I will revoke the rental contract.'

'You can't do that!'

Karina smiled thinly, flipped a page of the contract and

pointed out a chicken-scratched clause on page four. *Laziness may result in eviction at landlord's discretion.*

'What?' I exclaimed. 'I never saw that! You just added that in!'

Karina shrugged. 'I guess we'll never know. But there is your signature at the bottom, Miss America. So I suggest you get up and get dressed immediately.'

I gaped at her. 'Why? Where are we going?'

Her wide lips curved into a smile. 'Out,' she said simply. 'I'll be back in five minutes.'

She shot me one last evil look and disappeared out my front door, her hair and skirt swishing behind her. 'Five minutes,' she repeated, before slamming the door behind her.

I stared at the door. She can't make me go out, I said to myself stubbornly. And yet, a minute later, I found myself standing up and heading into the kitchen to examine my outfit choices. I'm not going out, said the voice in my head, but if I was, this floaty white blouse and this A-line skirt would look nice, right? Maybe with my long gold necklace, a pair of gold hoops, and my gladiator sandals?

Five minutes later, when Karina walked back in my door, I was standing in the bedroom, my hair pulled back into a sleek ponytail, all dressed to go out. It was like this Italian nutcase had some sort of power over me.

'Wow,' she said, regarding me with amusement. 'Impressive.'

I rolled my eyes. 'I have no idea why I'm even doing what you say.'

'It's because you know I'm right.'

'Or because I think you're crazy and I'm afraid of what you'll do to me if I say no.'

Karina's lips curled into a slow smile. 'Perhaps,' she said. 'But either way, you are dressed.'

She looked me up and down and then laughed. She shook her head.

'What?' I asked.

'You Americans are funny,' she said.

I looked down at my outfit. I thought I looked cute – especially considering I was dressing from the inside of a teeny kitchen. 'What's wrong with the way I look?'

She laughed again. 'Nothing,' she said, rolling her eyes. 'You look lovely.'

Confused into silence, I followed her out of the apartment, wondering just what I was getting myself into.

F ive minutes later, we were on our way through the
back streets of the city. I was practically jogging to
keep up, and my knees felt wobbly beneath me. I thanked
my lucky stars I'd decided to wear flats tonight; otherwise,
I surely would have caught a heel in the cobblestones in
our massive, inexplicable rush.

I had no idea where we were going, and I got more and
more lost by the moment as we wove quickly in and out of
back alleys and side streets. Everything felt like a blur; I
was growing increasingly sure that it was a horrible idea
to have taken a prescription sleeping pill and then to have
departed for a night out on the town with a woman who
might or might not have been entirely crazy. I looked in
vain for a street name I recognized, but we seemed to be
working our way deeper and deeper into Rome through
secret back roads.

'Um, where are we going?' I asked, as we ducked into
an alley that seemed darker than the rest.

'What is wrong?' Karina asked in amusement. 'Don't
you trust me?'

'Should I?' I grumbled.

Karina stopped in her tracks and turned to face me.

'Listen, Miss America,' she said. 'I have not decided yet whether I like you.'

'*You* haven't decided whether you like *me*?'

'That is what I said. You may not realize it yet, but I am a good friend to have.'

'Yeah. Who couldn't use a friend who breaks into her apartment?'

Karina glared at me. 'It is still *my* apartment, even if I am renting it to you. I did not break in, as you say. I am trying to help you. A little gratitude would be nice.'

'I'm supposed to say thank you for dragging me out at midnight?'

Karina grimaced. 'No,' she said. 'You are supposed to thank me for taking a little lost American under my wing. You do not think I have enough responsibilities?'

I was sick and tired of being the little lost American. 'I think you needed the rent money,' I said.

Karina gazed at me evenly. 'You do not know as much as you think you do, Miss America.'

She started walking again at double her previous pace. I stared after her for a moment and then jogged to keep up. 'Look,' I said. 'I'm sorry.'

She waved a hand dismissively.

'It's just been a long couple of days, you know?' I tried again.

'You are not the only one with problems,' she said.

Just then, she veered sharply off to the right, turned down another alley and, with me following, finally emerged onto a bustling street. 'We are here,' she announced abruptly.

I looked up, catching my breath from the hurried walk, and saw that we were standing in front of an old-looking building with two torches burning outside, lighting the awning-covered entrance to a bar that spilled people into the courtyard outside. Loud music and raucous laughter greeted us, and dozens of Italians seemed to be clustered outside the doors, smoking cigarettes or taking big swigs of beer and small sips of wine.

'Oh,' I said, regarding the place warily.

'Now what's the problem?' Karina asked with a sigh.

'I didn't know we were going someplace so trendy,' I said. 'I feel underdressed.'

Karina rolled her eyes. 'Oh, come off it, Princess Ann. You look fine and you know it.'

'Princess Ann?' I asked in confusion. But she only rolled her eyes again then turned away, gesturing for me to follow. I paused, then hurried after her.

Inside, the room was dimly lit with two long, stained wooden bars lined with people. A cover band was playing at high volume in the corner, rocking out to an old Beatles song. From the sounds of it, they were most likely Italian without a full grasp of English; the lyrics were just slightly off. Somehow, they had managed to change 'Love Me Do' into 'Love Me Too', which, when you thought about it, actually made more sense.

'Over here!' Karina beckoned. 'I know the bartender!'

I followed her to the far right corner of the bar, where she led with her chest and a smile and squeezed between two men who didn't look the least bit annoyed to be pushed aside. If anything, they looked grateful as they eyed her up and down. She grabbed my hand and pulled me in with her until I was pressed up against the bar too. I glanced back and was surprised to realize that the men were giving me the eye as well.

'Ignore them,' Karina said, without even looking. 'They're stallions.'

'What?' I asked, startled. I felt a little heat rise to my cheeks.

'That's what I call Italian men like that,' she continued. The guys had backed away now, sour expressions on their faces. 'They go out all dolled up, like prize race horses, with their greased-back hair and their sleek clothes and their wandering eyes. They pick out a woman, usually an American, who looks like easy prey, and they go for it. They have all the lines down, but it's a different girl every night, you understand? If you want to be loved for six hours – and that includes five hours and fifty minutes of them snoring loudly into your pillowcase – they're your guys.'

I giggled and glanced back at the men. Now that Karina mentioned it, they did look like a type. They had matching, greasy black haircuts, similar white shirts that were unbuttoned nearly to their navels, and tight designer jeans.

Come to think of it, they looked a lot like Francesco.

'See their crucifixes?' Karina asked. I followed her eyes to the big gold cross that each man had hanging from his neck, amidst his chest hair. She winked at me. 'They have no idea they are even being ironic,' she said.

I laughed.

'Seriously,' Karina continued. She seemed to be warming up as she went. 'They have no problem sleeping with different women six nights a week and then taking their mamma to church on Sundays and kneeling in front of *Gesù Cristo*.'

I wondered if this was why Karina seemed, in some

ways, so bitter and quick to judge. Perhaps she'd been hurt badly by one of these smooth-talking men. Although I couldn't imagine Karina being suckered in by some greasy guy's moves. She seemed like she'd been born too smart for that.

Karina ordered two drinks in rapid-fire Italian. The bartender, a cute, fair-haired guy about our age, bantered with Karina for a moment with a grin on his face while he prepared our drinks. When he pushed them toward us on the bar and she reached for her purse, he shook his head and held up a hand. She argued back in Italian and then laughed and shrugged.

'On the house, as you say in America,' she said. She handed me a drink, which was bright red.

'A Campari spritzer?' I guessed.

She laughed. 'Not tonight,' she said. 'That is an afternoon drink, typically. This is that drink's big brother, the negroni. Emmanuel here makes them perfectly.' She nodded to the bartender, who grinned at her adoringly. '*Cin-cin*,' she said, turning back to me. 'To an American in Roma,' she said.

I smiled. 'To an American in Roma,' I agreed, clinking glasses with her.

I took a sip of the drink, which was sweet with a strangely bitter aftertaste. It was cool and tasted strong, and in fact, after a few sips, I could already feel it. Yet Karina was downing hers like it was going out of style. A few minutes later, when she pushed her empty glass across the bar, Emmanuel had a new one waiting.

'And for you, *signorina*?' he asked, eyeing me, his English slow and halting.

'No, thank you.' I shook my head. I planned to drink

much more slowly. Plus, I had the feeling the sleeping pill was starting to kick in again.

Karina and I toasted again, and I felt a little woozier.

'Are you okay?' she asked, looking at me closely.

'Yes, I'm fine.' I stifled a yawn.

She wagged her finger at me. 'No yawning,' she warned. 'We are going to have fun tonight.'

The band launched into a Hootie and the Blowfish song, but instead of the real lyrics, they were singing, 'I'm tangled up in glue,' which nobody seemed to notice but me. It made me giggle.

I scanned the room. People were packed in clusters into every corner of the dark bar. It wasn't anything like the bars I'd frequented as a student here. My classmates and I used to spend many an evening at places like the Drunken Ship on the Campo de' Fiore, or the Fiddler's Elbow near Santa Maria Maggiore, both of which might as well have been plucked straight from a New York street corner. Even the patrons were ninety per cent American, British or Australian. I had loved those places, because they felt like pieces of the home I'd left thousands of miles away.

But tonight, I felt like Karina had ushered me into another realm of Rome. All around us, darkly tanned women with tumbling ebony curls like Karina's looked warily at heavy-lashed, olive-skinned men. Everyone was gesticulating wildly. A few newly formed couples braved the dance floor, the men looking their dance partners up and down hungrily. People *cin-cin*ed, tipped back tall glasses of beer or potent shots, and moved dangerously close to each other.

'The Italian way is to seduce by getting right up next to

someone, attempting some silly pick-up line and then, if that doesn't work, resorting to grabbing,' Karina said as we surveyed the scene.

I laughed and nodded. 'Sounds a little like men in New York.'

The smile immediately fell from her face. 'Italians,' she said, her voice suddenly icy, 'are nothing like you Americans. Don't ever say that again.' She muttered something about having to use the bathroom and strode quickly away before I could even reply.

I stared after her with an open mouth. I didn't know what I'd said to offend her.

Less than a minute after Karina had disappeared, her spot was filled by a tall man wearing what appeared to be the male uniform here – designer jeans and a white button-down shirt, with the top several buttons open.

'*Ciao, bella*,' he said, looking me up and down unabashedly and then licking his lips, as if he had just stumbled upon an all-you-can-eat buffet.

'Um, *buona sera*,' I said warily. I glanced around, hoping that Karina was simply being dramatic and would reappear at any second. No such luck.

Winking at me, the man unleashed a rapid string of Italian words I didn't recognize. I shook my head. '*Non parlo l'italiano*.'

I expected him to back off, but instead his eyes lit up like he'd won the lottery.

'Ah, an American!' he said in a very thick accent. 'I love America!'

'You've been there?' I asked, trying to be polite. I glanced around once more for Karina, but she was nowhere to be seen.

'No, no. But the women, they are all so nice.'

'Oh,' I said. 'Thank you.'

The guy's brown eyes sparkled as he leaned in closer. 'And you? You like the Italian men?'

'Not at the moment,' I muttered.

'*Non capisco*,' he said.

'Um, yes, Italian men are, um, fine,' I said, looking around again for Karina. Seriously, what could be taking her so long?

'Ah, yes, you think Italians are fine,' the guy said, bobbing his head enthusiastically as he drew out the last word. 'Good, good.' He took a step closer until he was standing practically on top of me. I wanted to move back, but I was pinned against the bar, meaning that my personal space had all but vanished. He smelled like salt, cologne and cigarette smoke, and as he leaned closer I could almost taste the Peroni on his breath. 'So, would you like to go? With me?'

'What?'

'Go? Would you like to, em, leave with me? This bar? To my home?'

I stared at him, startled. After having spent a summer here as a twenty-two-year-old, I should have been more prepared for this kind of behavior, these unabashed come-ons, this brazen expectation. But most of my previous summer here had been spent linked with Francesco, and prior to that I'd always been one of a gaggle of American girls, and I was never the prettiest or the bubbliest or the most outgoing, so I was usually an observer while my classmates giggled at Italian men's advances and often disappeared with them into the night. *I know better*, I used to tell myself, perhaps a little smugly.

And then there'd been Francesco, and common sense had abandoned me.

'Well?' The Italian guy was waiting for an answer.

'No,' I said firmly, embarrassed that I'd even hesitated. It wasn't that I'd been considering his offer; I'd just been marveling at the audacity of it.

'But why is this?' he asked. He was wearing a wounded sulk now. 'You do not like me?'

'I do not know you,' I said, searching once again for Karina.

'Ah yes, *bella*, but how better to get to know me than to accompany me home this evening?' he asked. 'You want to, no? I can see it in your beautiful eyes.'

I rolled my beautiful eyes. 'No,' I said.

He looked at me in consternation. 'But it is the natural way of things, you see.'

'What?'

'I am a man. You are a woman.'

'Yes, thanks for clearing that up,' I said.

Now he looked even more confused. He reached down and took my right hand in his. His touch was surprisingly gentle, which is why, I think, I didn't pull away immediately. 'But *bella*,' he said. He tilted my chin up to face him. 'Listen to your body,' he said.

The way he drew out the i in 'listen' and the o in 'body' made the words sound almost lyrical – but way too practiced, like he'd used the ridiculous line on many an unsuspecting American.

'What?' I choked out while trying to stifle a laugh.

He apparently mistook my amusement. 'Listen to your body,' he repeated more firmly, flashing me a smile that was, no doubt, intended to charm.

'Does that line actually work?'

He looked at me blankly. 'A line? I do not get your meaning.'

'Okay,' I said. 'Well, hang on.' I paused and cocked my head to the side.

'What are you doing?' he asksed after a moment.

'I'm listening to my body.'

His eyes glistened hopefully. He looked me up and down once more, his eyes lingering a little too long on my chest. 'And is your body speaking to you?'

'Hmm,' I said thoughtfully. 'Yes, yes, I'm getting a message.'

'Yes?'

'It's saying *no*.'

He looked taken aback. '*Che cosa?*'

'Yes, loud and clear. It's saying *no*.'

The guy stepped even closer and was just about to say something else when I caught the eye of another man a few feet behind him. He was broad-shouldered with curly, sandy-colored hair, pale green eyes and richly tanned skin – classic northern Italian good looks, the kind you found all over the place in Venice and many people associated more with Austria than with its neighbor to the south. He looked back and forth between me and the dark-haired guy, seemed to assess the situation quickly and stepped forward.

'*Tutto bene?*' he asked, looking intently down at me as he stepped between us. 'Are you all right?'

I hesitated and nodded. 'I'm fine,' I said. 'Thank you.'

He looked uncertain for a moment, then he nodded. He turned and said something to the man in rapid Italian.

The dark-haired guy grumbled something in return, shot me one last look and shuffled away, leeching on to the next group of women he came across.

'You are visiting from America?' asked the light-haired man, turning back to me.

I nodded. 'How did you know?'

'Your accent,' he said. 'And your clothing.'

I looked down, wondering what he meant.

'And,' he added, 'the fact that Giuseppe was drawn to you right away. He has American radar. In any case,' he added, 'I am sorry about Giuseppe there. He is impossible.'

'You know him?' I asked, surprised.

The light-haired man shrugged. 'When you live in Rome, it is like you know everyone.' He smiled down at me.

'Well,' I said, suddenly feeling nervous. Despite the fact that the room was still swimming in front of me, I could tell that this man was very attractive. And he'd been kind enough to save me from an ill-intentioned Romeo. 'Thank you,' I said.

'It is not a problem,' he said. He tipped his head slightly and winked. 'Enjoy your evening. And my country. We are not all like Giuseppe.'

And with that he vanished back into the crowd, leaving me alone before I could even ask his name.

Just then, Karina reappeared beside me with a cross expression on her face. 'I see you were having a chat with Giuseppe,' she said sourly.

'You know him?' I asked.

She rolled her eyes. 'I know *all* of them, Miss America,' she said.

She turned to the bartender and ordered two shots. She handed me one and nodded at it.

'Drink,' she said simply.

I studied the shot. 'I really shouldn't,' I said. 'I took a sleeping pill a couple hours ago, and—'

Karina cut me off. 'Stop being so good. It must get exhausting.' She clinked her shot glass against mine and tilted her head back, pouring the brown liquid straight down her throat. I hesitated and then did the same, against my better judgment. It tasted like licorice and went straight to my head.

Karina cracked a small smile and took my shot glass from me, stacking it with hers and placing it on the bar. Her face looked a little softer now. 'I'm sorry I left you alone for so long. I forget sometimes how much these men like to bother American women.'

I shrugged. 'It's fine.' I scanned the bar for my sandy-haired rescuer, but I didn't see him.

'I mean, you bring it on yourselves,' Karina continued. 'All those college girls who come over here with their money and their fake blond hair and their egos that need stroking. Americans are easy prey.'

'I'm not like that,' I said right away.

'You are very defensive,' Karina shot back.

After a few minutes of surveying the dance floor, Karina suggested we walk outside to get some air. I agreed; it was hard to hear anything inside other than the lyric-mangling cover band, and besides, I'd noticed since Karina had returned from the bathroom that many of the men were looking at us warily and avoiding our area of the bar. I found this amusing; clearly, Karina had quite the reputation here.

I followed her, and we sat down on a bench outside the bar. The night air was humid and warm, but not uncomfortably so. Karina pulled out a pack of cigarettes and tapped one out. She put it between her lips and glanced at me.

'I didn't realize you smoked,' I said.

She looked at me sharply. 'I don't,' she said. She pulled a book of matches out of her pocket, struck one and lit the cigarette with it. She inhaled deeply then gracefully removed the cigarette from her lips, tapped the ashes on the edge of the bench and took another drag.

'Okay,' I said dubiously.

She sighed and rolled her eyes. 'Are you the moral police?'

'No, I just—'

She cut me off. 'I almost never smoke. Not that it's any of your business.'

'I didn't mean to be rude.' I felt like squirming under her icy gaze.

'I don't smoke at home,' Karina continued after a moment. 'I quit after I found out I was pregnant with Nico. I only have a cigarette here and there, okay?'

'Nico?' I asked.

She took another drag and closed her eyes. 'My son.'

I stared at her. 'You have a son?'

'Is that so hard to believe?' she asked. She looked almost amused as she glanced at me. 'What, you do not think I am mother material?'

'I didn't say that,' I said quickly, aware that I was turning red. 'What I meant was . . .'

'That I'm not a good mother,' Karina filled in dryly. She

glanced at me. 'It is okay. I don't care what you think, though. I am a good mother to him. I am.'

'I believe you,' I said. We were silent for a moment. 'How old is he?'

'Six,' she said. She smiled and added, 'Six going on thirty-six, I sometimes think.'

'Six,' I repeated. I just couldn't envision wild Karina joining a Mommy and Me group or taking a little boy to the playground. 'Where is he?'

'I left him home alone,' Karina said. Then, seeing my horrified expression, she laughed and said, 'You are so gullible. Of course I would not leave him by himself. He is with my mother, his grandmother. He stays with her during the days while I work. I asked if she could watch him tonight too.'

'You did?'

Karina rolled her eyes. 'You are like a little lost puppy, Miss America,' she said. 'I needed to get you out. Besides, the best way to learn about someone is over a drink, no? And I must know you if you are to live in my apartment.'

I nodded, lost in thought. I wondered what it would have been like had I had a child. The women I knew back home tended to quit their jobs and move out to the suburbs the moment they found they were pregnant. I'd always thought that seemed impractical. It didn't fit with my logically laid out career track. Yet Karina seemed to go right on living her life, simply making her son a part of what she already had. I wondered if I would have been like her, had I been a mom.

'You do not have any children?' Karina asked, as if reading my mind.

I paused. 'No,' I said, glancing away. 'I'd like to one day. But I'm not getting any younger.'

'You are very negative, Miss America,' Karina said softly. But she dropped the subject.

I felt myself yawning again, my eyelids feeling heavier than ever.

'You're a mess,' Karina noted with a wry smile. 'You can't handle the alcohol?'

'It's not that,' I protested. 'I told you I took a sleeping pill. I guess it's not out of my system yet.'

Karina rolled her eyes. 'You Americans,' she said. 'You think a pill is the magic answer to everything.'

I shrugged, once again feeling like I was being held responsible for all my culture's apparent shortcomings.

'All right,' Karina said. She smiled and stood up. 'We shall go, okay? I don't want you falling asleep in the streets of Rome.'

I smiled weakly. 'I'm sorry. I'm not trying to be boring.'

'I know.' Karina smiled mischievously. 'But sometimes, when you're really good at something, you don't have to try.'

Perhaps I should have felt insulted, but I was starting to warm to Karina's good-natured ribbing. She seemed to run hot and cold; one moment her temper was on fire; the next, she was sweetly understanding; and the moment after that she was devilishly sarcastic.

We stood to leave, and I felt unsteady on my feet. It wasn't quite like the sensation of being drunk, because I was coherent. It was just that all my limbs felt heavy. It felt like it took a great effort to even put one foot in front of the other to follow Karina out onto the street.

'Are you okay?' she asked.

'Can we take a cab?' I asked weakly, recalling the quite long walk we'd taken to get here.

Karina laughed. 'There is a *sciopero*.'

'What?'

'A *sciopero*,' she repeated. 'I believe you call it *strike*?'

'There's a strike going on?'

'*Si*. All transportation workers. Including taxi drivers. Until tomorrow night.'

'They have a strike schedule?'

Karina looked surprised. 'Of course,' she said. 'It is printed in the newspaper. How else do we know they are striking?'

I was puzzled. 'But what are they striking for?'

Karina shrugged. 'Who knows? Better wages, maybe. Or shorter hours. Or maybe they are just having a *sciopero* because they haven't had one in a while. Along with *futbol*, it is our national pastime, you know.'

I smiled wanly, wondering how on earth my feet would carry me all the way home before the rest of me collapsed. My head was spinning a little, and I longed to lie down.

'Come on,' Karina said, taking me by the arm. 'It is not that far.'

We started back along the way we'd come, weaving through back alleys and side streets. I tried to keep up with Karina, but my tired limbs couldn't maintain the pace.

'Miss America, I don't have all night!' she snapped over her shoulder. I could see her temperament changing again. She didn't look as warm or as pleasant as she had earlier. 'Can't you keep up?'

'It's just that I'm so tired . . .'

'We've already stayed out way too late,' she said

sharply, like it was my fault. 'Now I'll be exhausted all day tomorrow at work.'

'I'm sorry,' I said meekly.

'Phh!' She made a noise of annoyance.

I tried to quicken my pace. 'So,' I said, trying to make conversation so I stayed awake. 'Tell me about Nico.'

'What do you want to know?' She turned a sharp right and then a sharp left into another alley, with me dragging behind, panting now.

'I don't know,' I said. 'What's he like?'

'He's six,' she said. 'He's like a six-year-old.'

'Oh,' I said, feeling dumb.

Karina sighed and slowed down a little bit to wait for me. 'He's very smart,' she said. 'He knows how to write his name already, and he knows how to count in a few different languages. He speaks English and Italian, like me. I want him to be bilingual.'

'Wow,' I marveled. 'A bilingual six-year-old?'

'It's not a big deal.' Her face was a little flushed. 'He likes to be read to. I read him Harry Potter every night, in English, but I leave out the scary scenes. He is too young.'

'What about Nico's father?' I asked after a moment as I tried to drag my tired feet along after her.

Karina stopped so quickly in her tracks that I almost slammed into her. She turned around and looked at me. 'What about his father?' she asked slowly, her voice suddenly icy and dangerous.

Startled by her sudden coldness, I took an inadvertent step backwards. 'Nothing,' I stammered. 'I . . . I was just wondering where he is.'

'He is not here,' Karina said. Her eyes had narrowed into two catlike slits as she stared at me.

'Oh,' I said. I struggled for words.

'And it's not any of your business, Miss America.'

I held up my hands defensively and tried a smile. 'I was just making conversation.'

But Karina just looked angrier. 'This is your idea of conversation?' she demanded. She laughed harshly. 'You know what? You can make your conversation somewhere else. I don't need someone – especially not some American – coming in and telling me I've made a mess of my son's life.'

I stared at her, stunned. 'But I didn't mean—'

'Enough!' Karina said sharply, holding up her hand to stop me. She closed her eyes for a moment, and when she opened them again they were filled with anger and focused on me. 'I don't need you judging me, Miss America. You're not so perfect either, you know.'

And then, before I could say another word, she strode quickly away, her hands clenched in fists by her sides and her hair swishing rhythmically behind her like a manic pendulum.

'Wait, Karina!' I yelled after her. But she had already turned a corner without looking back, and the sound of my voice echoed off the buildings lining the alley. A dog started barking somewhere nearby, no doubt awakened by the volume of my voice. I swallowed hard and hurried along in the direction Karina had gone.

But when I got to the end of the alley and looked right, in the direction I'd seen Karina disappear, the road was empty. 'Karina?' I asked hesitantly. The sound echoed again, bringing on a cacophony of barking dogs. I looked around guiltily and began walking down the road as quickly as I could, even though my legs were still dragging, and I longed to curl up and go to sleep. 'Karina?'

But she was nowhere to be found. I looked down alley after alley, street after street, but there was no trace of her. I couldn't even hear the sounds of her footsteps, heels against cobblestone, echoing between the buildings. The street was deathly silent.

Finally, I stopped walking and looked around. I had no idea where I was. We'd gone through such a maze of city streets to get here that I'd lost all sense of direction. I paused and listened for anything that might give me a clue – a nearby street filled with traffic noises, for example, or the lapping of the water against the banks of the River Tiber. But all was still.

I began walking again until I saw a small street sign a few blocks ahead. *Via Paloma*, it said. The name meant nothing to me. I cursed myself for not bringing my Rome map with me tonight; Karina had been in such a hurry to get going that I'd forgotten it. Besides, I'd assumed that I'd have her as my guide. I *never* left home without an idea of where I was going.

'Don't panic,' I said to myself. 'No reason to panic.'

After all, how hard could it be to find a main street and ask for directions?

Twenty long minutes later, I felt like I was on the verge of collapse, but I finally emerged onto the Via dei Fori Imperiali. I breathed a huge sigh of relief. It was a street name I knew; in fact, it was a street that anyone would know had they spent time in Rome. I knew it cut a straight line across Rome from the Piazza Venezia to the Colosseum. Indeed, I looked right, and behind me I could make out the looming ancient structure, dark, hulking and foreboding in the dead of night. I shuddered and tried not to think of all the death that had taken place there, all those scenes from the movie *Gladiator* that had stayed imprinted on my mind.

But the road, normally busy, was nearly deserted, probably because of the late hour – it was almost two a.m. – and the strike. I began walking away from the Colosseum, because my rudimentary knowledge of the city indicated that the Pantheon was in that direction. The crumbling Forum rose up from the shadows to my right. Five minutes later, I saw a young couple hurrying along the street toward me. I breathed an enormous sigh of relief.

'Excuse me!' I said, hurrying up to them. 'I'm sorry to bother you, but can you tell me where the Pantheon is?'

The couple stopped and looked at me warily. They exchanged glances. Close up, they were younger than I'd thought.

'*Cosa?*' the young man asked, squinting at me.

'Um, the Pantheon?' I asked hesitantly. 'Where is it?'

The man shook his head. '*Non parlo l'inglese,*' he said uncertainly.

I racked my brain for basic Italian. 'Um, *dov'è il panteon?*' I choked out haltingly.

The couple exchanged looks again. Then the woman began speaking to me in rapid Italian, gesturing wildly and pointing this way and that. I gazed at her helplessly. '*Non capisco,*' I said miserably. 'I don't understand.'

The woman sighed heavily and rolled her eyes. Her boyfriend said something to me in rapid Italian, gesturing in the direction I'd been headed.

'It's that way?' I guessed. 'The Pantheon is that way?'

'*Si, si,*' the man said, looking relieved. But I didn't feel comforted. He didn't seem to know what I'd just said.

'*Grazie,*' I said finally. They nodded at me and hurried on their way.

I continued walking in the direction they'd pointed, feeling wearier with every step. I wasn't even sure we'd been communicating. For all I knew, they were sending me to Vatican City or the Spanish Steps. Besides, I realized, once I found the Pantheon, how would I find the apartment? I actually had no idea where it was. Karina had led me through a series of back streets, and although I knew it was only a short walk from the famed dome, I could be wandering the twisting alleys all night trying to find it.

The realization made me feel even wearier. Exhausted now, I was walking at a snail's pace, searching in vain for another person to ask for help. Stupidly, I hadn't brought my wallet with me, only my passport and forty euros, twenty of which I'd spent at the bar. I had no choice but to continue on in hopes of stumbling upon my apartment. At least I had thought to bring my keys – the one small saving grace of the evening.

A few minutes later, my exhaustion got the best of me. I could barely put one foot in front of the other anymore. And then, like a mirage in the desert, I noticed ahead of me a little brick wall, about the height and width of a bench, by the side of the street. 'Thank God,' I murmured. I dragged toward it and flopped down on it. I sighed in relief. It felt incredibly good to sit, to take the weight off my weary feet.

I closed my eyes and sighed. My head was spinning, and with my eyes shut I felt almost normal for a moment.

'I'll just sit for a second,' I murmured to myself.

I leaned back and breathed in deeply, feeling amazed at just how inviting the cold brick surface was. At that moment, it outclassed my feather bed at home a thousand to one. It was almost unbelievably comfortable.

I opened my eyes and gazed out on the street, turning my head slowly from side to side as I strained to keep my eyelids from falling again. I vowed I would never take another sleeping pill. This was horrible. I looked from side to side. The road was deserted, but for a stray car here and there, zooming by.

I'll just close my eyes for a moment, I reasoned. I won't go to sleep. I'll just rest here for a second. Then I'll be on my way. I'll feel better once I sit for a few minutes.

That train of thought finally gave me permission to close my eyes. I took a few deep breaths and tried to relax. I knew I should get up and move, but sitting there felt so good. It was such a relief. I was so tired . . .

Those were my last thoughts before I drifted off into a blissfully ignorant sleep.

Strangely, I dreamt of Michael Evangelisti. The dream was vivid, but it was nonsensical. I was on the same little brick wall, but when I opened my eyes in the dream, the bench had relocated to the corner of Columbus and West 93rd in New York, just outside Michael's restaurant. I tried to get up and move, but found that I was stuck. I couldn't budge.

Michael came out of the restaurant just then and gazed at me with amusement. 'I knew you'd come back,' he said.

I tried to ignore the attractive way his eyes sparkled. 'I'm stuck,' I said. 'Can you help me?'

'I can help you with a lot of things,' he said. He sat down next to me and folded his right hand over mine. 'If only you'd give me a chance.'

I hesitated. I really did need help getting unstuck from this wall. It was like I'd been superglued there. But what else was Michael suggesting? 'I don't give chances to married men,' I said coldly.

He looked wounded, and for a moment I felt bad.

'You don't understand, Cat,' he said gravely.

'What is there to understand?' I demanded. 'You're married. Why doesn't that mean anything to you?'

'But Cat, you're the one I want.'

My blood boiled. I hated the way he was teasing me, pulling at my heartstrings when they weren't his to pull. 'Oh, go screw your wife!' I said irritably.

'What?' he asked, but suddenly, his voice sounded very far away and had taken on the trace of a foreign accent.

'Go screw your wife,' I repeated more resolutely.

Michael looked hazy all of a sudden, and from nowhere, I felt a firm grip on my shoulder. I looked at Michael in confusion, noting that both of his hands were in front of him. Who was grabbing my shoulder?

Then, as clear as day, a sharply accented deep voice spoke in my ear. 'Well, I don't have a wife, so that might be a little difficult.'

The voice was enough to snap me out of my dream. I blinked a few times and realized, to my horror, that not only was I not on a street corner in New York with the married restaurateur but I was also on a dark, deserted road in Italy with a sandy-haired man sitting beside me, his face inches from mine, looking into my eyes.

I screamed and scrambled away. Startled, the man let go of my shoulders and jumped back too.

'Relax, relax!' he said, holding up his hands. 'I was just trying to wake you. I was worried.'

'Who . . . who are you?' I demanded, shrinking away to the far corner of the bench. As my hammering heart began to slow, I realized with a start that it was the sandy-haired guy from the bar, the one who had stepped between me and the persistent Giuseppe.

'Well, I'm not Joe Bradley,' he said, raising an eyebrow at me. 'But do not worry. I'm not trying to hurt you. I just wanted to make sure you were okay.'

'I . . . I'm fine,' I said, wondering who Joe Bradley was and why that was relevant. I studied his face and realized that I kind of liked the way his green eyes sparkled in the light of the street lamps.

He grinned at me and, with a fake, exaggerated American accent, said, 'You should try to get up; a young woman like yourself shouldn't risk getting in trouble with the police. Not his exact words, but close, I think.'

I stared at him. 'Police?'

He laughed and rolled his eyes. 'Classic,' he said.

'What and who are you talking about?' I demanded. 'And why are you talking like that?'

'What, like Joe Bradley?' he asked, now back in his Italian accent, looking amused.

'Who's Joe Bradley?' I demanded. I was utterly confused now. I scooted away. Was this guy crazy?

'Oh, come on,' he said, shaking his head and smiling at me. He looked pointedly at my outfit.

I crossed my arms over my chest. 'What?' I demanded.

He laughed again. 'Okay, if you want to play it that way,' he said. 'But you *are* okay, right?'

I hesitated and nodded. 'I think so.'

He seemed to consider this for a moment. 'Okay,' he said. 'But may I ask why you are sleeping at the side of the road in the middle of the night?'

I opened and closed my mouth, but I realized I didn't know what to say. After all, where would I begin? New York, where I'd made the decision to shake up my boring life? The airport in Rome, where I thought I was falling into the arms of a man who loved me? This morning in that same man's apartment, when he told me to get out?

Or this evening, with my crazy landlady storming away from me in the street while the sleeping pills gradually muddied my brain?

The man stared patiently at me and then sighed. 'Okay, this is very charming, but don't you think you're taking the *Roman Holiday* thing a little too far?'

I looked at him blankly. 'Huh?'

He shook his head again and said something in Italian under his breath. Then he said, 'I mean, we run into this in Rome all the time. American tourists who want to think they're Audrey Hepburn in *Roman Holiday*. And really, it's fine if you want to play make-believe. But you can't just go around sleeping on streets by yourself. Not all Italian men are as nice as me.'

He smiled. I still wasn't following. I'd never seen *Roman Holiday* or any other Audrey Hepburn movie. I'd avoided them quite deliberately.

'Audrey Hepburn?' I asked flatly.

'You don't have to pretend,' he said. 'It's very clear what you're doing.'

'No, no, no,' I said quickly. 'I've never even seen *Roman Holiday*. I swear. I had a fight with my friend – well, not even my friend, really, my landlady – though I don't even know how, and we got separated, and, well, now I have no idea where she lives or how to find her place. I think I'm even more lost now than when I started. And I was just so tired . . .' I was embarrassed to feel my throat closing up. I blinked back tears and stood up. 'Look, I'm sorry,' I said. 'I'll be fine. I just . . . It'll be morning soon, and I'll find her, okay?'

The man stared at me for a long moment, as if trying to figure out if I was telling the truth. Then he extended his hand formally. 'I'm Joe Bradley,' he said. I hesitated and reached out, letting him shake my hand.

'But I thought you said you *weren't* Joe Bradley,' I said. 'And what kind of a name is that for an Italian guy, anyhow?'

He just looked amused. 'And I presume you are Anya Smith?'

'No, I'm Cat Connelly. What are you talking about?'

'You're not going to quote a Shelley poem to me?'

'What? Why would I quote a poem?'

'Okay,' he said. He looked me up and down, shrugged and extended his hand again. 'My name is Marco Cassan. And I apologize for any misunderstanding.'

I shook his hand hesitantly.

Marco looked satisfied. 'Shall we?'

'Shall we what?'

'Shall we go?' he asked. I raised an eyebrow in disbelief. Was he hitting on me? Trying to get me to go sleep with him? But he didn't seem to be looking at me in the vulture-like way the men at the bar had.

'Go where?' I asked tentatively.

'I can't just leave you here sleeping on the street the rest of the night.'

'I'm fine,' I insisted.

Marco made a face. 'No. This is not safe. You will come home with me.'

'I will not!' I declared hotly. 'And listen, just because I'm by myself sitting on the street in the middle of the night does *not* mean I'm that kind of girl!'

Marco raised an eyebrow. 'Yes, thank you, I realize that,' he said calmly. 'Nor am I that kind of man, as you say. I just meant that we could go to my apartment, and you could sleep on the couch while I sleep in my bed.

You understand? Just so that the Roman version of Jack the Ripper doesn't come get you in the middle of the night.'

'How do I know *you're* not the Roman version of Jack the Ripper?' I asked.

He shrugged. 'I don't know. Do I look like Jack the Ripper?'

'No,' I muttered. 'But you never know.'

'Princess Ann,' he began.

'Cat,' I corrected.

He smiled. '*Si*, Cat. I would never forgive myself if something happened to you.' He paused and added, 'My mother wouldn't forgive me either, to be honest. She raised me to be a gentleman. And I think that includes not allowing lost women to sleep on benches in dangerous neighborhoods.'

'Look,' I said, 'honestly, this is very nice of you, but maybe I should just head back to where I think Karina's apartment is. She's somewhere near the Pantheon. I'm sure I could find it if you just point me in the right direction.'

'I would be happy to,' Marco said. 'But if you don't know where she lives, it might be an impossible mission. There are so many streets around the Pantheon that looking for one building will be like, how do you Americans say it, finding a needle in a haystack?'

'Still,' I said, 'I should probably try.'

He shrugged. 'As you wish. I live in that direction in any case.' He offered his hand again, and hesitantly I took it and stood up. 'It's this way,' he said as we began walking. Then he winked at me and said, 'Come along, Princess Ann.'

*

An hour later, we had walked circles around the Pantheon, but I didn't recognize Karina's building. I was growing more tired by the moment – the result not of the sleeping pill, I suspected, but of the fact that I hadn't slept for more than a few hours at a stretch in two days. And Marco seemed to be dragging too.

But the more we walked and talked, the more comfortable I grew with him. His English was nearly perfect – he told me he'd spent summers in the United States with his grandparents when he was a kid – and he chatted pleasantly as he indulged me in a fruitless search for my apartment. I felt like an idiot.

He seemed nice, normal and kind, and I couldn't help but notice, as I snuck furtive looks at his sharp profile, that he was really handsome. Not in the powerful way some of my Wall Street boyfriends back home had been or the slightly dangerous way that Francesco was . . . just handsome in a *nice* sort of way.

'So?' he asked finally after we went down what felt like the thousandth unfamiliar side street. 'Do you think perhaps we can return to my apartment for a few hours of sleep? It's nearly four in the morning, and I have to be at work at ten.'

'I can't sleep at your apartment,' I said.

'Why not?'

I stared at him for a moment. Perhaps this was just a more advanced game than Giuseppe had played. 'I don't even know you!' I said hotly. 'And besides, I am *so* not that kind of girl.'

He looked confused. 'The kind of girl who sleeps?'

'The kind of girl who sleeps with a stranger!' I declared. 'I don't know who you think you are, but—'

He cut me off. 'I do not intend to sleep with you,' he said, perhaps a little too firmly. 'I plan to sleep in my bed while you sleep on my couch. Because the only other option is wandering around the streets all night.'

'I'm fine. You can just leave me here,' I said.

'You and I both know that I will not and cannot do that,' he said. 'So you have two choices. You keep me up all night and therefore ruin my day tomorrow. Or you come home with me and get a few hours of sleep, and then I help you again in the morning.'

I swallowed hard. I felt foolish. 'Fine,' I mumbled. 'Are you sure?'

'Yes,' he said. 'It's better than leaving you out on the street. Okay?'

Marco lived about a fifteen-minute walk from the Pantheon, in a lovely old building with a vast, flower-filled courtyard and a broad, winding staircase. I followed him up to the fifth floor, where he unlocked a big wooden door and held it open for me.

'It's small,' he said. 'Princess Ann might even call it an elevator.' He winked. 'But you wouldn't know anything about that.'

It was about the size of the apartment I was renting from Karina, maybe a little bigger. I stepped inside and felt immediately at home. It wasn't neat, but it wasn't messy either. Books and CDs, some in English, some in Italian, seemed to overflow from every surface.

'You like to read?' I asked, eyeing the ubiquitous stacks.

He nodded. 'I love it,' he said. 'I can't afford to travel as much as I'd like. What better way to see the world?'

I nodded and smiled.

'You sleep in the bed, and I'll take the couch,' Marco

said. 'I have an extra T-shirt and pair of boxer shorts you can wear, if you'd like.'

The thought of wearing his boxers sent a strange tingle through me. I shook it off and tried to remain nonchalant. 'No, no,' I said. 'I'll take the couch. You're already being so kind to let me stay here.'

'I insist.' He opened a drawer and withdrew a couple of items of clothing. He turned to hand them to me. 'These are what we call pajamas,' he said, mimicking an American accent again.

I looked at him blankly. 'Um, yeah. I'm familiar with the concept of pajamas.'

He laughed and shook his head. 'Unbelievable,' he said, lapsing back into his native accent. 'You really haven't seen the movie.'

I looked at him blankly. I went into the bathroom and changed quickly into the faded soccer T-shirt and black boxers he'd given me. I took a quick look in the mirror and was mildly relieved to see that I didn't look nearly as bad as I'd suspected I would.

When I emerged from the bathroom a moment later, he had already changed into track pants and a T-shirt. He smiled. 'I'll set the alarm for nine, okay?' he said. He glanced at his watch and sighed. 'That'll give us four and a half hours of sleep.'

'I'm sorry,' I said, looking down. 'This whole situation is ridiculous, isn't it?'

'Actually,' he said with a smile, 'I think that might have been the most fun I've ever had wandering around Rome.' He grabbed one of the two pillows that lay on the bed and stretched out on the couch. 'Can I get you anything before we go to sleep?'

I shook my head. 'Are you sure you won't let me sleep on the couch?'

'No,' he said. 'I'm fine. Like I said, my mother would never forgive my terrible manners.'

I thanked him again and climbed into his bed. The sheets were cool, smooth and, admittedly, a lot more welcoming than a brick wall on a wide Roman thoroughfare.

Marco turned the lights off, plunging us both into darkness. Within a few minutes, from a few feet away, I could hear him breathing evenly in the rhythm of sleep. I eventually drifted off too, finally giving in to the exhaustion that had overwhelmed me all night.

I slept until Marco's alarm went off the next morning at nine. It took me about twenty foggy, sleep-soaked seconds to remember where I was. But when I did, I sat up with a start.

Marco was already up, moving around the kitchen with his back to me. It sounded like he was humming to himself. For a moment, before I said anything, I studied his frame. He was tall, with broad shoulders, a muscular back beneath his tight white T-shirt, strong legs and curly, sandy hair.

I must have sighed audibly, for he turned around and smiled.

'Ah, you're awake, your royal highness,' he said with a grin.

I could feel the heat rise to my cheeks. He was obviously making another *Roman Holiday* reference I didn't understand. 'Morning,' I mumbled.

'Espresso?' he asked.

I nodded numbly.

'Very good,' Marco said properly. He poured dark

liquid into two small espresso mugs, grabbed a pot of sugar and two spoons and walked toward me. 'May I?' he asked, gesturing to the edge of the bed.

'Of course.' I scooted over a bit. He sat down beside me, and despite myself his proximity in the bed made me flush. 'Look,' I said after I'd taken a first sip of the thick, dark espresso. He gazed at me intently with his pale green eyes as I went on. 'I'm so sorry about last night. I really am.'

Marco stirred his coffee. 'It's nothing,' he said with a shrug.

'How can I repay you?'

Marco looked up in surprise. 'That is not necessary. I couldn't just leave you there.' He paused and stirred his coffee again thoughtfully. 'But perhaps you can come see me sometime at work, okay? And we can meet properly? You know, when I'm not strolling the streets of Rome picking up lost tourists, I work in a little café not far from where I found you. It's called Pinocchio.'

I nodded. 'I'd love to come.'

'Good. It is settled.' He stood up from the edge of the bed. 'I must leave for work. Would you like to take a quick shower first? I'd offer to draw a bath for you, like in the movie, but there really isn't time.'

Marco seemed to enjoy playing a one-sided game of *Roman Holiday* without me.

Twenty minutes later, I had showered, changed back into my outfit from last night, and used what little I had in my purse – a powder compact, mascara and lipstick – to make myself somewhat presentable.

Marco took a quick shower after me, and he emerged from the bathroom already wearing what I presumed was his work uniform: a crisp white shirt and black pants. His hair was still a little wet, and his curls glistened in the light.

'Ready?' he asked, grinning at me.

I nodded, and together we left his apartment. He said hello to a few neighbors who gazed curiously at me. I wondered what they must have thought. Marco didn't seem fazed.

Marco asked if I minded walking; the transportation strike was still in effect. I told him to go ahead without me; I could find my way back to the café where Karina worked on my own.

But he refused. 'Oh no,' he said. 'I am not letting you roam the streets again by yourself.'

I felt foolish having him walk me back to the café where I'd met Karina, but he assured me it was, more or less, on the way to his job anyhow.

Marco made small talk along the way, chatting about how much he'd liked America and how much he wanted to go back there someday soon, especially now that the euro was strong against the dollar. I responded pleasantly to his questions about the States, how I liked New York and which restaurants I'd recommend there. But I was feeling more and more foolish by the moment, and it was hard to carry on much of a conversation.

I parted with Marco just down the block from Karina's restaurant. It was nearly ten; I figured she probably wouldn't be there yet. But I could certainly sit outside and wait. On the outside chance that she was, in fact, already there, I certainly didn't need her glaring at me for showing up with a strange man after going missing all night.

'You sure you're okay?' Marco asked as he leaned down to give me a platonic peck on the cheek.

I nodded. 'Yeah. Thanks again.'

'And you'll come see me at work? At Pinocchio?'

I nodded again. 'I promise,' I said.

Marco shifted from foot to foot and jammed his hands in his pocket. 'You are sure you're okay?' he asked again.

I smiled. 'I'm sure. Really.'

He studied me for a moment and nodded, seeming to have made up his mind. 'Okay then.' He paused, and the corners of his lips curled upward into a smile. 'And you don't need me to lend you any money?'

I stared at him. 'No, thank you. Why would I need money?'

Then I noticed that his eyes were twinkling in amusement. 'Just one final Joe Bradley gesture,' he said. He laughed. 'Very well. I will go. It was very nice to meet you, Cat Connelly.'

It wasn't until he had vanished down the street, leaving me staring after him, that I realized he'd finally addressed me by name instead of calling me Princess Ann.

12

Karina was already at work, sponging off the outside tables, when I arrived in front of the café. Her back was to me, and she was working quickly. I noticed she was missing swipes of dirt here and there. She seemed distracted.

I stood behind her for a moment before loudly clearing my throat.

Karina whipped immediately around, and her eyes widened.

'*Dio mio!*' she exclaimed. She dropped her sponge and, to my surprise, rushed forward to embrace me tightly. Shocked, I let her hug me, but I didn't hug back. 'Where have you been?' she demanded into my shoulder, squeezing me so tightly that it felt for a moment like I couldn't breathe. 'I was so worried, Cat! What happened to you last night? Where were you? Are you all right?'

I pulled away, extricating myself from the bone-crushing embrace. 'I'm fine,' I said stiffly. 'Don't worry about it.'

'But where did you sleep?' she demanded.

'I don't want to talk about it,' I snapped. I didn't want to admit to Karina just how pathetic I'd been – or that I'd gone home with a complete stranger who kept referencing *Roman Holiday*. So instead, I just said coldly, 'If I can just get my rent back, minus the one day, I'll be on my way. I'm sure I can find another place.'

The truth was, I doubted that was possible. But she didn't need to know that. It got in the way of my haughtiness.

Karina's jaw dropped. 'Oh, no, no, no, my dear Cat!' she exclaimed. 'Why would you say such a thing? I am so sorry that I argued with you. It was all my fault. It will never happen again. I promise! You can't leave!'

I stared in disbelief. 'Karina, I think it's pretty obvious that you don't want me here,' I said coldly. 'After all, you—'

But I never had a chance to finish my sentence, because Karina cut me off with a strange expression on her face. 'An American,' she said simply.

'What?'

'An American,' she repeated. She took a deep breath and gestured for me to sit down.

I shook my head. 'I'm fine,' I said, trying to keep my voice icy.

'Please, sit,' Karina said. She pulled out a chair and sat down. She cleared her throat. 'Please. I must explain.'

I stared for a moment, considering her words. Then, reluctantly, I sank into the chair opposite hers. 'Explain what?' I asked.

Karina was quiet for a moment. She looked at her lap silently, and I almost got up to leave. But then she looked up with eyes that appeared to be a little watery. 'An American,' she repeated. 'Nico's father, Massimo, ran off with an American woman six and a half years ago, when I was eight months pregnant with Nico. He has never even seen his son. He does not care.'

She paused and looked down at her lap. I stared at her.

'It is why I do not like American women,' she said a moment later, still looking down. 'I told you that you could stay here because I needed the money. And because you know Michael Evangelisti, so you cannot be all that bad.'

I looked away, trying not to consider the irony that it was my affiliation with a cheating man that made Karina feel comfortable with me.

'But you,' she said softly, 'maybe you are okay. Maybe I misjudged you. Maybe it is not fair to judge all American women based on one.'

The words hung in the air between us. It wasn't exactly an apology, but I had the sense she was trying the best way she knew how.

She looked up after a moment, and as her eyes met mine, I was struck by how nervous she looked. I'd only seen her before when she had it completely together; when she was happy, or angry or self-righteous. Nervous didn't quite seem to fit on her strong-featured face, her enormous, eyelinered eyes, her overall aura of self-possession.

'Please say something,' she said after a moment.

I sighed. 'I don't know what to say,' I said. 'You can't blame Nico's father's leaving on *me*. And you can't treat me like I'm responsible.'

The words, coming from my own mouth, surprised me. I'd never been particularly good at standing up for myself. In fact, when your mother leaves, your father falls apart and your little sister needs some consistency, you learn to take whatever blame is laid at your feet without even thinking about it. That's who I'd grown up to be, and it felt strange to stand up to a woman I barely knew.

Karina looked embarrassed. 'I know,' she said. 'I made a mistake. And I am asking you to give me another chance. I think you are not so bad.'

'And you need the rent money,' I muttered.

She turned a little pink. 'Yes, I do,' she said. 'But I also want you to stay. I think it would be good.' She paused and added softly, 'For both of us.'

I thought about it for a moment. It had seemed like a good idea to storm in here and angrily demand my rent money back from this temperamental woman. But I hadn't really thought it through. Where else would I go? I had already decided I wasn't going home. Not just because of the potential shame involved, but because I had realized just how much I loved it here. And I hated to admit it, but I was almost looking forward to visiting Marco at Pinocchio. There was a small part of me harboring an irrational hope that maybe in a different setting, when I didn't look sleep-deprived and I wasn't lost in the middle of the night, he might even find me somewhat attractive. Maybe that was worth sticking around for.

Besides, although I'd never say it to her, I could understand where Karina was coming from. I'd been hurt by men too many times to count, but nothing I'd gone through could have compared to being left by a man you thought loved you when you were eight months pregnant with his child.

I cleared my throat. 'I'll consider staying,' I said. 'As long as you can point me back to the apartment.'

Karina exhaled loudly, visibly relieved. 'That is wonderful,' she said. 'Wonderful! Let me just tell my boss

I'll be gone for a few minutes, and I will walk you home, okay?'

A few minutes later, chattering nervously, Karina walked me back to the apartment. This time, I made sure to note the names of the streets and the route that we took.

Karina hugged me tightly at the doorway to the apartment. 'I am glad you are staying,' she said sincerely. 'Now go upstairs. Get some sleep. You look exhausted.'

I rolled my eyes. Talk about the understatement of the year.

'I will be home after the lunch shift,' Karina continued. 'And then, if you like, you will meet my son, Nico.'

Late that afternoon, after I'd slept for nearly six hours, I awoke to an insistent knocking. I dragged myself out of bed, rubbing the sleep from my eyes, and opened the door.

Karina stood there, looking a little sheepish. 'I woke you,' she said.

I shrugged. 'I needed to get up anyway,' I said. 'Besides, it was much better to wake up to a knock on the door than to a crazy Italian woman sitting on top of me.'

Karina looked at me for a minute, like she wasn't sure whether I was kidding or not. Then she broke into a grin. 'You are funny, Miss America,' she said. 'Now. Would you like to go with me to pick up Nico from my mother's apartment?'

I hesitated and nodded. What else did I have to do?

Karina waited in the hall while I splashed some water on my face, put on a bit of makeup, pulled my hair back into a ponytail and changed into capris and a striped T-shirt. Karina regarded me with amusement when I emerged from the bathroom.

'What?' I demanded.

She laughed. 'You look a little like a gondolier.'

I felt myself flush. 'I do not!'

'Yes, you do.'

I stared at her for a moment, but she just shrugged helplessly, as if she couldn't be held responsible for simply stating the facts. Grumbling, I went back into the tiny kitchen, picked out a yellow sundress and changed quickly into it. 'Better?' I asked when I emerged.

'*Si*,' she said. 'Much.'

Together, we set off on a brisk walk through another series of winding alleys and side streets. This time Karina walked at a moderately normal pace, which allowed me to keep up.

'You will like my son,' she said. There was something different about her face now. I wasn't sure whether it was because she'd decided she could trust me or because we were on our way to see the child she loved, but she didn't look hard, sarcastic and defensive anymore. 'How do you know Michael?' she asked after a moment.

I sucked in a deep breath. It wasn't like I couldn't have anticipated the question. 'He's an acquaintance from New York,' I said tightly. She glanced at me, and I added, 'My sister's wedding reception was at his restaurant. I know him through that.'

'Ah, yes,' Karina said. 'I have heard that his restaurant is beautiful. It is?'

I nodded. 'It is,' I admitted. 'How do you know him?'

'He spent summers here in Roma when he was a boy,' she said. 'He was several years older than me, so we were never really that close. But he was always kind to me. I remember he used to teach me English words when I was a little girl. My father, before he died, worked with Michael's uncle. They worked in a restaurant together before Michael's uncle owned his own restaurant.'

'Are you close with Michael?' I asked suspiciously.

She shook her head. 'No. He hasn't been back in years. Still I think of him fondly.'

I held my breath for a moment and asked a question I wasn't sure I wanted to know the answer to.

'Have you met his wife?'

Karina looked surprised. But then she nodded. 'Yes. A few times. Such a beautiful woman. Very kind.'

'Oh,' I said tightly. I realized a small part of me had been hoping that there was a massive misunderstanding and that she'd say something like, 'Wife? What wife? Michael is single and loves tall, brunette American women!'

We walked in silence the rest of the way.

Karina's mother lived in an old building near Piazza Navona, a massive rectangular piazza with a Bernini fountain in its center, framing a tall, slender Egyptian obelisk. The fountain featured four men that reminded me of Greek gods, facing out in stone, water flowing from beneath them. A small gaggle of preschool-aged children rode circles around it on tricycles, giggling and shouting things at each other as we passed. As I slowed to gaze at the massive fountain, Karina said, 'The four statues at the four corners are supposed to represent rivers in the four corners of the world.' She smiled at me. 'Beautiful, no?'

I nodded. 'Yeah.' The piazza itself seemed to be brimming with life. Places like this, to me, epitomized the spirit of Rome. Late afternoon was *aperitivo* time, and all around the bustling square people overflowed from restaurants and waiters hurried back and forth, balancing trays laden with slender, colorful drinks and glasses of wine and prosecco for happily chattering customers. Haphazardly placed umbrellas shielded people from the late-day sun, and at various spots around the piazza painters had set up small easels and were slowly and meticulously sketching the domed buildings or the fountain itself, or using their paintbrushes and palettes to capture the aqua of the fountain's water or the pale cream color of its statues.

'Ah, Nico!' Karina exclaimed suddenly, falling to her knees and holding her arms wide open.

From across the piazza, a little boy who'd been playing with a soccer ball glanced up, smiled happily and came running over, leaving the ball abandoned. He was followed a moment later by a woman who looked just like an older version of Karina, a little heavier around the hips and middle, but with the same black curls, albeit hers were streaked with grey, and the same wide, beautiful features and olive skin. The woman picked up the soccer ball just as Nico threw himself into his mother's arms.

'Mamma!' he shouted. She scooped him happily up. His hair was fiercely dark like his mother's, with unruly curls that flopped over his forehead. His cheeks were flushed, and he was wearing an adorable pair of denim overalls over a red collared shirt.

'Mio Nico!' Karina exclaimed, hugging him. I smiled. It was as if they'd been separated for months instead of mere hours.

The little boy rattled off something in rapid Italian, and Karina, still kneeling, smiled and laughed. She pinched his cheek tenderly and stood up. By this point, the older woman had reached the spot where we stood, and she was gazing at me curiously.

'Cat, this is my mother, Signora Milani.'

I nodded and smiled at the woman. 'Hi. It's nice to meet you.' The woman looked at me blankly.

'Mamma,' Karina said, turning to face her mother. She said something in rapid Italian, and I recognized the words *la ragazza Americana*, the American girl, and *mio appartamento*. The older woman nodded a few times at Karina and then turned to me with a smile.

'*Piacere di conoscerla,*' she said. Her eyes, I noticed, were the same as Karina's: big and piercing, lined with dramatic eyeliner. I recognized one of the common phrases of Italian greeting.

'*Piacere,*' I said. 'It's nice to meet you too.'

Karina leaned her head in. 'She doesn't speak much English. But Nico here does.' She gestured for Nico and said to him in English, 'Nico, this is my new friend Cat. She's going to be staying in our extra apartment.'

Nico studied me gravely, as if trying to decide whether I met his requirements for tenants. I was struck in that moment by how old and wise his eyes looked. They were big and brown and inquisitive and looked out of place in his young, slender face. '*Buon giorno,*' he said quite seriously, still studying me with interest.

'*Buon giorno,* Nico,' I replied.

Karina smiled and nudged him. 'Nico, she's from America.'

His eyes widened into little saucers. 'America?' he asked. '*Si?*'

I laughed. '*Si,*' I said.

'But I love America!' he declared in perfect English.

'Really?' I asked him. I glanced at Karina, who was rolling her eyes and trying to hide a smile. 'Have you been there?'

The little boy shook his head. 'No,' he said seriously. 'Not yet. But I plan to go someday. I am practicing my English so that I am ready.'

'Really?' I asked. 'You're very good at it.'

'Grazie!' He glanced at his mother. Then he looked back at me. 'Where do you live in America?'

'New York City.'

His eyes widened even further. 'New York City?' he repeated, incredulous. I nodded, and he said, 'That is the best place in all of America!'

Surprised, I laughed again. 'Well, I think it is, too.'

'It is, it is!' he said instantly. 'I want to go there someday. Maybe I will live there. I want to be a fireman.'

'A fireman?'

'Si, si!' he said excitedly. 'I see them on the television. The best fire department in the world is in New York, no?'

I smiled and nodded, feeling a surge of pride for my city. 'Yes, they are,' I said. September 11 flashed quickly into my head, and it occurred to me that Nico hadn't been born, hadn't even been a spark in his mother's eye, when my city had been forever changed. Yet this little boy from halfway around the world still considered our heroes to be his heroes too.

'Mamma reads me books in English every night,' he announced. 'And we watch American programs on the television. But only some American programs. Mamma says that some are too old for me.'

'He's a little too young for sex and violence,' Karina said under her breath, 'although half the time I feel like he's the parent, and I'm the child.'

Looking into Nico's wide, intelligent eyes, I could see exactly what she meant.

'That's wonderful that you like my country so much,' I said to Nico after a moment. I didn't know what to say, but he seemed to be waiting for a reaction.

He nodded vigorously. '*Si!*' he said. 'Maybe you will tell me about it someday? I do not know many Americans. Mamma does not like Americans.'

I glanced at Karina, who had turned a little red. 'Nico, that's not true!' she said. She glanced guiltily at me.

'But Mamma, you said—' Nico began.

'That is enough,' Karina interrupted him smoothly. She shot me a look and said something to him in rapid Italian. He shrugged and muttered something under his breath.

Karina spoke to her mother for a moment, and the two women exchanged kisses on the cheek.

'It is nice meet you,' her mother said haltingly, nodding her head at me. 'Nice American.'

'It is nice to meet you too,' I said warmly. '*Piacere di conoscerla.*' She leaned in and kissed me on the cheek too. The action both startled and touched me.

Karina said a few more things to her mother, and then Nico kissed his grandmother goodbye. She handed him his soccer ball, and he waved goodbye as we made our way back across the piazza.

'Can I hold your hand, Signorina Cat?' Nico asked as he skipped along between Karina and me.

Karina glanced at me, and I could tell again that she was trying not to smile.

'Of course,' I said. He tucked his soccer ball under his skinny left arm and grasped my left hand with his right. He continued to skip between us, occasionally looking up at me curiously and squeezing my hand. As we made our way back toward Karina's neighborhood, Nico alternated between chattering about America ('The taxis are *giallo* . . . how you say, yellow?') and announcing street names ('This is Corsia Agonale!' 'Signorina Cat, this is Via del Salvatore!'). He was like a little human GPS system.

'He likes maps almost as much as he likes America,' Karina said, shaking her head.

'He's really smart,' I marveled, looking down at Nico, who beamed up at me.

Karina shook her head. 'You're right,' she said. 'In a few more years, I won't be able to keep up with him.' She smiled, but there was something behind her eyes that told me she wasn't entirely joking.

'Mamma, I like Signorina Cat!' Nico announced as we turned the corner onto our block and saw the apartment building up ahead. 'Can she stay with us for a long time?'

Karina looked at me. 'We shall see,' she said. 'But Nico, you are right. I like Signorina Cat too.'

That night, I was sitting in my apartment, re-reading *Tender Is The Night*, my favorite Fitzgerald book, and feeling a little lonely, when there was a knock on my door. I opened it to find Karina standing there with a plate of lasagna in her hand.

'I put Nico to bed,' she said. 'And I thought maybe you had not eaten yet.' She held up the lasagna like a peace offering. I hesitated, but my stomach growled, giving me away. We both laughed.

'You're right,' I said. 'Thank you.'

She nodded and followed me into the apartment. Once inside, I hesitated, realizing that there was nowhere for both of us to sit together, unless we balanced on the edge of the bed. Karina must have noticed the same thing.

'Would you rather come down to my apartment?' she asked. 'As long as we talk quietly, we won't disturb Nico.'

I nodded, and together we walked downstairs.

Karina led me into the small dining room, which overlooked the street below from a pretty picture window framed in wispy curtains like the ones that covered the window over my bed. She opened the window and a breeze wafted in, along with the faint noises of passers-by talking on the street below.

'Before I was pregnant with Nico,' she said, with a faraway look in her eye, 'Massimo and I would sit here and smoke and watch the people on the street below go by. I felt like I knew everything that went on in this neighborhood, all the little secrets. But after Nico, well, I don't sit at this window much anymore.'

Karina opened a bottle of Chianti and poured us each a glass.

'*Cin-cin*,' she said, clinking her glass against mine. I repeated the toast and we smiled at each other. We each took a sip, and I savored mine for a moment, feeling the wine warm my throat all the way down.

'Try the lasagna,' Karina said eagerly.

I dug my fork into the edge. I took a bite, and my eyes widened. It was truly the best lasagna I'd ever had. 'Karina, this is amazing! Did this come from the restaurant?'

She shook her head. 'No. I made it.'

I took another bite. Indeed, it was delectable. The marriage of parmesan, fresh tomato sauce, garlic and basil was heavenly. And the layers of pasta were so thin and numerous, I felt almost as if I was eating a Greek baklava instead of a hearty Italian dish. 'You made this?'

She nodded, a little bit of color rising to her cheeks. 'It is not a big deal.'

'Are you kidding?' I asked. 'It's a huge deal! This is incredible!'

Karina was beaming. 'It was nothing,' she said dismissively. 'I just like to cook, you know?'

I shook my head in astonishment. 'You should be doing this professionally,' I said. 'Like at a five-star restaurant.'

She laughed. 'I *should* be doing a lot of things,' she said. 'But I have to support my son. I can't afford to go to school to become certified as a chef to work at that level. I had a lot of dreams. But life gets in the way, no?'

I raised an eyebrow and nodded, my mouth full of lasagna again. Karina was right. Life got in the way of a lot of things.

'So Nico liked you,' Karina said after watching me eat for a moment.

I smiled. 'I liked him too. He's a really nice boy.'

'Thank you,' Karina said. She paused and watched me as I tried to scoop up the remaining sauce and cheese on the plate with the edge of my spoon. 'You are very good with children,' she added.

'Thanks.' I pushed the empty plate away and put a hand on my stomach. 'Wow, Karina, that was maybe the best meal I've ever eaten.'

She ignored me. 'Why do you not have any children?' she asked instead.

The question startled me. An unexpected pang shot through me. 'I don't know,' I said slowly. 'The time hasn't been right yet.'

'But you want children,' Karina said. It was a statement, not a question. I hesitated for a moment, and she added, 'I could see it in your eyes. With Nico. You would be a good mother.'

'I don't know if that's what life has in store for me, you know?' I wasn't getting any younger. I didn't seem to be able to hold down a relationship. And much as I wanted a child and loved being around other people's children, it was something I just wasn't sure I could handle.

'Why would you say that?' Karina asked. 'You are still so young.' She took a sip of her wine and looked at me intently.

'I'm not that young. I'm about to turn thirty-five.'

'Thirty-five is very young, Cat,' she said simply.

'I'm just not sure I'd be a good mother,' I admitted. I looked down, but I could feel Karina's eyes on me, penetrating, piercing. And then, just when I thought we were lapsing back into a comfortable silence where I wouldn't have to discuss my lack of parenting abilities, she spoke.

'It's your mother, isn't it?' she said.

I looked up sharply. 'What?'

Her eyes were gentle as she gazed at me. 'This is about your mother. The one who left you when you were young. You wrote it on your rental application.'

'No,' I said, shaking my head. But my voice wavered, and I knew I didn't sound resolute.

Karina sighed. 'Cat, you are not your mother,' she said. 'You are a different kind of woman.'

'How do you know?' I asked, startling both of us with the sharp edge to my voice. 'How do you know?' I repeated more softly.

'Because the way you talked to my son,' she said after a moment, 'is not the way someone who is capable of leaving talks.'

I started to interrupt, to say that a twenty-minute conversation was hardly indicative of my ability to be a mother, but she cut me off.

'You are a kind woman,' she continued. 'I was horrible to you, and you forgave me. This Francesco was horrible to you thirteen years ago, and you forgave him. It may not always be a good thing, but you are a woman who tries to make things work. You are a woman who doesn't walk away.'

It felt like she had knocked the breath out of me. 'But . . .' I began, and found myself at a loss for words.

'But what if your mother was that way too?' Karina filled in gently. 'Is that what you are trying to ask?' I nodded; it was exactly what I'd been thinking. Karina shook her head resolutely. 'She wasn't.' I started to protest, but she cut me off. 'She wasn't,' she repeated. 'A woman like you would never become a woman who walks away.'

I let the words settle on me. Karina took another sip of her wine. My mind was swirling. I'd never had this conversation before.

'Your mother, she is Italian?' she asked after a moment.

Surprised, I nodded. 'How did you know that?'

Karina smiled. 'Because you have the Italian spirit,' she said. 'And you haven't been here long enough to have earned it on your own.'

I smiled and shook my head. We were silent for

another moment. I sipped my wine, lost in my own world.

Then Karina spoke again. 'Is she from Roma?'

'Yes,' I said simply.

'Is she here now?'

I felt another pang. I realized I hadn't told Karina what had happened after my mother walked away. 'No,' I said. 'She died. When I was eighteen.'

'I'm sorry,' she said.

'It's okay,' I said. It was my rote response.

She looked at me for a long moment. 'This explains a lot.'

'What?' I asked.

'This is why you came to Rome the first time, no? Thirteen years ago?'

I shook my head. 'No. She was already gone.'

'*Si,*' Karina said. 'But you came to be with her past, didn't you? To discover where she came from? Where you came from?'

I opened my mouth to protest. But Karina was looking at me like she could see right through me. 'Maybe,' I admitted.

'Does she have family here?'

'I think so,' I said.

'You never found them?'

I hesitated. 'I never looked,' I admitted.

Karina arched an eyebrow at me. 'Why?'

'I wanted to,' I said. I thought for a minute. 'I think maybe I planned to when I came here. But I don't know. I was scared, I guess.'

'Scared of what?'

I shrugged. 'That they wouldn't want me. That they would see whatever my mother saw in me that made me so easy to leave.'

I felt choked up the moment the words were out of my mouth.

'She didn't leave because of you,' Karina said.

'I know, I know.' I waved her words away like I was swatting flies.

'No, you don't know,' she said. 'She didn't leave because of you.' She repeated the words slowly, enunciating as firmly as she could.

I looked down at my lap and tried not to cry. I felt humiliated, stripped bare.

'Well,' Karina said after a moment. She clapped her hands together decisively. 'We will find them, then.'

'What?' I looked at her in confusion.

'But it is what you are here for, no?' Karina asked.

'No!' I exclaimed. 'That's all in the past. I came here to see Francesco.'

'And yet you are still here,' Karina said. 'There is something in this city that won't let you leave.'

I shook my head. 'No.'

But Karina just shrugged, like finding my mother's family was already a foregone conclusion. 'It is the only way you will see the situation for what it is.'

She stood up before I could protest and took my empty plate into the kitchen. I stared after her, open-mouthed, wondering what had just happened.

When she returned, it was like someone had flipped a switch. She was smiling again, and she poured us each some more wine. 'So,' she said brightly. 'Are you going to tell me where you went last night? Or am I going to have to pull that out of you too?'

Her abrupt change of subject jarred me. But I was so relieved to move away from talking about my mother that

I almost didn't mind being asked about the previous night.

'It doesn't matter,' I mumbled, looking down.

'Hmmmmm,' Karina said. 'Who is he?'

I stared at her. 'Who is who?' I asked, hating how guilty I sounded.

'The man you went home with,' she said with a hint of a smile. 'I assume you went home with a man.'

'Not exactly,' I said. She looked at me in surprise. 'I mean, I did,' I clarified. 'But not in the way you would think.'

Slowly, I told her the story of Marco's defending me in the bar and then finding me on the bench, and how he was convinced that I was trying to re-enact a scene from *Roman Holiday*. Karina was curious, too, about why I'd never seen the famous film, but, as I had with Marco, I dodged the question. I couldn't handle another Dr Karina psychoanalysis tonight.

'So he was handsome?' she asked when I was done.

I felt the color rise to my cheeks. 'Yeah.'

'And kind.'

'Well, yes,' I said. 'You'd have to be to take home a lost stranger with no ulterior motive, right?'

'Then you will go see him.'

'What?'

Karina smiled patiently. 'Tomorrow. You will go see him. At Pinocchio. I know this restaurant. It is close to here. You will go see him and meet him properly.'

I hesitated. 'I can't.'

'Phh!' Karina made her dismissive noise. 'Of course you can! And you will!'

The next morning, I woke up at eight. Apparently, my body was finally beginning to adjust to Italian time. I lay in bed for a little while, listening to the morning street noises below and thinking about what I'd do with my day. I wasn't used to having nothing planned. But today was blissfully, entirely free. I made a mental note to myself to call my father and sister later to check in and let them know where I was staying. They could certainly reach me on my cell if they needed to, but I supposed it would be smart to tell them that I had stormed out of Francesco's and was now staying with a crazy Italian woman. But it was only two in the morning in New York, and I doubted they'd appreciate a middle-of-the-night call. I'd phone them this afternoon.

An hour later, after a long shower, I headed out of the building in a cream-colored sundress and my gladiator sandals, with my brown leather bag slung over my shoulder and my hair back in a ponytail. It was going to be a hot day, and I planned to do a lot of walking around the Eternal City. Before I left, I tucked the address of Pinocchio in my wallet, just in case. But would I really go there? I was sure Marco was just being polite, and I certainly didn't want to out myself as a fool by showing up there like I thought his invitation was a genuine one. Still, Karina had seemed convinced that I had nothing to lose. And maybe she was right.

I started off at the church of Santa Maria sopra Minerva, just a stone's throw from the Pantheon. We had passed it on the way home with Nico yesterday, and it had piqued my interest. I'd heard of it, but I'd never gone inside. The summer I'd lived here, I'd been absorbed in my studies – and in studying Francesco – and I hadn't seen nearly as much of the city as I should have. Sure, I'd done the obligatory trips to the Pantheon, the Forum, the Colosseum and Vatican City, but I'd missed so much of the heart of the city. I vowed to make up for that this time round.

The outside of the church was relatively unimpressive; the cream façade was plain and rectangular, punctuated by three dark doorways and three oddly circular windows. In front of the church was a curious statue – a stout Egyptian obelisk that reminded me of the Bernini statue from the Piazza Navona, growing from the body of a somber, tusked elephant on a pedestal. I stopped and gazed at it for a while; it seemed oddly out of place in Rome, and particularly in front of a church, as it seemed to have no religious significance. I searched my mind for a Bible story about an elephant in Egypt, but I came up empty.

Shrugging, I checked my watch. It was just past nine, and I wasn't sure whether the church would be open yet. But the front door pushed in easily, and I entered, my eyes adjusting to the interior light.

I blinked a few times and stared. Nothing about the

plain, unassuming façade could have prepared me for the stunning interior of the church. It seemed to stretch on for the length of a football field, a series of arching columns that held aloft brilliant blue vaults in the ceiling. They reminded me of canopies over a childhood bed. The ceiling shone with golden stars and paintings of cherubic angels, separated by red ribs arching toward gilded domes. The marble floor glistened and led toward an altar that shone with several tall candles, backlit by pale stained-glass windows.

I took an English language brochure from the receptacle near the doorway and sat down in a back pew to read. The church, it said, was the only Gothic church in Rome, and it had been built atop the ruins of an ancient temple dedicated to the goddess Minerva. Completed nearly six hundred and fifty years ago, it housed the remains of Saint Catherine of Siena, who had died nearby, as well as a few popes who had died hundreds of years ago. There was also a Michelangelo statue to the left of the main altar.

I fished in my shoulder bag for my camera and pulled it out gingerly. I hadn't used it since Becky's wedding. It felt nice to have it in my hands again. I always felt different, somehow, when I could see the world through its lens.

I glanced around, wondering if I'd run into a nun or a priest who would scold me. But the church seemed to be empty. And I figured that as long as I left the flash off, I wouldn't be doing any harm.

I walked toward the altar, stopping here and there to take pictures of the expanse, which seemed bathed in the ceiling's brilliant blue color. I adjusted the aperture and shutter speed a few times, almost by rote, until the pictures were coming out perfectly, almost jumping off the two-inch screen. I smiled at the images and then focused on the lovely ceiling for another series of shots. I didn't want to forget the power of standing beneath the canopied, stardusted sky conceived centuries ago.

By the time I reached the altar, I was fully absorbed in what I was doing. I snapped photo after photo of the light pouring in through the stained glass, of the candles flickering on the massive pedestal. I got close-ups of some of the intricately detailed rose windows, of the massive columns, of the walls full of religious artwork.

To the left of the altar was the Michelangelo statue I'd read about in the brochure, a larger-than-life marble likeness of Christ looking over his right shoulder while clutching the cross on which he'd be crucified. I gazed at it for a while before beginning to take pictures. I was transfixed by the incredible realness of the statue. Although I'd gone to a Catholic school, I wasn't exactly the most religious person in the world. I couldn't remember the last time I'd gone to church or the last time I'd opened a Bible. But there was something about the resoluteness Michelangelo had sculpted onto his Christ's face, something about the way the man was standing, as if embracing his fate instead of running from it, that made something swell within me. I stared for a long time before shaking my head to snap myself out of it.

I raised the camera and began shooting, zooming in alternately on the statue's face, on his strong hands grasping the cross, on his perfectly formed knees and on his realistic feet, which seemed slightly more worn than the rest of the statue. I marveled at the visual contrast between the pale marble of the sculpture and the darker, shadowed marble of the wall behind it. I knew without looking at the screen that these would be amazing images.

By the time I emerged from the church into the morning sunlight a little while later, I felt breathless and exhilarated. It had been weeks since I'd last worked with my camera, and even though I was on the other side of the world, I somehow felt more at home than I had in a very long time. While I had my camera out, I took several shots of the elephant statue and of the church's façade. I also snapped a few street shots, just normal Romans going about their daily business, before finally returning the camera to its case and slipping it back into my shoulder bag.

I sighed and checked my watch. It was ten thirty. I stared in disbelief. I'd been in the church for nearly an hour and a half? It didn't seem possible.

I felt my stomach growling as I stood outside in the sunshine, and I realized I hadn't eaten yet. It was still early, but I knew I could make my way back toward the apartment, where there was a bakery open all day. Or I could try to find my way to Pinocchio and see if Marco was there. My heart jumped a little as I considered it. I took a deep breath. Why not?

I checked the address and then located it on the map of Rome I'd brought with me. It wasn't far. I thought about it for a moment, checked my makeup and hair in the compact mirror I dug out of my bag, and headed off in that direction.

Ten minutes of twisting, cobbled streets later, I found myself standing down the block from the restaurant, a tiny corner spot with a pale red canopy bearing the restaurant's name and a little picture of its long-nosed namesake. I took a deep breath and started toward it.

I wasn't sure whether it was open or not; there didn't seem to be anyone there. I walked through the little outside courtyard and cracked open the door. The dimly lit interior, filled with closely spaced, red-clothed tables, was empty too. Of course; like most Roman restaurants, it probably didn't open until at least eleven, if not later.

I sighed and turned away. I was just about to leave when Marco came bustling out of the kitchen, balancing a tray full of dishes and whistling as he swooped out through the swinging kitchen door and made his way to a sink in the corner of the room. He put the tray down, picked a towel up, and, still whistling, began drying dishes. He didn't even look up.

I watched him for a moment. I couldn't help admiring, as I had the other day, the smooth contours of his tanned face, the way his broad shoulders filled out his crisp white shirt, the way his black pants hugged his hips beneath his apron. He looked so happy, so content, that I almost didn't want to disrupt him. The longer I watched, though, without saying anything, the sillier I felt. This was stupid. What was I doing? It had been a mistake to come.

I began to back up, back out the door, hoping to tiptoe away unnoticed. Unfortunately, in my hurry to escape, I managed to smash into the hostess stand, sending a stack of menus crashing to the floor with a tremendous thud.

Marco looked up in surprise, and as his eyes met mine he blinked a few times in recognition. I held my breath, waiting for a reaction.

'Cat!' he exclaimed. He broke into a huge, infectious grin. 'You're here!'

'Um, yes,' I confirmed unnecessarily. I bent down to pick up the menus, my leather shoulder bag flopping noisily to the floor beside me. I couldn't have felt more conspicuous. 'I'm sorry,' I mumbled as I hastily gathered the menus into a stack.

Marco crossed the restaurant quickly. He bent down at my side and touched my shoulder. 'It's fine, Cat,' he said. 'That's a terrible place for the menus anyway, don't you think?'

It sounded almost patronizing, but when I snuck a look at his face his eyes just looked kind, and a little amused. I swallowed hard.

'I'm sorry,' I said, still squatting awkwardly by my pile of menus. 'I shouldn't have come in. You're obviously closed, so—'

'Cat, it is nice to see you,' Marco interrupted firmly. He scooped the remainder of the menus into his arms and smiled at me. 'Please, why are you worrying?'

I straightened up and handed Marco the stack I'd gathered. 'I, um, just wanted to say thank you again,' I said hastily. 'So, um, I'm sorry. I'll be on my way now. It was nice to see you.'

Marco looked at me for a moment with a half-smile on his face. Then he said patiently, 'Cat, stop being silly. Have a seat. I'll brew you come espresso, and we have a wide assortment of pastries. Okay?'

I hesitated. 'But you're closed.'

'And now we are open,' he said right away. 'For you, anyhow.'

I opened my mouth to protest again, but he cut me off with a raised hand and a smile. 'Stop,' he said. 'You are here now. No reason for you not to eat. You look hungry.'

I began to protest, but Marco was already picking up my bag from the floor and gesturing for me to follow him across the restaurant to a seat by the window. 'What do you carry in here, Cat?' he asked as he walked. He pretended that the bag was pulling him down with its weight, and he turned to grin at me over his shoulder. 'It feels like you are walking around with a ton of bricks!'

'It's a camera,' I mumbled, feeling silly.

'You are a photographer?' he asked.

'No,' I said quickly, embarrassed. 'I mean, it's just something I like to do for fun, you know?'

Marco nodded. He pulled out a seat for me and waited while I sat down.

'I'll return in a moment with your espresso.'

'You really don't have to—' I began.

But Marco cut me off again. 'I never do anything because I have to,' he said. 'I do things because I want to. You should too.'

His words silenced me long enough for him to walk away. I watched him go, my heart pounding.

Marco returned a moment later with two cups of hot, steaming espresso. 'Princess Ann,' he said formally, winking at me as he set mine down in front of me. He eyed the chair opposite mine. 'Mind if I join you?'

'Of course not,' I said.

He smiled and put his mug down. 'Wonderful,' he said. 'What can I get you for your *prima colazione*, for breakfast?'

'Oh, no, just the coffee's fine.'

'I insist. We have many pastries. What will it be? How about a cornetto?'

'If you're sure . . .'

'I am.' He got up and returned a moment later with two cornettos. He handed me one and put the other beside his coffee. He sat down and regarded me seriously. 'So, Cat, what brings you here this morning?'

I shrugged. 'Nothing,' I said. I took a bite of the croissant-like pastry, which was perfectly flaky, and, oddly, reminded me a little of Karina's lasagna from last night.

'Were you taking photographs?' he asked, nodding at my bag. He took a bite of his own cornetto and leaned back in his chair, looking perfectly relaxed.

I hesitated and nodded. 'Yes. Of the Santa Maria sopra Minerva church near the Pantheon. Do you know it?'

Marco smiled. 'Of course. It's beautiful. Did you see the Michelangelo statue?'

I nodded. 'It was amazing.'

'*Sì.*' He paused and gestured to my bag. 'May I see? The photos?'

I hesitated. 'They're not really that good.'

'I'm sure they're fine.'

I paused and shrugged. I dug into my bag and pulled the camera out, feeling silly. I handed it to Marco, who took it out of its case and examined it carefully, turning it over in his hands a few times.

'This is nice,' he said.

'Do you know cameras?' I asked.

He nodded. 'A little. I took a course at university. Photography has always interested me.'

'Me too.'

He smiled at me and turned the camera on. I showed him how to access the images, and he began flipping silently through the pictures I'd taken that morning, pausing for several seconds on each one.

His silence made me nervous. I sipped my espresso, wondering what he was thinking or what he'd say. I shouldn't have cared so much; it wasn't like I was a professional photographer or anything, or that he was a photography critic. But somehow his opinion seemed very, very important to me.

He reached the end of the morning's shots and studied the last one longer than the others. Then he handed the camera back to me and looked at me for a long time.

'What?' I finally asked with a nervous laugh.

He shook his head.

'You hated them, right?' I guessed. 'You thought they were terrible? That I did a really pathetic job of capturing the most beautiful church in your city?' I laughed to soften the words.

But Marco just shook his head again. 'No,' he said finally. 'The photos were amazing. I'm astonished.'

I was taken aback. 'Astonished?'

He nodded. 'They are very professional. The kind that someone would hang on their walls to remember a trip forever. The kind that a stranger would buy because the colors reach out to them.'

I swallowed hard. 'That might be the nicest thing anyone has ever said to me,' I admitted.

Marco laughed at this. 'That can't possibly be true, Cat. I am just speaking the truth. You shouldn't be so modest.'

I looked down at my lap, feeling silly and a little overwhelmed. 'Well, thank you,' I said after a minute. I took my camera back, turned it off, put it in its case and placed it back in my bag while he watched me curiously.

We sipped our coffee in silence for a moment, and I finished my pastry.

'What time do you open?' I asked after a moment in an attempt to change the subject.

'Usually? Noon,' Marco said. 'But this morning was a nice exception.'

'So you have to get here early and set things up?'

He nodded. 'The staff is very small. But you did not come here to talk about the operation of Pinocchio, did you?'

I laughed. 'No. I suppose not. I came to say sorry.'

'Sorry?'

'For the other night. It was a really weird situation to put you in, and it was incredibly nice of you to take me home with you the way you did. I don't know what I would have done without you.'

'Yes, well, I suppose another Joe Bradley would have come along,' Marco said, regarding me in amusement.

'I told you I haven't seen that movie,' I said.

'Yes, about that,' Marco said. He leaned forward. 'You must be the only American who has ever come to Rome without seeing the film.'

I shrugged. 'So?' I realized I sounded defensive, and I tried to soften the sharp word with a small smile.

Now Marco looked intrigued. Too intrigued. 'Why?' he asked simply.

'Why what?'

'Why haven't you seen it?'

'I just haven't gotten around to it.' I averted my eyes.

Marco shook his head. 'I don't believe that. What is the real reason?'

I considered this for a moment. The real reason sounded stupid to me, and I had no doubt it would sound stupid to him too. 'I just don't like Audrey Hepburn.'

Now he was staring at me like I was completely insane. I regretted saying anything. He wouldn't understand. No one would.

'What?' Marco asked with a laugh. 'How can you not like Audrey Hepburn?'

I shrugged. 'I just don't, okay?' I mumbled.

Marco looked skeptical. 'No,' he said. 'Not okay. There must be a reason.'

I shrugged and looked down.

'You don't like her haircut?' he asked.

I laughed, despite myself. 'No, her hair is fine.'

'She's too small, and small people make you uneasy?'

I laughed again. 'No.'

He thought for a moment. 'She reminds you of a woman you once loved?'

I looked up sharply. He was grinning at me, obviously kidding. The smile fell from his face after a moment, though, when I didn't respond.

'Oh,' he said. He looked embarrassed. 'I didn't mean. I mean, I didn't realize . . .' His voice trailed off and he fiddled with his espresso cup for a moment. 'I mean, I just assumed you liked men.'

I laughed, despite myself. 'I do,' I assured him.

'Oh,' he said. He looked confused. 'Um, and women?' he asked.

'No.' I shook my head. 'It's not like that.'

I could see from the expression on his face that I wasn't explaining myself well enough; he obviously thought now that I'd had a torrid love affair with an Audrey Hepburn lookalike. 'Okay,' he said uncertainly.

I sighed and closed my eyes. 'My mother,' I said finally. I couldn't believe I was talking about the woman for the second time in the space of twenty-four hours. I hardly ever mentioned her anymore, and most of the time I succeeded in banishing her from my mind.

'Your mother?' Marco asked. He looked just as confused, but at least he didn't seem to be creating any imaginary lesbian scenarios for me anymore.

'Yeah,' I said. I glanced at him. He was looking at me intently, waiting for me to finish. 'My mother's name was Audrey,' I said finally. 'Her parents were both extras in *Roman Holiday*. They lived here in Rome, and they met on the set. My mother's mother, my grandmother, I guess, apparently idolized Audrey Hepburn. When she became pregnant, she had to marry my grandfather quickly to avoid a scandal. They named her Audrey, after their favorite movie star. In fact, her middle name is even Hepburn. Audrey Hepburn Verdicchio. How about that? And strangely enough, she grew up looking a lot like Audrey Hepburn.'

I felt a strange pang as I said the words. It was the story my mother had told me many times during my early childhood – minus the out-of-wedlock pregnancy part, which my father had filled in later. My mother had always said it was the most romantic thing in the world. And she had worshipped the ground her namesake walked on. When I was younger, I had begged to watch the movies my mother talked about so often, especially *Roman Holiday*, of course. But she'd told me I was too young and could see them when I was a teenager.

Of course my mother had disappeared from our lives a year before I turned thirteen. And by the time she came back, I had sworn off Audrey Hepburn forever, illogically lumping her in with my mother as someone who was to be avoided at all costs.

I looked up at Marco after a moment.

He still looked confused. 'That's interesting,' he said

finally. I could tell he didn't understand but was trying to.

I hesitated again. 'My mother left us when I was a kid,' I said.

'Oh,' Marco said. His eyes looked genuinely sad, which touched me in a strange way. 'I'm sorry.'

I shrugged. 'It's no big deal,' I said.

'Where is she now?' he asked. 'Back here in Rome?'

I sighed again. I hated having to say the words. 'She died,' I said simply. 'A long time ago.'

'*Dio mio*,' Marco said softly. He sat back in his chair without taking his eyes off me. I was suddenly aware of how still and silent the restaurant seemed. The quiet made me uncomfortable. I shifted nervously, waiting for what he had to say. 'I'm so sorry, Cat,' he said finally, his voice soft and his eyes wide. 'I had no idea.'

'It's fine.' I waved my hand dismissively.

'No, it is not,' Marco said. 'And I made it worse by insisting on talking about *Roman Holiday* with you. *Che idiota!*'

I smiled. 'You're not an idiot. How would you know that I had some weird issue with Audrey Hepburn?'

He groaned. 'You must have wanted to hit me.'

'No, not at all.' I paused and smiled again. 'I just didn't know what you were talking about. So see? I really *wasn't* trying to be Princess Ann or whatever. And I still have no clue who Joe Bradley is, although I'm assuming he's a character from *Roman Holiday*.'

Marco smiled. 'Yes, he is.'

'Well,' I said. 'Maybe I'll watch it someday.'

'Yes?' Marco looked skeptical.

I thought about it for a moment. 'Maybe,' I said finally. 'Maybe it's time to stop letting my life be ruled by ghosts.'

I spent the next three days wandering the streets of Rome with my camera slung over my shoulder. I trekked through the dust of the Forum to capture the way the light reflected off the crumbling ruins. I spent almost a full day in Vatican City, photographing everything from the columns that lined St Peter's Square to the statues that sat atop the basilica. I shot nearly a hundred photos at the Colosseum, and detailed the Spanish Steps and Bernini's Fountain of the Barcaccia, which sat at their foot.

But the best shots I got were the ones I hadn't planned, the ones that were en route to the tourist sites.

On the way to the Forum, I crouched in a doorway and took pictures of a lone boy kicking a ball around a fountain in the Piazza Barberini. Halfway to Vatican City, I photographed two old men smoking pipes in the entrance to a butcher's shop and a trio of giggling teen girls in a huddle together, pointing furtively to a trio of boys across the way who were pretending not to notice. Before I reached the Spanish Steps, I captured two little girls with gap-toothed grins, jumping rope while singing *Se Sei Felice Tu Lo Sai*, the Italian version of *If You're Happy And You Know It*. By the time I wandered home late the third afternoon, having taken the long route past the Tiber so that I could snap some shots of the river glistening in the sun with the gritty Trastevere neighborhood rising up behind it, I had taken over five hundred photographs.

Best of all, I felt so exhilarated from all the picture taking that I'd managed to keep my mind off the things I'd discussed with Marco and Karina. Any time my mother popped into my head, or I saw a Roman woman with a haircut that looked like my mother's perennial Audrey Hepburn bob, I simply refocused, adjusted the aperture and lost myself in the world I could see through the lens. I loved the control that gave me, the way I could select the things that mattered and exclude the things that didn't.

I'd never felt so free in all my life. And to my surprise, I liked the feeling.

After returning home on the third day, I booted up my laptop, plugged in my USB cord, set my camera to automatically upload all the pictures on its SD card, and finally sat down to call home.

I called Becky first. I felt guilty that I'd dropped off the map for a few days, but in truth, they could have called me on my cell if they needed me.

Becky answered on the first ring, her voice sounding cheerful and close enough to be in the next room.

'Hi, sis!' I chirped, happy to hear her voice. 'It's me!'

'Cat! Where are you?' she demanded instantly.

I was taken aback. 'In Rome. You know that.'

'But I called you yesterday! Your cell didn't work, so I called that Francesco guy since you gave me his number, but he said you'd moved out! I've been worried sick!'

I paused and clicked over to the email box on my

laptop. I scanned the twenty-seven new messages I'd received since yesterday. None were from my sister.

'But Becky, if you were worried, why didn't you email?' I asked.

She made a huffing sound and said, 'I shouldn't have to play detective to track you down!'

I rolled my eyes. She was right; but I also shouldn't have to report back to her – or anyone, for that matter – either. That was one of the beautiful, liberating things about being single. But I didn't want to pick a fight with her now. Not over this. Not from four thousand miles away. So instead, I just said, 'I'm sorry. I'll call the cell phone company and see what the problem is. I didn't mean to worry you.'

'Well,' Becky said, 'you did. You can't just go disappearing like that. What if Daddy or I had needed you?'

'But you didn't, did you?' I asked in a small voice.

'That's not the point.'

I took a deep breath. 'Okay.' I paused. 'So. How's married life?'

As I knew would be the case, the change of topic worked perfectly, and Becky launched into a fast-paced, bubbly, long-winded tale about how Jay had tried to vacuum the carpet the other day but had tripped over the power cord and knocked over a lamp which made her *so* mad because it was her *favorite* lamp in all the world.

When she was done, she was silent for a moment and then asked, 'So? How are you? What's new?'

It was strange, I thought, that she hadn't asked about Francesco. Or why I was no longer staying there. But I figured I had to tell her anyhow.

'Well, I'm actually living in a little apartment near the Pantheon for the next few weeks,' I said. I took a deep breath. 'Things didn't exactly work out with Francesco.'

Becky was silent for so long that I thought we'd been disconnected. 'Hello?' I finally asked tentatively into the silence.

'I'm here,' she said. 'I just can't believe what I'm hearing.'

'What? What do you mean?' I was taken aback. It was about the last thing I had expected her to say.

Becky sighed dramatically. 'Come on, Cat,' she said. 'You go all the way over there and then you blow it with the guy you went to see?'

I was silent for a long moment, mostly because my jaw had dropped and I couldn't quite seem to get it to cooperate. Finally, I managed to squeak out, 'What?'

'Well, no offense, Cat. And I'm just saying this because I love you and I'm worried about you. But don't you think you're being a little too picky? I mean, you keep choosing all these guys and then changing your mind about them.'

'Becky, I didn't change my mind about Francesco,' I said. I shook my head. I didn't even know where to begin. She had never understood the concept of breaking up with men you knew were wrong for you; her philosophy was more along the lines of staying with them as long as they did things for you. 'He changed his mind about me,' I added softly.

Becky was silent for a minute. 'Are you sure you didn't just push him away?' she asked at last. 'Like you do sometimes?'

I could feel my skin beginning to crawl. 'No, Becky,' I said through gritted teeth. 'I didn't push him away.'

'Don't get defensive,' Becky said. 'I'm just trying to help. Because I love you.'

I closed my eyes for a minute and tried to calm down. 'I know,' I said finally.

'So when are you coming home?'

'In two and a half weeks. Same date as I originally planned.'

Silence. Finally: 'You're staying?'

'I like it here, Becky,' I said. 'I feel happy here. And it's nice to take a break.'

'Is there another guy?'

I shook my head. Apparently that's all she could think of. 'No,' I said. As soon as the word was out of my mouth, I thought of Marco. Did he count?

'So you're just alone?'

'Yes. And I'm happy.'

'Okay.' She paused. 'Well, that's good.'

'Thanks,' I said simply. For the first time in a while, I was feeling pretty secure about the decision I'd made.

'Oh, I almost forgot to tell you!' Becky said suddenly. 'That guy who owns the restaurant where the reception was? Michael? He called to ask about you.'

My heart stopped for a moment. 'What?'

'Yeah, well, he had my cell phone number from when we were planning the reception, and he just called out of the blue to ask if I knew how to get in touch with you.'

'And what did you say?' I asked carefully.

'I told him you were in Rome with your old boyfriend.' She giggled.

I swallowed hard. 'And what did he say?'

'What does it matter? He's *married*, Cat.'

'I know.' I paused. 'But what did he say?'

'He got all silent for a minute, and then he mumbled something about how he hadn't realized you had a boyfriend, but he wanted to clear up a misunderstanding with you.'

I shook my head. 'A misunderstanding?'

'Yeah. Look, Cat, you're not thinking about getting involved with some married guy, right?'

'No.'

'Because, I mean, now that *I'm* married, I would be personally offended.' Becky sniffed.

I closed my eyes and gritted my teeth. As usual, it was all about her.

'I would never do that,' I said. 'You know that.'

'Yeah, well.' She made another huffing noise and said, 'I just don't want to hear later that you got involved with him over there in Rome.'

'In Rome?'

'He said he was going over for work. But it's not like he has any way to find you.'

I closed my eyes. I was staying in his old friend's apartment. Of course he could find me. My heart was suddenly pounding rapidly, and my palms felt sweaty. 'Did he say when he was coming?'

'I don't know. This week, I think. Does it matter?'

'Of course. It doesn't.' I blinked a few times and tried to steady myself. 'Well, I'd better get going.'

'Oh, right,' Becky chirped, back to her cheerful self.

'Will you tell Dad I said hi? And let him know that I've moved apartments and will try to get my cell phone working?' I didn't think I could handle a second family conversation today about what a failure I was.

'No problem. Talk to you soon!' And with that the phone clicked off on her end.

I sat holding the phone for a while until it started making noises at me. Then I cut the connection and called the cell phone company, who promised to sort out the problem with my cell within twenty-four hours. Finally, I turned back to my laptop.

I watched blankly for a while as my photos loaded, each one crystallizing momentarily on the screen as the files were saved. It was like being in the middle of a slide show, reliving my last three days in Rome. The longer I watched, the more I began to breathe again. The photos relaxed me, reminded me of where I was, outside the pressures of having a boyfriend, of dealing with Francesco, of thinking about Michael.

Michael. I sighed and shook my head. I couldn't believe he was coming to Rome – or, given my sister's sketchy recollection, might even be in Rome now. The odds on my running into him were, of course, slim. But just knowing that we were, or would soon be, in the same city unsettled me. I tried to shake off the thought.

Just then, there was a knock at the door.

The first thought that flashed into my mind, just because I'd been thinking about him, was *Michael*. But that was insane, wasn't it? Surely Karina would have warned me.

Still, when I opened my door and found Nico there, there was a tiny, ridiculous part of me that felt disappointed.

'Hi, Signorina Cat!' he said excitedly.

'Well, hi there, Nico,' I said, smiling down at him.

'Mamma sent me up to see if you wanted to come

down to dinner. At the restaurant. It is slow there, and she says she has not seen you in a few days.'

I nodded. 'Yes, I've been sort of busy.'

'Doing what?' He blinked up at me.

I hesitated. 'Taking pictures, actually.'

'Pictures? Of what?'

'Of Rome,' I said. I realized it sounded silly, but Nico just looked curious.

'May I see them?'

I glanced over my shoulder at the computer. 'I have them on my laptop if you want to watch as they upload.'

'Oh, yes, please!' Nico said. He grinned at me and walked into my apartment. He sat down on the edge of my bed and stared at the screen of my Thinkpad. 'I've never seen a computer this small before!'

I looked at the laptop. 'You haven't?'

He shook his head. 'Mamma and I just have an old one. It doesn't do pictures very well. But I can email!'

'Well, that's exciting.'

'Yes,' he agreed. He stared at the screen for a moment. 'You took all these photographs?'

'Yeah.' I sat down beside him, and together we watched photo after photo materialize on the screen.

When they were finally done loading, Nico looked up at me. 'Those are really good,' he said solemnly.

'Oh yeah?' I smiled. 'Well, thank you, Nico.'

'Do you have any of America?' he asked, looking at me hopefully. 'On your computer?'

I paused. I wasn't accustomed to showing my photos to anyone. But it was silly to feel self-conscious about showing them to a six-year-old, wasn't it? 'Sure,' I said. I leaned over to the computer, clicked open a folder and started the slideshow function.

Nico sat transfixed for ten minutes while image after image of New York popped onto the screen. There were street shots of New Yorkers going about their days, businessmen absorbed in cell phone conversations, women hailing cabs, kids playing in Bryant Park, couples strolling in Central Park. There were black and whites of Magnolia Bakery and the Empire State Building, bright-hued photos of springtime in Central Park, sepia photos of the park's boathouse. As I watched with Nico, I smiled. I, too, was feeling transported to the Big Apple from the edge of a twin-sized bed in Rome.

When the slideshow was finished, Nico turned to me with wide eyes. 'Those were amazing,' he said.

I smiled. 'Thanks. They're nothing special.'

His eyes widened further. 'You are crazy, Signorina Cat! They were the best pictures of New York I've ever seen!'

I laughed. 'Well, thanks,' I said. 'But I'm sure there are many pictures out there that are much more beautiful than mine.' After all, how many photos of New York could one little Roman boy have seen?

He shook his head. 'No, no,' he said. 'I have seen hundreds! Thousands! Mamma takes me to the library every week, and I check out the books about New York. But these pictures, these are the best.'

I looked at him in surprise. 'Really?'

'Really!' He nodded vigorously. 'And the pictures of Roma, they are beautiful.'

'Well thanks, Nico,' I said. 'I don't know what to say.'

He thought·for a minute. 'Say you will take some

pictures of me and Mamma before you leave,' he said. 'And maybe Nonna too.'

I smiled. 'Of course I will, Nico.'

'Good, good.' He seemed to think for a moment, his little face growing solemn. 'So we shall go to dinner then? Before Mamma gets angry?'

I laughed. 'Yes. Let's go to dinner.'

After a delicious dinner of cold, rice-stuffed Roman tomatoes with salad and a glass of prosecco, eaten with Nico chattering away about America and Karina dropping in to sit with us every few moments, I went back up to my room. I wanted to do some laundry in the sink and then head to bed so that I could get an early start tomorrow. I planned to be outside Vatican City by dawn with my camera, in time to see the sunrise over the Tiber as it lit the buildings of ancient Rome on the east side of the river.

I was just hanging my dresses up to dry on the narrow pole that ran the horizontal length of the shower when there was a knock at my door. I opened it to find Karina standing there with her hands on her hips.

'Nico said you showed him some pictures of New York,' she announced without any ceremony, sweeping into my room and sniffing. 'What are you doing in here?'

'Washing clothes,' I said, holding up a damp dress as evidence. 'And yes, Nico came in and looked at some pictures. He seemed to like them.'

Karina rolled her eyes. 'You cannot just go getting him excited about New York.'

I looked at her in confusion. 'What? Why not?'

'It is not realistic.'

'I don't understand what you mean.'

Karina sat down on the edge of my bed. 'He will want to go there. And I cannot afford to take him.'

'Oh.' I sat down carefully beside her and considered my words. 'I'm sorry. But I'm sure he'll get to go someday. I'm sure *you'll* get to go someday.'

'Who says I want to?' Karina snapped.

I was taken aback. 'Oh. I'm sorry. I just assumed . . . I mean, since you are teaching him English, and since you speak such good English yourself.'

She shook her head. 'You don't know as much as you think you do.'

She stood up from the bed and began pacing distractedly. I watched her, feeling a little amused, considering that this was a difficult apartment in which to pace. Karina was able to take only three small steps before she had to turn back around and head in the opposite direction.

Suddenly, she stopped abruptly. 'Can I see them?'

'See what?'

'The pictures,' she said impatiently. 'The photographs.'

'Oh. Of course.' I paused. 'The ones of New York?'

'What else do you have?'

I shrugged. 'I took some of Rome too,' I said. 'In the past few days.'

She looked at me for a long moment. 'Why?'

I squirmed uncomfortably. 'I don't know. I like taking pictures.'

Karina nodded. She gestured to my computer. 'So?'

I felt uncomfortable, but with her plopped on the edge of my bed I couldn't exactly say no. So I booted up the laptop, pulled up the New York photos first and pushed play.

I pretended to be absorbed in the laundry, but I kept sneaking looks at her face to see how she was reacting as the photos flashed across the screen. I kept expecting judgment, criticism, or, at the least, Karina's signature sarcasm. But she just continued to stare, wide-eyed, as the images materialized. She barely even blinked. As I watched her out of the corner of my eye, it struck me how very similar to her son she was when she wasn't posing or yelling or thinking about how she looked.

Finally, Karina looked up at me. 'The pictures are done,' she said softly.

'Oh.' I crossed the room to the computer and cleared my throat. 'Um, want to see the Rome ones too, then?'

Suddenly, I felt her hand on my arm. She didn't say anything, so finally I looked up.

Her eyes were still wide, and she was staring at me. 'Those were amazing, Cat,' she said.

I shrugged. 'They're just pictures.'

'They're beautiful pictures,' she protested. 'Like Nico said, they are art.'

Art. I'd certainly never thought of them that way. 'No,' I said. 'They're just photos.'

'They are art,' Karina repeated firmly. 'And don't you dare tell me they are not.' She looked a little angry. I shrugged again.

'It's no big deal.'

She thought for a minute. 'This is what you do for a living at home? In New York?'

'What? No. I'm an accountant.'

She looked confused. 'What?'

'An accountant. Um, I work with a bunch of businesses.

I do their taxes, figure out their expenses. Things like that.'

'But I don't understand. What do you do with the pictures?'

I stared at her. I didn't understand what was so difficult to grasp. 'Nothing. I just like taking pictures. It's just a hobby.'

'A hobby?'

'Yes, you know, something I do for fun.'

'I know what a hobby is,' she said sharply. 'I was not looking for a definition.'

'Oh,' I said. She seemed to be glaring at me now. 'Are you angry with me for some reason?'

She shook her head. 'You are just foolish, that is all.'

'What?'

She paused and glanced back at my computer screen, which was illuminated with the final photo from my New York series, a shot straight up from the base of the Statue of Liberty at dusk, with a few stars already dotting the darkening sky overhead.

'You are foolish,' she repeated. 'You are an artist, Cat. And for you to waste your talent would be like . . .' She paused and seemed to search for the perfect analogy. Her face suddenly lit up. 'It would be like Leonardo da Vinci painting bathrooms. Or Michelangelo constructing pool decks.'

I laughed. 'Did they have pool decks in Michelangelo's day?'

Karina glared. 'You are missing the point.'

I was at a loss. I just shrugged.

Karina looked at me for a moment. 'Can I see the Rome ones?' she asked.

'Are you going to criticize me for those too?'

'I am not criticizing you,' she said sharply. 'Do you not know a compliment when you hear it?'

I raised an eyebrow at her. She had a strange idea of what constituted a compliment. But I acquiesced and pulled up the Rome pictures I'd taken over the last few days. 'I haven't had a chance to edit these or anything,' I mumbled. 'I just uploaded them today.'

Karina made a face at me and pushed play. Slowly, I sank down on the bed next to her and watched as, one after another, my photographs illuminated the screen. There were hundreds of them, and I was sure Karina would get bored. But she didn't move a muscle and didn't say a word. She uttered an *mmm* sound here and there, but I honestly wasn't sure if it was supposed to be a compliment or an insult. Looking at my photos of New York was one thing. But seeing her own city through the eyes of an American camera-toting outsider was probably quite another.

When the slideshow ended, Karina sat silent for a very long time while I took slow, shallow breaths, waiting for her reaction.

Finally, she stood up and took a few steps toward the door. I thought she was going to leave without saying anything. But then she paused, her hand on the door knob.

'Cat, what do you want from your life?' she asked softly, not looking at me.

'What?' It wasn't a question I'd expected.

'What do you want from your life?' she asked again. She looked up, and for a moment her eyes looked sad, which I couldn't understand. 'If you really had to choose, what do you want to do with your life?'

I shook my head. 'Karina. I'm about to turn thirty-five. I'm already doing what I want to do. I have a good job. I live close to my family. I'm happy.'

'No. You're not.'

I half laughed, but her words made me feel uncomfortable. 'Yes, I am.'

She stared at me, long and hard. 'So your life's goal is to calculate taxes and live close to your father and sister in case they need anything?'

I didn't answer.

She rolled her eyes after a moment and said, 'Yes, very fulfilling.' She paused, and her eyes bored into mine. 'Cat, what do you *really* want to do? If you didn't have to worry about bills or taking care of other people?'

I was about to protest again that I was completely content with how my life was now. But there was something about the way she was looking at me that gave me pause. I closed my mouth and thought about it for a moment. 'Maybe I'd be taking pictures,' I said finally in a small voice. I shook my head, dismissing the notion. 'But that's silly, Karina. It's not practical. So what's the point in even thinking about it?'

'I don't understand how it's silly,' she said right away, shaking her head.

I shrugged. 'I have things I need to take care of, responsibilities. There's no guarantee I'd make money taking pictures. And I like my job. It fits me.'

Karina looked down at the floor for a long time. When she looked up again, I could have sworn there were tears in her eyes before she blinked a few times, banishing them. 'Cat, you have no idea about responsibilities,' she said softly. 'I have dreams too. I always have. But now I have Nico to take care of, so it's not about me anymore. And that is fine. But you, you are alone. And I know you sometimes think this is a bad thing. But Cat, you are *free*. You can do what you want. And you are wasting that chance.'

The words hung in the air between us.

'But I have bills to pay, and I can't be irresponsible,' I said. 'I've always been the responsible one. For my sister. For my dad. At my job. Changing all that, well, it's not that easy.'

'Yes, it is,' Karina said. 'It *is* that easy. You just choose. You choose to make things different. You take a chance. Because if you do not, one day you will wake up and find that life has you in a corner, and there is no way out.'

She blinked a few times, more rapidly now.

'Is that how you feel?' I asked softly.

'No,' she said sharply. 'I have no regrets. Not about Nico. But this is my life now. I've made my decisions. You, you still have all your life before you, all your decisions left to make. And you have chosen to put yourself in a corner, because you're scared.'

Her words startled me. 'I'm not scared.'

'Then what do you call it when you always choose the safe way?' Karina asked.

15

I was still thinking of Karina's words the next day. In fact, as I rose before the rest of the city, staked out a spot along the Tiber and watched through my lens as the sky transformed from ash to fire, it was nearly all I could think about.

I avoided Karina all day and decided to wander through Rome instead, pulling out my camera now and then to shoot street scenes that piqued my interest. But by three in the afternoon I was hot, dusty and exhausted, thanks to my mostly sleepless night and the early hour that I'd gotten up. I was walking back toward the Pantheon when I made the snap decision to swing by Pinocchio instead.

I hadn't seen Marco in days, and I wasn't even sure he'd want to see me again. I'd been a little worried he hadn't known how to react to my story about my mother. Either way, Karina's words about always choosing the safe way had made me think, although I'd never admit that to her. To stay away from Pinocchio forever would be to err on the safe side. To go there would be brave and unlike me. It meant taking a risk, the risk of seeming foolish, the risk of being rejected. It felt like something I had to do.

The restaurant was practically deserted when I arrived; three thirty was just past the lunch rush and before neighborhood patrons began streaming in for the lively *aperitivo* hour on the patio. The only people inside were a couple sitting by the window, a mostly empty bottle of wine between them, gazing into each other's eyes and whispering. The woman was giggling every now and then, and the man kept glancing out the window every time she looked down. I had the urge to pull out my camera and shoot them, but it would have been too conspicuous here, of course.

I stood in the doorway for a moment, trying to let my eyes adjust to the inside light. I didn't see Marco, although I caught a glimpse of another waiter slowly folding napkins in the back of the restaurant. He hadn't seemed to notice my entrance.

I considered leaving. After all, I'd come to see Marco and he wasn't here. But wasn't my decision to come as much about me as it was about him? Besides, perhaps it would be nice to sit down at a table to escape the heat of the day and to sip a glass of prosecco. It would be nice to relax and look through the photos I'd taken today.

I flagged the waiter down, and he rushed over with apologies in Italian for not noticing my arrival. I waved dismissively. '*Non è un problema,*' I said. 'Um, *una tabella per una, per favore?*'

'*Soltanto uno?*' he asked, looking behind me, presumably to see if someone else was coming.

I nodded. '*Sì. Soltanto uno.*' It was the story of my life, seemingly.

'Ah, *buon, buon,*' he said, nodding nervously. Then, in English, he added, 'Follow me, please.'

I ordered a glass of prosecco, and the waiter hurried back a moment later with the drink and a small bowl of glistening, crispy potato chips. Many of the restaurants in Rome that served *aperitivi* served complimentary chips with them, which never failed to remind me of America, although the Italians considered it a custom distinct to their culture.

I was just about to take a sip of the sparkling wine when I heard a deep voice from across the room. 'Drinking alone, Princess Ann?' I turned and saw Marco standing across the restaurant, grinning at me. He had an apron on, and he was holding a massive bunch of basil in his hands. He said something to the other waiter, set the basil down and crossed the room toward me.

I could feel the blood rising to my cheeks. 'Er,' I said.

Marco winked at me. 'One must never drink alone,' he said. 'It is bad luck. Perhaps you will allow me to join you?'

I swallowed hard and gestured to the empty seat at my table. 'Of course,' I said.

He nodded. *'Meraviglioso,'* he said. 'Do you mind to wait one minute?'

I shook my head and stared after him as he disappeared back into the kitchen. He emerged in a moment with the apron gone and a second flute of prosecco in his hand. He crossed the room and sat down.

'Cin-cin,' he said. I smiled and clinked glasses with him, averting my eyes.

'Wait!' Marco said sharply, just as I was about to take a sip.

Startled, I paused with the flute halfway to my mouth. 'What?'

'You must look at me while we toast!' he exclaimed.

'What?'

'This is serious,' he said. 'There is an old superstition about not meeting someone's eyes when you toast them.'

'What's the superstition?' I asked.

Now, Marco looked a little embarrassed. 'Honestly?' he asked.

I nodded.

'The superstition says that if you avoid someone's eyes when you toast . . .' he paused and leaned forward conspiratorially, 'it's seven years of bad sex.'

I could feel my face heating up again and thought that I was probably tomato red.

Marco studied me for a moment in apparent amusement. 'Well,' he said finally. 'I can see we have a lot to toast.'

He repeated the toast and this time, despite my embarrassment, I looked into his eyes as we clinked glasses and as I took my first sip. Then I looked away and took long swallow, feeling the tiny bubbles tickle my tongue and my throat on the way down. We drank in silence for a moment, me averting my eyes and trying not to blush, Marco staring at me.

'Cat, why are you here?' he asked abruptly, cutting the silence short.

I swallowed hard. 'I just wanted to get a drink,' I said a little defensively.

'No, not here at the restaurant.' He laughed. 'Here in Roma, I mean. Why are you really here?'

I took a deep breath. I didn't know what to say. There were so many answers on so many levels. 'I don't know,' I said. 'I just needed a break from my life in the United

States.' It wasn't a lie. Coming to Rome *had* been a break from my boring, routine daily grind at home.

But Marco didn't seem to be buying it. He was looking at me closely. 'Please, Cat,' he said, his expression graver than I'd ever seen it. 'Tell me the truth.'

I paused.

He looked intently at me and added softly, 'The one thing I ask of people is that they are honest all the time. Lies only get us in trouble.'

'I'm not lying,' I said defensively.

'But you are not telling the full truth either,' he said. 'If you are not comfortable discussing it, that is fine. But truth is always the best.'

I thought about what he'd said.

'Fine,' I said. I took a deep breath and looked him in the eye. 'I came for a guy.' And with that, I launched into the story of Francesco, pausing here and there when Marco interjected with words of astonishment. When I finished, I held my breath, waiting for his response.

'Cat, this Francesco is a fool,' he said finally. 'You are beautiful, intelligent and interesting.'

'No one else seems to think so,' I said lightly.

'No, I think it is quite the contrary,' Marco said thoughtfully. 'I think this Francesco did realize all those things about you. But that is not what he was looking for.'

'What?'

He paused. 'Some men are not looking for a partner. They are looking for someone who needs them, who worships them. And you would never feel that way about this Francesco.'

I shook my head. 'That's not true,' I said. 'I could have loved him. I *did* love him at one point.'

'It's not about love,' Marco said. 'Not for some men. They want to feel they are needed. Not that they are loved. And you, you are mature. You are responsible. You are smart. For a man like this, that is not enough. He is not looking for an equal. He is looking for someone to make him the center of her universe. And that is not you.'

I looked at Marco for a long time. 'How do you know all this?'

He shrugged. 'I like to study human nature,' he said. 'The way you like to photograph things that move you.'

He paused. 'But that isn't all, is it?' he asked after a moment. He was gazing at me evenly, and I had the disturbing sense he could see right through me.

'What?'

'That is not what drew you to Roma,' he said. 'Perhaps it was the push you needed to come back. But it is not why Roma captured your heart in the first place.'

I looked down at my lap and took a few deep breaths.

'It's your mother, isn't it?' Marco said after a moment.

I nodded. I didn't say anything. I didn't need to.

'It is not so easy to confront ghosts,' he said.

I shook my head, still not looking at him.

After a moment of silence, Marco said, 'I have an idea. I will return in a moment.'

He took our empty prosecco flutes and hurried into the kitchen. I saw him talking to the other waiter, and then he logged onto a computer and scrolled through a few screens. He made a phone call, turning his back to me, and I could hear a few strains of unintelligible Italian. When he hung up and came back a moment later, he was smiling.

'If it is okay with you,' he said, 'we will go now.'

I glanced around. 'Go? Where?'

He smiled. 'There are some things I would like to show you.'

'Don't you have to work?'

'I talked with Antonio,' he said, nodding at the other waiter, who was drying and stacking dishes. 'He's fine here alone. The dinner staff will be here in less than an hour.'

'But where are we going?'

His eyes seemed to sparkle. 'You shall see,' he said. 'Do you trust me?'

I hesitated, but only for a second. 'Yes,' I said.

I followed him out the door, wondering what I was getting myself into.

Marco led me around to the back of the restaurant, where there was a silver Vespa parked up against the wall.

'Get on,' Marco said, nodding to it with a slight smile.

'It's yours?' I asked.

He nodded. 'Have you been on one before?'

'Not for years. They seem more dangerous now than they did then.'

'I promise I'll keep you safe,' he said. 'But you have to trust me.'

I hesitated. 'Okay.'

Marco offered his hand, and I stepped onto the scooter, wishing I had worn pants today instead of a skirt. I wasn't sure how to sit gracefully. I adjusted myself so I was sitting side-saddle.

'Is this okay?' I asked, feeling a little foolish.

He laughed. 'I would say it's perfect.' He shook his head, muttered something in Italian with an amused expression on his face and climbed on in front of me. 'Put your arms around me,' he said.

I hesitated and then did as I was told. I was surprised by how taut and muscular his back and shoulders felt through his plain white shirt.

'Hold on tighter,' he instructed as he gunned the engine. I wrapped my arms around him more tightly, and as I pressed into his back a powerful wave of attraction swept over me. Even in the broad daylight, out in public, there was something that felt very intimate about touching him this way.

'Ready?' he asked.

'Ready,' I said. We lurched forward. I shrieked a little, startled, and he laughed.

'Just hang on,' he said. 'You'll be fine.'

We set off through the streets of Rome, darting down alleys on the scooter. Even with the size of the thing, I still felt safe. I somehow believed that Marco wouldn't let anything happen to me.

I closed my eyes for a moment and felt the wind in my hair. I held a little tighter to Marco, enjoying the solid, safe feel of him.

'You okay?' he asked.

I opened my eyes and smiled. 'Yeah,' I shouted over the engine.

We whizzed by fountains and churches with aging stone façades, apartments with clothing lines outside, little parks with kids sliding down slides, piazzas with teenage girls sitting on steps fluffing their glossy, dark hair. We passed tourists taking pictures, street vendors hawking their wares, mothers walking toddlers. Finally, we pulled up in front of the crumbling Colosseum. Marco pulled to the side of the street, cut the engine and turned to smile at me.

'I *should* take you inside,' he said. 'But we only have a half a day. And I want to make sure we get everything done.'

'What do you mean?' I asked, confused.

'You'll see,' he said mysteriously. 'But you have been inside before, correct?'

I nodded. 'Yes.'

'Good then. We'll continue. Hang on.' He gunned the engine again, and off we went, shooting back into the streets of Rome.

A moment later, we pulled up to a stop sign, and Marco turned around to talk to me. 'Now I know you're probably hoping to kick me off, so you can ride around by yourself and get us in trouble,' he said with a mysterious smile. 'But I'm afraid we can't do that today. I don't have my American News Service card on me.'

'What?' I asked, thoroughly confused.

But he just laughed, shook his head and took off down the street again. 'Hold on!' he yelled a moment later. I squeezed tight, and he took a sharp right onto a side street. A street market had been set up, and as I stared, wide-eyed, hanging on for dear life, he steered the Vespa deftly between stands selling cheese, wine and meat, and around vendors waving scarves, toys and flowers in the air. When he emerged on the other side, miraculously without mowing down any innocent bystanders, he braked and turned to look at me. 'You okay?' he asked.

My heart was hammering a mile a minute.

I stared back at him for a moment. And then, to my surprise, I started laughing. 'What did you do that for?' I asked, glancing over my shoulder and then back at him. I couldn't stop giggling. I think it was a combination of nerves and amusement at the whole situation. Risky as it had been, it had also been exhilarating.

'It's all part of the plan,' he said mysteriously. 'Hold on.'

We set off again, zipping southward on the broad Via Celio Vibenna, with a sprawling green park to our left that Marco identified as the Parco Ninfeo di Nerone. We turned right after the park and cut toward the river. Finally, Marco drew to a halt in front of a large, brown church with several arched entryways and a bell tower.

'It is called Santa Maria in Cosmedin,' he said. He got off the scooter and held out his hand. 'Come on.'

He must have seen the reluctance on my face, because he laughed, took my hand and said, 'Trust me, Cat.'

'*Cosmedin* means beautiful,' Marco explained as we walked toward the structure. 'If I remember correctly, it received the name in the eighth century after it was dubbed one of the loveliest churches of its time.'

'I feel like I should be paying you for a tour,' I teased.

He made a face at me. 'Just listen,' he said. We continued strolling toward the church. 'It has quite a history,' he said. 'There were two popes elected here and one anti-pope. And its bell tower is the tallest medieval belfry in all of Roma.'

We had reached the steps of the church now, and Marco led me toward the dimly lit entrance. He smiled at me and then pointed down the portico to a huge, cream-colored, circular marble decoration on the outside wall, through a series of half a dozen arches. 'Do you know what that is?' he asked.

I looked at it for a moment. It appeared to be a man's face, with a flowing beard and sockets for the eyes, nostrils and mouth. It was chipped and cracked at the edges and seemed to be decaying with age. It looked vaguely familiar to me, perhaps from some textbooks I'd studied of Rome, but I'd never seen the real thing before. 'No,' I said finally.

Marco smiled. 'Good.' He led me down the hall and up to the circular sculpture. He nodded at it. 'It is called *La Bocca della Verità*, the Mouth of Truth,' he said, 'and it was brought here in the seventeenth century. It probably came from an ancient Roman fountain. The legend is that if you put your hand in the mouth, and you've been lying, your hand will be bitten off.'

My eyes widened. 'What?' I looked from the carved face up to Marco. 'You're kidding, right?'

'No, not at all,' he said gravely. 'It is true. The truth is very important.'

I stared at the statue. The mouth was just tall enough for a man's hand to be inserted comfortably. And although the face had looked benign just moments before, knowing the legend somehow made it look a little sinister. In fact, the longer I stared, the creepier it looked. I made a mental note to return one day, when the lighting was better, to photograph it.

'So?' Marco asked after a moment. 'Would you like to go first? Or shall I?'

I looked up at him in surprise. 'Go first?' I repeated. 'Do you mean you think I'm going to stick my hand in that thing's mouth?'

He laughed. 'That's the general idea.'

'Well, you go first,' I said quickly.

He arched an eyebrow at me. 'What's wrong? Are you scared?'

'No!'

'Then go ahead.'

I looked up at him, startled that my heart was hammering to such an extent. It was just a carved marble head; what did I think was going to happen? But it was impossible to see into the depths of the carving's mouth. How did I know what was behind the wall?

'Well?' Marco urged.

I took a tentative step toward the wall and reached my hand out, little by little, toward the sinister face. With every inch, my trepidation multiplied. What if there was someone behind the face, waiting to grab my hand? What if something in the stone shifted and collapsed? What if the legend was true and the carving somehow knew that I was lying to myself about my feelings for my mother and her family?

'I can't,' I admitted, pulling my hand back and shuddering.

Marco laughed and shook his head.

'Well, let's see you do it!' I said, feeling a little silly.

He laughed again and shrugged. 'If you say so.' He took a few steps forward and slowly inserted his hand into the mouth. I held my breath. He pushed his hand further and further in, and I watched his fingers disappear into its depths, then his entire hand. He turned to smile at me, and then a look of pure agony crossed his face.

'Augh!' he yelled, twisting back to the statue. His hand seemed to be struck. He twisted and writhed, trying to pull away.

I screamed and rushed toward him, pulling at him from behind. Moaning, he finally pulled his hand from the mouth of the evil face.

'Oh my God!' I cried. 'What happened?'

Marco held his hand up for me to see. It was fine.

'What happened?' I demanded again.

'I was joking with you,' he said with a wink.

I stared at him, open-mouthed. My heart was still pounding. 'You jerk!' I exclaimed, punching him play-fully in the arm. 'I can't believe you did that! You scared me!'

I shook my head and tried to catch my breath. Marco was smiling at me, and when I looked up to tell him again what a jerk he'd been he silenced me by pulling me into his arms in a tight hug. 'I'm sorry,' he murmured into the top of my head. 'It had to be done. You'll appreciate it later.'

I pulled back a little and looked up at him, confused. 'I'll appreciate that you just scared the heck out of me?'

'Yes,' he said cheerfully. 'You will.'

He pulled me back into his embrace, and we stood there for a long time, wrapped together, until I could feel the beat of his heart as the solemn face, which didn't look quite so evil anymore, looked on.

That evening, after we dropped by Marco's place so that he could change out of his waiter uniform and by my place so that I could leave my camera at home and change out of my own sweaty, dusty clothes into a clean sundress, we went to dinner at a little café just around the corner from Squisito. It nestled just to the right of the Pantheon, and while I had been showering in my apartment Marco had called ahead to ask for one of their outside tables. We were seated along the street with a breathtaking view of the Pantheon's façade and the obelisk and fountain in the middle of the Piazza della Rotonda.

Marco ordered champagne for both of us to start. Once it arrived, Marco smiled and we clinked glasses. I made sure to look into his eyes this time.

'To Rome,' he said. Then, as he looked closely at me, he added, 'And to us.'

'To us,' I echoed.

We chatted through our salad courses. I told Marco about my father and sister and about the recent wedding, and he told me about his three brothers and three sisters and how he'd come here to Rome to open a branch of the family restaurant his father had started in Venice.

'You're from Venice?' I asked.

'*Si*,' Marco said. 'I worked in the restaurant there for years, but I've always wanted to have my own. So I came to Rome five years ago with all the money I'd saved up and a dream of opening a place.'

I stared at him. 'Pinocchio is yours?'

'*Si*,' he said.

'Oh.' I was surprised. 'I didn't realize.'

'Ah, so you're not after me for my money,' Marco teased.

I laughed. 'No.'

'Good,' he said. 'Because I have none. I've spent it all on the restaurant!'

As he began to talk about the challenges of opening a new restaurant in Rome, and how gratifying it was to see his dreams come to fruition, my mind wandered a little, back to Michael. I'd never known a restaurant owner before, and it seemed a strange twist of fate to be sitting here with a second one while the owner of Adriano's in New York still lurked in the corner of my mind. It was foolish, of course, that he was even still in my realm of thought, especially when I was having dinner with the handsome, kind and, most of all, available Marco.

'Don't you think?' Marco asked, concluding a chain of thought I hadn't entirely heard.

I shook my head. 'I'm so sorry,' I said. 'My mind was wandering. What did you say?'

He laughed. 'I'm boring you already?' He winked at me. 'I was just saying that I opened the restaurant because I think it's worth the risk to pursue your dream, even if you don't know if it will work out. Don't you think this is the case?'

I hesitated. 'I'm not sure,' I said. I thought of Karina's words. 'Apparently, I like to live life on the safe side.'

'There is value in that too,' he said. 'But I think that is the difference between living a small life and living a big one.'

'What do you mean?'

He thought for a second. 'I mean, I think it's perfectly acceptable to live a safe life,' he said. 'I wouldn't have been unhappy if I had stayed in Venezia. I probably would have continued to work in the family restaurant; I would have gotten an apartment in Mestre near my family, and I would have married, had children, played on the family *futbol* team at weekends and one day inherited the restaurant along with my brothers.

'But my world would have been so small. You understand? I might have traveled, and I might have done little things here and there. But my dream would have died in my head. And I never would have made any real difference in the world.'

I nodded. Suddenly, my heart was pounding. 'I know what you mean,' I said softly.

'But here in Roma, things are different,' he said. 'For a year I barely had enough money to eat, and I had no time. I was working twenty hours a day setting up the restaurant. And at the beginning, we had no business. It was terrible. I felt like I was going to fail. But I didn't let go of my dream. And today I am so happy, Cat. My life is not perfect, but it is good. That is all I can ask for.'

'That's amazing,' I said. I didn't know what else to say.

'Do you have dreams too?' he asked. 'Beyond what you are doing now?'

I thought for a minute. 'Yeah,' I said. 'Maybe I do.'

16

After a wonderful dinner of fried seafood – a Venetian specialty, Marco explained – and a bottle of Pinot Grigio, followed by espresso and a shared dessert of tiramisu, Marco said that he had another surprise for me, if I would trust him.

We climbed onto the Vespa and set off through a series of small city streets, eventually winding up on the Via dei Coronari, heading toward the river. I closed my eyes and held on tight as we drew closer to the water. I could smell the salt wafting in on the evening air.

Marco finally parked the Vespa near the Ponte Sant'Angelo, the marble pedestrian bridge that spanned the Tiber with a series of arches, overlooking the Castel Sant'Angelo. It had always been my favorite place in Rome. The bridge was flanked with ten angel statues, all of them holding things like a crown of thorns, a cross, or whips. I'd read somewhere that all ten angels carried instruments of Christ's crucifixion. Although I wasn't deeply religious, there was something about the statues that had always moved me.

'This is one of my favorite places in Rome,' I said to Marco as he took my hand and we began strolling toward the bridge. I briefly remembered discussing it with Michael, the look on his face when I said it was my favorite spot to be alone. But I shook off the thought just as quickly. 'How did you know?'

He looked surprised. 'I didn't,' he said. 'But it is a place I've always loved too.'

I expected us to cross the bridge toward the towering, cylindrical *palazzo*, which looked almost magical bathed in pale yellow light. But instead, Marco took a sharp turn to the right as we reached the bridge and led me down a series of stone steps toward the river bank below.

'Where are we going?' I asked.

He squeezed my hand and continued down the stairs ahead of me. 'You'll see.'

As we descended, I could see a small boat docked up ahead. It looked as if it had been hastily strung with several strands of sparkling white lights. Marco shouted something to the man standing on the deck of the boat, and the man waved back.

'You know him?' I asked.

Marco nodded and smiled at me. 'It's my friend Nari. He is the only person I know with a boat. I asked him to meet us here.'

I looked at him, puzzled, as we reached the base of the stairs and began walking toward the boat. 'You did? Why?'

'I looked everywhere for a barge that was hosting a dance tonight,' he said with a mysterious grin, 'but I could not find a single one. So I had to make my own.'

'A barge hosting a dance?'

'You will understand later,' he said. 'But tonight, it is just a dance for two. Well, three, if Nari stays. But I think

I can persuade him to go get an espresso while we use his boat.'

I was completely confused now, but I followed Marco aboard the small, white vessel and shook Nari's hand when we were introduced. The man barely spoke English, so Marco translated a few pleasantries between us and then slipped into a rapid conversation in Italian while I looked around the boat.

It was small, the kind we might have taken out on Long Island to sunbathe on for a few hours in the summer. It looked like there was a small cabin below. There was a big, shiny, wooden wheel toward the back of the boat, and behind it a motor. At the front of the boat, on the flat, wooden deck, there were two small seats set up, facing the river, and a small stereo tied up to the capstan, presumably so that it didn't pitch overboard.

'Nari is going to take my Vespa and get some coffee,' Marco said finally, turning away from his conversation. Nari, who was standing behind him, nodded to me, smiling. 'He said we can use the boat for a couple of hours while he's gone.'

'But where are we going?' I asked.

Marco smiled. 'Nowhere.'

Puzzled, I shook Nari's hand again and watched as he hopped nimbly from the boat to the bank and made his way up the steep stone stairway toward the bridge. A moment later, he vanished, and I turned to Marco.

He smiled and offered me his hand. 'Would you care to dance?'

I laughed. 'Here?'

'Where better?'

I paused, shrugged and put my hand in his. He bent to turn on the stereo with his free hand, and then he fiddled for a moment with the tuner until he found a station playing what sounded like old-time big band era classics. '*Perfetto*,' he murmured. 'Shall we?'

He pulled me onto the makeshift dance floor and put his right hand on my waist. He lifted my right arm in the air, into a proper ballroom dancing stance, and we stood together like that for a moment. The song changed, and Marco smiled, twirled me around and dipped me. When he pulled me back up again, he moved his left arm to my back and drew me closer.

We swayed that way to the music for a few songs, without saying a word. I pressed my head against his chest and listened to his heartbeat as we rocked back and forth to the music, with the boat moving gently beneath us. I looked out on the river, and at the glowing Castel Sant'Angelo on the opposite bank, its windows blazing bright, its cross seemingly illuminated from within. It looked like a magical palace under a dark sky full of bright stars. Up above, the moon was nearly full and filtered down onto the water, where its diluted reflection rippled and winked at us. Occasionally, a small boat would motor by, or we'd hear a faraway voice from the bridge above, but for the most part it felt like we were all alone in the midst of this city of two and a half million people.

'This is amazing,' I murmured.

'Yes,' Marco agreed. 'It is.'

I looked up, and slowly he titled his head down, and his eyes met mine. We stood holding each other for a moment, staring into each other's eyes. And then, in what felt like slow motion, he slowly lowered his head and touched his lips to mine for the first time.

I don't know whether it was the fairy-tale setting in the shadows of a glowing castle, or whether it was the soft romance of the music, or whether it was simply the way a first kiss with the right person was supposed to feel, but when Marco kissed me, gently at first, it felt like magic.

I don't know how long we stood on the deck of the boat, swaying in the moonlight and kissing each other. It might have been mere moments; it might have been an hour. Time seemed to collapse around us, and I didn't care. Marco didn't seem to be in a hurry to make this more than what it was. There seemed to be no rush, no urgency. Being forced to savor the moment that way was absolutely delicious.

Finally, Marco pulled away and gazed down at me. 'You are an incredible kisser,' he said softly.

'You too,' I said. I smiled up at him, my heart pounding like it had earlier at the Mouth of Truth, but for entirely different reasons this time.

Marco stroked my hair. 'Let us sit and enjoy the moonlight on the river for a little while,' he said.

We settled on the bow of the boat, facing out to the river, Marco's arm wrapped tightly around my shoulders. We sat in silence for a while, then Marco turned and pointed up to the bridge. 'Do you know the story of the angels that guard the Ponte Sant'Angelo?' he asked.

I shook my head.

'Long ago, the bridge was called the bridge of St Peter, because it was the bridge that pilgrims used to reach the Basilica di San Pietro,' he began. 'But legend has it an angel appeared above the castle to announce the end of the plague, which is why the castle and the bridge were both renamed. Angels became very important to the meaning of the bridge after that.

'In the late 1600s, Bernini launched a program to create ten angels to watch over the bridge, at the request of the Pope,' he continued. 'The ten angels, sculpted under his guidance by his students, carry the tools of Christ's crucifixion. They are said to watch over the city, angels guarding Rome from all evil.'

'That's beautiful,' I said.

'*Si*,' Marco said. He kissed me on the top of the head. I smiled into the darkness and closed my eyes.

A few moments later, we heard footsteps behind us and turned to see Nari returning with a paper bag in his hand. He smiled at us and stepped aboard the boat as we stood up. He and Marco chatted for a few minutes, and he handed the bag to Marco.

'He brought us cannoli from the café,' Marco said.

'Oh, *grazie*,' I said to Nari, smiling at him.

'*Prego*,' he replied.

He and Marco chatted for a moment more, and then Marco took my hand. 'Are you ready to go? I have something else I'd like to show you.'

I shook my head and laughed. 'There's more?'

Marco smiled. 'If you don't mind.'

I smiled back, and nodded. After saying goodbye to Nari, we made our way up the stone steps and climbed onto Marco's Vespa. Twenty minutes later, we were walking through the door to his tiny apartment. He poured us each a glass of wine and offered me a seat on the couch. He sat down beside me.

'*Cin-cin*,' he said, raising his glass to me. I met his eye, and he added in a slow, deliberate voice, 'To making the ghosts go away.'

I clinked glasses with him, but I wasn't sure what he meant. Then he leaned back on the sofa and studied me carefully.

'I was thinking a lot about what you said about your mother and her family here,' he said, 'and about getting rid of ghosts.'

I swallowed hard. 'Yes,' I said. I looked down. 'It sounds silly. But I'm not sure that I'm ready.'

Marco nodded. 'Yes, you are,' he said firmly. He put his wine glass down and stood up. He crossed the room to a small bookshelf in the corner and pulled out a DVD. '*Roman Holiday*,' he said, holding it up for me to see. 'I think we should watch it.'

I stared at the box in his hand like it contained anthrax. 'Why?'

'Do you trust me?' he asked, instead of answering my question.

I hesitated. 'I think so,' I said. 'Yes.'

'Then trust me about this,' he said.

I regarded him warily.

He smiled gently and went on. 'You will understand when you watch the movie,' he said. 'But I wanted to change the meaning of it for you. I think you will find now that when you watch *Roman Holiday* it won't just be about your family. It will be like a souvenir of today.'

'I don't understand,' I said.

'You will,' he said.

I took a deep breath and looked at the DVD case in his

hand. Audrey Hepburn, who reminded me so much of my mother, beamed happily out, perched on a scooter, her arms wrapped around Gregory Peck, with the Colosseum in the background.

I looked down at my lap. My mind was reeling, my heart pounding. It was ridiculous; I knew it was just a movie. But it was a movie that had haunted me since I was twelve, something that represented everything I loved and hated, everything I'd had and lost. But Marco knew that. And maybe he was right.

I took a deep breath and closed my eyes briefly. 'Okay.'

Marco smiled at me. 'Good.' He put the movie in, pushed play and sat down on the couch beside me. He put his arm around me and pulled me close. 'This is a good thing, I think,' he said. 'But if you want to stop, just tell me. We can stop anytime.'

I nodded. 'I think I'm okay,' I said.

The movie began, and I felt strangely empty as I watched the opening sequence of Audrey Hepburn's character, Princess Ann, traveling around Europe to various functions. I smiled slightly as she struggled through an official appearance in Rome, and later, as she gazed out her window at the sparkling city below, I felt a swell of pride that Rome was, for the time being, my adopted city too.

'Are you okay?' Marco asked, squeezing my shoulder.

I nodded. 'So far.' And I was. But I still didn't understand what Marco meant.

On the screen, the princess snuck out of her room, hitched a ride into Rome and wound up sleepily wandering streets that looked familiar to me. When she finally settled in for an inadvertent nap on a little brick wall near the Forum, my eyes widened.

'Oh my God, that's right around where you found me, isn't it?' I asked, looking up at Marco.

He laughed. 'Now you see why I was so convinced that you were just another American trying to re-enact the movie,' he said.

I stared. 'Oh no,' I murmured, shaking my head in disbelief.

I laughed as Joe Bradley happened upon Princess Ann and had an exchange that sounded eerily similar to the one I'd had with Marco. And then, when Joe Bradley was forced to take the princess back to his small apartment, I turned to Marco again.

'This is unbelievable,' I said. I sank back into Marco's arms to watch the movie, but to my surprise I found that instead of desperately trying to scan the crowd of extras for the faces of my grandparents, and instead of disliking the Princess Ann character because of everything she represented to me, I was watching the movie to pick out the places Marco and I had gone together.

I watched in disbelief as the day's adventure unfolded on the screen in black and white. Joe Bradley took Princess Ann on a Vespa ride to the Colosseum, and I understood why Marco had made the comment about wishing he had more time to take me inside. As they whizzed through the outdoor market, knocking things over, I saw why Marco had made his strange detour through vendor stalls today and why he'd made the comment about not having an American press card. I laughed aloud as Joe Bradley and Princess Ann visited the Mouth of Truth, shook my head in wonderment as they dined just across from the Pantheon, and finally felt tears in my eyes as they made their way down the steps near the

Ponte Sant'Angelo to a big dance party on a barge in the river.

'You did all of that for me?' I asked as Joe and Ann danced together on the deck of the barge.

Marco nodded. 'I wanted you to be able to look at this movie as something other than the picture that represented your mother,' he said. 'Now it's about you and your time in Roma. Good memories, I hope, to replace the bad ones.'

We watched in silence as the movie ended, and my eyes filled with tears in the final scene.

We sat quietly while the final credits rolled in the darkness. I felt shaken. *Roman Holiday* had always represented something larger than life to me, and now it had taken on a different meaning entirely. It felt disconcerting, as if I really had let go of something.

'Did you like the movie?' Marco asked.

I hesitated for a moment. 'Yes,' I said. 'I really did.' And I meant it.

'Good,' he said. 'I wanted to give you that. But the rest, it is up to you.'

I looked at him. His face was illuminated oddly by the black and white light from the TV screen, making it appear almost as if we were in our own black and white movie. 'What do you mean?'

'I mean that this movie, it was your most important ghost, right?' he said. 'And now you have faced it. And you are okay. The world has not ended. You are still here. So the rest, the rest is up to you.'

'The rest?'

'You have two more weeks in Rome, right?' he asked. I nodded.

'Then figure out how you can change your life in that time,' he said. 'Stop being haunted by the past.'

I thought about his words for a moment and nodded. 'I'll try,' I said.

He looked me in the eye. 'You have the power to change things,' he said. 'It starts here, in Roma.'

I spent that night with Marco, both of us pressed together in his bed, unlike the last time, when he'd stretched out on the uncomfortable couch. We kissed for a while, but nothing happened beyond that. I was an emotional wreck, and Marco knew it. I dozed off for a while and woke up with tears running down my cheeks. Marco was already awake, wiping them away. He pulled me closer, and when I fell asleep again I slept deeply, feeling safer than I had in ages.

17

The next morning, Marco cooked breakfast, and we laughed about how he was obviously not cut out to be a chef; he overdid the eggs, burned the toast and even spilled the orange juice on the counter.

'At least the coffee is perfect,' he said with a laugh as he poured me a small cup of thick, dark liquid from a little metal pot on the stove.

'Hard to believe you own a restaurant,' I teased, examining my charred toast.

'I know!' He laughed. 'I don't know what I'd do if my chef ever quit. The place would go to ruin.'

After breakfast, Marco drove me home on his Vespa and kissed me goodbye. 'I'm out of town for the next couple of nights, to visit my family in Venezia,' he said. 'But when I am back, we should get together.'

His words gave me a strange sinking feeling. My days here were growing fewer, and it was profoundly disappointing to know that I couldn't spend them all with him, although I had no right to expect that. But when he smiled at me there didn't seem to be any regret in his eyes, any disappointment at having to miss some time with me.

'Okay,' I said. I smiled at him. 'Yesterday was amazing.

I don't even know how to thank you.'

'You can thank me by thinking about things,' he said. 'You only live once, and nothing should hold back the adventure.'

He kissed me again, asked me to come by Pinocchio in a few days and said goodbye. I watched him as he rode down the street. As he reached the corner, he turned and waved. Then he disappeared.

I smiled to myself and turned to walk inside. I was startled to see Karina standing in the shadows of the doorway, her arms crossed over her chest, regarding me with an amused expression.

'Well, good morning, Cat,' she said, grinning at me. 'I see you have found a souvenir in Rome already.'

I felt myself turning red. 'It's not what it looks like,' I said. 'Nothing happened.'

I didn't even know why I was defending myself. But she looked amused by it.

'Then you are crazy!' she exclaimed. 'He was gorgeous! Who is he?'

'The guy from Pinocchio,' I said. 'The one I told you about.' I quickly recapped my day and night with Marco as she stared at me, wide-eyed.

'Forget *Roman Holiday*,' she said when I was done. 'This sounds like you are starring in your own romance movie.'

I laughed and shook my head. 'I don't know,' I said. 'There's definitely chemistry there. We'll see what happens.' I was still thrown by the fact that he was vanishing for a few days. And he hadn't even suggested I might go with him, even though he knew I had nothing scheduled, nothing keeping me here in Rome.

'So, you watched the movie?' she asked. 'And you weren't upset?'

I thought for a minute. 'No,' I said. 'I think I needed that push. And the way he created a whole new set of memories to go along with the movie . . .' I paused and shook my head, 'it was amazing.'

Karina nodded. 'I am glad,' she said. 'Good for you.' She reached over to give me a spontaneous hug. 'Yes, Cat Connelly, I am starting to like you.'

I showered and changed and headed out on my own for a while, toting my camera. I intended to make my way over to the Trevi Fountain today to shoot there, but instead I found myself thinking about *Roman Holiday*. Clearly, it was fiction and thus a silly thing to be taking into consideration. But there was something about Princess Ann's courage in changing her entire life, if only for a day, that inspired me. How was it that at nearly thirty-five, I'd never done that? Not even for a moment. Sure, it had been somewhat brave to come to Rome – both when I was twenty-two and now – but both times, I knew the arrangement was temporary and wouldn't really change my life in any major way. Didn't that mean I was hardly taking a risk at all?

I was thinking about that when I spotted a barbershop up ahead on the left, just down the block. I stopped in my tracks and stared, thinking of the scene early in the movie where Princess Ann gets her hair chopped off, an act that sort of symbolized a definitive break with her past and with the guarded person she had been all her life.

I reached up and touched my own brown hair, which fell a few inches below my shoulders in the same haircut

I'd had since high school. It was one of those cuts that didn't really change with the times. I'd gotten the ends trimmed, like clockwork, every eight weeks for as long as I could remember. But my hair had almost become a safety blanket, one of those things by which I identified myself. Maybe by changing that, I could begin to change everything else too.

In that moment, I knew it was something I had to do.

I took a deep breath and, before I could second-guess myself, I darted across the street and pulled open the door of the barber's.

Inside, it looked much like the shop where Princess Ann had gotten her locks chopped off. It wasn't a beauty salon, by any stretch of the imagination; it was a pared down, stark place with four gleaming chairs, two sinks and three barbers standing around in white smocks. There weren't any customers there.

All three men stared at me as I walked in. One said something in Italian, and I shook my head. '*Non parlo l'italiano,*' I said. '*Parla inglese?*'

Two of the barbers shook their heads, but the third, the youngest of the trio, nodded. 'I do,' he said. 'A little. I understand a little.'

'Good.' I sighed in relief. 'I would like a haircut, please.'

He nodded. 'I understand,' he said. He gestured to one of the chairs. I sat, and he picked up a small handful of my hair. 'A little bit?' he asked, pinching a lock between his thumb and forefinger, a half-inch or so from the bottom.

I took a deep breath and channeled Princess Ann. 'No, higher.'

He raised his eyebrows and went up an inch.

'More,' I said.

He glanced at me skeptically in the mirror. I smiled back. We could be here all day if we played this game. 'I'd like it cut into a bob, please,' I said.

He looked confused. '*Non capisco.*'

I lifted my right hand and made a line just below my right ear. 'Here,' I said. 'I want it to here.'

'*Si?*' he asked, looking uncertain. He said something in rapid Italian, and I told him I didn't understand. He collected his thoughts and put his hand where mine had been, showing me the length he thought I wanted. '*Qui?*' he asked skeptically.

'*Si,*' I said. '*Qui*. Here.'

He shook his head and said in English, 'Okay. I will cut.'

He didn't look too sure about it. He walked slowly around me once, examining my hair. He wound up in front of me and held a hand in front of his forehead. 'The front too?' he asked, mimicking bangs.

I hesitated and nodded. '*Si,*' I said. 'With bangs.'

'*Come desiderate,*' he said. He circled me once more and then leaned in with his scissors. As he began cutting, I saw one huge chunk of my hair fall to the ground. I closed my eyes. I couldn't watch.

'Done,' he said several minutes later. 'I am finished.'

I cracked open my eyes and looked into the mirror. My jaw dropped as I saw my reflection.

Gone were my long, plain, stick-straight strands. In their place, a lively, layered bob glistened, with long bangs framing my face.

'You like, *signorina?*' the barber asked nervously.

I reached up in wonderment and touched my hair. I couldn't stop staring.

'*Signorina?*' he prompted, looking worried.

'I love it,' I said. 'I love it.'

The barber sighed in relief and wiped imaginary sweat from his brow. '*È bello,*' he said. 'It is beautiful.'

He beamed at me. Smiling, I paid him and sauntered out, feeling the breeze on the back of my neck for the first time as I stepped outside into the fresh air. Part of me had expected to regret the cut as soon as I emerged back into reality. But as I walked down the street, glancing at my image in shop windows, I felt only relief, like the hair on my head finally reflected who I was meant to be.

Two nights later, I still hadn't heard from Marco. He should have been back from Venice by then, and I figured he was probably busy. But still, I found myself feeling vaguely uneasy, wondering if he'd changed his mind about me just as I began to let myself feel something for him. When Karina popped her head in at just past six to ask if I wanted to join her for a drink that evening, I jumped at the chance as a way to distract myself from waiting pathetically by the phone.

A few hours later, after I'd taken a brief nap and changed into a pair of black J-Brand jeans and a dark gray tank top, with a pile of faux pearls and black peep-toe heels, Karina appeared at my door.

'Wow,' she said, looking me up and down and then staring at my hair. 'You look amazing.'

'Thanks,' I said, smiling self-consciously.

'You cut your hair.'

I nodded. 'It was time for a change.'

Karina looked at me for a long moment and then smiled slowly. She knew I was talking about more than just my hair. 'I am proud of you, *bella,*' she said.

Together, we set off down the street, our heels click-clacking on the cobblestone. Karina was dressed up too, in a low-cut little black dress. 'There is a man named Raffaele who said he would be here tonight,' she mumbled without meeting my eyes. 'He is a waiter at another restaurant nearby.'

'Ah,' I said, smiling at her. 'Is this someone you're interested in?'

'No!' she snapped immediately. But her red face gave her away. 'Maybe,' she amended. 'It is foolish, perhaps. But he seems very kind. And he is always so nice to Nico.' She shrugged. 'There is a celebration tonight with all of the other waiters from his restaurant. Some party for something or other; he didn't explain. Raffaele invited me to join them.'

'Well, that sounds good,' I said. I glanced at her as we hurried down the street and was amused to see that her cheeks still looked a little flushed. The seemingly unflappable Karina was nervous.

The bar was just off the Piazza della Rotonda, the plaza in front of the Pantheon. In fact, I was surprised I hadn't noticed it before. But the entrance was nondescript and tucked into the first doorway of an alleyway near the restaurant where I'd eaten with Marco. 'This bar is always fun,' Karina said as we walked in. 'A lot of the people who work at the restaurants come here.'

Inside, it was dark and already packed with people. Off to the right was a long wooden bar with three bartenders rushing around behind it. To the left, tucked into a little alcove, was a live three-piece band with a guitar player belting out lyrics in English, which, unlike the last time

I'd gone to a bar with Karina, actually sounded pretty accurate.

'Come on,' Karina said, grabbing my hand. 'There's Raffaele.'

She took my hand and led me across the room to a cluster of five tall, athletic-looking men who were all around six feet. The man in the center of the group, a dark-haired guy with chiseled features that reminded me of the statues I'd seen around the city, grinned from ear to ear the moment he spotted us.

'Karina!' he exclaimed as we drew closer. '*Siete venuto!*'

Karina squeezed my hand once more, glanced at me with a small smile on her face and stepped forward to kiss the man on both cheeks.

'*Buona sera*, Raffaele,' she said. She turned and gestured at me. '*Ciò è la mia amica, Cat. È una Americana.*'

'*Ciao*, Cat!' Raffaele said pleasantly. He reached out to kiss me politely on both cheeks, then rattled off a few sentences in rapid Italian. I shrugged and looked helplessly at Karina.

Karina smiled. '*Non parla l'italiano,*' she said, nodding to me.

'Ah,' Raffaele said. He thought for a moment. 'It is a pleasure to meet you,' he said formally, in slow, decisive, heavily accented English. 'I am learning the English now. It is good with the restaurant.'

'Your English is very good,' I said, smiling at him.

'*Grazie,*' he said. 'Thank you.'

He and Karina introduced me around to the other waiters, all of whom grinned at me and tried to say something in English.

Karina made an effort to include me in the conversation, but it was clear to me that I was holding her back. She was giggling at Raffaele's jokes and then making an attempt to translate them for me. I knew she didn't mind. But I knew I had to be a good friend too and make myself scarce for at least a little while.

I told Karina I was going to get a drink, and after she had worriedly asked if I was okay, and I had assured her that I was, I made my way through the crowded room over to the bar. I ordered a Stella and turned to survey the room. Karina was already in her own little world with Raffaele. Her head was inclined toward him as she listened to something he was saying, and he had his arm wrapped gently around her waist, pulling her close as he spoke into her ear above the din of the bar. Her face was flushed, and she was smiling. She looked happy.

I sipped my beer and gazed around the room for a while. The band was playing the Beatles' 'Something,' which had always been one of my favorite songs. I smiled and followed along with the words until the tune ended. Then I grabbed my beer and set off to find the bathroom.

After waiting in a seemingly interminable line to use the women's stall, I made my way back to Karina's group. As I approached from the back, I saw that two new people had joined their group, a tall, broad-shouldered man with a thick shock of dark hair, and a small, balding, older man with stooped shoulders.

Karina, who was still tucked under Raffaele's arm, spotted me and waved as I walked toward them. She had just opened her mouth to say something to me when the two newcomers turned around to see who was coming.

My eyes locked with those of the younger man, and my jaw dropped. I stopped in my tracks, still a few feet away from the group.

'Cat?' the man asked, looking just as incredulous as I felt.

It took me a few seconds to catch my breath. 'Michael?' I said.

Karina grinned at me. 'Isn't this a wonderful surprise, Cat?' she asked. 'I had no idea he was going to be in Roma!'

I didn't respond. Instead, I continued to stare at Michael. 'What are you doing here?' I finally mustered.

'This is my Uncle Armando,' he said, nodding to the older man beside him. The man nodded at me and smiled. 'He owns a restaurant very near here. Didn't I tell you that? These guys are his waiters. Two of them,' he nodded to the two men closest to him, 'are my cousins, Gianni and Lorenzo.'

Karina was looking at me strangely. 'I should have remembered to tell you that Raffaele works at Michael's uncle's restaurant. I didn't even think of it.' She paused. 'Are you all right?'

'No,' I whispered, still staring at Michael.

'Cat, what are you doing here?' Michael repeated.

'I . . . I live near here,' I stammered uncertainly.

'She lives in my spare apartment,' Karina clarified. She still looked mystified. 'Didn't you give her my number, Michael?'

He nodded slowly. 'I didn't realize she had come to stay with you, though.' He paused and looked me straight in the eye. 'She hasn't returned any of my calls.'

This rubbed me entirely the wrong way. 'I wasn't

aware we had anything to talk about,' I said stiffly, my annoyance at him returning now that the initial shock of seeing him had begun to wear off. He looked disturbingly handsome in a dark button-down shirt and dark jeans. His eyes looked brighter that I remembered them, which just made it harder to look away.

I glanced at Michael and then back at Karina. I hated that there was suddenly an ache in my chest.

'Cat, we really need to talk,' Michael said quickly. He took a step toward me, but I backed away.

'So, you didn't bring your wife and kid on this trip?' I asked. 'No mother-in-law?'

Karina looked startled. Her eyes darted to Michael and then back to me. For a moment, I hoped that she'd laugh and tell me I had somehow misunderstood everything. But instead, she didn't say anything. She just glanced at Michael and then looked away. Michael stared at me and slowly shook his head.

'How sad to have to leave them behind,' I said coldly.

'Cat,' Michael said again. He reached forward to touch my arm, but I shook him off.

'Karina, I'm not feeling very well,' I said. 'I'm going to go home, I think.'

Karina looked nervously back and forth between Michael and me. 'What's going on?'

'Why don't you let your friend Michael explain?' I said. I hated that the ache inside me was growing worse. I shouldn't be aching for a man like him. I hated that however much control I was able to exert over most of my life, I couldn't quite seem to master the art of telling my heart to stop wanting something it simply couldn't have. And I hated that, apparently, this was the universe's idea of a funny joke, to drop the married man I'd had a perfect evening with into my path, halfway across the globe.

'Cat, *please*, let me explain,' Michael said.

'There's really nothing to say,' I said. I forced my eyes away from him and turned back to Karina. 'Thank you for inviting me out this evening,' I said with forced formality. 'I hope you have a wonderful time.'

'Cat, you don't—' she began.

But I cut her off. I took a step forward and kissed her on both cheeks. I told Raffaele it was nice to meet him, and I said goodbye to the other waiters. I nodded to Michael's uncle, and then I took one last look at Michael's face. He looked stricken, as if he couldn't possibly have anticipated that I would still be unwilling to embark on an affair with a married man. It made me feel almost ill.

'Don't come after me,' I said to Michael. 'I don't think there's anything to say.'

'But—' he began.

'No,' I said firmly. And before anyone else could say anything, I turned on my heel and walked quickly away without looking back.

Once outside the restaurant, I broke into a run, as fast as my heels would take me. I had the feeling that Michael would try to follow me, and I didn't want to hear his explanation. As far as I was concerned, there was nothing he could say that could make any of this excusable or understandable.

I initially headed toward the apartment, but as I drew closer I realized that Karina would probably come back soon to find me. I didn't want to talk to her tonight, not about Michael. I needed to be alone.

I hailed a cab and asked to be taken to the Ponte Sant'Angelo. I would have walked, but with the heels I had on I suspected my feet would have disappeared in a mass of blisters before I got there. I paid the fare and walked slowly across the bridge toward the Castel Sant'Angelo, which was casting a glow over the river beneath it. I finally settled near one of the statues on the far side, the angel holding a cross, and leaned into the marble railing. All around me, Rome glowed in the darkness.

I closed my eyes and let the breeze from the water tickle my face gently.

I knew that my anger at Michael was out of proportion. I barely knew the guy, and in truth we'd had an undeniable connection, but it had lasted only a few days, until I found out the truth.

What bothered me most, though, and what made me feel so terribly angry with him, was that seeing him try to cheat on his wife was like watching my mother at work. I had no doubt that, in the time she was gone, she'd had many affairs. And wasn't Michael doing the same thing to his spouse and children?

I sat on the bridge, lost in my own thoughts, until I heard church bells in the distance tolling midnight. Then I shook myself out of it. There had been a small, foolish part of me that had hoped, a little bit, that Michael would come find me on the bridge. I had, after all, told him it was my favorite place in Rome. If he really had something to tell me, if there were some explanation I was missing, he would have come after me, wouldn't he?

But the truth was, there was no excuse. He was married. I was just as alone as ever.

I picked up my phone, took a deep breath and called my father, the one person who had never let me down.

'Hi, Cat!' he said when he answered the phone. 'How are you, sweetheart? How's Rome?' It was still early in New York, just past six p.m., and I knew he was probably tuning into the evening news while he cooked himself a dinner for one – Hamburger Helper, maybe, or a frozen meal. I could almost see him in my mind, and it made me miss him and miss my life back in New York.

'Hi, Dad,' I said. I closed my eyes for a moment. It was good to hear his voice. 'Rome's been great. I'm sorry I haven't called.'

He laughed. 'You don't have to check in with me, honey. I'm doing just fine.'

'Good,' I said. I took a deep breath. 'Dad, I need to know something.'

'Sure, sweetheart. What is it?'

I paused, not quite sure how to phrase it. 'Dad, when Mom left, why did you wait for her?' I asked.

He was quiet for a moment. 'What do you mean?' he asked in a flat voice.

'I mean, why didn't you ask her for a divorce?' I said. 'Why did you wait for her to come back to you? Why did you let her hurt you?'

He sighed. 'Cat, it's not as simple as that.'

'What's not simple about it?' I asked. I could feel my temper rising a little, as it did every time I heard my father defend my mother.

'Cat,' my father said slowly, 'I know your mother made a lot of mistakes. And the biggest was to walk out and miss most of your childhood.'

I swallowed hard, but I didn't say anything.

'But, honey,' he continued, 'I wasn't perfect either. Your mother and I had a lot of problems, and I did some things to push her away.'

'So what?' I asked. 'Couples fight. That doesn't mean one of them gets to leave while the other one hangs on.'

'Cat, I loved your mother with all my heart,' my father said slowly. 'She made a lot of mistakes. But so did I.'

'Dad, you can't blame yourself for what happened,' I said.

'Cat,' he said firmly, 'you don't understand everything.' He paused, and his voice softened. 'What is this all about, honey? Are you okay?'

'I'm fine,' I said quickly. I was blinking back unexpected tears.

'Then why all the questions?'

'I don't know.'

He paused. 'Are you planning to see your mother's family over there?'

'No,' I said instantly.

The silence stretched on so long that for a moment I was sure we'd been disconnected. 'Cat, I think maybe you should,' he said.

I looked out at the dark street, the buildings of the ancient city casting shadows all around me. 'No,' I said. 'I think maybe I should let Mom go and forget about her.' Before my father could respond, and before he could hear my voice shaking, I said a hasty goodbye and told him I'd call him later in the week.

'I love you, Dad,' I added.

'I love you too,' he said slowly, his voice sad.

I hung up, and, blinking back tears, I flagged down a cab and asked the driver to take me to Marco's.

'Hi,' Marco said, blinking sleepily at me from his doorway when I arrived fifteen minutes later. His sandy curls were flattened by sleep, and he was wearing only a pair of boxers with little frogs on them. 'What are you doing here?'

I felt instantly foolish. My mind had been spinning with thoughts of Michael and of my parents; I hadn't even stopped to consider how inappropriate it would be to drop in on Marco unannounced in the middle of the night. Not to mention the fact that he had returned from Venice today and hadn't called me yet.

'I'm sorry,' I said quickly, looking down at my feet. 'I shouldn't have come.'

I could feel his eyes on me as my face flamed. 'Of course you should have,' he said finally. He reached out and pulled me into his arms, pressing me into his bare chest. 'You can always come here.'

I felt the hot moisture of my tears on his chest before I even knew I was crying.

'Cat,' he said in a soothing voice, stroking my hair. 'What's the matter?'

'I don't know,' I said, sobbing harder. 'I don't know what's wrong with me.'

'Shh,' he whispered into the top of my hair, ruffling it with his breath. The sensation sent chills through me. 'It's going to be all right.'

He pulled me into his apartment, kicking the door gently closed behind us.

'Do you want to talk about it?' he asked after a moment.

I shook my head. 'No,' I whispered.

I looked up. Our eyes met first, and then I closed mine, and a moment later I could feel his lips pressing against mine, gently at first. I responded with a hunger I didn't realize I had, pressing myself into him as our kisses became deeper and more intense. Since his studio apartment was so small, we had only a few steps to go to reach his bed, and we tumbled onto it clumsily, both of us working to tug off first my shirt, then my jeans.

'Are you sure?' Marco asked as he fumbled with the hook to my bra.

'Yes,' I said firmly, into his mouth.

'You want to do this?' he asked. 'You're sure?' he asked again.

'Yes,' I repeated. I wasn't thinking; I was on autopilot as I helped him with my bra and then reached down for his boxers.

A moment later, after scrambling to find a condom in his underwear drawer, Marco was inside me. I closed my eyes and lost myself in the moment, holding on to him tightly, afraid that if I let go I'd drift away forever.

I left the next morning before Marco woke up, kissing him lightly on his forehead and then again on his lips after he stirred. I stared silently out the cab window on the way home, numbly wondering what I'd just done. My emotions had been stripped raw.

Karina had slipped a note under my door, but I didn't read it; I picked it up and put it on my bedside table, then I changed quickly into pajamas, washed the day off my face, and crawled into bed.

When the phone rang a few hours later, I felt like I'd fallen asleep just moments before. I cracked an eye open and squinted at the clock. It was ten in the morning. I looked at the caller ID. It was my father. It was the middle of the night in New York. Something had to be wrong for him to be calling.

I grabbed the receiver, fully awake, a panicky feeling inside me.

'Cat?' It was my father.

'Dad, are you all right?' I asked right away.

'Yes, yes, everyone's fine,' my father soothed me quickly.

'Oh,' I said. My heart slowed and I took a deep breath.

'So what's going on? It's like four in the morning there.'

'I know,' he said. 'I'm sorry to call like this. But I've been thinking about your phone call all evening.'

'I'm sorry,' I said. 'I didn't mean to make you upset.'

'I know you didn't.' He paused. 'But there are some things you should know.'

'What things?'

There was a long silence. 'Dad?' I asked tentatively.

'I cheated on your mother, Cat,' my father blurted out.

I think my heart stopped beating. 'What?' I whispered.

'It was just a one-night stand,' he said quickly. 'It didn't mean anything. But it was a few months before she left, and when she found out about it, I think it was the final straw.'

'You cheated on Mom?'

He sighed. 'Things had been bad between us for a while. But there was no excuse for what I did. None. I tried to apologize. I tried to tell her it didn't mean anything. But she said it had ruined everything. I had betrayed her trust. And she was right.'

I was speechless.

'Cat, honey?' my father asked after a moment of silence.

'Why didn't you tell us?' I said softly. 'I mean, when we were older, at least?'

'Because your mother asked me not to,' he said. He sounded choked up. 'She knew how badly she had hurt you by leaving. She didn't want you girls to hate me too. Even when she came back, she made me promise to never tell. "The girls need someone they can respect," she always said. She said it would never be her, because of what she had done to you by leaving. She wanted you to be able to respect me.'

I was silent.

'Cat?' My father said tentatively after a moment. 'Say something.'

'I don't know what to say.'

'If you want to hate me, honey, that's okay,' he said. 'I hope you don't. But if you do, I understand. I spent years there hating myself. Blaming myself for your mother's leaving.'

I thought about it. 'Dad, you didn't make her leave,' I said finally. 'No matter what happened, you didn't make her leave her family. That was her decision. She left us.'

'I know, honey,' he said. 'She regretted it the rest of her life. I know she did. And you have every right to feel the way you do.' He paused. 'I guess I just needed you to know that it wasn't all as black and white as it might have seemed to you at the time. And it's a big part of why I never wanted to give up on her. We loved each other, Cat. We always did. We just both made a lot of mistakes.'

I thought about love and loss, decisions and consequences. 'Why are you telling me all of this?'

'Your sister, she's okay,' my father said. 'I've never worried much about her. But you, you're still carrying around this heavy heart about your mom.' He paused. 'Knowing that you're over there, where she came from, still refusing to let yourself forgive her, well, it breaks my heart.'

'You think she deserves to be forgiven?' I asked him.

'I think everyone deserves forgiveness, Cat,' he said.

My father told me sadly that he knew it was a lot to take in but that he hoped I would think about things and call him when I was ready. I agreed, and, still shaken to the core, said goodbye.

I sat there on the edge of my bed for a while, thinking about things.

My dad's revelation hadn't really changed anything, had it? I mean, sure, perhaps my father wasn't the faultless martyr I'd made him out to be in my mind. But I'd known that anyhow, on some level. I had never expected an admission of cheating – he didn't seem the type – but I knew he had an Irish temper, and I have many memories of my parents screaming at each other in the living room when they thought Becky and I were asleep. I used to crawl into bed with her and cover her ears so that she wouldn't hear them, but when I was protecting her there were no hands left to cover my own ears. I always heard every word through our apartment's thin walls.

He used to yell at her that she had ruined his life, and she would shout back that she should have married someone, anyone, but him. He would tell her that before her he had had all sorts of dreams and she had taken them all away. She would tell him that he had his head in the clouds and would never have made good on his dreams regardless. One of them would end the argument with a top-of-the-lungs 'I hate you,' and my father would usually storm out for a few hours. I'd always hear him come home in the middle of the night, long after I should have been asleep. He'd tiptoe into the living room, sometimes knocking into the coffee table in the dark, and I'd hear him open the door to the bedroom he shared with my mom. I'd hear them murmur softly to each other, and I knew everything was okay. Then and only then would I be able to fall asleep.

Sometimes, when we were young, one of them would casually ask Becky and me whether we'd heard anything strange the night before. Becky, who always slept through it all, would shake her head and say no. I would force my own face into a blank expression and tell them I didn't know what they were talking about. They would always exchange relieved glances and go back to pretending things were okay.

So to know that there was discord between my parents before my mother left was no major revelation. But to know that my father had cheated, and that he had hurt my mother in those final months of normality, somehow shifted things in my mind. The shift was slight – not enough to make me blame my father or feel furious that I hadn't known before. But it was enough to enable me to see my mother as someone wounded, not just as someone heartless. It didn't change what she had done, and I didn't think I would ever be able to understand how a mother could leave her children. But it did provide another piece to the puzzle. And it made me realize that even though I thought I knew the situation inside and out, maybe there were still a lot of pieces missing.

Maybe it was time I went about putting the puzzle back together instead of turning my back on it.

I showered, threw on a casual cream-colored sundress and left with my camera slung over my shoulder before Karina could arrive. I had the feeling that she'd come knocking on my door to talk about Michael as soon as she got a break at the restaurant. But I still wasn't ready to talk about him. I didn't even want to think about him.

Instead, I set off toward Piazza Colonna, a square off

the Via del Corso that I'd never been to before. In fact, I'd deliberately avoided it, although it housed an impressive monument, the Column of Marcus Aurelius, an intricately detailed, 135-foot marble column that had been completed just before the end of the second century. But it wasn't the column I was interested in seeing today. It was the tiny scarf store on a side street off the main plaza.

I'd known about it for years. I didn't even need to consult a map to get there. I'd traced the path there on paper so many times that it was burned into my mind. And yet I'd never gone. I'd never wanted to. Until today.

The streets were quiet, so grabbing a cab near the Pantheon wasn't a problem, and we didn't have to fight much traffic to get to our destination. I had the driver drop me off on the east side of the piazza and I crossed it quickly, barely looking at the column and its beautifully carved scenes as I hurried by.

I wound through the side streets like I'd been doing it all my life until I reached the Via della Guglia. I saw the shop right away, up ahead on the right. It was small and unassuming with a big picture window in front displaying an array of brightly colored, beautiful scarves. Big, cursive letters on the window identified it as *Sciarpe dalla Famiglia dello Verdicchio*. Scarves by the Verdicchio family. Scarves by *my* family.

I stared for a long time, transfixed by the sight of something I had always imagined but never seen. I'd met my mother's family only once, when I was a toddler. I remembered almost nothing about them, other than that my grandfather had smelled like smoke, and my grandmother had smelled like licorice. In family albums I had flipped through before my mother left, my mother and her sister Gina, just eighteen months younger than her, looked so similar that my mother always said they were mistaken for twins. I had committed the faces of my grandparents and aunt to memory from those albums, and from the Christmas cards they would send each year. But the cards stopped coming the year that my mother died, so the most recent images I had of these people were seventeen years old. I didn't know if I'd recognize them. I didn't even know if they were still alive.

It was early still, and the street was nearly deserted. The lights were off inside the store, and there was no one inside. I stopped to peer in, pressing my nose to the glass.

The dark space seemed to throb with muted colors. Neatly folded silk scarves hung from racks, separated by colors. Scarves in brilliant blues and purples sat in the center of the store, while pinks, oranges and reds led off to the left, yellows and greens to the right, and blacks, beiges and whites toward the front. The whole right wall was lined with wooden shelves, on which sat folded pashminas in every color of the rainbow. Through the darkness of the interior, I could just make out the glass-enclosed case on which the cash register sat. The case, too, was filled with small scarves in all colors of the spectrum.

I stood there for a while, just looking. I knew it was just a store, of course, but there was something that moved me about knowing that my family's hands had touched every scarf, that they had decided where the racks would go, that they had laid out the colors and the patterns, that they had probably hand-picked all of the merchandise. Hands that had touched my mother, held her hand, pinched her cheeks, stroked her hair, had also touched everything in this store. And in a strange way, that took my breath away.

After a while, I checked my watch. It wasn't quite eight thirty yet. The store probably didn't open until ten or eleven, and I wasn't sure what I'd do when it did. I needed time to think.

I backed away from the window and crossed the small street. Two doors down was a building with a small stoop out front, five wide stairs running up to a big front door. I sat down two steps up and waited.

After a while, I pulled out my camera and absent-mindedly began flipping through pictures on the screen. I'd deleted most of them from the SD card after uploading them to my computer, but I had saved a few, and as I looked through several shots of my neighborhood in New York, taken just a month ago, I felt a wave of profound disconnection.

I didn't belong here in Rome, on this dusty side street thousands of miles from the world I lived in. This place wasn't my home, much as I wanted to feel like it was, much as I wanted to feel like I was meant to be here. Home was the brownstone I saw on my LCD screen, the street teeming with people, the coffee shop on the corner. Home was the pair of pigeons perched expectantly on a Central Park bench, the man who sold bagels from a cart on the corner, the glistening eaves of the Chrysler Building. Home was the view of Ellis Island from Battery Park, the gaudy green, white and red of Little Italy, the dilapidated charm of Chinatown. Home was Becky and Dad.

But what if part of me belonged here too? It was almost as if a piece of me had been here all along. From the moment I had arrived in Rome thirteen years ago, it had all felt so familiar, as if I had been here before. What if

Rome had been passed down to me through my mother's blood, a map of the city written as a sort of genetic blueprint that composed who I was to become? It sounded crazy, but what if the ghosts were more real than I'd given them credit for? Something had drawn me back here. And perhaps I needed to put that something to rest before I could re-join my own life.

I turned off the review screen on my camera and picked it up slowly. I looked through the lens and zoomed in on the scarf shop across the street. From this angle, I could just see the bright silk glistening in the window, beneath the bold lettering of the sign that declared the place to be, like me, a piece of the Verdicchio family.

I snapped a single shot. I looked at it on the screen. The composition of the photo was all wrong. I looked through the viewfinder again and zoomed further. The colors jumped into the forefront of the screen, and I snapped again. I looked at the screen, and again I didn't feel the shot worked. I took a deep breath and stood up from the stoop. I walked a couple of doors down until I faced the shop directly, and, still standing across the street, I began shooting.

As sometimes happened when I was able to hide behind my camera's lens, I became lost in the images as I worked, snapping from every angle. I moved left and right, squatted, perched, moved to catch the best angles as the sun crested the stout buildings and began to pour its rays over the street. People were beginning to emerge from the buildings around me, some dressed for work in the office, some dressed casually to take children to school or run errands. But I barely noticed them. I was lost in the world that existed for me inside the twelve-inch cylinder protruding from my camera. It was like a kaleidoscope that isolated everything else and brought its own images into sharp, unignorable focus.

After a while, I settled back onto the stoop to wait. I wasn't sure what I was waiting for, exactly. I knew I wanted to catch a glimpse of my aunt or of my grandparents, but then what would I do? What would I say? Would I even recognize them after so many years? Would they even still be here? What if the store had been passed on to cousins, or to strangers who had decided to keep the name the same? Suddenly, I felt paralyzed by fear and uncertainty. What if I'd mustered the courage to come here this morning for nothing?

Thirty minutes later, I saw the lights go on in the scarf shop. I blinked a few times. I hadn't seen anyone go in the front door. Perhaps my mother's family lived above the store, or perhaps there was a back entrance. Suddenly, my heart was pounding double time.

A moment later, a woman in her mid-sixties with shoulder-length, glossy black hair streaked with a few ribbons of gray stepped out the front door with a rag and a spray bottle of blue liquid in her hand. I recognized her immediately as my Aunt Gina, a woman I knew only from pictures. She began spritzing the window and wiping it off. I stared, mesmerized, as she worked quickly. She looked so much like my mother, so much like what my mother would have looked like had she lived another two decades. Although I'd been stockpiling resentment toward her since I was twelve, holding on to it like currency, it sent a powerful wave of sadness through me to see someone who so strongly embodied what could have been.

As I watched her work, I raised my camera and

focused on her through the viewfinder. I zoomed in and studied the familiar contours of her face, the way she held her shoulders just like my mother, the way she was smiling to herself absently as she wiped, an expression that reminded me so much of my mother that it hurt.

I began snapping photos, almost without thinking. I was hitting the shutter in rapid-fire, suddenly not wanting to miss a single second of this woman's expressions and motions. It was suddenly desperately important to me to capture it all.

She was just about to finish the window when she turned around and looked straight at me. I snapped a quick shot of her before I could think, and then I guiltily lowered the camera and tried to act like I was looking somewhere else. My heart hammering, I feigned calm and turned around to photograph a trash can to the right of the stoop. I didn't know if she was still looking at me, so I pretended to be incredibly absorbed in the red bicycle tied to a lamppost two doors down. I shot several frames of it too.

By the time I glanced back to the storefront, she was gone. I breathed a sigh of relief, but I felt a surprising tinge of sadness too. There had been something about looking at her, even through my lens, even from afar, that made me feel closer to my mother than I had in years. And to my surprise, I liked the feeling. Perhaps the walls I'd built around my heart weren't as high as I'd thought.

I sat on the stoop for a while catching my breath, trying to gather myself. I felt like an emotional wreck. Slowly, I turned the camera back on and began flipping through the images, studying my aunt's face, her posture, her expression in each one.

Suddenly, I heard footsteps approaching. I shook myself out of my trance and looked up. My eyes windened in horror as I realized that my Aunt Gina had come back outside and was not only staring at me but was now just a few yards away, charging toward me with determination. I stood up quickly, fumbling with my camera and almost dropping it.

She was saying something in rapid, sharp Italian, waving her arms around dramatically, but I was too stricken by the familiarity of her voice to muster any kind of logical response. She sounded so much like my mother, whose voice I had been sure I'd forgotten. I knew she was berating me for taking her photo without asking; I was sure she was probably wondering why I had done so. But all I could do was stare.

Finally, she stopped talking and seemed to be waiting for a response. I swallowed hard a few times, trying to dislodge the lump in my throat. '*Non parlo l'italiano,*' I managed to choke out. I added weakly, 'I'm sorry.'

She opened her mouth right away to say something else, but then she stopped. She looked at me for a moment and took a step closer. Something in her eyes changed. And just like that, I knew that she knew.

'Catarina?' she asked softly. My heart jumped into my throat. 'Cat?' She paused and shook her head, like she couldn't quite believe it. 'You are Cat, aren't you?' she asked. But this time, although it had been phrased like a question, I knew she meant it more as a statement.

'How did you know?' I asked softly.

But she didn't answer. Instead, she stared for a moment longer, motionless, before drawing me into a fierce, tight hug that expelled the rest of the air residing in my already breathless lungs.

'You are Audrey's daughter,' she said softly as she pulled away. It was like she was telling herself again so that she had no choice but to believe it. 'You are Audrey's daughter, here in Rome.'

I hadn't been referred to as my mother's daughter since I was a little girl and she was walking me to my piano lessons and ballet classes.

'Yes,' I confirmed softly. 'I am.'

She hugged me again and then drew back a foot or so and cupped my chin in her hand. She stared into my eyes. 'You look so much like her,' she murmured.

I swallowed hard. 'You do too.'

'What are you doing here?' she asked. 'Did you come to Roma to see me?'

Her expression was hopeful. I had been worried about how she'd feel about me should we ever meet. Had my mother told her how hateful I'd been when she'd come home? How I'd told her I could never forgive her, could never accept her as my parent again? Did my aunt know how much I had probably hurt my mother during her final days? A wave of guilt washed over me as I looked into eyes that looked so much like the ones I had last seen seventeen years before.

'No,' I answered honestly. 'I came here for me.' I took a deep breath and added, 'But I think coming here to see you is a part of that.'

I wasn't sure if the sentence made any sense, but Gina nodded slowly, like she understood. 'I always knew you'd come,' she said. 'Your mother told me you would.'

'What?' I asked.

She smiled gently. 'Will you come inside the store with me?'

I hesitated, took a deep breath and nodded. I stuffed my camera back into my bag and hoisted it over my shoulder. As I began to follow her, she surprised me by taking me gently by the hand. She squeezed hard.

I followed her into the shop, which was dimly lit and smelled faintly of lavender and orange blossom, an enticing scent that reminded me of the perfume my mother used to wear. Gina motioned for me to wait while she brought a chair out from the back. 'Sit,' she said with a smile. I did so, and she settled onto a stool behind the cash register. She leaned forward and studied my face for a moment. 'You are beautiful,' she said softly. 'It is like looking at Audrey.'

I felt tears in my eyes. I shook my head and looked down. 'I look like my father too,' I said. I immediately regretted it; it sounded combative and ungrateful. But Gina didn't seem to take it that way.

'Yes, you do,' she said. 'Your mother always loved that about you and your sister. She said you two had taken on the best elements of both of them. She loved you girls very much.'

I snorted and looked away. Gina was silent, perhaps waiting for me to say something. But there were no words to say. How did you tell a woman that her sister didn't know the first thing about love?

'Do you know where she went, those years she disappeared?' Gina asked after a while.

The question startled me, and I jerked my head up. My mother had always been secretive about where she'd gone; I'd always assumed that she'd moved in with a man somewhere else, trying to build a different life for herself. As a teenager, I had lain awake at night and vividly constructed tales of her departure in my head. I always imagined she had gone out west somewhere, Las Vegas, maybe, or Los Angeles. In the scenario I visualized, she had moved in with a man who was taller, darker and more handsome than my dad. And I imagined that this mystery man had a couple of kids from a previous marriage, maybe two girls, whom my mother coddled and fawned over, allowing her to forget about her own kids.

'No,' I admitted finally. 'She never told us.' I had hated my mother a little bit more for never explaining where the black hole that engulfed her had been. My father wouldn't tell us, either; in fact, I wasn't sure he even knew. I had asked for the last time the year she died. After that, I had decided that it didn't matter where she had gone, that I shouldn't care. All that had mattered was that she had left us without looking back.

Gina looked at me for a long moment. 'She wanted you to know,' she said finally. 'But only if you came looking. Because if you came looking, it meant that you were ready for the answer.'

'What are you talking about?'

'She came here, Cat,' Gina said softly. 'She came home. To Roma. To us.'

'What?' I stared, incredulous. I hadn't imagined that my mother had fled her children in favor of her parents. If she had, surely they would have sent her back, right? Surely they would have told her that it was inexcusable to abandon one's kids, that family was the most important thing in the world, that the tie between mother and child was the one link that was meant to never be broken. 'Why?' I asked weakly.

Gina looked down at her hands for a long time. She

turned her right hand over, palm up, and traced her lifeline with her left index finger. Finally, she looked up at me. 'She was sick, Cat,' she said gently.

'Sick?' I repeated. I didn't understand. 'What do you mean?'

Uninvited images of a valiant battle against cancer filled my head. But that couldn't be right. If she'd been sick, she would have stayed at home with us and fought it.

Gina sighed. 'In the head,' she said softly. 'She was ill. Very ill.'

'What?' I stared, uncomprehending.

'Your mother always struggled with depression,' she said slowly. 'Did you know that, Cat? Did you know that about your mother?'

'No,' I whispered.

Gina smiled. 'Good,' she said. 'She did not want you to. Not when you were young. And for a while, she was sure that loving you girls, loving your father, would save her, would end the sadness.'

I felt tears in my eyes. 'But it didn't?'

Gina shook her head. 'I don't think depression like that is a choice, something that can be turned on or off,' she said. 'For a while, she was able to fight it. But it was always there. She would lash out at your father sometimes, for no reason, right? And sometimes she would become angry at you girls?'

'Yes,' I whispered, a flood of memories pouring in, sad memories of my mother crying or yelling or throwing things, memories I had locked away.

Gina nodded. 'I know. She felt very guilty about that. She would tell me she was sure she was ruining your lives. She always said you and Rebecca deserved better.'

'But she left us,' I said. My voice sounded very small, almost as if I had regressed to the age of eleven. 'How could she have left us?'

'I don't know that I will ever understand that, Cat,' Gina said. 'You may never understand either. But please know that when she came home to Roma, to us, she spent every day thinking of you and your sister and your father. She cried about it all the time. But she thought she was doing the right thing. She thought you were better off without her.'

'But—' I stalled. I didn't know what to say. 'This is impossible. She didn't love us enough to stay. If she had loved us, she would have stayed.'

Gina's eyes filled with tears. 'Cat, she didn't leave because she *didn't* love you,' she said. 'She left because she *did*. She did love you. More than she could bear. And she thought she was hurting you by staying there with you. She thought you would be better off without her. I tried to persuade her to go back to New York, but Mamma and Papà, they were just glad to have her home. They didn't want her to be in America. They never liked your father. They felt he had taken your mother away. So they let her stay, and they told her it was okay. They blamed America for her depression. But it wasn't America. It wasn't her life there. She was just sick.'

'This isn't possible,' I said softly.

Gina looked at me sadly. 'It is the truth,' she said. 'She finally began seeing a doctor. And, slowly, things got better. She began taking medication. She learned to deal with things. And when she felt ready, she went home to try to become a part of your family again.'

I could feel tears streaming down my face now, rapid

and unbidden. I wiped them away, angry that my emotions were spilling over. 'Why didn't she tell me?' I whispered. 'Why did she just let me hate her? Why didn't anyone tell me?'

'She thought it was a sign of weakness,' Gina said. 'And she felt she deserved your hatred. She wanted to win you back on her own. She wanted to show you that you could trust her, that you could love her. She wanted to spend every day making it up to you.'

I thought about how many times my mother had tried to talk to me, how many times she had listened as I told her I hated her, how many times she had simply said, 'I love you, Cat. I always have, and I always will,' instead of fighting back. Sitting here with her sister, with a woman who looked so much like her, I could almost hear her voice in my head now.

'But then she died,' I said softly. The tears were rolling down my face in rivers now, and I was having trouble catching my breath.

'Then she died,' Gina repeated, her own eyes growing watery.

I was sobbing now, full force. 'I never told her I loved her,' I said. 'I never said it after she came back. But I never stopped loving her. I just didn't want to. It was easier to hate.'

Gina looked at me for a moment. Then she stood up and gathered me in her arms, letting me sob into her shirt. 'But she knew, Cat,' she said softly. 'She knew you loved her. She always knew.'

With the truth out on the table, there was nothing left to say. I needed time to digest everything. It was like my whole world had changed.

My mother had still left us without a word and without an explanation. No matter the reason, that fact would always haunt me, and it would always hurt. I didn't think I could ever fully forgive her for that.

But for the first time in my life, I understood that it didn't have to do with us. Not entirely. She hadn't left because she didn't love us. It was because she was fighting demons she couldn't understand, and because she didn't want to drag us down with her.

It meant it wasn't my fault.

On a logical level, especially as an adult now, I realized that when a couple split from each other it generally was between the two of them, not because of anything that had happened with their children. I knew I shouldn't be carrying the blame around on my shoulders. But when you're twelve and your mother walks away, it's impossible *not* to blame yourself. So even though my father would tuck me in at night and tell me that our mother loved us and would be back soon and that her leaving had nothing to do with us, I never quite believed him. Maybe if I'd cleaned my room better, picked on my sister less frequently, stopped arguing about staying up past my bedtime, she would have stayed. Maybe if I'd been better organized, had been able to take care of myself, had helped out more around the house, she wouldn't have felt so much pressure.

And so I became the person I thought she wanted me to be. I stopped fighting with Becky; I did my best to take care of Dad; I vacuumed, did dishes, cleaned up after all three of us, learned to cook dinner, and did everything I was told. I never went through a rebellious phase as a teenager, because what if rebelling made my father want to leave us too? I never took chances, because what if they didn't turn out right and something bad happened to me? Who would take care of Becky?

I had become the woman I was today because I thought my mother had left us because we weren't worth the hassle, weren't worth loving. I had become who I was because I thought that if I could just make myself better, I'd be easier to love, and she'd come back.

But it hadn't had anything to do with me. She hadn't fled our family in favor of a mysterious stranger. She hadn't left us to love another set of kids. She had left because she didn't know how to take care of herself, and she didn't know how to ask for help.

Her solution had been to run away from what was inside herself, from what was right in front of her. And hadn't I spent my entire adult life doing nearly the same thing?

Karina listened that afternoon, open-mouthed, as I poured out the story of meeting my Aunt Gina that morning.

'I'm so proud of you for doing all this,' she said softly. 'So where are your grandparents? Did you meet them too?'

I looked down. 'Gina said that my grandmother died five years ago, and my grandfather died last year,' I said. 'She runs the store alone now.'

'I'm sorry,' Karina said.

I shook my head. 'No,' I said. I felt tears in my eyes. 'I actually think it's okay. It means they're probably with my mom, right?'

Karina nodded quickly, and I looked up in time to see tears glistening in her eyes too. She blinked them quickly away. 'So what are you going to do now?' she asked.

I shrugged. 'I don't know. I don't know that there's anything *to* do. I have a lot to think about, you know? I just can't stop feeling guilty about how horrible I was to her when she was going through all that.' I paused and swallowed a lump in my throat. 'When she came back, she spent every day telling me she loved me. And I spent every day telling her I hated her guts. She died thinking I hated her.'

Karina was silent for a long time. I was sure she was judging me, and she had every right to. I'd been a horrible daughter. A horrible person.

'Say something,' I said finally into the silence. 'If you think I'm the worst person in the world, just tell me.'

'No,' Karina said firmly. She took a deep breath. 'I need you to listen to me. Look at me.' She paused and waited until I looked reluctantly into her eyes. 'Listen to me closely, Cat. She knew.'

'What?'

'She knew,' she repeated firmly.

'Knew what?'

'Knew that you loved her,' Karina said. 'Knew that, much as you wanted to, you could never hate her.'

I shook my head. 'How would you know that?'

Karina waited until I was looking into her eyes again before she responded. 'Because I'm a mother,' she said. 'And a mother always knows. A mother can read her child's eyes like a book. A mother can see into her child's heart. A mother always knows.'

'But she was gone for five years.' I shook my head. 'I'd changed. She couldn't still know me.'

'A mother knows,' Karina repeated. 'No matter how you thought you felt, and regardless of the words you said, I know she could read the truth in your eyes.'

I started to protest. But there was something about the expression on Karina's face that stopped me. She meant it with every ounce of her being.

'You have nothing to regret,' she added after a moment. 'Cat, you were just a child. A hurt, sad child. None of it was your fault.'

I stared into my mug for a long time, as if the answers to my own darkness lay in my coffee's murky depths.

Karina was silent for a while. Then, gently, she said, 'Cat, I need to talk to you about Michael Evangelisti.'

I jerked my head up and stared at her. 'Michael?' I laughed harshly. 'What is there to say? He's a married guy who doesn't care that he has a wife and child.'

'Cat,' Karina said slowly, 'he's not married.'

'What?' I said. I shook my head. 'No, you're wrong. His mother-in-law called the restaurant the night I went out with him. She lives with them, for God's sake. And you said yourself that you know his wife!'

'No,' Karina said. 'I said I'd met her. I didn't say I *know* her.'

My insides went cold. 'What?'

'Her name was Linda,' Karina said slowly. 'An American. She was quiet, but she seemed very kind.' She paused. 'They had a daughter together. Annie. She's about Nico's age.' She hesitated again and looked at me. 'Linda died four years ago. In a car accident.'

'*What?*'

Karina nodded. 'Annie was in the car with her. She barely had a scratch. But Linda was killed. Michael was devastated. He came back here, to Roma, to his family, for a year. In fact, Nico and Annie used to play together when they were little. But he wanted to raise Annie in New York, where he had built his life, so he moved back, and he opened a restaurant there. Linda's mother moved in with him to help care for Annie, because he was working such long hours to get the restaurant off the ground, and he didn't want his daughter to be raised by a nanny.'

I felt like someone had just punched me in the gut.

'He's not married?' I whispered.

Karina shook her head. 'No. He explained the misunderstanding he had with you. He feels terrible. I told him I didn't even know he had started dating. He said he hadn't; you were the first person he's asked out since Linda. He said he didn't know he was ready until he saw you sitting on a barrel of olive oil in his kitchen.'

'He said that?' I asked.

Karina nodded. 'Yes,' she said. 'I think he really likes you.'

'Oh, God,' I said. I put my head in my hands. 'What have I done?'

'It was a misunderstanding,' Karina soothed me. 'I'm sure you can work it out.'

I looked up. 'Where is he now?'

She hesitated. 'He's gone back to New York,' she said. 'He waited for you last night. But you didn't come home.'

Guilt poured through me like the flood of a burst dam. 'No,' I said.

Karina nodded. 'He left you a note,' she said. She fished her in apron pocket. A moment later, she drew out a folded piece of paper. 'Here,' she said. 'I have to get back to work now. I'll come by after my shift. But read this. And think about it. Okay?'

I sat down in my apartment a few minutes later, still holding the note in my hand. I was dying to know what it said, but there was a part of me that wasn't entirely sure I should read it.

After all, it was scary to let someone in. It had almost been easier when I could write Michael off as a lying, cheating scumbag. That I could handle. That I was used to. But meeting someone who took my breath away for the right reasons was a different story altogether.

And there were so many reasons not to give him a chance. If I was the first person he'd been out with since his wife, chances were he was emotionally vulnerable, and I'd be his dating guinea pig, right? And then there was the fact that he had a child. If, by some chance, it worked out between Michael and me, was I really ready to be a stepmother to a little girl? I had always worried I'd be a terrible parent, that I would fail the children I was supposed to love, just like my mother had. I knew I was getting much too far ahead of myself – I'd only been out with Michael once, and here I was superimposing myself onto his family blueprint – but it was something I knew I had to consider. Another person's life hung in the balance here. What kind of mother – or stepmother – was I capable of being?

And then there was Marco. Sweet Marco, who had seen my sadness and fear and done more to open my eyes and my heart than anyone had in years. And that was the bottom line. He was a good man. And I wasn't a woman who walked away. I never walked away. I wasn't my mother.

I slowly unfolded the letter and began to read.

Dear Cat,

I'm sorry. I'm sorry that I didn't tell you about my wife and my daughter. I'm sorry I didn't know how to explain it to you that night at the restaurant. And I'm sorry if I hurt you or made you feel like I had betrayed you at all. I'm assuming Karina has explained it to you by now. It's still really hard for me, the whole situation, and I'm not sure what to do. I haven't dated since Linda died. I haven't wanted to. My life is my daughter and my restaurant. I didn't think I had room for anything else.

And then I met you, and you were the first person who made me want to take a chance. I know it sounds crazy, and of course I barely know you, but I felt something that day at your sister's wedding. And of course I've screwed it all up now, and I don't know if I've scared you away for good. If I have, I don't blame you. It's my fault. But if you can find it in your heart to give me another chance, I'd like that very much. I'm not sure I'm ready. But I'd like to try.

Maybe there was a reason that I ran into you in Rome. Your sister told me you'd come here. And I knew I'd told you that my family owned a place near the Pantheon. So I was hoping that maybe I'd see you somewhere around. I didn't realize you had moved in with Karina. I wish I'd known. Maybe we would have had a chance to talk. Instead, I've spent the last few days wandering the streets, looking for your face in the crowd. I had given up. And then I saw you across the bar. I couldn't believe it. But maybe that was the way it was meant to be.

I'm sorry I had to leave without saying goodbye. I know you're in Rome for a little while longer. But please, take some time to think about this. There's no rush. And you know where to find me when you're back in New York . . . if you want to. It's up to you.

Ciao,
Michael

I read and re-read the note several times. Then I folded it carefully, put it into the side pocket of my handbag, and sat back down on my bed to think.

Karina came up to my apartment just after nine. She'd put Nico to bed, and her mother was downstairs, watching TV. 'I thought you might want to talk,' she said. 'Want to go get a bite to eat?'

I nodded, and together we walked out of the apartment. Ten minutes later, we had settled into two seats on the patio of a little café just around the corner, in the opposite direction from the Pantheon.

'They have wonderful pizza here,' Karina said. 'The

best pizza in the city, I think. Would you like to share one?'

I nodded, and when the waiter came over Karina took care of ordering. The waiter returned a moment later with a bottle of Chianti and two glasses of water. He poured us each some wine, and after he left Karina raised her glass in a toast. 'To mothers,' she said.

I smiled. 'To mothers.'

We each took a sip of our wine. I was trying to think of how to ask a question that had been weighing on my mind. 'Karina?' I finally said.

'Yes?'

'How did you know you were ready to be a mother?'

She laughed. 'I didn't. At all! It was the last thing I would have planned for myself. But it happened when it was supposed to. And the moment I saw Nico's face for the first time, I knew everything was going to be all right.'

'But you always knew you'd be a good mother, right?' I asked. 'I mean, your mom seems perfect.'

Karina smiled. 'I thought I'd be a horrible mother,' she said. 'I loved to smoke. I loved to drink. I have a terrible temper, as I'm sure you've realized. I am selfish, and I didn't think I could love a child the way I was supposed to. I thought I'd want to spend my money on clothes and shoes and going out with my friends. But then everything changed.' And for the first time in my life, I feel like I'm exactly where I'm meant to be.'

I thought about this for a moment. I nodded.

'Is this about Michael?' she asked softly. 'And Annie?'

'I don't know,' I confessed. 'I don't know how to feel about that. I'm scared of dating someone with a child. I'm terrified, actually. Not because I don't want a child. But because I'm not sure I'm a good enough person to be part of a child's life.'

Karina laughed. 'Cat, that's the craziest thing you've ever said. You're one of the best people I know.'

I swallowed hard. 'But what about Marco? I started something with him too. Don't I owe it to him to see that through?'

Karina shrugged. 'I don't know the answer to that,' she said. 'I think you have to look inside yourself and see what feels right.' She was silent for a moment and then added, 'I have realized that when you do your best to do the right thing, life has a way of working out. So if being with Marco feels right, then do it. But if it doesn't, well, you're doing him good by walking away before he gets too involved.'

'I'm not sure,' I said. It still felt like walking away from a good person, something I had vowed I would never do. But maybe the world wasn't as black and white as I'd thought it was. Maybe I was ignoring a whole spectrum of colors. Funny how I could see all those complexities so sharply through the lens of my camera, but without it to hide behind I reverted to the safe simplicity of wrong or right, without considering all the shades in between. It had always seemed like the perfect way to view the world, because it left little room for error. But now, I was realizing that perhaps the viewpoint itself had been one big error all along.

Our meal arrived, and Karina changed the subject by telling funny stories about things Nico had done. She was right: the pizza was delicious. The crust was thin, flat, and perfectly crispy at the edges, and it was topped with a thin layer of perfectly melted mozzarella, followed by thinly sliced tomatoes and whole basil leaves that I was sure had just been plucked. On top of that lay several thick slices of soft, tender buffalo mozzarella. The combination of flavors and the freshness of it all made my taste buds sing. This was Italy; it was all atop this pizza, in a medley of freshness and flavors that I'd never seen duplicated across the Atlantic. I wondered for a moment why it was so hard to do something so simple. Couldn't a New York chef duplicate this exact meal in a Stateside kitchen? Or was the fact that it couldn't happen, that it didn't happen, just another piece of evidence that my two worlds, New York and Rome, could never be reconciled with each other, could never be one?

When we were done, we ordered two espressos and split a tiramisu.

'I was thinking about what you said,' I began as we leaned back in our seats to watch the people walking by on the sidewalk outside the restaurant. It had been a slow but steady parade all night, of young families going home, hopeful couples heading out, and friends making their way down the street arm in arm. It was life.

'What did I say?' Karina asked. She laughed and added, 'I say lots of things.'

I smiled. 'What you said about how I've always lived life on the safe side.'

She blushed a little. 'I'm sorry. It wasn't my business.'

'No,' I said. 'It was. And I'm glad you said it.'

She looked at me, waiting.

I took a deep breath and continued. 'I've always loved photographs,' I said.

'I know,' she said. She smiled, and I had the sense she knew exactly what I was about to say. Perhaps she'd even known it before I had.

'I think I'd like to try to sell some of them,' I concluded.

'Well, that is good news,' she said. She paused. I could tell she was trying to hide a smile.

'It is?'

'Yes,' she said. 'Since I have already contacted a photo gallery in New York about your photos.'

'*What?*' My eyes bulged out of my head.

Karina nodded calmly. 'Yes. They are too beautiful to be kept to yourself, Cat. And I knew you would realize that someday too.'

I wasn't understanding. 'Wait, wait, wait. What do you mean you contacted a gallery?'

'I used the Internet to find a photo gallery in New York that specializes in Italian photographers,' she said with a nonchalant shrug, like it was no big deal. 'The owner is American but spent many years living in Italy, and when I called I just explained that I was an agent who had discovered a new talent in Roma and would like to send along a few photographs for her consideration.'

'Wait, you said what?'

'That I am your agent,' Karina said with a smile. 'And by the way, I will be taking my ten per cent.'

I stared at her. 'And you sent pictures to the gallery already?'

'Yes. Three of them.'

'How?'

'I have a key to your apartment, remember? And they are all on your computer.'

'You broke into my apartment to steal pictures?'

'No,' Karina clarified a little sheepishly. 'I opened the door to your apartment to *share* your pictures.'

'And you sent three random pictures to some stranger in New York?' I pressed on.

'No, I spent an hour and a half deciding which three pictures captured the heart of Roma the very best,' she said. 'And I sent them to a gallery owner whom I'd spent the last hour telling how wonderful and talented you were.'

I couldn't believe what she was telling me. 'What did the gallery owner say?'

She smiled. 'She said that they were three of the most beautiful pictures of Roma she had ever seen. She said they truly captured the heart of the city she loved. She said they made her feel inspired.'

My job dropped.

Karina smiled and continued, 'She said she'd like to start off with a collection of ten of your photographs. She'll blow them up and frame them, and they'll hang in her gallery for thirty days. If they sell, you will get paid seventy-five per cent; she takes twenty-five per cent as her gallery fee. She said it gets renegotiated down to twenty per cent once a photographer has exhibited there successfully for six months.'

'What did you tell her?'

'That I would talk to the photographer and get back to her.' She paused. 'She asked for your name, but I didn't tell her. I didn't know if you wanted to use your real name or not.'

I thought about it for a moment. I couldn't believe this was happening. I knew I should have been angry with Karina for sending out my photographs without my permission. But I was blown away by her enthusiasm, her wide-eyed belief that of course someone would want to buy my pictures. And the crazy thing was, someone did. A stranger in New York, someone who had been to Rome, saw my pictures and felt inspired.

Still, I wasn't entirely sure that I wanted to put my own stamp on the photographs yet. Although I knew that at nearly thirty-five I should be more secure, I was still terrified of failing. But what else could I call myself?

I thought for a moment about what had brought me to this place, what had initially made me decide to hide behind the lens of a camera, what had made me seek out answers in this city that would never quite be mine.

I suddenly felt like a giant weight had been lifted from my shoulders. I smiled.

'Tell her,' I said slowly, 'that the photo credit should read "Audrey H. Verdicchio."'

Marco called the next day. I met him for coffee at Pinocchio and filled him in on my big few days, leaving out any mention of Michael for now. I still hadn't decided how I felt about him. Or about Marco. But I didn't think one situation should necessarily influence the other. Not yet.

'I am so happy for you,' Marco said after I had finished. 'And so proud of you, too, for going to see your aunt.'

I nodded. 'I felt like it was the right thing to do.'

Marco studied my face for a moment. Then he reached across the table to gently brush the hair out of my face. 'You've only been here for a few weeks,' he said. 'And it's like you've become a different person.'

I thought about it for a moment. 'No,' I said. 'I think it's that I've finally become me.'

Marco nodded slowly. 'There is nothing better for each of us to be than ourselves, is there?'

I shook my head, thinking of all the time I'd wasted trying to be someone more loveable, more reliable, more organized and less easy to leave. And the one big thing that had been missing had been staring me in the face all along. All I had to be was *me*. Imperfect, hasn't-got-it-all-figured-out-yet me. Cat Connelly, the daughter of Bruce and Audrey, two people who didn't quite have it all figured out either. Two people who loved their daughters, even if they didn't always know how to show it. Maybe being loved didn't always have to be something I earned, something I fought for. Maybe it could just *be*, when the time was right.

'So the photo gallery has asked to see a wider variety of Rome photographs before they choose my initial ten,' I concluded. 'Karina sent them a selection of the photos I've taken so far. But the gallery owner wants more.' I paused and felt myself blushing a little. 'Karina says that this woman thinks there's going to be a high demand for these photos once she begins exhibiting them.'

'When will that happen?' Marco asked.

'In about three weeks,' I said. 'She's about to take down a display from a photographer in Tuscany. A series of sunflower shots that just aren't selling very well. She wants to put my exhibit in its place. Apparently, historic urban art is hot now.'

'This is wonderful, Cat.' Marco beamed at me. He leaned forward to kiss me on the cheek. 'You must be so happy.'

'I am.' I smiled back. 'So. I have eight more days here. And I need to find some shots that capture the soul of Rome. I want to bowl this gallery owner over, Marco. I want to go in with images like nothing she's ever seen.'

I felt excited for the first time in a very long time. A nervous, apprehensive, fluttery kind of excited, where I felt like everything could cave in on me suddenly . . . or the whole world was about to open up. I just didn't know which way it would go yet.

'Let me help,' Marco said.

'What?'

He grinned. 'Let me help you. This is my city. I fell in love with it the moment I first came here from Venice, and I've spent so many hours wandering the streets here and taking it all in. I can take you to my favorite places, and I can help you find your own.'

I hesitated. 'Are you sure you want to do that?' I asked. 'You have to work.'

He shrugged. 'Of course I do. But I do not have to be here all the time. And I want to help you. I want to see my city through your eyes. And I want you to see my city through mine.'

I smiled. 'You're pretty great, you know that?' I paused and tried to remember a line from *Roman Holiday*. 'You've helped give me faith in relations between people,' I paraphrased a line from the movie's final scene.

Marco got it immediately. He grinned, reached across the table and squeezed my hand. Then he leaned across to kiss me, gently and tenderly, on the lips.

For the next week, Marco met me each morning and took me to a different spot in Rome – the Arco di Constantino, a beautiful arch covered in ancient battle scenes, one day, and the Terme di Caracalla, the towering ruins of public baths used until the sixth century, another day. I'd discovered that Rome was at its most beautiful in the mornings, before the sun rose too high in the sky, and I enjoyed shooting the ancient monuments, the beautiful domes, and the Roman people going about their daily routines when the pale light softened the edges of everything, giving the city a magic, ethereal glow.

Marco helped me carry my heavy camera bag, laughed

at my jokes, told me about his family and kept me amused with funny stories of growing up in Venice, in the world of gondoliers, tourists, and a slowly sinking city steeped in legend and mystery. I told him about life in New York, and for the first time in years I also found myself sharing stories about my mother that I had locked away long ago in the back corners of my mind. As we walked from photo shoot to photo shoot, I found that my mother's memory was becoming clearer and clearer in my mind as I laughed about silly things she had done, smiled at memories of birthday parties she'd thrown for us, and recalled vividly what it was like to snuggle into the crook of her arm while she read me fairy tales, in Italian, from a big, illustrated book she had had since she was a little girl.

The more I let my mother's memories back in, the more I felt. It was like a tidal wave of emotion, sneaking up on me. But each night when I went to bed, I felt steeped in powerful waves of happiness and sadness. Sometimes I woke up with a smile on my face; sometimes I woke to tears I hadn't remembered crying. The more my life came together, the more I seemed to be becoming an emotional wreck. But I knew that this was exactly what I needed to be doing, strange as it seemed. Perhaps it was the result of twenty-plus years of emotions being squashed deep down inside. There was nowhere else for them to go as they bubbled toward the surface.

The more time I spent with Marco that last week, the more confident I grew that if I stayed here, if I allowed myself to, I could fall in love with him. He was a good man, and I knew he cared about me. I also knew that he cared enough to respect whatever it was I was going through. I knew he had sensed me backing off, and although he probably didn't understand why, he didn't push me. He simply spent time with me, tried to make me laugh, comforted me when he saw the shadows on my face. We spent hours kissing – in front of beautiful fountains, atop hills overlooking the city, in front of churches that had been there for centuries upon centuries. But it didn't go any further than that again. I had never known a man like him, and if the timing had been other than it was things might have gone a very different way.

But as the days ticked by and my heart continued to open up, I knew with increasing certainty that I just wasn't ready. It didn't have anything to do with Michael. I wasn't ready for him either. It was just that the more I became *me*, the more I realized how much time I'd need to get to know this version of myself, which I'd spent so long locking away.

While Marco worked dinner shifts at his restaurant, I spent several evenings with Karina. Nico often joined us too before Karina put him to bed. Over incredible meals of spinach ricotta pasta, sage butter ravioli or rosemary pork, which Karina seemed to whip up effortlessly, she chattered happily about the conversations she'd had with Gillian, the gallery owner in New York, while Nico went on and on about how he couldn't wait to tell all his friends that he knew a top photographer. I couldn't help but laugh.

One evening, four days before I was due to leave Rome, I went to the park with Karina, Nico and Karina's mother. As Nico kicked a soccer ball around with a few other little boys whose parents had brought them out to play, I sat on a bench with Karina and her mother and realized that I really felt like part of a family over here. I couldn't remember the last time I'd felt like that, even with my father and my sister at home. It was like we'd all retreated into our separate corners when my mother had died, and we hadn't quite known how to reconnect since then, although I knew we all loved each other. I promised myself that once I got my own life back on track, I'd work on mending my family too. I bet it was what my mother would have wanted.

I snapped photos of Nico and his friends as the sun dipped below the tree line and the light began to fade. It was still forty-five minutes before sunset, but it was that time of the day in Rome where the shadows began to creep in and the evening snuck toward the city.

'Maybe Gillian will choose one of the photos of Nico for her gallery!' Karina said excitedly as she watched me shoot.

I smiled. 'That would be perfect,' I said.

Twenty minutes later, as Karina helped Nico gather his things and they started back toward home, I told her I wanted to take a walk by myself for a little while. There were two more shots I wanted to get before I felt my work was done.

First, as the sun began to sink into the horizon, setting the western sky on fire with a palette of oranges, pinks and deep blue, I squatted on the sidewalk of the Via dei Fori Imperiali, just in front of the Forum, and took several snapshots of the little brick wall where Marco had first found me. I must have looked insane to passers-by as I got down almost level with it, so that I could get a wide-angle shot. But I wanted to photograph it, along with the crumbling ruins of the Forum behind it, backlit by the fiery sky of sunset. Just as I was getting ready to shoot, two pigeons fluttered over and landed on the edge of the wall, right beside each other. I watched them, transfixed for a moment. And then I began shooting, watching through the lens as the birds hopped around, faced each other, stood beak to beak. When I sat up a few minutes later and brushed the dust off my clothes, I checked out the images on my camera's screen. I smiled. They were perfect. Exactly what I'd been going for.

As the last rays of saturated sky deepened to a dusky, dark blue, I made my way toward the Ponte Sant'Angelo, a place that still felt magical to me. I snapped photograph after photograph of the illuminated bridge, watching the angels spring to life in sharp focus. And for the first time I wondered if perhaps what had always made me feel so comforted here was that there really was something angelic about this bridge. Maybe, just maybe, the legend of the angels guarding the city from atop the bridge was true. And if it was, maybe my mother's ghost visited here from time to time too, to look out over the city that had once been her home. The thought, however irrational it might have been, made me smile.

I strolled up and down the Tiber's nearside bank, crossed the bridge, shot the angels close up and far away, photographed the Castel Sant'Angelo from across the water. I must have snapped a hundred photos altogether, most of them of the bridge in its entirety, from all different angles as the sun vanished from the sky, finally leaving the bridge bathed only in the lights of Rome.

Three days later, I awoke to my last full day in Italy. Hundreds of digital proofs had been sent off to Gillian in New York, and she had promised to get back to us within the week about which ones she'd like to use. Karina had initially been joking about deducting a ten per cent commission, but I wouldn't have it any other way. She had been the one to listen to me and to take the initiative to help me break out of my shell of safety. She had worked hard. And I wanted her to reap the benefits too – if there were any. I told her I'd love it if she'd officially be my agent and accept a ten per cent commission for everything she was able to sell. The thing was, I still wasn't sure if this was just an overly enthusiastic, overly hopeful dream. For all I knew, Gillian had terrible taste, and the photos would never sell to anyone.

'Does this mean I get to sell your photographs everywhere?' Karina had asked, rubbing her hands together excitedly.

I smiled. 'I give you full control . . .' I paused and added, 'to sell Audrey Verdicchio's work wherever you please.'

She stared at me for a moment. 'Good,' she said. Then, in a tone that made her sound like she'd been doing this forever, she added, 'I'd like to see some line sheets of New York photographs within the next week or so, so that I can start selling those over here. Americana pays, you know.'

'Okay,' I said with a laugh.

'And of course if your Roma pictures sell well in America, you'll have to come back often to visit,' she said. 'For work purposes, of course. You'll need to take more photographs.'

I grinned. 'If you say so. I can't ignore my agent.'

Karina had organized a going away dinner for me that evening, with her, Nico and her mother, and Marco and my aunt Gina. I was excited that they were all going to meet. There were a few things I needed to do before the dinner, though, so I headed out early on that last day.

I stopped by a print shop to pick up an order I had placed two days before, and I emerged carrying a big, bulky bag. I considered walking the twenty minutes or so to Gina's shop, but knew it would take forever lugging my purchases. So instead, I flagged down a cab and gave him the address. Ten zigzagging minutes later, I emerged in front of the scarf store. I hadn't told Gina I was coming, but I hoped she would be happy to see me.

Her face lit up the moment I entered. She was helping a customer, an elderly woman who seemed to be having trouble deciding between a gray scarf and a beige one. I couldn't understand the Italian conversation, of course, but Gina seemed to be patiently talking the woman through the decision, letting her make up her own mind. I smiled as I watched them. It reminded me of my mother talking to Becky when she was little, waiting patiently for her to choose which fairy tale she wanted to have read to her that night.

Finally, the woman made her decision and went to the register to pay. When she finally left the shop, Gina came over and hugged me.

'My dear Cat!' she said. 'I was not expecting to see you until tonight. But now you have made my day twice as happy! What do you have in the bag there?'

I smiled at her. 'I wanted to bring you something that means a lot to me.'

'What is it?'

I felt shy and a little nervous as I slowly pulled one of the 20x30 photographs out of the bag. I hadn't had time to frame them. They had been matted in white cardboard, though, and could be easily slipped into a standard-sized frame.

I slowly turned the big photo around and showed it to Gina. Her eyes widened as she stared at it.

'*You* took this?' she asked, sounding incredulous.

I nodded, feeling a little color rise to my cheeks.

'Cat, it is beautiful,' she said softly.

I smiled, feeling a swell of pride. I had given her my favorite photo of the Ponte Sant'Angelo at twilight. I supposed I wanted to give a little piece of the magic I had felt there to the one person on earth who had made me feel like I had a second chance with my mother. Seeing her apparently genuinely impressed with my photograph made me feel a little bit like I was getting my mother's blessing too.

'Thank you,' I said.

'But how did you know?' she asked after she had studied the photograph for a while. She looked up at me, her brow creased.

'How did I know what?'

'How did you know this was your mother's favorite place?'

I felt the breath go out of me. 'I didn't,' I said after a moment.

She looked puzzled. 'But why did you give me this photograph?' she asked. 'Of all the places in Roma?'

'Because it has always been *my* favorite place in Rome,' I said.

We stared at each other for a long moment. Somehow, my mother and I had both chosen the same spot in the city to claim as our own. It wasn't like choosing the Spanish Steps or the Trevi Fountain or the Colosseum or any of the other monuments that graced postcards and calendars. It was like choosing a needle in a haystack.

Finally, Gina smiled. 'Perhaps, then, your mother is not so far away after all.'

'I think maybe you're right,' I said after a moment. We chatted for a few more minutes, and then I gave her directions to Karina's apartment and said I'd see her at seven thirty. She kissed me goodbye on both cheeks.

Next, I made my way to Pinocchio, where I knew I'd find Marco working.

'Cat!' he said happily as I came in through the front door. He was standing near the sink, drying glasses. 'Come in, sit down!'

I shook my head. 'I can't stay long,' I said. 'I just wanted to bring you a gift.'

He looked puzzled. 'But it is you who are going away,' he said. 'You should not be giving me a gift.'

I smiled. 'I wanted to.'

We sat down together at a table near the back of the restaurant. I took a deep breath and pulled his 20x30 photo out of the bag.

He stared for a moment, his eyes moving around the image slowly. Then a smile spread across his face. 'It's the place I found you sleeping,' he said.

'Yeah.' I nodded and looked at it with him.

It was the best of the photographs I'd taken a few days earlier. In it, the two birds that had landed on the edge of the wall were facing each other, their beaks nearly touching. It almost looked as though they were kissing, or perhaps preparing to tell each other an intimate secret. It was sweet, and I felt it fitted perfectly with what I wanted Marco to remember about me, about us.

He gazed at it for a long time. 'Princess Ann,' he said finally. 'I will treasure this forever.'

I leaned forward to hug him, as we both blinked tears out of our eyes.

I left the rest of the photographs with Marco and asked if he'd bring them to Karina's tonight. I'd printed three for her, and I wanted them to be a surprise. Plus, I had one more thing I needed to do before I left Rome.

I set out from Pinocchio thinking a bit about the restaurant's namesake and the meaning of the truth. I followed the map I'd printed out earlier, and within twenty minutes I was standing at the door to Francesco's apartment building, feeling very much like I'd come full circle.

I took a deep breath and went inside. I walked up the four flights to his door, held my breath and knocked.

I told myself that coming here had been enough. If he wasn't home, it didn't matter; it wasn't meant to be. I listened for footsteps, but I didn't think I heard any. I knocked one more time just to be sure. Nothing.

I breathed a sigh of relief. There was a part of me that wanted to tackle my last remaining ghost, but a bigger part of me was relieved that I wouldn't have to see the man who had hurt and humiliated me just four weeks earlier. Despite all that had happened since then, the wound was still raw.

I was just about to turn away and retreat down the stairs when the door swung open, revealing Francesco standing there, shirtless, with just a pair of tight jeans and bare feet.

'Cat?' he asked, surprised. He glanced from side to side. 'What are you doing here?'

I stared at him for a long moment, wondering how it

was possible to have felt so much for him when I stepped off the plane, but to feel absolutely nothing for him now. And it wasn't just that I didn't like him anymore; I didn't hate him either. I just felt incredibly, refreshingly indifferent. 'I need to talk to you,' I said.

He smirked at me a little, and I could swear he sucked his gut in a bit, as if he was conscious, despite himself, about how his body looked to me. 'I didn't know you were still in Roma,' he said.

'Yes,' I answered simply. I didn't owe him an explanation.

'What did you do to your hair?' he asked. 'You look good.' He looked me unabashedly up and down, then waited for a response.

I knew I was supposed to answer in kind, but instead I simply smiled and said, 'Thank you.' Then I added, 'I know.'

He looked a bit startled to have not had his ego stroked in return. He blinked a few times and cleared his throat. 'Do you want to come in?'

I thought about it and shook my head. 'No,' I said. 'I have just one thing to say to you, and I think I can say it here.'

He swallowed hard. It was finally hitting him that I hadn't come here to beg him to take me back, or to tell him how much I missed him, or to ask him for one last roll around in his bed. '*Cosa?*' he asked cautiously.

I took a deep breath.

'Thirteen years ago, you had a fling with me, and that's all it ever was,' I said. 'It meant too much to me. And when I was gone, you moved on to the next young, foolish girl.'

He looked at me for a moment and shrugged. 'It was not just a fling,' he said. 'I had some feeling for you, Cat. But yes, I moved on quickly. I think that you loved me. And I did not love you the same way.'

I shook my head and smiled slightly. 'But that's just the thing,' I said. 'I don't think I loved you after all. I thought I did. I was young and foolish. Which is exactly what attracted you to me in the first place. But you know what, Francesco? I think I loved the feeling of being wanted and needed. And I blamed myself when it didn't feel like that between us anymore. But it was never about loving you. It was about me trying to complete something that felt empty.'

'I don't understand.' He was staring at me blankly. 'Why are you telling me these things?'

'Because I think it's important to be honest.' I took a deep breath. 'I also wanted to come here to thank you.'

'For what?' he asked.

'For being you,' I said.

He looked at me warily, as if he wasn't sure whether I was making fun of him. I wasn't. I meant it.

'What do you mean?' he asked.

'You're a complete asshole,' I said. I hardly ever cursed, but I knew it was fully deserved this time. He opened his mouth to protest, but I held up a hand to stop him. 'And I'm glad that's who you are,' I said. 'Because if you'd been a better person, if you'd been a decent man, I might still be here with you. And I would have missed having the best four weeks of my life.'

'I don't understand,' he said, looking at me in confusion.

I smiled. 'And you never will.'

And with that, with my head held high, I walked away from Francesco for the last time. I could feel his eyes following me as I left, but I didn't turn back. There was no reason to. He was in the past. As I walked down the stairs and finally emerged into the sunshine outside, I felt like I was walking straight into the future.

The dinner party that night was lovely but bittersweet. It was wonderful to be surrounded by the people who had come to mean so much to me in Rome but terribly sad to know I wouldn't see them again for a while. The sadness, however, was tempered by the fact that I knew I'd be back someday soon. It was a promise I'd made to myself already. Regardless of whether the photography thing worked out, I'd vowed to begin living my life. And now, a big part of my life was here. I had the feeling I'd only begun to discover it.

Karina served a panzanella salad of crispy bread chunks, thinly sliced onions, wedges of sweet tomatoes and a homemade balsamic herb vinaigrette, followed by a small starter course of creamy risotto with asparagus, zucchini and mint. The main course was perfectly crisp, thin pieces of chicken parmesan, flavored with rosemary and served on a bed of handmade fettuccine with a light, creamy sauce, sprinkled with toasted pine nuts.

'This is amazing,' Marco, who was sitting to my right, whispered to me at one point when Karina got up to bring in more freshly baked bread from the kitchen.

'I told you,' I said with a smile.

He shook his head and took another bite. 'Maybe I could use her at the restaurant . . .' he said, his voice trailing off.

'I think you should talk to her about it,' I whispered, trying to hide my smile, just as Karina returned to the room.

Gina was sitting on the other side of me, and I kept catching her staring at me. Each time, she shook her head and looked quickly away. Finally, she softly vocalized what I knew she was thinking. 'You look so much like her,' she said.

I nodded, accepting this. 'You do too,' I said. 'Being with you feels a little bit like she's still here.'

Gina nodded and squeezed my hand under the table. 'She is.'

Gina and Karina got along wonderfully, and for the first time I saw Karina's mother open up and laugh too. I should have felt a little left out as the three women gossiped in Italian, and Nico drilled an amused Marco with a series of intense questions, but instead I sat back in my chair, watching them all, sipping my coffee and feeling more at home than I ever had in New York. In less than four weeks, these people had become my family, however little common ground we had had to start with. And it warmed my heart to see my mother's sister, a woman I'd just met but was tied to forever, getting along so well with Karina, who I knew would be my friend for years to come.

After a dessert of the most delicate, delicious flaked almond pastry I'd ever tasted, Nico got up from the table and came around to my side.

'Signorina Cat?' he asked.

'Yes, Nico?'

He paused and looked at his feet. 'I am really going to miss you.'

I blinked back tears. 'I'm going to miss you too, Nico. Very, very much. But I will come back and visit.'

'Do you promise?' he asked, looking up hopefully.

'I promise,' I said firmly.

He paused. 'Maybe Mamma and I can come to New York too. I speak very good English.'

'Yes, you do,' I said with a smile. I remembered Karina saying that she couldn't afford a trip to New York, so I didn't want to encourage him. But at least they would have a place to stay now, and I hoped that might be enough to change her mind at some point.

Nico looked down again and added softly. 'My papà lives there.'

I blinked a few times and recovered quickly. 'He does?'

Nico nodded and leaned forward to whisper in my ear. 'Mamma does not talk about him very often. But she says he lives in New York. I would like to meet him someday.'

'Maybe you will,' I said after a moment. I wanted to tell Nico that sometimes the people who are supposed to love you will break your heart. I wanted to tell him that his father might not be the man he had imagined him to be. I wanted to tell him that holding on to hope might be a mistake. But he was six. He didn't deserve to have his bubble burst yet. And besides, I was a week away from thirty-five, and I certainly didn't have it all figured out either. Maybe Nico was right. Maybe people deserved a second chance, even when they hadn't earned it.

Nico hesitated again and looked a little nervous. 'Just one thing, Signorina Cat,' he said.

'What is it?'

'You promised you would take photographs of me and Mamma and Nona,' he said. He looked down, as if embarrassed to be asking me. 'Did you run out of time? Maybe you can take them the next time you are here.'

I smiled at him. 'Well, Nico, I am glad you mentioned that. I actually didn't forget.' I leaned forward and whispered in his ear, 'There's a big, flat bag in the corner of the living room, behind the sofa. Could you go get it for me?'

Nico grinned and nodded. He disappeared, and a moment later he came back carrying the bag. As he entered the dining room, the conversations around the table slowed, and everyone looked at it with curiosity.

I cleared my throat as I stood up and took the bag from Nico.

'Karina?' I said. I looked around the table. Everyone was smiling at me. I took a deep breath. 'I can't begin to thank you for everything you've done for me. Four weeks ago, I was a complete mess. If it hadn't been for you, I might have given up and gone home. And I wouldn't have met Nico, or your mother, or Marco or Gina. And now you've all become my family.'

Around the table, everyone exchanged looks. Marco and Gina clinked glasses.

'It's not much,' I continued, 'but I wanted to give you a small gift to say thank you. Of course I'll be back to visit – if you'll have me – but in the meantime, I wanted to give you a piece of your family to tell you how much you mean to me. You've made me feel like I belong here.'

'A piece of my family?' Karina repeated, glancing at the bag.

I nodded. 'Yes.' I pulled the first of three 20x30 matted photos out of the bag and turned it around to show to the table.

'*È oi!*' Nico cried out. 'It's me!' Karina gasped and smiled as she gazed at the photo, which I'd taken several days ago at the park with Karina, her mother, and Nico. It was a black and white photograph of Nico kicking a soccer ball, his face scrunched up in concentration. He looked older and wiser than his six years, and his eyes glistened as he looked into the unfathomable distance.

'Oh, Cat!' Karina exclaimed. 'It is beautiful. I will treasure it forever.'

I smiled. 'Wait. I'm not done.' I pulled a second photograph from the bag and turned around to show it to the table. It was another black and white, shot the same day. Karina and her mother had been sitting on the park bench, watching Nico. When I'd gotten up to photograph him at one point, I turned around to glance at them and saw them laughing at some joke. I turned the lens quickly their way. In the photo I'd captured, they were both mid-laugh, leaning toward each other, looking into each other's eyes as they giggled like schoolgirls. They looked like best friends as much as mother and daughter, and I'd known from the moment I shot the image that it would be one of those meaningful portraits that captured the subjects' personalities perfectly.

'Oh, Cat!' Karina exclaimed again, placing a hand on her chest and blinking a few times. 'It is wonderful!' Her mother was nodding enthusiastically and smiling.

'One more,' I said. I pulled the third and final photograph out of the bag and turned it around for them to see.

Karina's eyes filled with tears as she gazed at the portrait. 'Oh, Cat,' she said softly.

I smiled. It was one of my favorite pictures. Black and white like the other two, it was shot from behind with my zoom lens. When Karina, her mother and Nico had walked away from the park the other day, and I'd gone in the other direction, I had glanced back over my shoulder and seen them walking hand in hand. I had turned around immediately to shoot them from a distance. Karina was in the middle, one hand holding her mother's and the other hand holding her son's. Her mother carried a bunch of sunflowers in her free hand, and Nico's soccer ball was tucked beneath his bony upper arm as he skipped to keep up. In the photo, Karina was saying something to Nico, who was gazing up at her with a huge smile on his face. Karina's mother had her head turned to the side to look at them, just enough so that, even in the shadows, you could see clearly the expression of love and pride on her face as she gazed at her daughter and her grandson. In the background of the photo, in the direction the three of them were walking, lay ancient Rome, its old buildings casting long shadows on the ground as the sun sank toward the horizon.

'*Dio mio*,' Marco said softly. 'Those photographs are amazing, Cat.'

I beamed. 'Thank you.'

Karina's mother looked at me with what appeared to be new respect. 'Beautiful,' she said simply, the word spiked with her Italian accent. '*Grazie.*'

'*Prego*,' I responded with a smile. 'You're welcome.' I turned to Karina. 'Your family has come to mean so much to me.'

'Well,' she said, glancing back to the photo and then at me again. 'You are part of our family now.'

Nico came over and gave me a big hug. As I glanced around the table, at all the people I'd come to love in such a short time, I knew the words were true.

After dinner, when Nico and Karina's mother had gone to bed, I walked outside to say goodbye to Gina and to see her safely into a cab.

'I'm so glad you came to find me,' she said.

'I am too.'

She reached up and brushed her thumb gently across my cheek. She smiled at me sadly. 'Your mother, I think, would be very proud.'

I swallowed a lump in my throat. 'I hope so,' I said. A month ago, I would have sworn that my mother's opinion meant nothing to me. But now, everything was different. I took a deep breath. 'Gina,' I said. 'I'm sorry.'

'For what?'

'For not coming sooner,' I said.

She shook her head. 'No,' she said. 'Do not apologize. You came when you were ready. And that is all that matters.'

I looked down. 'But I think of all that time I wasted, feeling so angry at her.'

She reached for my hand. 'Cat, that time was not wasted,' she said. 'Your mother, even though she meant well, she hurt you. You needed time to come back to her on your own. She was always very sorry for what she did to you. And she never blamed you for being angry.'

I swallowed the lump in my throat and nodded.

'I don't blame you, either,' she added. 'You are a very

strong young woman. I see the best parts of your mother in you.'

'You do?'

'*Assolutamente,*' she said. She reached out to embrace me tightly. 'Come back to Roma soon,' she said into my ear. 'You always have family here. This is your home too.'

I nodded. 'I know,' I said.

She kissed my cheek, smiled at me and climbed into the cab. Before she shut the door, she reached into her handbag and pulled out a gift bag. 'I almost forgot,' she said, handing it to me. 'For you. To remember us.'

She smiled and shut the door to the car. I watched as they drove away. As they turned the corner at the end of the street, she raised her hand in a small wave. I waved back, feeling sadder than I expected to. When she was gone, I reached into the gift bag and pulled out several small items wrapped in tissue paper, and one larger one. I smiled as I unwrapped them. She had given me gorgeous silk scarves from the family store in three different colors – teal, beige and pale pink. She had also given me a beautiful pashmina wrap in black.

There was a little notecard enclosed with the gift. *You will always be a Verdicchio*, it said in perfect, ornate cursive.

I smiled, unfolded the pashmina and pulled it around me. It was soft and warm, and as I stood in the moonlight on the steps of the building I'd called home for the last few weeks, I felt a bit like I was being embraced.

Marco and I helped Karina clear and wash the dishes, and, after thanking her for the wonderful meal and agreeing to meet her in the morning before I left for the airport, I set out with Marco.

He laced his fingers loosely through mine, and we walked in comfortable silence for a while. All around us, Rome glowed in the moonlight and under the street lamps that now dotted the ancient roads. I felt very sad to be leaving this place.

We strolled until we emerged on the Piazza Venezia, and suddenly I knew where Marco was leading us.

'Are we going to our spot?' I asked with a smile.

He smiled back. 'Where it all began.'

Five minutes later, we had reached the Forum and the stout brick wall where I'd fallen asleep four weeks ago. It felt like a lifetime.

Marco pulled me into a hug. 'I'm going to miss you, Princess Ann,' he said.

'I'll miss you too,' I said. I took a deep breath. 'I need to talk to you about something.'

He nodded, and I could see in his eyes as we sat down that he already knew what I was going to say.

I took a deep breath and tried to slow my pounding heart. 'Marco,' I began, 'you have changed my life, and I don't know how to thank you for that.'

He reached for my hand and squeezed it. He smiled sadly at me, but he didn't say anything.

I closed my eyes for a moment and then opened them again. 'Marco,' I said, 'I don't even know how to say this to you. But I don't think I'm ready. I'm not ready to be with someone yet. It sounds crazy, because I'm almost thirty-five, but I think that in the last four weeks, everything has changed. And I have some growing to do.'

'I know,' he said, nodding at me, a serious expression on his face.

'It's not you,' I said. 'I think if the timing were

different, we'd have a chance. And maybe that'll happen in the future. I don't know. But for now, even though it sounds silly, I think I need to take some time to myself.'

Marco looked down at our intertwined hands. 'It does not sound silly,' he said after a moment. 'I think it sounds very wise.'

'I'm sorry,' I said softly.

'Do not be sorry,' he said. 'It is the right thing.'

I took a deep breath. 'I don't want you to hate me,' I said.

He smiled. 'That would never be possible.'

'I'm sorry I didn't say something sooner,' I said. 'I didn't know what to do. I've never felt this way before.'

He nodded. 'Neither have I,' he said. He took a deep breath. 'I think I knew you were going to say this. But it is harder than I thought.'

'I'm sorry.'

'I know,' he said.

'I'd like it if we could keep in touch,' I said. 'And when I come back to Rome, I'd like to see you. Maybe things will be different in the future.'

He thought for a moment. 'I do not think so,' he said. 'I think this is not your home.' He smiled at me. 'It would have been nice, maybe. Me and you. But you are from America. I am from Italy. And I think that we would never be able to fully be a part of each other's worlds.'

'Sometimes things like that work out,' I argued.

'Yes,' he said. 'But more often they do not.'

The words hung between us in the awkward silence. Finally, Marco stood up.

'I think I should go,' he said.

I stood up too, feeling suddenly panicky. Was I making a huge mistake? I didn't want to let him go. 'Can we just sit here for a while?' I asked, feeling silly the moment the words were out of my mouth.

He hesitated and shook his head. 'No,' he said. 'I think I need to be alone.' He paused and added, 'I will walk you home, if you like.'

I shook my head. 'That's okay.' I managed a faint smile. 'This time, I know the way back to the apartment.'

Marco smiled half-heartedly. 'Cat, I am sure that we will be friends one day,' he said. 'But please, let me contact you. I will when I am ready.'

I took a deep breath. I was trying not to cry. 'Okay,' I agreed.

We hugged goodbye, and for a moment I didn't want to let go. I wanted to tell him that I could move to Rome, that maybe I could be with him forever. What if that was the right thing to do? What if I was making the biggest mistake of my life?

'Thank you,' I said softly as I finally let him go. 'For opening my eyes.'

He shrugged. 'No, Princess Ann,' he said. 'I think you did that yourself.' He paused and smiled sadly. 'Besides,' he continued. 'This is the way the movie ends, isn't it? We're supposed to go our own separate ways.'

I was silent. I was trying not to cry.

Marco smiled sadly. 'To paraphrase the movie, life isn't always fair, is it?'

'No, it isn't.' I paused and struggled to recall one of the last lines from the movie, as Princess Ann and Joe Bradley are parting. Remembering movie lines has never been one of my strong points – after a few seconds the best I could come up with was: 'I don't know how I'm supposed to say goodbye to you. I just don't have the words.'

Marco smiled at me for a long minute. Then he leaned forward and kissed me once more, a lingering, closed-mouthed kiss on the lips, and then, without another word, he turned to go. I watched him until he turned left at the end of the street, finally disappearing around a building.

He didn't look back once.

The next morning at six, I was getting ready to leave when there was a knock on my door. Surprised, I opened it to find Karina there, fully dressed and ready to go.

'What are you doing up so early?' I asked.

'You didn't think I was going to let you go to the airport alone, did you?'

'But I'll be fine!' I said. 'I can say goodbye to you here. It's a long cab ride.'

Karina shrugged. 'It is early. I will be back in time for work. And I would like to say a proper goodbye.' She paused. 'Besides, if I remember correctly, your suitcase is a mess. You'll need help carrying it.'

I laughed. 'Okay. Thank you.'

She helped me drag my bags down the stairs. We left them in the entryway to the building and went back upstairs so that I could say goodbye to Nico.

Karina's mother was sitting in the living room, reading a book and sipping an espresso. She got up when I came in and crossed the room to hug me tightly. She said something to me in rapid Italian, and Karina smiled.

'She said that you are like a daughter to her,' Karina translated, 'and that she hopes you will return to us soon.'

'I will,' I promised. I searched my mind for the proper

Italian phrasing, and as I said the word I hoped it was coming out right. '*Rinvierò*,' I said to Karina's mother. 'I will return.'

Karina laughed. 'You are fluent already!' she teased.

Nico was still asleep, so I went in to wake him up. I sat on the edge of his bed and whispered his name. He opened his big brown eyes and blinked at me a few times. He smiled, and then I could see the realization dawning on his face. He had forgotten for a moment that I was leaving.

'I'm on my way to the airport,' I said softly.

He looked at me for a long moment and sat up. 'I don't want to say goodbye.'

'Then don't,' I said. 'Let's say instead, "I'll see you soon."'

He studied my face, as if trying to decide whether I meant it or not. Finally, he smiled a little. 'Okay,' he agreed. 'I will see you soon, Zia Cat.'

I blinked back tears. It was the first time he had used the endearment, which meant 'aunt.'

'I will be back, *il mio nipote*,' I said, returning the endearment by calling him my nephew. 'I promise.'

He thought about it for a moment. 'I know,' he said finally. 'And maybe Mamma and I will come visit you in New York.'

I reached out and hugged him for a long moment. 'I hope so,' I said into his thick, dark hair.

'We will not say goodbye,' Karina said as we got into a cab and set off toward the airport, 'because it's not really goodbye. I am your agent, right? We will need to talk often about your photographs.'

I laughed. 'Of course,' I said, 'although perhaps I'm crazy to think anyone will possibly want to buy my pictures.'

Karina shook her head. 'No,' she said. 'You are crazy to think that they won't sell. You have to believe in yourself once in a while, Cat.'

We rode in silence for a few minutes. 'Karina?' I asked hesitantly as we pulled out of the picturesque area of the city and into the more nondescript areas of the suburbs as we headed for the airport. 'Nico told me that his father lives in New York.'

Karina sucked in a deep breath but didn't say anything.

'Is that true?' I asked after a moment.

She hesitated and nodded. She looked out the window, effectively turning her back to me.

'I didn't realize you were in touch with him,' I said.

The silence stretched on for so long that I was sure she wasn't going to answer. And then, suddenly, she blurted out, 'I wasn't, for a long time. And I don't want to be.' She still wasn't looking at me. She was gazing out the window, and her voice sounded muffled. 'He left me, Cat. He left *us*. He chose another woman over me, and he left us in Rome while he went off to start a whole new life in America.'

'I'm sorry,' I said softly.

She shook her head vigorously. 'No. It is nothing to be sorry about. It happened. It is done.' She paused. 'But he is Nico's father. And Nico deserves to know his father. I found him in New York last year, and I've been sending him pictures of Nico.' She paused, and added, 'One day, they should meet. But I am not ready yet.'

'I understand.'

'I should have asked him to stay,' she said after a moment. 'If I had begged him, when I was pregnant with Nico, he would have stayed, I think. But I was too proud.'

I thought about it for a moment. 'Karina, you shouldn't have to beg someone to stay with you,' I said.

'But Nico would have had a father,' she said. She finally turned away from the window to face me. I could see the pain and regret in her eyes.

'No,' I said. 'Nico would have had a sad, angry household to grow up in. His parents would have resented each other, and he would have felt it.' I thought of my own childhood, of all the horrific fights between my parents, and of the relative calm after my mother left, the way that instead of the constant waves of anger from my parents there was suddenly only fierce, powerful love from my father, who would have given us the world had he been able to. 'Instead,' I said, and I wasn't sure whether I was referring to myself or to Nico anymore, 'instead, he's had a relatively happy childhood with a parent who would do anything for him.'

Karina looked at me for a long time and nodded.

'When you're ready,' I said, 'come to New York. Stay with me. And I'll go with you to see your ex-husband, if you want to.'

I expected her to protest. But instead, she just looked down and murmured, 'Thank you.' After a moment, she added, 'You're going to make a wonderful mother someday, if that is what you choose.'

'Thank you,' I said simply. I didn't know if that was what my future held or not. But I was no longer scared that I'd be like my mother. I think I already was like her in some of the good ways. And the bad things, well, I'd learn from her mistakes. And it would make me better, stronger, more prepared for the job of motherhood.

We rode in silence for a while, each of us lost in our own thoughts. As we began seeing signs for the airport, I said quietly, 'I told Marco I couldn't see him anymore.'

Karina looked at me in surprise. 'You did?'

I nodded. 'It was the right thing to do.'

She nodded slowly. 'So it's Michael, then? You'll call Michael when you get back to New York?'

I hesitated and shook my head. 'No,' I said. 'I think I'll just spend some time alone for a while.'

I didn't know how she'd react. I knew Karina liked Michael and probably wanted me to give him a chance. And I didn't know how to explain to her that right now, it wasn't about the guy. It was about me. I needed to just be with *me* for a while.

But Karina looked at me for a long time and smiled. 'Good for you, Cat,' she said.

I knew she understood.

'Are you going to tell your sister about your mother?' Karina asked after a moment.

'Someday,' I said. I paused, and then tried to explain. 'My mother didn't want us to know unless we came looking. And my sister never felt the same way about my mother as I did. She forgave her. She was happy to have her home. I think I'm the one who struggled with it.'

'And your dad?' she asked.

'I think he knew. On some level, anyhow,' I said. 'But if he ever asks me, I'll tell him about seeing Gina.'

We hugged goodbye for a long time outside the taxi, until the driver honked his horn and gestured for Karina to hurry up and get back in.

She rolled her eyes and grinned. 'Roma,' she said. 'What can you do?'

I laughed. 'I still love it here,' I said. 'Rude cab drivers and all.'

Karina hugged me again, quickly this time, and when she pulled back there were tears in her eyes. 'I'm glad to know you, Cat Connelly,' she said.

'Me too,' I said.

She quickly wiped her tears away and climbed back into the cab. The cab driver peeled quickly away from the curb. Karina pressed a palm against the window in a silent wave. I waved back and watched her until the cab disappeared.

A few hours later, as my plane lifted off and Rome rose up below us, a dusty collection of pale domes, patchwork green parks, glittering crosses and maroon rooftops, I felt a strange sort of melancholy. I knew I was going home. But I also knew there was a part of me that would forever be at home in the city below me, the city that gradually slipped away beneath the clouds until I could no longer make out any trace of its magic.

22

Three months later, almost to the day, I was standing in the baggage claim area of JFK Airport, waiting for Karina and Nico to come through customs. I hadn't been back to Rome since I left, although I was planning another trip there the following month. So I'd been beyond thrilled when Karina called and said she was thinking of bringing Nico over to meet his father for the first time.

There was another reason for her trip, too. My photos had been selling so well at the Gillian Zucker Gallery that I'd decided to quit my accounting job at Puffer & Hamlin three weeks ago. It had been a huge leap on my part – not just because of the inherent financial insecurity, but because of the fact that I'd never been a person who lived without a safety net – but so far it was working out. I'd be making less than I had as an accountant, and I'd have to pay for my own health insurance, but I'd have more time to travel. And of course I'd still have my accounting degree and all my connections in that world as a fallback if photography didn't work out long term. But it was time I took a leap of faith in my life.

Gillian, whom I still hadn't met face to face, had asked

Karina if 'Audrey H. Verdicchio' could take another set of Rome pictures and perhaps work on a series of shots of the Amalfi coast too. I had agreed and was looking forward to the assignment. Karina had also just sold a number of New York black and whites to a small gallery in Rome, and already the photos I'd just taken in early September, of the swan song of summer in Central Park, were selling well.

Of course it was Karina's ten per cent commission from all the sales that was helping to finance her trip. Plus, while she was here, she had meetings arranged with three other galleries in New York and two in Boston, to show them my work. Nico was thrilled that he'd get to see not one but two big American cities. He had already called me twice to ask me if I'd be coming with them to see the ducks in Boston's Public Garden. I'd promised that I would, and I was planning to borrow my father's car to drive the three of us up there in a few days.

Karina didn't know it yet, but I was planning to reimburse her for her flights over here. After all, she was going to be doing business on my behalf while in the States. She shouldn't have to pay her own way, although I suspected she would have come regardless. As she had said to me on the phone when I asked her if she was sure she was ready to see her ex, Massimo, again, 'It is time.'

I saw Nico come through the customs door first. He spotted me right away and broke away from Karina to run across the room. He threw himself into my arms and hugged me tight around the waist. 'Zia Cat! Zia Cat!' he said excitedly. Then he launched into an excited stream of Italian, his eyes wide and his words flowing rapidly.

I laughed as he finally let me go and stepped back,

waiting for a response. 'Nico, I don't speak Italian, remember?'

He stared at me for a moment and laughed too. 'I didn't even realize I was speaking Italian!' he exclaimed. 'That is how excited I am to be here in New York City!'

He hugged me again, and as I hugged back I couldn't help but notice that he seemed a little taller – and that he had lost a front tooth. It made me sad to think that by being apart just three months I was missing seeing him grow up. I already loved him the way I knew I would love my own niece or nephew – who was due to arrive in just under five months. Apparently, Becky and Jay had started trying for a baby on their honeymoon, and it had worked out right away – as Becky's life almost always did.

There was a part of me that used to resent the way she stumbled through life, with everything working out perfectly, while I had to fight for everything I ever had. But something had changed in me this year, and now I was nothing but happy for my sister. I was looking forward to having a new member of our family to love.

Karina was close behind Nico, dragging a giant suitcase behind her. Once Nico let go of me, I rushed forward to help her. She smiled in relief and dropped the bag for a moment to hug me tightly. 'Well, this is a change,' she said with a grin as we both reached for the suitcase handle again and began pulling. 'You helping me with an oversized bag.'

I laughed. 'Don't get too used to it,' I said. 'I'll be back in Rome soon enough, making you carry my luggage.'

She rolled her eyes and laughed as I led them outside to the taxi stand. Ten minutes later, we were in a minivan cab headed toward Manhattan. Karina and I were in the middle row, and Nico was in the back, his face pressed against the glass as he waited for the skyscrapers of my city to come into view.

'Thank you for having us,' Karina said softly as Nico babbled to himself in the back seat.

'Oh, please,' I said, rolling my eyes at her. 'You're like family now.' I paused and added, 'But you'd better not charge me rent the next time I come to visit you.'

She laughed and promised I could sleep in her guest room free of charge any time I wanted to.

'So how's work going?' I asked, trying to hide a smile.

Karina looked worried. 'It is going well,' she said slowly. 'But there is something I must tell you.'

'What is it?'

She hesitated. 'I am no longer working at Squisito,' she said.

I feigned ignorance. 'Really? What happened?'

She hesitated. 'Please do not be angry with me. But Marco – your Marco – asked me a few weeks ago if I would come to work for him, as his executive chef.'

She paused and studied my face as if trying to figure out whether I'd be upset. She continued rapidly, 'I had to try out, of course. I had to cook all the items on his menu and talk to him about improvements in the food and new dishes we could try out. But he gave me the job, Cat. I start next week.' She paused. 'Are you angry with me? I should have asked you. It was terrible that I did not ask you.'

I smiled at her. 'I honestly couldn't be happier for you,' I said. She looked surprised. 'Really,' I added firmly. 'Besides, I've known about it for weeks. Marco asked me not to say anything to you until he had officially offered you the job. But he called to ask me if it was okay before he even got in touch with you in the first place. How do you think he got your phone number?'

She stared at me in shock. 'So you've been talking to Marco?'

I nodded. 'A little bit,' I said.

'And?' she asked, looking at me hopefully.

I smiled. 'And nothing. He's a good guy. And I know we're going to be friends for a long time. But I don't think he was the right one for me.' I paused and added, 'Plus, he's dating someone.'

'What?'

'Remember the weekend he went to Venice?' I asked. 'The weekend we went out and ran into Michael Evangelisti?'

Saying his name sent a strange pang through me. I had decided not to contact him when I got home to the States, and although I thought of him often, I hadn't been ready to see him. In fact, I had deliberately avoided the entire Upper West Side for the last three months.

Karina nodded. 'I remember.'

'Marco ran into a girl he had dated in school that weekend. They went on their first date just before I spent the night with him. So maybe it was bad timing for both of us. That's who he's seeing. She's been coming to visit him every weekend.' It made me a little sad, because the closer Marco became with this new girl, the more it meant that that door was closed to me forever. But I was happy for him too. He deserved to find someone, and I knew in my heart that it wasn't me.

'Wow,' Karina said. 'I did not know that.' She paused and looked at me closely. 'And Michael? Have you seen him?'

I shook my head. 'No,' I said simply. I left it at that.

Just then, Nico shrieked from the back seat. 'I see it, Mamma! I see it! The Empire State Building!' Sure enough, off in the distance, we could see the distinctive peak of the city's most famous tower. And as our taxi took us closer to the city, Nico bounced up and down and announced other things he could see: the Chrysler Building, the UN building, the trees of Central Park.

'He sure knows New York,' I said to Karina with a laugh.

She rolled her eyes, but I could see pride in her eyes. 'He has been dying to come here since the day I first put a book about New York in front of him.'

The next day, I went out to shoot Central Park in the morning while Karina took Nico to see his father for the first time. I had offered to go with them, but she'd said no. It was something she had to do on her own, for her son. She'd been mentally preparing for months.

So I wandered through the east side of the park, shooting foliage. The remnant of an Indian summer had given way to fall a few weeks ago, and now the air was crisp and the leaves were at their most colorful. The park seemed to be aglow with every imaginable shade of red, orange and yellow. The leaves had just begun to fall from the trees, thanks to high winds two nights earlier, and so in addition to photographing the trees and the cityscape behind the vibrantly colored Sheep Meadow I was able to catch kids in bright jackets and blue jeans running, shrieking and playing in the leaves. It made me smile. I had the feeling the shots would sell well in Italy; they were a perfect slice of Americana.

By the time I returned to the apartment, Karina was already sitting at my kitchen table, both hands wrapped around a coffee mug as she stared into space. I was surprised; I had expected them to spend the day with Massimo.

'Where's Nico?' I asked, glancing around. She focused on me slowly.

'Asleep,' she said flatly. 'He didn't sleep much last night, because he was so excited to be here. And the time change has thrown him a bit.'

I sat down at the table with her. 'So?' I asked carefully. 'How did it go?'

Karina took a deep breath. She exhaled slowly. 'Massimo is a terrible person,' she said finally.

'What happened?'

She shook her head. 'Nico was so excited to see him. But do you know, Massimo had a *futbol* game on the TV in the background? And he barely even looked at Nico; he was too busy watching the game. Nico was asking him questions and he kept telling Nico to be quiet so that he could hear the *futbol* announcers. After an hour, he asked us to go; he said he had a busy day and couldn't spend it all with a family reunion.'

'What?' I was incredulous.

'It broke my heart,' she said. She blinked away tears, and I reached for her hand. 'Not for me, of course,' she continued, 'but for Nico. I think he had imagined all sorts of things about his father. And it is my fault for letting him. I never told him what a horrible man his father was. I thought that perhaps Massimo would change if he had the chance to see his child.'

'I'm so sorry,' I murmured.

'There is no reason to be sorry,' Karina said. 'In a strange way, I feel a little better. And I think Nico will too, once he has some time to think about it. Massimo is exactly the man I thought he was. And the fact that he doesn't want to be in Nico's life, that he couldn't even pretend to be interested for a few hours . . .' She paused and shook her head. 'Well, I don't feel so badly anymore about the way things ended between us.'

'You shouldn't have anyhow,' I reminded her.

'I know,' she said. 'But sometimes it is easier to see that from the outside. Now I know I did not make a mistake.' She paused and added, 'I just don't know how to forgive myself for hurting Nico this way.'

'It's not your fault,' I said.

She shook her head. 'It *is* my fault when I can't protect my child from things that hurt him.' She got up from the table and walked into the bathroom, shutting the door behind her, before I could say anything else.

I had my father over for dinner that night so that he could meet Karina and Nico. I invited Becky and Jay too, but they already had dinner plans with one of Jay's friends. And I don't think Becky realized how important my little Italian family of two had become to me.

Nico was quiet and reserved at first. He still looked stricken after the encounter with his father, and Karina was sitting protectively close to him, stroking his hair. But after chatting with Karina for a little while, my dad began asking Nico questions about what he liked best about New York, and soon the little boy opened up. By the time we had finished the meal, he had moved to sit next to my dad and was showing him pictures of New York he had drawn back in Italy.

'I save them,' he explained intently, his eyes wide as my dad nodded, flipping through each picture like they were the most important things he'd ever seen. 'I keep them in my pocket sometimes, to remind me of New York City. And now Mamma and I are here!'

'These are wonderful, Nico,' my father said seriously.

Nico nodded. 'That is the Empire State Building. It is my favorite building in New York City. And this one,' he said, flipping to the next picture, 'is a building called the Flatiron. Do you know it?'

'Yes, I do,' my father said with a smile. 'Maybe we can go there later.'

Nico's eyes widened. 'Really?'

'Really,' my father said. He glanced at Karina, who was looking at him carefully, a half-smile on her face. 'In fact, I happen to know a pretty good ice cream place near the Flatiron building. Maybe I could take you there, if your mother says it's okay. Maybe she and Aunt Cat would like to come along.'

Karina smiled at my father. She seemed to be thinking about something. 'If you don't mind,' she said, 'perhaps you and Nico could go alone. There is something I would like to show Cat. I was going to do it tomorrow, but now would be perfect.'

'What is it?' I asked.

'I found out a few days ago from Gillian at the gallery about a place that has bought eighteen of your 20x30 photographs and has used them as interior décor,' she said. 'I thought you might like to see it.'

My heart thudded. I had deliberately avoided the gallery, because I hadn't wanted to announce in any public way that I was the so-called Audrey H. Verdicchio.

'No one has to know it's you,' Karina said, apparently reading my mind. 'But I think it will be wonderful to see a whole room full of your photographs. Don't you think?'

I hesitated, long enough for my father to say firmly, 'Yes, she'll go.' He shot me a look and added, 'You should be proud of yourself, kiddo. Go enjoy it.'

'I don't know,' I said uncomfortably.

'Look at it this way,' my father said. 'If you don't go, you'll be interrupting Guys' Night Out. And Nico and I have some serious ice cream eating to do.'

Nico laughed and my father high-fived him. Seeing my dad interact so naturally with the boy – and seeing Nico warm to my dad so quickly – was amazing. I glanced at Karina and shrugged. 'Okay,' I said warily.

'Good,' she said. 'Go get dressed.'

I looked down at the faded jeans and T-shirt I'd put on after coming home from the park. 'Aren't I dressed already?'

She rolled her eyes at me. 'You have to look better than that to see your photographs on display for the first time.' She nudged me and grinned. 'Show a little respect.'

So I said goodbye to Nico and my father, who promised not to let Nico eat too much ice cream. Nico threw his arms around me before he left and whispered in my ear, 'I like your father, Zia Cat.'

'Good,' I whispered back. 'You can borrow him any time you want, kiddo.'

He beamed at me and, after he had kissed his mother goodbye, he and my father left hand in hand.

After they were gone, I did as I was told and changed into my back J-Brand jeans and my favorite grey cashmere long-sleeved tee, the one that always received compliments. As an afterthought, I tied the teal scarf from my aunt Gina around my neck. It always felt nice to be reminded of her.

Karina nodded approvingly at my outfit and insisted I put on a little makeup too. 'You must look good to see your photographs,' she said seriously.

I rolled my eyes at her. 'You're bossy.' But I did as I was told. A few minutes later, we were in a cab, pulling away from my curb.

Karina handed the driver an address scribbled on a piece of paper.

'Where are we going?' I asked.

'You'll see,' she said mysteriously.

As we cut across the park, I began to get a funny feeling in the pit of my stomach. 'Karina?' I asked suspiciously as we emerged on the west side and the driver turned right to head further uptown. 'You're not taking me to see Michael, are you?'

'No,' she said innocently. 'I told you, I am taking you to see your photographs.'

But when we turned down West 93rd Street and crossed over Columbus, finally pulling to a halt in front of the familiar façade of Adriano's, I turned to glare at her.

'Karina,' I said. 'I specifically asked you if you were taking me to see Michael. You lied.'

'No,' she said, not making eye contact. 'I actually have no idea whether he's here or not.'

I glanced up at the restaurant, not understanding. I looked back at Karina, who was still avoiding my gaze. 'What are you talking about?'

The cabbie turned around and grunted something that sounded like, 'Are you getting out?' We both ignored him as the meter continued to run.

'I am being honest,' Karina said after a moment. 'I do not know if Michael is here or not. But I wanted you to see this.'

'You're telling me that it's Michael Evangelisti who has just randomly bought eighteen of my photos?' I asked dubiously.

Karina nodded. 'But it's not what you think,' she said quickly. 'He has no idea they are yours.'

I stared at her.

She continued, 'I called him a couple of months ago and said that I'd heard of a new photographer who was exhibiting at a gallery in SoHo. I promise, I did not say it was you. He has no idea. But when he was in Roma, he was talking about how he would like to make his restaurant feel more authentically Italian. And when I called, I suggested this might be the way.

'He sounded doubtful at first, but he promised to go check the photos out. Gillian called me a few weeks later and told me she'd made our biggest sale yet – eighteen 20x30 photos, framed, sold to the owner of a restaurant called Adriano's on West 93rd Street.'

I shook my head. 'You mean he looked at all the photos in her gallery,' I said slowly, 'all the different photographs she has of Italy, and he chose eighteen of mine?'

Karina nodded slowly. 'Amazing, isn't it? And whether you see Michael or not, whether you talk to him again or not, I think you should see your photographs displayed the way they were meant to be.'

I thought about it for a moment. I was at a loss; I didn't know what to do or how to feel. I looked at Karina uncertainly.

'I know it is not total coincidence,' she said after a moment, 'since I am the one who suggested he go to the gallery. But I swear, I told him nothing about you. Does it not mean something that he chose to surround himself with your art?' She paused and added, 'Now, every time he sees Roma, he sees it through your eyes.'

I swallowed hard. I looked up at the entrance to Adriano's. Then I looked back at Karina. 'Okay,' I said. 'Let's go in.'

Karina grinned, quickly paid the muttering cab driver and tumbled out of the car. I followed more slowly and stood on the sidewalk for a long moment after the taxi had peeled away. I stared up at the restaurant. I didn't know why I felt so scared. I had liked Michael – a lot. And if it hadn't been for a stupid misunderstanding, perhaps I would have begun dating him months ago. But now, I wasn't so sure. Did he hate me after the way I'd been so rude to him – on not one but two continents? And if he didn't, how did I even know he was available? Perhaps he was dating someone else, and by allowing even a sliver of hope in I was setting myself up for heartbreak. And even if he wasn't, was that a road I wanted to go down? It would be complicated to date a widower with a daughter. What if he wasn't ready? What if his daughter hated me from the start?

'Are you going to stand there and think of all the

reasons you shouldn't go in?' Karina asked. 'Or are you going to act like an adult and walk through those doors to see your hard work on their walls?'

'Er,' I said. I was still thinking about it. 'The second choice, I guess.'

'Good.' Karina grabbed my hand and dragged me into the restaurant.

The hostess – the same girl who had delivered the news that Michael's mother-in-law was on the phone – looked us up and down with a bored expression on her face. 'Table for two?' she asked.

'No,' Karina responded immediately. 'We are just going to walk around and see the photographs in the dining room.'

The hostess snapped her gum at us. 'I don't know if that's allowed.'

Karina stared her down. 'I know the owner,' she said. 'And I'm sure it's fine.'

She took me firmly by the hand again and dragged me into the main dining room before the hostess could protest.

As soon as we got through the doorway, we both stopped in our tracks.

The room looked entirely different from the way it had last time I'd been here. Gone were the nondescript prints of old Italian paintings, as well as the fake vines and grape bunches that had lined the walls. The entire interior, in fact, had been redesigned. The curtains were a lovely black velvet now, and the tablecloths were a rich black too, which looked striking against the exposed brick walls.

But the most obvious difference was my photographs,

which were spaced evenly around the room, six on each of three walls. All together, they looked larger than life in their stark black and white.

I stood motionless for a moment, staring at the work I'd done. I'd never seen them collected this way before, and certainly not eighteen of them together at this size. They were all framed in shiny black wood, lined with silver, which enhanced their sharp, black and white movie quality. As I gazed around at the walls, I felt like I was reliving my month in Rome in vivid detail.

I recognized a scene from the Ponte Sant'Angelo, and two angles of the Trevi Fountain. There were several shots of the Forum and one shot of a café off the Piazza Venezia. There was a shot of the Pantheon and two of the banks of the Tiber river. There were three photos of Vatican City, and one of the Mouth of Truth, which reminded me, of course, of *Roman Holiday* – and of Marco. And there were also several shots of Romans going about their daily business – two old men playing chess outside the bakery near Karina's apartment, a trio of old women hobbling down the street, two teenage girls on a stoop leaning together and obviously gossiping about a boy who was passing by. Most striking, though, were two pictures that sat side by side in the center of the back wall.

One was a shot of a little boy playing soccer in the park. You couldn't see his face, and, since it was dusk, it was hard to make out any distinguishing details.

'That's Nico, isn't it?' Karina asked softly.

I nodded. 'Yeah,' I said. It was strange to see him on the back wall of Michael's restaurant.

But perhaps even stranger was seeing the shot beside it. It was the picture I'd snapped of Aunt Gina as she was cleaning the window of the store, the day I'd met her. She had just turned around, as if she knew she was being watched, and her eyes met mine through the lens, just before I snapped a final shot and turned away, pretending that my attention was elsewhere. I had, of course, seen the photo on the screen of my computer before agreeing that Gillian could show it in her gallery. But I'd never seen it blown up to such a large size. Even from a distance, you could see Gina's deep eyes, her smile lines and her worry lines, and the expression of curiosity on her face as she stared out from the photo. I took a few steps closer, oblivious of the diners around me, and gazed at my aunt, feeling a pang of sadness as I thought about how far away she was and how much I missed her.

'That one was my favorite,' said a deep voice behind me that I recognized immediately, 'because the woman in the picture kind of reminded me of you.'

I whirled around. 'Michael,' I said flatly. I swallowed hard. He was just a few inches away from me, looking at me closely. I glanced around for Karina, who had backed all the way across the room and was watching us with an amused expression. She gave me the thumbs-up sign.

'Hi,' he said simply.

'Hi,' I said.

We stood there, just looking at each other, for a long moment.

Then Michael blinked and cleared his throat. He glanced behind me. 'Is that Karina over there?'

I nodded. 'Yes. She and her son are visiting.' I glanced in her direction again and realized she had disappeared.

He looked confused. 'She didn't tell me she was

coming.' He paused. 'She told me about the gallery that sold these pictures, though. Is that why you're here? Did you come to see the photos?'

I hesitated, not sure what to say.

'They really make a difference, don't they?' he asked, looking around.

I nodded, but I still didn't say anything. I couldn't seem to find the words.

We stood looking at each other again. 'So, you've been doing okay?' Michael finally asked. 'It's, um, been a while.' I could tell he felt as awkward as I did. There was something comforting about that.

'I got your note,' I blurted out suddenly. 'I'm sorry I didn't call you. I just . . . I didn't know what to say. I felt like I'd screwed it all up, just by not listening to you. But I wasn't ready. I wasn't ready for anything. I wasn't ready for what might happen if I called. I . . . I know I was wrong not to, but I didn't know what to do.'

Once the words were out of my mouth, I felt strangely like a weight had been lifted from my shoulders. And now the butterflies were back as I waited to hear what Michael would say. Once I had opened myself up to him, admitted I was wrong, it was like I had reopened a closed road to my heart. I was handing him the power to reject me. And that was scary.

'It's okay,' he said finally. 'I'm sorry too, for not trying harder to clear things up with you that night.' He paused and thought for a second. 'I think I wasn't ready either. I wanted to be. But I wasn't. And I think I knew that deep down.'

'Oh,' I said softly. I wasn't sure what he was telling me. Was he still unready? Was he still scared?

'But I think I'm ready now,' he added after a moment. 'For what it's worth.'

I couldn't help smiling. 'I think I am too,' I said softly.

We stood there for another awkward moment. It was like the restaurant had faded around us, and it was just Michael and me, in our own little bubble.

'I kind of like standing here,' he said suddenly. I knew he was trying to alleviate the awkwardness. 'I feel a little like I'm in Rome.' He paused, and when I didn't reply he added, 'But I guess that sounds sort of silly.'

'No,' I said. 'It doesn't. That's how the pictures are supposed to make you feel.'

He laughed. 'You say that like you know the photographer.'

'I do,' I said. I looked up and met Michael's eye. I didn't know whether to tell him or not. But suddenly, I found that I wanted to. I was proud of this, and proud that the photos I had taken made him feel something. 'It's me.'

'What?' Michael asked, looking confused.

'The photographer,' I said. 'It's me. I took the pictures.'

He looked even more baffled. 'What? No. It's a photographer named Audrey something. A new talent, the gallery owner called her.'

'Audrey Verdicchio,' I said.

'That's it.' Michael snapped his fingers. 'How do you know that?'

I took a deep breath. 'Audrey Verdicchio was my mom's name,' I said. 'When I decided to try to sell some of the photos I'd taken in Rome – with Karina's help – I decided to use her name. I didn't want anyone to know it was me.'

He stared at me. Then he looked slowly around at all the photographs until his eyes landed on the one he'd said was his favorite. 'And that woman in the picture?' he asked.

'My aunt Gina,' I said. 'That's probably why she reminded you of me.'

'My God,' Michael said softly. He shook his head. Then he looked back at me, and after a moment a slow smile spread across his face. He laughed. 'So all this time, I've been surrounded by you. Literally.'

I laughed too. It was sort of funny when you thought about it that way. 'I guess so.'

'Well,' he said, 'I don't usually believe in signs. But there's got to be some cosmic message in all of this. Right?'

I hesitated and nodded.

'So at the risk of sounding like a fool,' he said, 'would you consider going out with me again? If I promise to you that I'm not, in fact, married? I haven't even been out on a date since that disaster date I had with you.'

'Well, the whole date wasn't a disaster,' I said with a half-smile.

'No, it wasn't,' he agreed. 'But the end was.'

I nodded and looked down. 'I'm sorry,' I said. 'I really am. Do you think we can ever forget about it? Can you forgive how stupidly I acted?'

Michael paused, and for a long moment, I thought he was going to say no. But then he spoke, his voice slow and deliberate. 'Maybe it's not about forgiving or forgetting,' he said. 'Maybe it's about remembering everything and being willing to start over anyway.'

'Even if it means you might get hurt,' I added softly. I thought of my father and my mother, how much more I understood now, and how much I'd probably never understand.

'But sometimes, it's worth the risk,' Michael said. He took my hand. 'Don't you think?'

I looked into his eyes, and for the first time in a very long time I had the feeling I was exactly where I belonged. I smiled back and let myself stare into his eyes deeply enough to reawaken the butterflies slumbering in my stomach. 'Yes,' I said finally. 'I do.'

little black dress

**brings you
fantastic new books like these
every month - find out more at
www.littleblackdressbooks.com**

**And why not sign up for our
email newsletter to keep
you in the know about
Little Black Dress news!**

You can buy any of these other
Little Black Dress titles from your
bookshop or *direct from the publisher*.

FREE P&P AND UK DELIVERY
(Overseas and Ireland £3.50 per book)

TO ORDER SIMPLY CALL THIS NUMBER

01235 400 414

or visit our website: www.headline.co.uk

Prices and availability subject to change without notice.